She had believed that when the man responsible for killing her sister was finally brought to book, she would experience some degree of peace; instead, she found herself deeply disturbed by the fact that he had at last stepped out of the shadows which had concealed him. Before he had been a faceless, nameless entity out there in the dark, unimaginable, incorporeal. Now, he had a name, an age, a presence.

Also by Susan Moody

Playing With Fire
Hush-a-bye
The Italian Garden
Misselthwaite

Falling Angel

Susan Moody

CORONET BOOKS
Hodder and Stoughton

First published in Great Britain in 1998
by Hodder and Stoughton
First published in paperback in 1998 by Hodder and Stoughton
A division of Hodder Headline PLC

A Coronet Paperback

10 9 8 7 6 5 4 3 2 1

British Library Cataloguing in Publication Data
Moody, Susan
Falling Angel
1.Detective and mystery stories
I.Title
823.9′14[F]

ISBN 0 340 68605 7

Typeset by Hewer Text Ltd, Edinburgh
Printed and bound in Great Britain by
Clays Ltd, St Ives plc

Hodder and Stoughton
A division of Hodder Headline PLC
338 Euston Road
London NW1 3BH

for Araminta Whitley
agent, friend and rottweiler

Prologue

Blood everywhere.

It's a phrase often heard, often read. People say: 'There was blood everywhere,' not meaning it to be taken literally, not blood *every*where.

But that morning, when she stepped into the room, that was what she saw.

Blood everywhere.

Upholstery stiff with it. Walls splattered with it. Curtains and carpeting dark where it had dried. The glass on the pictures, the books on the shelves, the silver, the Coalport tea service, sprayed with thick brown drops of it.

For a moment, she stood unsure, wondering if somehow this was the wrong house, a stage set, a joke. Then upstairs the child wailed and she was jolted back into reality. In front of the dead-embered hearth (blotched and smeared), lay something hideously unrecognisable yet, at the same time, all too instantly identifiable.

The horror of it – clothes hacked away, clotted slashes of flesh, a hand lying parallel to the arm from which it hung by a ribbon of skin – could temporarily be shelved by the urgency of the now-screaming child. She stepped over blood-soaked rugs towards the hall, hand at her throat, trying not to breathe the brassy air. At the door, she turned, steeling herself, to look at the . . . what was the best word: object? Thing? Shape? . . . To look at what lay on the floor between the sofas. Eye took in detail which brain wished forcibly to reject. Blood-stiffened hair. Slack mouth. The whiteness of teeth. Denim still blue between streaks and gobbets of dried blood.

The child paused to draw fresh reinforcements of air into its lungs and she called reassurance up the stairs, knowing as she did so that there could be no comfort ever again, not from here on in. Worst, most horrible of all, was the knowledge that this was her fault. Directly. Incontrovertibly. Her fault.

It was unthinkable. Impossible. Unbearable. This could not have happened. Yet the mind was working again now, already accepting that it had. There were the police to call, emergency services to alert, not that they could do anything now. The mutilated body had surrendered hours ago to death. Only the blood remained.

Everywhere.

Act One

Other mornings, when rain drizzled on the wild garden and threw light the colour of steel into the bedroom, or when reflected sunshine turned the room golden, the mark on the ceiling became more than a mark. It was probably nothing more than the result of rain seeping through the roof, but at different times it could resemble a barn owl in flight, a giant moth or a stylised fountain. Flora often conjectured more exotic reasons for its fine-spread outline, had fantasised a bird coming down the chimney to flutter sootily against the white-wash, a pair of rural lovers indulging in unusual sexual practices, a drunken husband hurling beer at a cowering wife.

But this morning, it was an angel. And angels only came on good days.

Light, sharp and brittle, poured into the white-emulsioned spaces round her bed, making it impossible not to begin negotiations with the day. Flora kicked back the covers, and stood at the window while she shrugged into her dressing-gown. Below her, the garden glittered. Frost had spiked each twig, each separate grass blade; ice encased the bare branches of the fruit trees in the orchard so that she imagined they would tinkle like bells if they knocked against each other. Beautiful, she thought, shivering, brushing her hair with goose-pimpled arms. Glorious. But bloody cold.

In the freezing bathroom, more light streamed through stained-glass windows depicting waterlilies and reeds. White and green: ice and peppermint. Her breath hung cloudy in front of her face. Didn't people in the old days get sewn into their clothes until winter was past? At the moment it was easy to see why. No one in their right mind would want to undress in temperatures like this, even for the sake of cleanliness. Definitely not just for sex. Though she had long ago folded away any thought of that: now, it lay dormant at the back of her mind like a summer dress waiting for the warmer weather to return.

Which at least made it easier to be without Oliver.

But it was too cold to think of him. To think of anything but keeping warm. Sucking breath in through her teeth, she hurried downstairs to the heat of the kitchen. The Aga had been her one extravagance on moving here; even though the rest of the house was chill, at least there was always somewhere comfortable to sit. Filling the kettle, she again glanced out of the window. At ground level, the sun-dazzle of the frosted garden had given way to colourlessness, like an old black-and-white film. The frost was bitter, devouring the uneven grass, gnawing at blackened stems and fallen leaves. At the edge of the rough winter lawn a twiggy bush of dogwood stood bunched, its red stems overlaid with hoar-frost. Fog loomed at the edges of the garden.

She put a cardigan on over her sweater, a skiing jerkin on over that, before wrapping herself up in the big tweed overcoat which had been Oliver's. Even after all this time – it was over a year since his voice on the answering machine had coldly informed her that his solicitor had been instructed to file for divorce – she fancied that it still retained his particular smell, some essence of the man she had loved so passionately.

Had loved? Still loved, try as she might not to. Mouth tucked in, eyes closed, she stood for a moment, recapturing Oliver. Morning exercises, some part of her brain insisted drily. Limbering up for a day she would spend trying not to think about him. It was more than that. Sometimes she was afraid she was losing him. Forgetting. The precise placement of his features, the length of his fingers, the way he talked, which was always rapidly, always as though he was afraid of being stopped before he'd told her everything he had to say, but the timbre of his voice, the almost transatlantic roll on the 'r's, the little drag on the vowels: these she was mislaying.

After what had taken place between them, she had known that this was the only solution. Being down here in the cottage, *their* cottage, learning to accept the way things had worked out. Getting on with her life. Finding her independence. Living without him seemed no easier now than it had the morning she moved in here permanently. He had always led; she had been content to follow. She had no experience of, as it were, fending for herself. Shopping, yes, cooking, domestic tasks. They were easy, undemanding. But filling the space around herself with . . . herself: *that* she had not yet come to terms with. And still sometimes the pain of his loss took hold of her like a giant hand. Crushing her. Bones breaking, veins bursting, heart clamping in agony. Were the pain ever to endure longer than the smallest possible measurement of time – microseconds, nanoseconds – it would kill her.

She tugged the back door shut behind her and ran across the frost-spiked grass to the stone barn which she used as a studio. The ancient stone walls oozed chilly damp; the inside of the windows were double-glazed with ice. Bracing herself against the cold, she lit the big calor gas heaters at either end of the long, tiled room. Warming her hands at the gently popping flame, she promised herself that this time next year there would be central heating, both here and in the cottage. She reached up for the tin of ground Italian coffee on the shelf above the long, built-in counter which stood against one wall of the barn, cursing as she always did the fact that she was too small to reach anything without straining for it, then set the percolator going on the hotplate, spooned in grounds from a silver-foil packet.

Oliver would have been lofty. 'Call that coffee?' he'd have said. 'More like river sludge. Dish water. Not *real* coffee.'

Once, she'd have accepted his judgement on this, as on everything else. Now, partially released from the umbrella of his influence, she might have challenged him. How do you define 'real' coffee? she could have asked, had he been there with her, walking round the room in his swift, unsettled way.

Is it the sweetish gritty stuff we were served in Istanbul? The wincingly bitter post-dinner brew that we drank in Paris? Georgie's coffee, boiling water poured over beans which have been ground in a hand-held wooden box with an over-sized handle sprouting from the lid? Smiling, Flora leaned against the counter while the pot chugged and chuckled. The multiplicity of possibilities, the lack of exactitude which surrounded things – coffee, colours, words – had always pleased her.

Holding the warm mug in both hands, she walked over to stand in front of her current drawing board. A half-finished painting showed a water rat nosing through reeds at the edge of a river. The detail was precise; the water rat only that, a wild creature, sleek, furred, cautious. Although she was in constant demand as an illustrator of childrens' books, she refused to indulge in anthropomorphism. She despised those cute animals in red waistcoats and brass buttons which filled the pages of so many books intended for the young: the Disneyed wolves in checked trousers, the sanitised bears. They cheated the children who read them; they were, besides, unnecessary. Most of her work was taken uncompromisingly from nature; she relied on the settings and backgrounds to ally the pictures with the storyline.

But today was for angels.

'What is an angel?' Oliver had asked suddenly one day. They were in Florence, looking at an Annunciation and he stood behind her, his hand kneading her shoulder. 'What exactly *is* an angel?'

Until then, believing that she knew, she had scarcely considered his question. But later, as they made love in the big *matrimoniale* which dominated their hotel room, she found herself considering it again and realised with surprise, that she did not. It continued to nibble at her long after they had moved on, down through Italy, across Europe, and home again. Later still, making swift sketches on the drawing pad she always carried, she had contemplated the sorts and conditions of angels: cherubim, putti, the winged figure of Thanatos. Laying paint on paper, drawing leaves, grasses, blossom, painstakingly colouring berries – hips and haws, brambles, blackberries, sloes – she thought about djinns and *hafaza*, of the resounding many-eyed archangels: Gabriel, Uriel, Michael, Raphael. Of Lucifer and the exhilaration of his fall. Of Thrones, Dominions, Powers, and the strange beauty of their stern androgynous faces.

And epiphanies. Instants of revelation. The Annunciation, for instance, the terrifying moment when a girl acknowledged an illicit pregnancy. Paul's blinding conversion on the road to Damascus. Winged Cupid, the personification of the moment when pure love strikes the heart. Jacob wrestling with his own confusions. And it came to her that angels were not messengers or guardians but simply clarifications of thought. Voices from the soul. Not believing in God, she realised, one warm summer evening, with gold-edged clouds cramming the sky above London, that the closest she could get to a definition was this: an angel is an epiphanic moment compacted and made solid, crystallised.

On her second board was a drawing she had begun a few weeks earlier. Something quite unrelated to her present work, it had suddenly appeared in her mind, demanding to be given substance. Perhaps it was inspired subconsciously by the mark on the ceiling, perhaps Oliver's question was finally demanding a concrete answer. It had proved to be the first of several; a tiny angel, balancing on a teaspoon, leaned forward, wings quivering as delicately as a dragonfly's. Behind it stood a flowered cup and saucer, a jar of Cooper's marmalade, the label painted so meticulously that it might have been a photograph. The angel had the cropped hair of a skinhead. Doc Martens showed beneath its ripped denim garment; an earring glinted in one ear. This was a twentieth-century angel; when it spoke, it would be with the authentic voice of the inner-city streets. She squinted at the drawing. There was something not quite right about it. She found her portfolio and spread it open on the plain wood table under one of the windows. Here were sketches of other angels, and she saw that all of them had the same fault: the wings. The unmuscled way she had attached them to the shoulders was wrong. No angel – no bird, for that matter – would be able to fly with wings set at that angle. She would have to do some research, get hold of some books, study the birds which flittered in the garden. Vaguely she remembered a painting by Saraceni in Rome, of St Cecilia with an Angel, an angel musician whose wings conveyed the utmost power and made her feel that this was a creature which really could have braved the wind.

She wondered what Oliver would have made of her angel. Would he have teased or encouraged? Although she had tried to keep it up, her drawing skills had diminished in the years of her marriage: there had never been time to produce more than hasty sketches here and there, and often not even for those, as the two of them criss-crossed the world. When she spoke of it, Oliver had been matter-of-fact, pointing out that it was like riding a bicycle, she would never lose her technique and once they were settled she could take up her work again and meanwhile, she knew how much he needed, how he depended on her. It had never happened: she had realised that her happiness lay in providing him with the calm he required in order to concentrate on his work.

The angel in the DMs had proved to be a catalyst. Instead of simply illustrating other people's books, she had asked herself why she should not write a book, a children's book, herself. Now the notion was beginning to take shape. What would he think, if he knew, Oliver, her incubus, her demon lover? Would he have been glad that he had been proved right? Would he care? In the bleak days after she had left him, she had begun the painful task of regaining her dormant skills; now she was making a living from them, just as she had originally intended. More importantly, should it matter whether he cared or not? He was no longer a reference point: they had gone their different ways. The problem was that although she knew she ought to keep him out of her mind, it was impossible. Through Oliver she mediated the past: for her, he *was* the past. She could not rid herself of the hope that he was her future too.

Halfway through the cold morning, the telephone rang. She set down her brush and wiped her hand down the front of her painting sweater.

'Hello?'

It was Georgie. 'Oh, Flo, oh thank God you're there,' she said, hysteria flowing like an harmonic variation beneath her words.

'What's wrong?' Flora looked down at her hands. Angel-coloured paint, lying along the bones and outlining the knuckles, gave them a spectral appearance. 'What is it?'

'Everything. I'm about to slit my throat.'

Once, Flora would have rushed in with cough-mixture words to soothe and comfort. Recently, she had been practising detachment. Especially from Georgie. Georgie and Oliver. The two people who mattered most. 'Are you?' she said.

'My throat or my wrists. You've got to help me, Flo.'

'Have I?'

'*Yes*!'

'Help you do what?' Flora said coolly. Jamming the receiver under her jaw in order to free her hands, she poured another mug of coffee, circling the palm of her hand over the black surface of the counter. It was only in the past couple of years, in the absence of larger pleasures, that she had properly come to appreciate such small ones as this present satisfying mattness of slate, the thick sound as a spoon connected with it.

'Oh, Flora,' moaned Georgie. 'Oh, Jesus.' In the room beyond her telescoped voice, Ella Fitzgerald languished darkly while behind her a trumpet and a tenor saxophone improvised sad accompaniments. 'I'm in trouble.'

'What kind of trouble?'

'The worst kind.'

'Have you murdered someone?'

'Don't be ridiculous. Murdered someone! Look, you know that tour we're supposed to be going on?'

'We?'

'The Ragbags, for God's sake: who'd you think I meant?'

'What about it? And why do you say 'supposed'? I thought it was all set up.'

'It was. *Is*. The opportunity we've been waiting for all these years. The break into the international scene.'

'You're already part of the international scene,' Flora said, rolling her eyes at the ceiling. Dammit: why did she always slip so effortlessly back into the role of comforter? Since the split with Oliver – since the *divorce* from Oliver – *she* was the one in need of comfort. 'The way I heard, you're hardly ever home these days.'

'Who'd you hear that from?'

'You, Georgina.'

'Well, it's not true.'

'Look, last year, you went to Amsterdam, Sydney and Stockholm. You've got a European tour lined up for the beginning of next year. And you were in the States not all that long ago—'

'Five years ago, to be precise. Last time, we were still trying to break into the scene. This could be our big chance. I'm talking the *States*, Flora. North America. You can imagine how important it is. The sky's the limit. And if not, there's all kinds of subsidiary work available for a good band. In fact, our manager's already talking to people in the record industry.'

'So what's the problem?'

'Oh, God.' For a few moments, Georgie gulped and sobbed. Without envy, Flora knew that emotion would not blotch Georgie's complexion, that her eyes would not redden, that even in extremity, her hair would remain in whatever elaborate style she had recently arranged it. 'Oh, Jesus,' she said again. 'What on earth am I going to do?'

'I'll tell you what *I'm* going to do,' said Flora. 'I'm going to put this damn phone down right now unless you tell me what's wrong.'

Another pause. Then Georgie said, in a voice made small by simplicity: 'I'm pregnant.'

It was scarcely an exaggeration to say that the floor seemed to rock beneath Flora's feet. Had she sat down with paper and pen and dreamed up scenarios to explain whatever predicament Georgie had got herself into, this was the one she would never have hit upon. Georgie, pregnant? Georgie, a mother? The two words simply did not fit together. And yet, thinking logically, why not? Georgie was twenty-nine, healthy, sexually active. The only real surprise lay in the fact that it had not happened before.

Flora cleared her throat, steadied her voice. 'When lovely woman stoops to folly, eh?'

'I knew I could rely on you to be flippant over something so dreadful.'

'*Is* it dreadful?' With her right hand Flora rubbed absently at the place above her left elbow where the long knife scar had healed ragged, blue-white.

'You know damn well it's absolutely the worst thing that could have happened!' screamed Georgie. She banged the receiver down on some hard surface and moved away. Flora could almost see her pacing up and down, hands digging into her thin hips, face screwed up with anger.

She waited. When Georgie picked up the phone again, Flora said: 'Worst, because of the tour?'

'Worst because I don't want it!' Georgie yelled. 'Can you imagine me with a baby?'

'No.'

'Well, then.'

'What about the father?'

'The father?'

'You know. The other half of the operation.'

'What about him?'

'Does he have any views?'

'None at all. Because I have no intention of discussing it with him. Now or ever.'

'Why not? Maybe he'll want you to have the baby.'

'That's too damn bad if he does. Because even if he did, I'm not going to have it. What would I do with a baby?' shouted

Georgie. 'I am not going to have it, Flo. I mean it. I really mean it. It's not just the tour. I don't want it. I really don't.'

Under the words lay much more than a desire not to be inconvenienced. Panic was there. And terror. None the less, Flora felt obliged to put an alternative viewpoint; why else would Georgie have rung, if not to be convinced? 'I think you ought at least to speak to the father,' she said reasonably.

'Flo, I'm not ringing you in order to be talked out of my decision. I'm ringing because I need practical help.'

'Then on this particular matter, you've got the wrong person.'

'You're my *sister*, dammit.'

Despite the difference in their ages, she and Georgie had once been almost inseparable. Marriage, travel, the demands of Oliver's career, on the one hand, and Georgie's on the other, had inevitably meant that they had grown apart; since Flora's divorce, their relationship had changed. Perhaps Flora felt defensive; perhaps Georgie was ill at ease with a sister whose life had altered so suddenly, so radically. Whatever the reason, they were increasingly edgy with each other. 'So I am,' Flora said, unable to keep the sardonic note from her voice. 'I thought you'd forgotten.'

'I've been busy, OK? The thing is, I know you'll help me, that I can rely on you.'

Once, perhaps, Flora thought. But now? 'Maybe the two of you could get married.' She tried to remember who Georgie was currently seeing, currently sleeping with, but failed to come up with even a name, let alone a face.

'Married? Are you joking?'

'No. Despite everything, I still believe marriage is – can be – a marvellously fulfilling and—'

'Oh, please,' said Georgie. 'Spare me the platitudes. Anyway, the – the other half of the operation, as you put it, is committed elsewhere.'

'Ah.'

'And even if he wasn't, I wouldn't want to marry him.' She thought about it. Added a heartfelt: 'God, no.'

'But you wouldn't have slept with him if you hadn't liked him,' said Flora. Under her layers of clothing, the scar throbbed.

'Wouldn't I? Oh Flora, you are so old-fashioned.'

'Did – *do* – you like him?' Was she old-fashioned, and if so, was that a bad thing to be?

'He's OK, I suppose. But I certainly don't want to *marry* him.' Georgie spoke through gritted teeth. 'I don't bloody well want to marry anyone. Have to give up my career, the way you did.'

'I did not.'

'Get real, Flora. Anyway, I like living on my own. I like doing the things I like doing, when I like doing them. I don't want to have to think about anyone else every time I get up in the morning. I don't want to have to explain what I'm doing every second of the day. I don't want to have to make arrangements when I go on tour, leave disgusting noodle casseroles in the freezer, make sure the ironing's done. Call me selfish, if you like, though you'd be wrong if you did because no one else is involved, but that's the way I like it and that's how I want it to stay.'

'I see.'

'Which is why you've got to help me. I have to have an abortion, Flora. There is absolutely no way I'm going to have this baby.'

'What makes you think I'd know anything about such things?' said Flora. 'And if I did, I don't know if I think you'd be doing the right thing by getting rid of it.'

'Are you suggesting I'm doing the *wrong* thing?'

'I'm wondering whether you maybe haven't entirely thought this through.'

'Oh, I've thought it through, all right. I didn't just wake up this morning and decide I want to get rid of it. I've been thinking of nothing else for days, believe me.'

'What about the NHS? Surely you can do this legally, can't you?'

'If you're prepared to have them prying into the most

intimate details of your private life – and you can convince them of your psychological need, etcetera, etcetebloodyra.'

'How long have you known about this?'

'I've kind of suspected for a while – but I've been so terrified of the result that I only got round to buying one of those test kits yesterday. And guess what . . . Oh, Christ!'

'It may sound like a stupid question, but aren't you on the pill?'

Georgie gave a bitter laugh. 'The way my life's been recently, there's hardly any need. Besides, those things are terribly bad for you. Do you realise I've been on the pill for over ten years?'

'Come on, Georgie.'

'OK. So maybe I missed a few days.'

'Pissed again, eh? Then why didn't you make him use a condom?'

'Let's just say that I was taken – we both were – by surprise.'

'It wasn't – oh, Georgie.' Hideous possibilities seized Flora. 'You haven't been—'

'Been *what*?'

'Raped.'

'Jesus.' Georgie drew in a deep breath of exasperation. 'No, Flora. It's *not* the result of rape.'

'You can afford to raise a child, can't you? Pay for nannies and things.'

'Yes.'

'And you know I'd help.'

'Flora.'

'What?'

'Listen to me, Flora.'

'I am.'

Georgie spoke in a low, emphatic voice. 'I do not want this baby. I do not intend to have this baby. I will *kill* myself if I can't get rid of this baby. And I need you to help me.'

'Surely the man involved has a right to at least know about it?' Flora persisted.

'He has no rights. None at all. Not over me, at any rate.'

'Is his marriage bad, perhaps? Maybe if he knew, he'd—'

'Make an honest woman of me, do you mean?'

'What's wrong with that?'

'Anyway, did I say he was married? All I said was that he was fucking committed.'

'If he slept with you, what kind of a commitment is it?'

'Jesus, Flora. Get a life, will you?' A thud at the other end of the line indicated that Georgie was slamming her fist down on something. 'Listen, this is a guy who would no more want to move in with me than I would want him to.'

'In that case, why is he having an affair with you?'

'I knew all about it when I let it happen. Besides, it wasn't exactly an affair.' Georgie sounded, for the first time, edgy rather than distraught.

'What was it, then?'

'There are complications which I don't want to go into, don't even want to think about at the moment,' said Georgie. Her voice rose. 'The main thing is that I must get rid of this damn baby.'

'What kind of complications?'

'They've got nothing to do with anything. And the man isn't part of the equation.'

'There was a pause in which Flora could hear the fierce sound of Georgie's sobs. Flora made her voice harsh. 'What you mean is that it could be one of several men, don't you? That you don't even know who the father is.'

Silence. Then Georgie said, pleading: 'Flora. You've got to help me. Tell me where I go, how I cope.'

'I'll help, of course I will. But only when I'm sure that *you're* sure about this.'

'I am absolutely certain. I *swear* it. Quite apart from anything else, think of it, Flora. Just think of it. Suppose I turned out like – like *her*'.

'That's impossible.'

'Not necessarily. She's my mother, after all: I've got the

same genes. I'd spend the entire time monitoring myself. Every time I was cross or slapped the kid's bottom, every time I was mean or unfair, I'd be wondering. I can't, I just can't face that.' More sobbing. 'Flora, help me.'

Sympathy welled, but Flora kept her voice cool. 'How far along are you?'

'Eight or nine weeks.'

'Then there's still time.'

'To set things up?'

'Mmm.' To dissuade her from getting rid of the child in her womb, Flora meant. 'Look, why don't you come down here to the cottage for a couple of days?'

'What, and freeze to death? No thanks. Besides, it wouldn't do any good.'

'We could at least talk it over.'

'Can't you come up here?'

'Do you want me to help you or not?'

'Jesus. All right. *OK*. I'll bring my fur coat. Just promise me there'll be plenty of booze.'

'You'll have to give up alcohol, won't you?'

'Are you out of your mind?'

'In your condition. It's terribly bad for the baby.'

'But I'm not going to have it, am I? And, Flora—'

'What?'

'Promise me you won't tell anyone about this. Please. Nobody. Not even your precious Oliver.'

'I never talk to him.'

'Well, if you do. OK?'

Flora didn't answer. Talking to Oliver was her secret vice, her luxury, the security blanket in which she wrapped herself when troubled by cold doubt. Not often, no more than half a dozen times in the past two years had she lifted the telephone and dialled his number, waited for his answering machine to kick in. Then closed her eyes when she heard his voice, leaned into it for the few seconds that his message lasted, let herself slip into him as though into a pool of warm and scented water.

'Flora,' Georgie said sharply. 'You do promise, don't you?'
'Yes,' she sighed.
'Don't tell anybody. Not yet.'
'I promise.'

The two girls were in the tree-house. Flora wasn't supposed to be up there, her mother said she was too big and heavy, she'd damage it, but the sisters knew that was rubbish since Georgie was already bigger than Flora. With the summer holidays nearly over and a new school term looming, Flora was rushing through her holiday task of reading *Nicholas Nickleby*.

A ladybird began a distracting trek across the page of her book; she watched it hesitate on the word 'Micawber' as though it held a personal significance, pause between two lines before changing direction, head towards the left. Shaking it off, Flora looked up at the tree soaring above her head, wondering if she could ever capture on paper the way the sun fell through the layers of overlapping, copper-edged leaves. Between them, glimpses of the sky showed, an uncomplicated blue. Next door's children squabbled amiably in their sandpit. Distantly, someone mowed their lawn. Above the faint roar she could hear the muted sound of a Test Match commentary.

She knew there had to be a word to describe this moment precisely. Peaceful was not right; it was too passive, it did not convey the lack of threat. Unharassed? Almost right. Carefree, she thought. Free of care. She smiled. Carefree was exactly right.

Last term, the girls in her form had moaned about having to read *Nicholas Nickleby*, but she loved the complicated weaving in and out of the characters, the farcical elements of their lives, the wisdom she glimpsed behind the author's humour. Even the sentimentality pleased her. So, especially, did Smike, poor bullied Smike.

Up at the house, a door was flung open. She sat motionless

as the afternoon dissipated about her. The leaves above her head gave a sudden shiver. Her mother's voice called, shattering the calm.

'Flora! Where are you? Come here immediately.' Squinting through the leaves, Flora could just see her standing at the tall windows of the breakfast room. The white beads at her throat, the flame-red of her cotton dress. The colour of hell. The colour of pain. Flora swallowed, feeling the thud through her veins as the adrenalin began to pump and flood.

'She doesn't like you much, does she?' nine-year-old Georgie whispered, as though afraid she might otherwise be overheard. Her breath still had the acetylene smell of the pear drops they had been sucking earlier.

'She hates me,' Flora said. And did not add: but not as much as I hate her.

'Don't you mind?'

Flora, four years older than her sister, shrugged. 'Who cares what she thinks?' she said, with an insouciance that neither girl was yet old enough to see as tragic.

The truth was that *she* cared. She ached, sometimes, to be loved as Georgie so clearly was, especially when she remembered that once she had been. She longed to be . . . fêted was the word she used to herself. *Celebrated.* With all the accompanying connotations of birthday candles, presents, of Christmas trees, of fanfares and warmth and laughter.

'*Flora!* Will you come here at *once*!'

'I'd better go,' Flora whispered, 'or she'll start looking.'

'What have you done this time?'

'What have I ever done? She doesn't need an excuse.'

'Is she going to hit you?'

'Probably.'

'Flora . . .' Georgie said hesitantly.

'What?'

'Is it . . . I mean, do all mums . . . is everybody else's mother nasty to her children or is it just ours?'

About to swing down from the tree, Flora paused. Georgie had never asked the question before and although Flora was only thirteen, she was old enough to know that saying yes might colour her little sister's view of how things ought to be, whereas if she said no, it would make their own particular situation seem even worse, isolate the two of them even more.

'Sometimes,' she said. 'Sometimes.' She swung down onto the slippery leaves at the tree's base and ran across the lawn towards the house. Her mother was standing in the hall, holding onto the newel post, her head thrown back as she stared into the gloom of upstairs. Her face was pinched with annoyance and dislike. 'Flora! You *wretched* girl. Are you up there or not?'

'I'm here.'

Her mother whirled round, red skirt curving behind her, and advanced across the hall. Seizing the flesh of her daughter's upper arm, she pinched it between thumb and finger. 'Creeping up on me like that—' she said. 'I've been calling you for ages. Didn't you hear me?'

'No.'

'Don't speak to me in that impudent tone.' Even though braced for it, Flora was still rocked back on her feet by the force of the slap which accompanied this. None the less, though the outline of her mother's hand flamed against her cheek and her eyes watered, Flora remained steadily staring up into her mother's hostile eyes until the older woman blinked and looked away. It was another small victory in the daily battle they fought. 'Have you been up in the tree-house?' she demanded.

Flora shook her head.

'You're lying, aren't you? *Aren't* you? You been up there although I've repeatedly told you not to. Can't you understand that it's not strong enough for both of you? If one of you fell . . . So it's Georgie's house, do you hear? *Georgie's.*'

'I didn't go up there,' Flora said. Despite herself, there was a tremble in her knees and the anticipation of pain.

'You're a bloody little liar. And you know how I hate liars. Almost as much as I hate mindless vandalism.' She pushed Flora's right arm up behind the girl's back.

One day, Flora thought coldly even as she bent over gasping with pain, as she dropped to her knees, as her mother pulled her head back by the hair and slapped her face again, one day she'll really hurt me, she'll break something, one of my ribs or my arm, and then I shall tell and maybe they'll put her in prison or something. But she knew she never would. She had no choice but to suffer, she had to bear it somehow, for Georgie's sake.

'Did my father tell lies?' she said, putting as much insolence into her voice as she could.

'What did you say?'

'You heard.'

'Since you ask, yes, Flora, he did. Just like you.'

'I *don't* tell lies.'

'And while we're at it, how many times have I told you not to mention your father to me?' Her mother began dragging Flora across the floor of the hall. 'How many times?'

Flora didn't answer.

'Don't talk about him,' her mother said. 'Do you hear? He's gone, and we've all got to forget him.'

'I haven't.'

'You know nothing about him,' her mother said through gritted teeth. From the top of the piano, she picked up the length of garden bamboo which she used as a cane. 'Nothing.'

Later, locked into her bedroom, Flora stared through tears into the sunny garden. Her face was streaked with blood where her mother's rings had cut into her cheek. Why had her father gone and left the two of them here? Sometimes she thought that if only she had the answer to that question, she could make sense of things. It wouldn't matter about not being loved, if only she could understand what had made her father go. There were red weals up the back of her legs where the bamboo cane had cut into her flesh. All she could hope, through the pain and the numbing hatred, was that Georgie didn't get the same punishment for allowing her into the tree-house.

* * *

There was no reason why she should have remembered that single afternoon, when there must have been so many others like it. Most of her mother's attacks had been bewilderingly random, flying at her with the sudden viciousness of a dart, making it impossible to set up defences for herself in advance. But after all these years, she still vividly recalled not only the beating but also the feel of the beech tree's smooth bark as she dropped to the ground, the particular shape of its ribbed leaves, the crunchy feel of beechnut kernels under the crêpe-rubber soles of her sandals.

Animosity had stained her childhood like spilled blood. Her mother's aversion to her was an impediment as crippling as any physical handicap. There was a girl at school with an arm withered by polio, one who wore a brace on her leg, another in a wheelchair, victim of some disease about which they never spoke. They were clinical disadvantages, visible, calling for compassion and an awkward pity. Her own affliction was emotional. Nobody offered sympathy because no one was aware of its existence. Like a squint, her lack of love was an aberration against which it would have been impossible to insure, because there could never have been any way of predicting it.

Older, she came to the conclusion that the animosity was related to the fact that their absent father had loved his elder daughter, where he did not, could not, love his wife. Could not even pretend to. After he had disappeared from their lives, vanishing one afternoon as unobtrusively as the smoke from his cigarettes, Flora's resemblance to him must have triggered the abuse from her mother which had left her with a permanent sense of her own lack of worth and unlovability. Plus the terror which still manifested itself in amorphous nightmares and sudden sweats of fear. As a child, all she could do to combat them was to lie in the darkness and hug to herself the certainty that her father loved her, that one day he would come for her.

It was years before she realised that he was not coming back, that she had been left to face her mother alone. That he had loved her, yes. But not enough to protect her.

* * *

Staring now at her teaspoon-perched angel, she reflected that it could not have stemmed from any failure in herself. She had always been conscientious, cooperative, dependable, where the doted-on Georgie was usually unreliable, often untidy, always rebellious. Flora obediently wore the unflattering frilly dresses and tucked blouses their mother insisted on, kept her hair brushed and her nails clean, ran errands, helped in the house, whereas Georgie slopped about in jeans and T-shirts, obstinately refusing to be the ladylike creature her mother yearned for. Yet it was Georgie who was loved. At some deep level, Flora had maintained the superstitious hope that if she was good, she might be loved too. It was not until adolescence that she perceived, in the cold places of her heart, that she never would.

Lucky Georgie took after their mother: pale-haired where Flora was a darker blonde, blue-eyed and undeniably cute despite her height. Even at nine, she was taller than her sister. Their physical differences could have pushed the sisters apart, but in fact they had been as close as twins, collaborators in the shared struggle to deliver Flora safely into adulthood. Georgie had early on learned the techniques of distraction, in order to draw the fire away from her sister. Her mother's attention was easily diverted from Flora by the sight of Georgie's tears, by scratches or bruises, by tousled curls and torn dresses; she had never realised that Georgie could cry at will and that her small wounds were often self-inflicted.

It was not until Flora left home and went to art school that she discovered not everyone came from a dysfunctional family. Some of her fellow-students actually liked their parents. Many of them appeared to like themselves.

Abruptly, Flora put down her brush and got up. How different Oliver's parents had been from her own. Everything she could have wished for. He was stocky, with wild white hair and hot blue eyes. She was small, a lively blonde with a colourful taste in clothes. Neither was in the least parental.

Analysing that first meeting afterwards, she realised that they had simply accepted her, welcomed her without expectation, without judgement. It was their great gift to assume that, unless it was proved otherwise, everyone they met possessed an intrinsic worth.

She poured more coffee from the percolator and went to stand at one of the pair of arched windows which gave onto the garden. A cold wind blew among the frost-stiffened tatters of leaf which hung from withered stems in the flowerbeds. The sky was ponderous with snow.

She remembered a snowy Boxing Day on Primrose Hill. Oliver in a red woollen scarf, excited as a child, organising everybody. Toboggan races, sledges, snow sparkling over London, children shrieking with delighted fear, blue light spreading across the park as evening came down. People living nearby had gone back to their houses and returned with thermoses of soup, turkey sandwiches, wine. New friendships had been made, old ones rediscovered. Voices chattering, laughter, a day-long impromptu outdoor party.

Oliver had made it happen. Oliver always made things happen. He had such a gift for fun, for improvisation, for . . . but she must stop thinking about him. She must. She would never be free to go forward until she could stop looking back. He would be forty soon; he had dominated her life for nearly fifteen years. It had to stop. She had to accept that he had gone. She was on her own.

Think, instead, of Georgie and the baby growing inside her.

Somewhere – was it in heart or in head? – Flora recognised her own grief. Georgie was pregnant, was going to have a baby. She herself never would. Georgie had mentioned their mother but that ought not to be a problem. She had been loved; surely she could be loving? Flora knew already that her arguments against abortion would sound weak. Whatever advice she offered, Georgie would demand to know who the hell Flora thought she was, by trying to persuade her sister she had to go through with something which she herself had always refused to contemplate. But, as she stared out at the cold white garden, Flora knew that whatever happened, this baby must not be consigned to a plastic bucket in a hospital theatre or flushed down some cistern, to float away, unloved and unknown, through the drains and sewers of the city.

She raised her head. Listened. Heard a car pull up, a door slam, brisk footsteps on the concrete path which ran from the front of the cottage to the back. She smiled, knowing who it would be.

He turned the handle of the door and slipped inside the studio, letting in as little cold air as he could. 'Flora. I hope you don't mind me intruding on your working day.' He came over and stood behind her, close enough for her to feel the shape of his body against her back.

'You know I don't.' She turned and looked up at him. 'Coffee?'

'Please.' He unbuttoned his thick sheepskin jacket. 'I waited until I thought you might be knocking off for a mid-morning break.'

'Kind Angus. Actually, I'm not getting on very well. There are too many other things to worry about.'

'Your sister, for one.'

'Right.'

'Is she still insisting on a termination?'

'As of yesterday's phone call, yes.'

'How much longer before it's not going to be possible to have an abortion?'

'Not very long. But she's coming down at the weekend to talk about it, so she's obviously still undecided.' Flora poured coffee into a mug, added milk and two sugars and handed it to Angus. She felt guilty about having defied Georgie's ban on telling anyone, but had decided that Angus couldn't, in the circumstances, count.

He was an architect met at a Sunday morning sherry party to which she had been invited after she came to live permanently in the cottage. The hosts had issued the invitation to both her and Oliver and refrained from asking questions when she turned up alone. Hesitating at the door of the drawing room, Angus had immediately caught her attention. There was a vitality about his gestures and the forceful way he spoke which reminded her of Oliver. Later, as she chatted to some of the locals about the forthcoming general election, she found him at her side. 'I'm Angus Macfarlane,' he said, neatly edging her away from the rest of the group. 'Are you new here?'

'Not really. Sort of,' Flora had said. 'I mean, we've had the cottage for a while but I live there now.'

'We?'

'My husband and – my *former* husband and I. We used to live in London – at least, he still does. Do you live down here?'

'I'm like you, a transplant from the Great Wen. After far too many years of working my buns off for various architectural firms, I decided it might be more effective to work them off for myself. So I set up my own company, and moved down here permanently about a year ago.'

'And how's it going?'

'Pretty good so far.' He smiled at her. 'Tell me about you.'

She told him. He was perhaps ten years older than she was, at first glance fairly ordinary-looking, chunky. The repressed energy which made him almost quiver with vitality even when standing still, not speaking, was engaging. A mover, a shaker, she thought, already amused by the gusto with which he attacked everything which came within his orbit, from a glass of sherry to a discussion of classical architecture.

As she was leaving, he asked if they might meet again. He was the first man to ask her out since she had split up with Oliver, and she agreed, well aware that she was accepting his invitation as much in the hope that he might help her to banish Oliver from her mind as for any pleasure she might find in his company. Perhaps he sensed this. He kept the evening formal, booking a table at a renowned restaurant, keeping the conversation impersonal, setting out to entertain her with anecdotes about the perils of working for himself, as though acutely sensitive to her wariness.

'There's another thing,' he said, smiling to indicate a certain self-mockery. 'If we're going to be friends, and I hope we are, I have to confess to an incurable addiction.'

'What's that?'

'I play the trombone in a band. Just amateurs, of course, almost-middle-aged family men trying to re-create their youth on alternate Friday nights.'

'Are you good?'

'Passable. We get a number of gigs. You'll have to come and hear us one weekend.'

'My sister sings with a band. Georgie Flynn: ever heard of her?'

'Georgie? Good heavens: I most certainly *have* heard of her. '*Falling Angel*' . . . I played with Jerry Long once – God, it was years ago.'

'Who's Jerry Long?'

'The man who wrote "*Falling Angel*" for your sister.'

'"*Falling Angel*"? Is that a song?'

'It's a classic: you must have heard it.'

'I don't think I have,' Flora said, ashamed.

'It's not just a song, but a classic. I heard her sing it in Newcastle once: wonderful.' He smiled, looking back into the past. 'When I say I played with Jerry, I mean he let me jam with him once. Listen, I've got a tape of Georgie Flynn singing with the Ragbags. Perhaps you'd let me come round some evening and play it to you.'

'I'd love that,' Flora said. 'Have you met Georgie?'

'Definitely. As a matter of fact, I . . . uh . . . know – *knew* – her quite well.' The way his eyes shifted made her wonder precisely how well. 'So she's your sister, is she? I'd never have believed it. She's so tall, for one thing. So impossible to miss. And beautiful, too. Whereas you—'

'—Are a tiny, mousy creature nobody gives a second glance at. Is that what you were going to say.'

He smiled. 'I'm not going to pander to your insecurities, Mrs Treffyn, and tell you that you are extremely beautiful, though in a completely different way from your sister. Nor am

I going to say that I have enjoyed your company this evening more than I can possibly say. But that won't stop me thinking it.'

She was embarrassed. Avoiding his warm gaze, she sat twisting the stem of her wine glass round and round on the tablecloth, while he told her about the disastrous village hop at which his band had last played.

It was not until they were driving home through moon-washed fields that the tone of the evening changed. Crossing the ancient stone bridge at Blewbridge, he said: 'It's a beautiful night. Shall we walk along the towpath for a while?'

Flora had been wondering whether to suggest it herself. The air was full of summer scents, and the moon was electrically bright. He took her arm and for a while they walked in silence, listening to the mild chatter of night birds. It was light enough to see the tower of Blewbridge Church square against the sky and bats zigzagging after insects.

Flora said: 'We've spent the whole evening together and so far the only thing I know about you is that you're an architect and you play the trombone.'

Angus walked on without replying, head bent. The river flowed past them, silent except for the whisper of water among the reeds near the banks.

'Angus?'

'My wife left me four years ago,' he said suddenly. 'For one of my oldest friends.'

'I'm sorry.'

'It's not easy to admit that your wife preferred someone else. Whatever tone you adopt, you end up sounding as though you're looking for sympathy and at the same time announcing that you've been a complete failure as a husband.'

'Why do you think you were a failure?'

'Must have been. Otherwise she'd have stayed with me.'

'My husband and I are divorced too. I don't think he considers he was a failure, any more than I think he was.'

'But I'll bet you think you failed as a wife, don't you?'

She was silent. Of course she did. Knew it for a fact. Was perfectly well aware that her marriage had broken up because of her deficiencies, and for no other reason.

'I'm managing to come to terms with losing her,' Angus said soberly. 'But I simply can't . . . I cannot handle the fact that since she left, I've scarcely seen our two little girls. You can't believe how much that hurts.' But she could, turning in the glimmering light to look at him, seeing the lines of pain enclose his mouth and shadow his eyes. 'Although I've got joint custody and unlimited access, she puts every possible difficulty in my way. Whenever I ask to see them, she says they're ill or they've got some vital school thing they have to do, or she's already taking them away that weekend.' His hand tightened on her arm. 'God, I hate men who whinge about their ex-partners, as though all the blame rests with the other person. But in this case, I really . . . Her latest ploy is to say that the girls don't want to see me, that they've asked her not to make them come and stay with me. And for all I know that may even be true, though I find it hard to believe.'

'Why doesn't she want you to see them?'

'She and Harry – that's my friend – have had another child together, and I think she wants to build a new family unit, one which doesn't include me.'

'How terribly sad.'

'Unimaginably so,' he said. 'They're my children too, and I love them at least as much as she does, if not more because believe me, I certainly wouldn't be putting obstacles in the way if our situations were reversed.'

'Isn't there any legal way to make her let you see them?'

'Probably. I no longer know what's best. Think of the repercussions for the children, as well as for me, if I went back to the court about it; the time it would all take. And if by any chance she *is* telling the truth, think of them being forced by law to spend time with a man who has become a stranger to them.' He stopped and gazed across the silver-lit water meadows. An owl swooped just above their heads and she heard the bark of a hunting fox from the wooded stands on the other side of the river. 'I tell you, Flora, that sometimes, in the middle of the night, I've seriously contemplated snatching them away from her, taking them abroad to live. Just so I can see something of my own daughters before they've grown up and it's all too late.'

Moved by his distress, she took his hand. 'I'm so sorry.' She wondered if that was why her own father had never once visited them, whether she had stumbled on yet another example of her mother's cruelty.

'Don't be,' Angus said violently. 'The last thing I want is pity.'

'It may be, but that doesn't stop me feeling it.'

'Perhaps if I'd done something differently, she'd have stayed.'

'And perhaps not.'

'You read about them sometimes,' Angus said. 'The kidnappers, the snatchers. I don't mean the men who take their daughters back to isolated villages in Pakistan and marry them off to brutish illiterates, but those poor sad bastards who end up stealing their children away from their mothers, not because they think the mother is doing a bad job, but just because they are absolutely desperate to know their own child.'

'There was a case recently in the papers, wasn't there? A man whose wife had taken their son to live in Italy?'

'That's right. God, I felt so sorry for him when the police finally caught up with him. You hear such a lot about anguished mothers whose ex-husbands take their children away. And read so many articles about mother-love and its power and strength. But nobody ever seems to write about father-love, and the desperation we, too, feel when we see our children being deliberately distanced from us. I know it's fashionable for women today to portray men as unfeeling sods who don't have a single finer emotion, but for most of us, that's not true at all.'

She squeezed his hand and said nothing.

'You haven't got children, have you?' he asked.

'No.'

'Is that from choice?'

Their acquaintance was still too new for her to want to talk about it. 'More or less.'

He was sensitive enough to leave the subject. They walked back to the car in silence and when they spoke, it was impersonally, about trivial things. At the gate of the cottage, he got out and opened the door of the passenger seat. 'I've really enjoyed this evening,' he said.

'So have I.'

'Flora. I'm sorry. I shouldn't have poured all my despair onto you.'

'I didn't mind in the least. It helps to talk about things.'

'Yes, but not to someone you're really hoping to impress. Someone you already know that you want to spend a lot of time with.'

She was silent.

'I've ruined it, haven't I?' he said softly. 'I've made you think I'm pathetic. I just wanted to have things straight between us from the start.'

'But you still love her, don't you?'

'I don't know,' he said, his voice so low she could scarcely hear him.

'Good night, Angus.' She reached down for the latch of the gate and began to walk up the path to the front door.'

'Flora,' he said.

'Yes?'

'Can we do it again, sometime?'

'Why not?' she said lightly. She did not expect him to call. She knew he regretted unburdening himself to her, and knew too that he could not have helped seeing the barriers behind which she herself was hiding. The break-up of her marriage was still too recent, her feelings still too raw, for her to wish to begin building new intimacies with someone. If that, indeed, was what Angus was suggesting. In any case, she had forgotten how – if she ever knew. She had met Oliver when she was eighteen and from then on he had been the only man she had ever wanted.

But Angus *had* called. Since then, they had become increasingly close friends; one of the many things she appreciated about him was the fact that, so far, he had never put any sexual pressure on her whatsoever. So now she said, 'Did you come to ask me something in particular?'

'Yes.' He put down his mug and took both her hands. 'I could have telephoned, but I thought it would be better if I asked you in person.'

'Asked me what?'

'If you would like to come to Madrid with me for a weekend. I've got to go over and see a client in a week or two, and if you're willing, I thought it'd be nice to take on a couple of extra days and go on a kind of culture-binge. See the Prado. Visit the Thyssen collection. Look at the sights. What do you think?'

They were both aware that he was asking for more than her company. She had always known that eventually he would want to sleep with her, though she had not yet decided what she would do when he asked. If she agreed, he would be the first man since her divorce from Oliver. It would be sad for her and difficult for both of them.

'Can I think about it?' she said.

It was part of what drew them together that she did not have to explain; he knew exactly where her hesitations lay.

Flora's days of docility had stretched long past childhood, enduring throughout her marriage. It was not until she had moved to the cottage, was alone, no longer responsible for anyone but herself, that she had discovered just how much of her energy had been left untapped. Sometimes, hearing herself, replaying conversations in her head, she was aware of how strong she sounded and was pleased. By managing to exist without Oliver, some inner courage of which she had been unaware had been released from the obscurity where for so long it had cowered. All her life she had been waiting for the years when she could finally step into her own clothes instead of wearing other people's cast-offs, stiff with expectations she could never live up to. She had always been either daughter or sister or wife. Now, at last, she could simply be Flora.

Whoever, whatever, that might be.

'There'll be other tours,' Flora said. 'And you've been to the States before.'

'I already told you that was different. Do you have any idea how long we've been trying to set up this particular trip?'

'That isn't the point.'

'Eighteen months,' said Georgie. 'More than eighteen months of negotiation and worry. We were going to open at the Rainbow and Stars in New York.'

'Were you? I'm sure they can find someone else.'

'Jesus!' Georgie exploded. 'You haven't got a clue what that means, have you?' She looked much thinner than when Flora had last seen her. Her hair had changed colour, too – deliberately, Flora supposed – from its usual dirty-looking blonde to a metallic bronze which reminded Flora of the kind of bracelet people wore in order to ward off rheumatism.

'No, but—'

'Can you imagine how the band's going to react when their lead singer says, 'Sorry guys, instead of coming along, I've decided to have a baby.' Believe me, they'll be really chuffed.'

'A baby is important,' said Flora.

'Oh yeah? Then why haven't you had one?'

'We're not talking about me . . . The point is that you *are* pregnant. That means you're going to bring another human being into the world, a whole new—'

'Jesus, Flora. Are you on Prozac or something?'

'—Whole new person. You can't just dismiss it as irrelevant.' Even to her own ears Flora sounded mawkish.

'The Ragbags is people too. And they need this tour as much as I do. They've all a living to make, and Frankie's got a mortgage as well as a wife and kids. Besides, where are they going to find another singer at this stage?'

'There are plenty who'd be glad to take your place.'

'You bet your ass there are.' Georgie ran her hands dramatically through her coppery hair. 'Oh, *God.* I must have been crazy.'

Drunk, more like, Flora thought uncharitably. Her sister's way of living didn't involve too many tea parties with the vicar. 'But you can go back – afterwards, can't you?' she said.

'Oh, sure.' Georgie reached for her drink, ignoring Flora's frown. 'Those are shark-infested waters out there, believe me. After letting them down, I just know the guys will be waiting with open arms to have me back.'

'Why didn't you think of that before you slept with him?'

'I already said, I was taken by surprise.'

Only too easily Flora could imagine Georgie's Limehouse loft, softly lit, the black velvet cushions, some handsome hunk invited back for a drink, Billie Holliday on the turntable, the hour late and both of them slightly tipsy. The kisses getting fiercer, the hands more urgent, the bodies demanding, yes, she could see how it might have happened. 'What's his name?' she asked.

'Whose?'

'The man's, Georgie. The baby's father.'

'Why?'

'I just wondered. Maybe if you don't want to talk to him, I could go instead and—'

'Flora, you are my only sister and I love you – I *think* – but I swear I will fucking *kill* you if you try pulling something like that. Can't you get it into your head that I don't want the man, I don't want the baby, I want to go back to where I was before all this happened? I liked my life, I don't want it disrupted. I don't want this effing baby.'

'Can't you postpone the tour?'

'At this stage?'

'Have the baby,' Flora urged. 'You can leave it with me. I'll look after it.' Then thought: what on earth am I saying? She wasn't sure she even liked children; she certainly didn't find them adorable. They were noisy. They demanded. They did not acknowledge the rights and existence of others except in so far as they touched upon themselves. She was not maternal: it was as simple as that.

'*You*?' Georgie said, with exaggerated disbelief.

'Why not? That way, it needn't interfere with your career, except for this single solitary engagement.'

'If I screw up this engagement, there won't *be* a career,' screeched Georgie. 'If I let the band down, my name will be mud in the industry. I'll be finished.'

'You're being ridiculously melodramatic. Other women in similar situations must find themselves unexpectedly pregnant. I've read about them. Opera singers, ballet dancers. Sportswomen. In fact, I'm sure I've heard that it improves the voice if you have a baby.'

'Sometimes I feel ten years older than you, Flo,' Georgie said. 'And at least twenty years wiser. Can't you get it into your head that my career is *over* if I go through with it?'

'You know you're exaggerating. You might lose this gig, but there'll be others.'

'How would you know?'

'Maybe you didn't plan it, but now it's happened, why not accept it? You know you can count on me to give you all the support you can possibly need.' Flora wondered just how much she meant it and whether the words were merely the means towards achieving an end she was, for various complicated reasons, determined upon.

'This is the woman who's too afraid of turning out as abusive as her mother to have any children of her own,' Georgie said sarcastically. 'Why should it be different with someone else's baby?'

'That's a vile thing to say.'

'But true.'

'It's not.'

'You've bored on about how unmaternal you are for so

damned long that I've finally started to believe you. I'd never dare leave my child with you, in case you beat it up.'

'That you can even say such a thing,' Flora shouted, furious, 'makes me realise how like *her* you are, after all. I've never really believed it, but now I can see it's true.'

'Fuck you very much. As an argument for abortion, you couldn't have stated your case more eloquently.' Georgie got up. Her face was red and determined. 'I spoke to Dave about it before I came down here – his girlfriend had one about six months ago. He's given me the name of a clinic and I'm going to contact them tomorrow morning, fix something up.'

Flora recognised that under the scathing words lay hope. If Georgie knew of a clinic where she could go for an abortion but had none the less asked her sister for advice, had agreed – however unwillingly – to come down here with her floor-length fur coat and her bottles of gin, then surely she must want to be persuaded to keep the baby? She, too, stood.

'I'm going to bed now,' she said. 'We'll talk again in the morning.'

'No,' said Georgie nastily. 'Talking is finished. I'll drive back to London tomorrow and sort it out.'

Flora shrugged. 'Do what you like.'

Death lies in her bed. Death is stronger than she is, irremediable. With death at her side, clocks cannot be put back, fresh starts made, new leaves turned. Sometimes, half-awake, by keeping her eyes closed and her body still, she can imagine she is a child again, and none of it has happened. But not today. With the whiteness of impending snow pressing on her eyelids, she cannot now pretend that he is ever going to come back to rescue her, to paint the world with brilliance.

She opens her eyes. Faces the morning. Another day to work through. More salvaging to be done.

'You don't know shit about life,' Georgie shouted. She was crying, her unbrushed hair tumbling down onto her shoulders, last night's make-up still blurring the contours of her eyes. She wiped them with the back of her hand, leaving mascara smudged across her cheek bones. The night before she had stayed up long after Flora had gone to bed, drinking and smoking until she had stumbled up the steep cottage stairs at four o'clock in the morning. Flora, herself unable to sleep, had heard her sister restlessly shifting about in bed, cursing and weeping, had smelled cigarette smoke and had stayed vigilant, worried that Georgie might set fire to herself or to the house. When Flora finally got up at dawn, Georgie came down too and the circular arguments started up again, back and forth, wearisome, irreconcilable.

'Nonsense,' Flora said briskly.

'You and your oh-so-happy marriage – at least, until it fell apart. You're living on another planet, Flo. You've never had to get out there on the street. You've never had to hustle for it. You've spent the last however many years travelling round with Oliver or sitting in this bloody freezing cottage doing your pretty little paintings, completely cut off from ordinary life. Fucking water rats, for God's sake.'

'You bitch,' said Flora quietly. 'That's totally unfair.' *Pretty little paintings . . .* She filled a kettle and banged it down on top of the Aga, still fighting back her anger at Georgie's carelessly disparaging remarks. *Pretty little paintings . . .* Despite the warm fug of the kitchen, she felt numb. 'There's no reason why it shouldn't be just a temporary blip in your career,' she said, trying to keep the coldness out of her voice. 'And it might do you good to have a break, not have to worry about anything for a while.'

'Except bringing this wonderful new person into the bloody world. And if I do go ahead and have it, I won't be able to just get rid of it when I've had enough. It'll be like a millstone round my neck until I die. A what-d'you-call-it . . . an incubus. I'll never be free, I'll spend the rest of my life worrying about it. That's what being a mother is about, in case you didn't know.'

'Unless it's our mother—' Flora stopped, but it was too late.

'Which is pre*cis*ely why I do not intend to be one myself, thank you *very* fucking much.'

'It'd be entirely different for you.'

'Would it? I've worked hard to get where I am. Christ, do you think I *like* the late nights, the booze, the come-ons and the gropes, smoke-filled nightclubs and shabby hotels, the coke, the junk they're all into and not wanting to look like a prude, not wanting to be left out of things? I put up with it all because it's taking me where I want to go. This damn baby's going to ruin everything I've worked for all these years.'

'Stop bullying me,' Georgie yelled suddenly.

'I haven't said a word for the past two hours.'

They were in the sitting room, with a fire of wood and coal burning in the hearth, the curtains drawn against the cold evening outside. The day had remained overcast, more snow falling in heavy flurries, darkness descending around half-past three. After lunch, Flora had managed to drag Georgie out for a walk, thinking that by tomorrow they might be snowed in and unable to get out at all. Home again, they had dozed over the Sunday papers, which were strewn on the carpet in front of the fire. Now Georgie sat staring into the flames, her fur coat wrapped round her, while Flora drew her teaspoon angel knee-deep in snow, shivering with cold, the hem of its garment soaked, a cardboard sign in its hand written in elegant liturgical script, reading **Hungry and homeless, please help**. If she showed it to Georgie, would it, too, be dismissed as a pretty little painting? She had no idea what the storyline behind her pictures might be, only that all of them would eventually link together.

'You don't need to speak,' said Georgie. 'Just the way you look at me is enough. You think I'm irresponsible to have slept with a man I don't love, and irresponsible to get pregnant and bloody outrageous to contemplate having an abortion.'

'No, I—'

'And don't say you fucking don't, because you do. I think it myself, so I know you must, too.'

'All I want to do is look at the possibilities, the options,' said Flora. Among the strewn newspapers, she could see a shrill headline about government policy, the restaurant column with a picture of the smugly plump food critic embracing a chef, the latest predictions for summer fashions. None of it had any relevance to the crisis taking place under this roof. 'And if you decide in the end that you really want to get rid of the baby, then that's what we'll do.'

'We? What's with this we? *I'm* the one who'll get rid of it and suffer all the consequences afterwards, and risk never being able to have a baby again. Not you. Not safe little Flora who's never lived in the real world for more than ten minutes. *I'm* the one who'll have all the depression and the regrets and the breakdowns. Not *you*—'

Flora did not point out that these were the very arguments she had been using to persuade Georgie that she should keep the baby. Instead, she said: 'What was Dave's reaction to your news?'

'If you must know, he thought it was brilliant.'

Flora nodded. 'Did he say why?'

'He said it would soften me. Said it might make me an even better singer if I could project some real emotion for a change.' Georgie poured another defiant gin. 'Real? I know all about real emotion, thank you.'

Flora got up and peered through the curtains. Snow had fallen overnight. Now, as she had hoped, it was snowing again, great soft flakes which were quietly building up on top of the layer already there. With any luck, they would be stranded by the morning. Which would give her the time she needed. At the moment, no one was on the baby's side except her. Somehow, she had to persuade Georgie to keep it. But why? Why was it so important to her that her sister go through with something she so clearly did not want to do? Answers exploded inside her head, jagged and dangerous, like the fragments of a nail bomb, but she did not want to examine them. Not now. Not yet. She did not feel ready to consider truths which she feared she would find unpalatable, uncomfortable. And mostly about herself.

Oliver Treffyn was two years above her, in his final year of art college. He was older than the other students, always the focus of attention, always the centre of a crowd. The girls who hung round him seemed unimaginably sophisticated or daring to Flora: they wore rings in their noses and had peacock-coloured hair; their clothes were made of patchwork and leather, they were hung about with bells and chains made of nails or light bulbs; they smelled of patchouli. Oliver Treffyn was out of her orbit, she knew that, he was not for her. But at least she could look at him, nobody could stop her doing that. So, in the college canteen, in the corridors, in the studios, she looked at him, observed. It seemed to her that he possessed a humming-bird quality; he vibrated with a happiness which she longed, more intensely even than she hoped for the painfully lingering death of her mother, to share.

Knowing that such an ambition was doomed, she tried instead to find out everything she could about him. At the same time, she was perfectly well aware that if she could not have him then there was no point in carrying on, there was no future, no hope: she resigned herself to an early grave because it was beyond the bounds of any fantasy to imagine that he would give her even a first glance, let alone a second.

She learned from other students, from her tutors, that he was studying theatre design. That he was brilliant, the adored only child of clever elderly parents. That his mother was a drama critic, that he had studied literature and drama at university, that even before he came to the college he had been commissioned to design sets in two or three provincial theatres. That he was destined for success.

She talked about him endlessly to Eithne Pascoe, the second-year student who had become her closest friend at the college. Eithne was a Celt, half-Irish and half-Cornish, a passionate, vital girl, over six foot tall, with brilliant red hair which fell down her back like a waterfall.

'You two are made for each other, darling,' Eithne said once.

'Oliver Treffyn and me? What do you mean?'

'He's used to adoration, and you're desperate to adore.'

'Am I?'

'If you could see the soppy expression on your face, you'd know the answer to that question. Now me, I like them quite the opposite, young and pretty and ready to be moulded.' She flexed her long red nails like a cat's paws and stared round the college pub where they were sitting. 'Like that one. Product of a one-night stand between a theology student and a nun, by the looks of him.' She nodded her head at a boy who stood against the bar, trying to pretend he was waiting for someone. 'I eat innocents like him for breakfast.'

'Poor Chris,' Flora said.

'Chris, is that his name?'

'Christopher Leon. He's in my year.'

'Well, young Christopher's about to graduate. Though not necessarily in art studies.' Eithne got up and tugged at her miniskirt.

'Be gentle with him,' Flora said, as her friend tottered across the room on her impossibly high heels and accosted the young man at the bar. She wished she had that kind of sexual assurance.

In the canteen one lunchtime, she saw Oliver Treffyn sitting with Philip Chapman, whom everyone knew was the most gifted and subversive student of his year. For a while she watched them. Then Oliver, leaning back to laugh at something Philip had said, caught her eye and smiled. Tentatively she smiled back. To her astonishment, he pushed back his chair, said something to Philip and came over to her table.

'You're Flora Flynn, aren't you?' he said, sitting down beside her.

'Yes.' How could he possibly know that? She blushed furiously: Eithne hadn't said anything, had she? Hadn't told him that Flora Flynn had a crush on him, for God's sake? 'Are you as young as you look?'

It seemed an odd question to ask, implying a prospective intimacy which excited her. 'I'm eighteen,' she said. 'That's what most of us first years are.'

'It's just that you look so untouched by life.' He reached forward, laid a finger against her cheek. Laughed. 'I've been wanting to do that since the first time I saw you.'

'Untouched?' The word was not nearly exact. 'Far from it,' she said lightly, then blushed again as she realised the implications of what she had said. 'I don't mean that I—'

But in fact there *had* been men, in the year she'd spent au pairing in Paris and, later, in Madrid. Not slept with. But certainly embraced, in more than one sense of the word. One man had even offered to set her up in a flat near the Prado.

His gesture implied that he knew what she meant. He crossed one leg over the other, easy with himself. 'I was telling my parents about you the other day and my mother said that your mother was the best Beatrice she had ever seen.'

Flora blinked. 'What?' This close, he was less of a humming-bird and more like a dusky angel.

'Your mother *was* Jessica Glanville, wasn't she?' He added, with a quick smile: 'Still is, I hope.'

'Yes. Yes, she was.' Her mother's theatrical career had long been subsumed in the disillusions of marriage and a betraying husband. Her daughters had grown skilled in shutting out everything but the warning signs of another approaching rage. They had digested the fact that she had studied at RADA, were aware there had been a season at Stratford, a run at the National Theatre: they knew little else, being more concerned to avoid rather than to converse with her. '*Is*,' added Flora.

'And her Benedick was Rupert Flynn.'

'He's my father.'

'I thought he must be, because of your surname.' He gazed at her. Added delicately: 'Ma said they'd had something of a tempestuous relationship.'

'You know more about it than I do,' she said.

His face changed. 'That's rather sad.'

'I suppose it is a bit.'

A picture flashed into Flora's mind: herself at the kitchen table, studying *Much Ado About Nothing* for 'O' Level. Her mother, reading over her shoulder, had offered three or four comments on the play which Flora, despite herself, had recognised as both knowledgable and sharp. Angry about one of her mother's autocratic vetos earlier in the day, she had not responded and had been surprised when after a moment, her mother turned and went out of the room without saying anything more.

What chiefly amazed her now was the fact that Oliver Treffyn should have discussed her with his parents. Why? He didn't know her. He had never even spoken to her before. How had he known who she was?

Seeing her surprise, he said, almost apologetically: 'My mother was the drama critic of one of the literary magazines for years and years. She's amazing, really. Not only has she seen just about everything that's ever been put on stage, but she can remember it all, down to the smallest detail.' He spoke fast, words tumbling like falling water from his mouth. If she closed her eyes, she could see a river dashing over a stony bed, and sunlight on wet rocks.

'M. C. Treffyn,' she said.

'Yes.'

'I always read her column. What does your father do?' Her researches had not uncovered these facts.

'He's into drama too. But an academic rather than a true hands-on theatre person. He writes books about it, though, rather than articles. Shakespeare. Congreve. Does some directing now and then as well, though not a lot. Which is what I'd like to do myself, one of these days.'

'I thought you were studying set design.'

'I am. But I don't want to be tied down to any single aspect. I want to keep all my options open. The whole man.'

'So the theatre's in your blood?'

'I suppose it is. As it must be in yours.'

It's not, she thought. I'm nothing like my parents. 'I can't act.'

'Everyone can act, if they have to.' He smiled at her. 'Look, you absolutely must come and meet my parents one day. They would be so thrilled. Could you bear to, do you think?'

To Flora's embarrassment, her eyes filled with tears. What a bloody stupid question, she wanted to say. I cannot imagine anything I would rather do than go home to your big house in Hampstead and meet your mother, who is a well-known critic and your academic father, who writes books and occasionally directs. Instead, she simply said: 'Yes.' And, always polite, well behaved, well brought up, added: 'Please.'

How typical of Oliver it had been to suggest that in introducing her to his parents, the thrill would be all on their side. Nothing could have been more calculated to make her feel at ease. Afterwards, he was to tell her that it was the wounded quality of her which had attracted him in the first place. That from the first moment he saw her, he had known he would marry her and so had set out to discover all he could about her. Just as she had done about him. 'You were so vulnerable, so tiny, so obviously starving for a kind word,' he said. 'Like a little sparrow. And when you looked at me with those huge brown eyes, I knew I wanted to protect you for the rest of my life.'

'You,' she said, 'were so beautiful that I knew I would die if I couldn't have you.'

Like her sister, Flora had at first been terrified that she might inflict on a child the kind of upbringing she'd had herself. Later had come a more selfish fear: that a child would interfere with her marriage, might dilute Oliver's love. She could not have borne that. In the beginning, Oliver had gone along with her. His career was taking off, keeping him fully occupied; he was in demand all over the world, and he liked to have Flora with him. After a few years, however, he had begun to suggest that it might soon be too late, that perhaps they ought to rethink the matter. 'I'm going to be based in

London for the foreseeable future. For the first time in our married lives we're settled,' he said.

'That's no reason to start having children.'

'But I want them.'

'I don't.'

'I'd like to be able to pass on to someone else all the things my parents gave me.'

She understood that. She wished that things were not as they were. She said nothing.

'I know I'd be a good father,' Oliver said.

'Yes.'

'This big house: it should be full of children, Flo. Mine. *Ours*.'

'No,' she said. To tell him the truth would alienate him for ever.

Over and over again they threw the same arguments at each other, the same reasons for and against, the same accusations. Never, Flora cried passionately, in their high, apple-green drawing-room, would she inflict on a child what she had gone through herself. And when Oliver tried with varying degrees of persuasion, cajolery and, eventually, threat, to reassure her that she would never ever be like her mother was, she didn't believe him.

'I can't do it.' Flora would throw herself back on the cushions of the sofa, would get up to pace nervously about the room or pour herself a drink, hands unsteady. 'It would be completely irresponsible.'

'But you don't *know* that you'd be a bad mother. How could you possibly? Don't they say that people bring up their children the opposite to the way they themselves were brought up?'

'That's rubbish,' Flora had screamed, nerves rubbed raw by exhaustion and guilt. 'If that was true, you'd be the worst father ever known.'

Their discussions grew more and more acrimonious. Sometimes, they would draw back and regard each other with dismay. How could this be happening to them. To *them*?

They loved each other, for heaven's sake. Adored each other. Theirs was the sort of marriage described as idyllic: how could it have come to this?

'When did you grow so hard?' Oliver asked and she knew she should have told him the truth long before: that she had been forced into it years ago, that she had always been hard, that it was the only way she had survived her childhood, that all the soft susceptibilities which he had loved in her were nothing but a sham.

A night had come when she yelled: 'If you're so keen on a child, go and find someone else to have it with!'

And he had looked at her, not with hatred, but with a sadness so deep that if she could, she would have had five children right then and there, if it would bring the smile back to his face, make him happy again. 'I don't want children with another woman,' he had said. 'I want them with you.' And had got up, and gone out. Watching through the window as he walked away down the street, shoulders hunched, a street light catching diamonded raindrops on the back of his coat, she had loathed herself.

She had moved into the spare room, unable to torture him – or herself – with nearness. They had begun to move away from each other physically, circling round the edges of rooms where the other was, always keeping obstacles – tables, sofas, glasses of wine, other people – between them.

Eventually, she had gone to live in their country cottage. Fatalistically, she had always accepted that Oliver could not really love her or want to be with her. Unlovable Flora. Plain Flora. Stupid, *clumsy* Flora. He was bound to go one day, so by going herself, she was only fast-forwarding the inevitable. Much better to leave first. And then he had rung her, so distant that she had scarcely recognised him. He had spoken of divorce in a voice so uncaring that she had listened to his plans without speaking and then softly replaced the receiver. It was now nearly two years since they had parted; sometimes she thought that her solution was working. Most of the time she knew it was not.

4

'Now you must paint me a picture,' her father said.

The paint-box was black and shiny, its lid raised into six soft-cornered rectangles. He watched her lift the lid and take in the little squares of colour inside. So many of them that Flora was overwhelmed. Colours she could not have imagined would be contained inside a box. Gold and silver. Purple. Turquoise. Under her fingers, the curved surfaces of the paints were soft and weighty; she could feel the promise they held, the power. With them, she would be able to paint anything. Anything. The whole of creation.

A cardboard chart, lying across the top of the paint-box, showed the names of the colours underneath. Her father read out some of them for her: burnt umber, Vandyke brown, rose madder, yellow ochre, the colours made richer by each having two names, rather than just one. The white was not simply white but Chinese white, conjuring up for her an exotic landscape on the other side of the globe, a special white, different from the whites to be found in England, whiter, somehow, and superior. And the greens were far more than mere greens: they were emerald and holly, Nile and leaf, meadow, moss, shamrock, bottle.

But it was the reds she liked best of all. So many reds: cochineal, magenta, cadmium scarlet, crimson lake. Distinctly she could picture the lake, lapping at its banks, brimming over the edges, staining reed and grass a brilliant, shining red like the wine in her father's glass at night. Dazzling ducks swam there, scarlet-plumaged; ruby swans dipped their long necks into water the colour of beetroot.

Two paint-brushes came with the box, lying in their own

special tray, varnished a shiny red, with silver letters running up the side, spelling out the manufacturer's name.

'Remember, you must never suck your paint-brush,' her father said, although until that moment the thought had never occurred to her.

'Why not?'

'Because it's bad for you.'

'What will happen if I do?'

'You'll rot your insides. Especially if the brush has got green paint on it.'

'What's wrong with green?'

'It's poisonous.'

'Enough to kill me?'

'Maybe.'

She imagined the poison eating away at the dark pink insides of her cheeks, turning her tongue green – chartreuse or jade, perhaps – then slipping down her throat to shrivel the soft bits inside her stomach. She expected that it would be bitter, like lemon juice on the tongue, yet later, when she tried it, challenging Death itself with her boldness – but how else could you produce the fine point on the brush except by sucking it? – it was strangely pleasant to the taste, tangy, like toothpaste.

Where were the others, Georgie and her mother? They must have been around on her birthday. Yet she had no recollection of them, only of her father's bright eyes, and the weight of the paint-box in her hand. He spread newspaper over the kitchen table, found blank paper, filled an empty fish-paste jar with clean water.

'Now you must paint me a picture—'

But, with the magic wand of her paint-brush ready in her hand, she was seized not with power but with a humbling sense of the vastness which lay beyond this kitchen.

'What shall I paint?' she asked.

'Anything you like.'

'Yes, but what?' She was suddenly terrified of worlds which she was not ready to explore. And how could anyone settle for just one thing, when they could choose absolutely anything?

He leaned towards her, smiling, and put his hand on her leg. 'Look inside your head, darling. Or look around you. You could paint a chair, like Van Gogh.'

'Who's Van Gogh?' She looked down at his fingers. She loved his hands. She wanted to draw the long fingers which rested on her tanned holiday skin.

'Another painter, like you.'

'But I don't want to paint a chair.'

'Then paint a garden, like Monet did. Or apples, like Cézanne.'

'Apples?' There was a bowl of them on the dresser and she stared at them doubtfully. Real artists didn't bother with ordinary things like apples, did they?

'Or you could become a surrealist,' he said, using the voice which meant he was teasing her. His fingers gently squeezed her thigh. 'And paint wine bottles turning into carrots. Or trains coming out of fireplaces.'

'That's silly,' she said, reproving.

'You're so severe,' he said fondly. 'Before you dismiss chairs with such scorn, have a look at Van Gogh's.' He slid her off his knee and took her hand, leading her into the dark little room to the right of the front door which was his study. He began pulling books from the crowded shelves which lined the room and laying them open on his desk. 'Look at this. And this. At these water lilies . . . these apples . . . this mother with her baby.'

She liked the chair, recognising in it something graspable, something on her own level. She liked the Madonna and child he showed her, the serene, wide-browed girl wrapped in blue velvet, the baby grasping a necklace of coral beads, angels with rainbow-tipped wings standing reverently on either side and in the distance, glimpsed through an arched and open window, a landscape with a peasant carrying a bundle of sticks on his back, and a sky of an unearthly blue.

Later, he took her on his knee and kissed her. 'You must keep the paint-box safely,' he said. 'Don't leave it lying about.' The words were wrapped in peculiar significance. Afterwards, she was often to wonder whether he guessed how things would turn out, and what pangs of conscience the knowledge might have caused him.

'Hide it, you mean?'

'Yes.'

'From Georgie?'

'Maybe.' He kissed her again. 'And always remember, you have the world to choose from, Flora,' he said softly.

A month later, he left.

'Do you remember our father?' she asked Georgie.

'How could I? I was only two or three when he went off.' Georgie, curled into a corner of the sofa, shivered inside her fur coat. 'God, it's cold in here, Flora. I don't know how you stand it.'

'You can't expect summer temperatures in late February.'

'Not outside, no, you're absolutely right about that. But inside . . . *Jesus.*'

Flora stood up and pulled the curtains across the window. With the sky darkening into dusk, the snow outside had turned the palest of blues (smoke blue? Powder blue?) Flakes still fell, dropping heavily past the window; she could see to the end of the garden and beyond, the blue-whiteness catching light from the sky.

'Don't you remember anything about him at all?' she said.

'Not from when I was child. But—'

'But what?'

'I wasn't going to tell you. But . . . I've seen him since.'

'What?' Stunned, Flora turned from the window, leaving one side still open to the evening. 'You've *what*?'

'A couple of years back. In Dublin. He showed up after one of our gigs.'

'But—' Flora felt her face grow hot. 'That's impossible. You can't have done. He's dead.'

'That's what she wanted us to think. But he's not. At least, he wasn't two years ago.'

'I don't believe you.' Flora's heart pounded, beating against her ribs with outrage. 'She *told* us. It was about the same time Gran died. She told us he was dead too.'

'Jesus. Look at that damn snow.' Georgie lit another cigarette. Her hands trembled.

How could she be so casual about something so significant? 'Why didn't you tell me, Georgie?'

'It was when you and Oliver were splitting up. I didn't want to add to your problems. And by the time you'd sorted yourselves out—' She shrugged.

'But you must have known—' Impotence made the word catch in Flora's throat, '—How much it would mean to me.'

'I decided it was better not to tell you.'

'Why *not*? Didn't you think I had the right to know?'

Georgie lifted her shoulders again, drawing deep on her cigarette, blowing smoke at the fire which Flora had built in the raised hearth. The flames hissed and spat each time snowflakes drifted down the chimney.

'I can't believe this.' Flora pressed a hand over her eyes. Behind her fingers the years tumbled and rolled, shaken like a kaleidoscope into stillborn might-have-beens. 'I can't believe you could be so cruel.'

'I wasn't trying to be. He'd never had anything to do with us before: what difference would it make to you to know he was alive?'

'That's my business, not yours.'

Georgie shrugged again, her shoulders guilty.

'How did he get in touch with you?'

'He was sitting in the foyer of my hotel when I came in after a gig. Me and Frankie and a couple of the others. We went towards the lifts and he came over, asked if he could have a word. Told me his name was Rupert Flynn. I honestly didn't take it in at first. Just registered that he had the same name as I did. And then . . . Flora, it was . . . If someone had hit me on the head with a baseball bat I'd have felt the same kind of shock. I was literally stunned. We went and sat down and . . . and talked. Ordinary sort of talk.'

'What was he like?'

'He was—' Georgie turned to stare at her sister across the back of the sofa. 'Handsome. Definitely handsome. And rather actorish. Wearing a long black coat and a white roll-neck thing underneath. He had one of those American private eye-type hats in his hand, as though he'd just stepped off the stage.'

'But what was he *like*?'

'If you really want to know, I thought he was . . . um . . . rather pathetic.'

All Flora had of him was a remembered smell, the blue of his eyes, the paint-box. And the names. Monet. Van Gogh. Breughel. Botticelli. Icons for a lonely childhood. She did not want to know that Georgie had found him pathetic. She wanted him to be the towering, wonderful man she remembered. She turned back to the window and pulled the curtains tightly shut. Her shoulderblades felt spiky with anger. 'How very patronising you sound.'

'I'm sorry if you want me to say something else, but that's what I thought.'

'Pathetic?'

'Extremely. And weak.'

'Weak?' Flora turned sharply. '*Weak*? If it was really him you saw, which you'd probably had too much to drink to be sure of, I just don't believe you could think he looked weak.'

'Suit yourself. I was there and you weren't.'

'Dammit!' Georgie shouted suddenly. She threw her cigarette at the fire. 'Can't you see, Flo? Don't you bloody understand how impossible it is for me to have this baby? What kind of future can it possibly have, with no father, and a mother who hates it?'

'You won't hate it.'

'You don't know that. Look how much she hated you.'

'Trust me,' Flora said.

'Why? What the hell do you know about it?'

Flora sighed. 'I know you'll love it. And it will love you.'

Over and over the two of them went, the same questions, the same answers, treadwheeling round and round until she fancied she could could feel the tilt of the carouselling earth beneath her feet and herself clinging on for dear life in case the whole thing span out of control before she could rescue the child lodged in her sister's womb. And now there was this further complication, if that was the right word. Rupert Flynn, Actor. Dilemma.

'How can you know?' asked Georgie.

'I promise, Georgie. I promise.'

That afternoon another angel had appeared on her drawing pad, unkempt, draggle-winged, tattooed. Its unruly hair was tied back in a ponytail and it was carrying copies of *The Big Issue*. The tip of its nose was red with cold; its denim robe was ripped and grubby. It had nothing to do with the lovely names of angels which swept like a winged army through her head: Peniel and Petahel, Kyriel, Eladel, Gabriel and Uriel. Man's need meant there were angels for almost every eventuality: Angels of the Sorrows of Death, Angels of the Sphere, Angels of the Seven Days, Angels of the Seven Heavens. On and on, pages of them, volumes of them, rank upon rank still quiring to the young-eyed cherubins . . .

Georgie started to sob, the sound hopeless against the hissing flames. 'If I have it, it won't have a father. And look at the way having no father has fucked us two up.'

'Are we fucked up?'

'God knows I am. And you're no better.'

'How do you mean?'

Georgie pressed her hands to her face; words escaped between her fingers. 'Living out in the sticks . . . in this fucking freezing hovel . . . you and your bloody badgers . . . If that's not fucked up—'

'I live here because I want to.'

Georgie sat bolt upright. Her face was flushed and tear-streaked. 'Because you wouldn't give Oliver a baby, you mean,' she screamed. 'And now, because you feel guilty about it, you're trying to force me to have one instead.'

'Calm down, for God's sake.'

'I'm not having it, Flora, and that's final. You can't make me.'

She wanted to reply: OK, Georgie, if that's how you feel, get rid of it, it's Rupert Flynn I'm interested in, not some tiny scrap of gristle in your belly. Instead, she said: 'Nobody's trying to make you do anything you don't want to.'

'Like hell they're not.' Georgie got up and rushed across the room towards the door. 'I'm going out,' she said.

'In this weather? Don't be ridiculous—'

But by the time Flora had got out into the hall, Georgie had already opened the front door and was outside, knee deep in snow, the long hem of her coat dragging behind her as she stumbled towards the sagging gate.

'Georgie! Come back!' Flora was beginning to tire of the fight involved in keeping this baby alive. Yet sometimes, half-asleep, she could almost see it, reaching towards her, begging for its life, and knew she must not give up until she had done everything she could for it.

Her sister struggled on towards the gate and out into the lane which ran in front of it. The air was bright although by now the night was fully advanced, the sky a dark blue, with a few cold stars sparkling here and there. Snow drifted in through the open door, forming fronded patterns on the hall tiles. Flora pulled her coat from the hall stand and threw it round her shoulders, pushed her feet into wellington boots and went out into the swirling snow after her sister. None of this really seemed to be happening: she still could not take in the fact that the father she had believed dead, whose loss she had wept over for years, was in fact still alive. And had even been in touch. With Georgie, at least.

The snow was deep, almost up to her thighs, so that each step required a major effort. She was aware of anger burning inside her. Not merely for the present situation – how had it happened? – but also for the past. She had thought she knew her sister; the knowledge that Georgie had seen their father and not told her about it seemed so near to betrayal that she could hardly bear to consider the unspoken falsities which must lie between the two of them.

Where the snow had drifted against the hedge, it was almost hip-deep. Her jeans were sodden and freezing by the time she caught up with Georgie. 'Come back to the house,' she pleaded.

'No.' Georgie shook her head and plunged on.

Flora stopped. Light from the bedroom window lay like treacle across the snow. 'Why didn't you tell me you'd seen him?' she said.

'I already said.'

'But that wasn't the truth.'

'It was.'

'Why?'

Georgie too stopped. Her bright hair sparkled with silvery flakes.

'Why, Georgie?'

'I didn't want him to be—' She broke off. 'He just wasn't—'

'Wasn't what?'

'All those years,' Georgie said. She turned to face her sister. Snow fell past her face. 'Imagining him. Thinking he was . . . he was something special, something out of the ordinary, a hero, a – a king. And all he turned out to be was a not very successful actor in a long black coat. I couldn't face it.' Her face twisted with pain. 'And, you see, if I didn't tell you, then I could hide it, pretend I hadn't seen him, and that way, I could still picture him the way I always had and the reality might not be true after all.'

'Oh, Georgie.' Flora felt she had never understood her sister more completely. She moved closer, but Georgie backed clumsily away.

'Leave me alone,' she said. 'Can't you just leave me alone?'

'I could. But I'm not going to.'

'Flo, I am so unhappy.'

'I know.'

'Having this baby won't change any of that.'

'It might.'

'I can't have a child just in the hope that it might cure my problems.'

Flora reached towards her. 'Come here, Georgie. Come back to the house with me.'

'It's no good.' Georgie moved further into the heaped drifts, her coat trailing after her. Her foot caught in some hidden obstacle so that she staggered, tried to regain her balance, then fell, plunging deep into the cushioning snow.

Flora stumbled forward, tripping in her turn, landing half on top of her sister. She tried to put an arm around Georgie. 'Come back,' she said.

Instantly, Georgie began to struggle. 'Keep away from me!' she screamed. 'Leave me alone.'

'Calm down.'

'Don't touch me. Get off!' Georgie moved frenziedly in the snow, clawing at her sister as though she was a savage beast. 'Go away.'

Flora tried again to embrace her, but Georgie struggled ever more frantically. 'No!' she said. 'No.'

Her coat had fallen open and Flora put her arms inside it. 'It's all right,' she soothed. 'I'm not going to hurt you.' And then wondered if that was really true. Her insistence that Georgie take a course of action which she was determined not to do, was that not causing hurt? Didn't Georgie know better than Flora how she felt about having an unwanted child? She tightened her hold, while Georgie uttered incoherent cries of grief and anger, her face wet with tears and saliva, her eyes, in the half-light, wild. The heavy snow was already beginning to fill the crater which the two of them had created.

When did I last hold her? Flora wondered. Her clothes were wet and cold. She held on tightly, murmuring as though to a frightened child, while Georgie thrashed and heaved beneath her. Her sister's body seemed like alien territory under Flora's hands. She could feel the nervous bones: a thinness of rib, a probe of hip, the nubbed line of her backbone under its cursory layer of flesh. My sister . . .

How long did they lie there together, while the silent

snowflakes fell? Time seemed suspended, feeling banished, the two of them locked in a physical struggle which Flora, so much slighter than her sister, none the less knew she had to win. When Georgie finally calmed into a trembling, gasping stillness, she felt as though she had breeched some impregnable defence.

'Come on,' she said tenderly. 'Let's go home,' and Georgie, her head hanging like a newly tamed colt, nodded. They tried to get up at the same time and floundered, beating the cold air with their arms while the newly fallen snow arced towards the sky like wings. By the time they got back to the cottage and had shut the door behind them, they were both soaked. It didn't matter. Both of them knew that some important milestone had been passed.

'A bath,' Flora said.

'And a whisky.' Georgie let her sodden coat fall onto the little drift of snow which had formed against the lower edge of the coffer in the hall and started up the stairs. 'I'll go and turn on the water.'

By the time Flo had brought glasses and a bottle upstairs, Georgie was already in the bath. Flora had not seen her naked for years; she felt shy. Painfully aware of her sister's gaze, averting her own, she slipped out of her clothes and climbed into the bath.

'You always had such a good figure,' Georgie said enviously. With both hands she held the glass which Flora had poured and sniffed at it.

'You were always the beautiful one.'

'I'm much too thin. Men don't like that, bones sticking into them, knees all knobbly in bed, and hips like nutmeg graters.'

'Have you had lots?' Flora said. 'Of men, I mean.'

'Hundreds. Well, dozens, anyway.'

Georgie lay back against the curve of the old-fashioned bathtub and squeezed hot water over herself from a sponge. 'At least you've got plenty of hot water: it's the only reason I've survived this past week.'

Her body gleamed just below the surface of the water. Flat

stomach, small, brown-nippled breasts, a mound of pale pubic hair.

'What's it like, sleeping with lots of different people?' asked Flora.

'Sleeping with. Oh, Flora. You're so old-fashioned. Why don't you say fucking, like everyone else?' Georgie sighed, putting her hand under her hair and lifting it so that it trailed damply over the edge of the tub. 'What's it like? Listen: you've had one man, you've had most of them.'

'It can't be true.'

'They're all the same, really. And they're all obsessed with size. I mean, let's face it, the equipment's pretty well identical in all cases, but none of them ever seems to realise that it's not how big it is that counts, it's what they do with it.'

'I've only ever had Oliver.'

'You don't know how I envy you.'

'You do?'

'Of course. You always seemed so together. I don't suppose either of you ever gave a second thought to technique. Vibrators and crotchless knickers and different positions, all that acrobatic crap. Who needs it? Love is the best sex aid I know.'

The thought of Oliver's stocky body, the way his hands used to linger over her breasts, the sounds he made as he came . . . Don't think about it, Flora told herself. Hide it away. It still hurts far too much. 'Have you ever been in love, Georgie?'

'Yes.'

'And are you in love at the moment?'

Georgie shook her head. 'No. But I wish I was.' She stretched her legs out on either side of the bath so that they embraced Flora's hips. 'God, how I wish I was.'

'Have you ever wanted to get married?' Asking the question, Flora wondered why she had never asked it before. Why it had taken the unwanted child inside Georgie's womb for the two of them to approach intimacy again.

'I almost did, a couple of years ago.'

'Who to?'

'This guy, Jerry, Jerry Long, plays with a group in San Francisco.'

'He's the one who wrote "*Falling Angel*" for you.'

'How did you know that?'

I ought to have known anyway, Flora thought. It shouldn't have taken a comparative stranger to tell me what my own sister is doing. 'Do you know someone called Angus Macfarlane? He told me he'd heard you singing in Newcastle.' And I should have heard her too. Instead, our lives have not so much drifted apart as simply not been joined.

Georgie stiffened. Frowned. 'Who?'

'You heard.'

'Angus,' Georgie said, as if dredging something up from the very depths of her memory. 'Plays a sax. Or is it a trombone?'

'That's the one.'

Georgie peered at Flora above her whisky glass. 'When you ask if I know him, do you really mean have I fucked him?'

'Something like that.'

'Do you mean recently?'

'Maybe.'

'What's your interest in him?' Georgie smiled knowingly. 'Aha! I begin to see it all now. He lives down here, doesn't he?'

'He does. But more importantly, he brought a tape over one evening, a tape of you singing that song. "*Falling Angel*". Georgie, it's wonderful. I – I didn't know you could sing like that.'

'Impressed, were you?'

'Very.'

Georgie tilted her glass against her mouth and sipped again. 'So you've been getting together with Angus, haven't you?'

'Not in the sense you mean. Not yet.'

'But definitely maybe, huh?'

'Or even maybe definitely,' said Flora.

'In that case, I shall say no more about him.'

'Anyway, this Jerry Long and his group: would I have heard of them?'

'No. They were just the support band when we played the Basement. But I really loved him. I'd have happily settled down with him. And bed was only a part of it, instead of just about all of it, the way it is with most guys.'

'What happened?'

'He decided he wasn't ready for it.' Georgie reached over the edge of the bath and felt around for the neck of the whisky bottle. 'The little house. The little woman. Not that he put it like that, the bastard.'

'How did he put it?'

Georgie filled her glass and poured more into Flora's. 'Said it wouldn't be fair to me, that his job meant he was away half the time, that he didn't want to put a brake on my career. So we had this really weepy farewell dinner when we were both doing gigs in Cancún and that was it.'

'It sounds sad.'

'Oh, it was.' Georgie closed her eyes. 'I pretended it was just one of those things and all the time, my heart was breaking. I looked at him across the table and I thought: I am going to die if I don't see him again, if I never sleep with him again, if I can't feel him beside me in the night, if I can't have him for my own. But there was nothing I could do about it, so I laughed and so did he, and we told jokes and then we walked barefoot on the beach – they have this kind of star-shaped sand there which never gets too hot – and remembered all the things we'd done together and – and—' Georgie's voice quivered and broke. '—And the tears were rolling down our faces the entire time.'

'I wish I'd known.'

'You and Oliver weren't around . . . Anyway, what's the point in telling someone else about your pain? It doesn't make it any better.'

'Sharing it does. Talking about it—' The sentence – the lie – trailed off into the steamy air. 'When we were children, knowing that you were there, sharing it, even if you didn't have to endure it, somehow made it not quite so bad.'

Georgie leaned forward, her breasts brushing the surface of

the water, and touched the long scar on Flora's arm. 'Flora, you can't imagine the hate I sometimes felt for her. And because I can't forget it, any more than you can, well . . . Can't you see why I don't want a child?'

'You wouldn't be like that. You couldn't.'

'Dare I be certain?'

'Do you still hanker after your Jerry?'

'Sort of.'

'Have you ever seen him since?'

'Yes. Actually, I have. The last time he came over from the US, as a matter of fact, a couple of months ago.'

'He's American?'

Georgie nodded slowly. 'Californian – which isn't always the same thing.'

'He's not the one who—' Flora gestured towards her sister's stomach, '—you know?'

'The father?'

'Yes.'

Georgie pressed a hand to her belly. Smiled secretly to herself. 'I'm not saying who is or who isn't.'

'Do you still love him?'

Georgie pondered. Her face was flushed with heat and alcohol. The damp was making her hair curl around her face. She looked, Flora thought, beautiful. 'I don't know. Maybe. You only get these feelings once or twice in a lifetime, I'm sure. Like you and Oliver.'

'Me and Oliver is finished,' Flora said.

'He'd come back if you'd have him.'

'How do you know that?'

'I just . . . feel it.'

'He's in love with someone else now.'

'Flora, for God's sake grow up.' Georgie straightened, sending water splashing up and down the bathtub. 'He may *be* with someone else, but he's not in love with her. Any more than you're in love with Angus. In fact, the reason you go out with him is because he reminds you so much of Oliver. He certainly does me. All that pent-up energy, that tiring enthusiasm.'

There were implications in her sister's words which Flora was afraid to examine. 'I like enthusiasts,' she said. 'And how do you know Oliver isn't in love with Annabel Black?'

'Because, if you really want to know, he and I talked about it once. After you left like that . . . He wanted to know if I thought you'd ever come back.'

'What did you say?'

'That I didn't have the faintest idea.'

'So he took up with Annabel Black instead. Who's years younger and fifty times more gorgeous than I could ever be.'

'And is also a first-class, high-grade bitch.'

'Is he happy with her?' Flora knew she ought to hope that he was. If she still had any feeling for him, how could she be glad to hear that he was not? Yet when Georgie did not rush in to assert that he was clearly miserable, she was conscious of deep distress. What right did he have to be happy, when she herself – despite Angus – was so disconsolate?

'Who knows?' Georgie said. She was still holding the bottle in her hand. She looked at it and then shared the remaining contents between the two glasses. 'He seems to be: I don't see him around that often, but I don't pick up any bad vibes when I do.'

'I see.'

'Besides, she'd be mad to do her usual Dragon Lady act round him. Hot-shot director like that: he could give her a hell of a career boost. Probably already has.'

'Oliver's not a director, he's a set designer.'

'See? That's what comes of burying yourself down here in an igloo and pulling the sealskins over your head. Didn't you know that he's in the middle of directing rehearsals for a brand new version of one of the Greek plays – can't remember which – and guess who's playing the leading lady?'

Flora rested her cheek on the edge of the bath. 'Oh no,' she said. '*Medea.*' Sobs backed up in her throat, clogging it. She began to weep. 'He's always wanted to direct it. He had so many . . . We used to talk about it all the time . . . When we finally stopped travelling, how he would—'

'You *are* still in love with him.' Georgie said, and for once her voice was gentle.

'No. I'm not. Really I'm not. I've had more than enough time to get over him. It's just that every now and then—'

Georgie rubbed her hand up and down her sister's leg. 'I know. I know. Sometimes, even now, I see someone in the street or hear a bass line in a club, and I think: It's Jerry! And my whole body seems to come alive again.'

Flora lifted her head. It seemed heavier than she was used to. 'Has he . . . Has the Dragon Lady had any children?'

'Not yet. Too busy clawing her way to the top, I should imagine.'

'Poor Oliver.'

'I know.'

They sat silently for a while until Flora said, the words emerging a little blurred: 'You're right. We're both completely fucked up.'

'I'll drink to that.'

'No wonder really. A bitch goddess for a mother and a father who didn't give a shit. Did he say where he lived or what he'd been doing all these years?'

'Our father? I can't remember what he actually said, but I got the impression he'd been living in the States. But maybe that's because he had an accent. It sounded American but it might have been Irish. I was so flabbergasted by the whole thing of meeting him that I couldn't think straight.'

'Why was he in Dublin?'

'He was in something at the Gate, I think. A Frank McGuiness play.'

'Did you go and see it?'

Georgie shook her head.

'Why not? Weren't you the slightest bit curious?'

'I thought about it, but in the end decided that if he couldn't be bothered to see us for all those years, I couldn't be bothered to watch his wretched play. Besides, I couldn't bear the thought of seeing him come on and do ten lines and then go off again, when he should have been playing the lead.'

A voice came back to Flora. His voice. 'An attendant lord,' she said. 'I remember him saying that to me. I was having my bath and he was sitting on the stool, talking to me. '*No, I am not Prince Hamlet, nor was meant to be. Am an attendant lord, one who will do to swell a progress, start a scene or two*.'

'Very modest of him.'

'He was supposed to be one of the finest actors of his generation.'

'Who said so: his agent?'

'We've always known that.'

'Even if it was true, his generation was so long ago that everyone's forgotten him.'

'Where did we get the idea that he was this great actor?' Flora asked. 'It can't have been from her.'

'Perhaps he was once. But not any more . . . If he's been alive all this time, why do you think we've never seen his name in the papers?'

'Drink, I imagine. Or was that just another of her lies?' Poor Daddy, Flora thought. Rage bonfired her body. Hatred of her mother ran along the whisky streams in her veins. She remembered her father sitting with her at the kitchen table – had he imagined then that he too had the world to choose from? And if so, when had it begun to shrink?

'Right,' Georgie said, 'I mean, you get the Peter O'Tooles and the Robert Stephens who go on the bottle but at least they kept on acting. Our poor dad – he must have dropped right out for a while, and by the time he tried to get back, it was all too late and far away.'

'Was he drunk when you saw him?'

'He didn't seem to be.' Georgie splashed water about. 'Honestly, Flora, there's no point asking me all these questions: I couldn't take anything in. I'd had a few myself: half the time we were talking, I was trying to persuade myself that he was real and not just an advanced case of DTs.'

'What did he say about us?'

'Practically nothing.'

'He must have done. He must have tried to explain, apologise, something.'

'You'd have thought so.'

'Did you ask him why he never came to see us? Why he abandoned us like that?'

'Not really.'

'Did he . . . say anything about me?'

'Asked how you were.'

'That's all?'

'It was while you and Oliver were still more or less together. I couldn't see the point of going into further details so I said you were very happy, doing well, stuff like that, and he said he knew Oliver's work. I told him why I was in Dublin: what else do you do when some guy you don't remember ever seeing before in your life stumbles up and says he's your long-lost father? There's so much to say that in the end it's not worth saying anything.'

Hungry for further detail, Flora said: 'Did he still have those beautiful eyes? And his hair: had he gone grey? Did he look old?'

'His hair was the best bit about him. If you caught sight of him across the room, you'd still think he was someone special.' Georgie swallowed the last of her whisky.

'Does the fact that he looked you up mean he's at least kept tabs on us?'

'Who the hell knows?'

'Georgie, you can't really feel that indifferent.'

'Can't I? Can't I just? Look, let's talk about something else. I find this all kind of hard to handle.'

'Why did she tell us he was dead? That's what I can't get to grips with. I wonder if things might have been different if he hadn't left.' And why did you keep such momentous news from me, Georgina, my sister, my rival?

'For us, they would. Maybe not for him.'

Flora said nothing. She felt that there had been more to the meeting than Georgie was admitting, but now was not the moment to try to extract what it had been.

Later, her head swirling from the whisky, she lay in the darkness of her bedroom. Her hands curled into fists against her sides. Why had they been told their father was dead? If her mother had come into the room, she knew she could quite easily have killed her. She tried to fit Georgie's description of Rupert Flynn onto the picture of the man she remembered but could not do so. She had photographs of him downstairs: head shots, publicity stills, a few family snaps. Even allowing for the fact that the professional pictures had been taken to show him to best advantage, he had been very handsome. Questions, so many questions. Behind her lids, disconcerting brightness made fireworks patterns in the dark. Why had he left them without a word? How could he have done that? Why had he finally contacted Georgie but not her? Why hadn't he got in touch with her since? There must have been a reason. Gran probably knew, but Gran was long since dead.

'It's Flora here.'

'Oh, my dear.'

The silence at the end of the sentence was so much a statement that Flora needed a moment to control her voice. A moment into which Oliver's mother said: 'Flora? Are you still there?'

'Yes.' This was even more difficult than she had anticipated. At the time of the divorce, Oliver's parents had written to express their dismay, emphasising that whatever might pass between their son and his wife, they hoped that Flora would continue to include them among her friends. At first she had been too distressed to answer; as the days and then the weeks and months went by, it became increasingly difficult and eventually impossible to do so. She hadn't seen either of them since her flight from London. 'Uh . . . Marguerite.'

'Yes?'

'Could I come and see you?'

'Make it soon; we've missed you so much.'

Flora sagged with relief. No reproaches for her long silence, no exclamations of surprise or delight, simply the calm acceptance which had always been Marguerite's chief characteristic.

'Would the day after tomorrow be convenient?'

'Perfect.' Another pause. Marguerite's silences were as much an art form as Pinter's. 'Is there any particular reason you want to come?' *After all this time* shimmered unspoken down the line.

'I'll explain when I see you.'

She bought a paper, any paper, to read on the train, as though it might act as a tranquilliser to her thoughts. The headlines titillated: another poor woman had been murdered in the Cotswolds and while pretending shock and horror, the details spared the reader nothing. Knifed to death in her own sitting room while her nine-year-old son slept upstairs. 'There was blood everywhere,' the police spokesman said. 'A vicious, unnecessary attack. I've never seen anything so—' The lacerations were described, the wounds detailed. 'We're linking it with the other attacks in the area.' The victim, only twenty-nine, a single mother, had put up a strenuous resistance before succumbing to the ruthless blade: attempting to defend herself had only made her dying the more excruciating and undignified. There was a diagram of where each of the previous bodies had been found, and photographs of the women so far murdered by the man they were calling the Cotswold Killer.

Flora stared out of the window, not seeing the landscape slipping away. What a hideous way to die. What a dreadful way to kill someone. Shooting was quicker and cleaner. Even strangling. But a knife, no single wound necessarily fatal . . . so much pain, so much blood. Horrible.

Somehow she had anticipated change to match that which had taken place in her own life, but the Muswell Hill street looked woundingly the same as it had during the years of her marriage. Spring was well advanced towards summer, the trees leafed, the gardens bright with urban daffodils. Nor was the house any different: the ornate front door was still a peeling red; the heavy brass knocker still tarnished. At the bow-fronted windows, the curtains were, as always, clumsily pulled back, announcing to the world that neither Theo nor Marguerite Treffyn had time to spare each morning for the niceties of draping the faded chintz when there was so much else to cram into the day which lay ahead. The familiarity of it was therapeutic. Climbing the worn marble steps to the front door, Flora felt the cloud of confusion, which seemed to have hung over her since the divorce, begin to break up.

Marguerite had not changed, either. Angular and beautiful as a flamingo, she was draped in brilliant mulberry velvet under a shawl of rainbow-coloured silks, lined with paisley wool. She held Flora for a long time in silence before leading her into the drawing room, strewn as usual with newspapers and files, piles of open books, playscripts and theatre programmes. Although both the senior Treffyns had their own studies elsewhere in the house, where possible they preferred to bring their work down here where they could be in each other's company. Marguerite's embroidery frame, holding a half-finished cushion cover, leaned against one of the shabby armchairs. Theo's gold-encrusted velvet slippers stood in the hearth, a sure sign that he was not at home. A smell of cold tobacco hung in the air.

'Su-Beth's still in love with Theo, I see.' Flora nodded at the slippers, the gift of one of Theo's former graduate students during the year he had spent as a professor at the University of Tennessee. Overestimating, perhaps, the amount of wear and tear that the slippers received, Su-Beth sent him a new pair each Christmas.

'Sweet, isn't it?' Marguerite said. Adding unconcernedly, as though the disorder had struck her for the first time. 'Oh, goodness, just look at this room.' She tried to tuck in some of the strands of hair, blonde merging with silver, which tumbled from the loose knot on top of her head. 'I really ought to tidy up in here.' She sat down and began pouring coffee into two mugs.

Flora realised that she had been presumptuous in coming here, in assuming she would still be welcome. The smell of the rich, strong brew brought back so many memories that, to her annoyance, the threat of tears gathered again at the back of her throat. In her retreat from her marriage, she had lost far more than a husband. All round the room were photographs of him: Oliver as baby, Oliver as choirboy, Oliver as wedding pageboy, angelic in white ruffles, Oliver as cricket captain, undergraduate, college actor, Oliver in swimsuit and morning dress. And, most painfully, Oliver marrying Flora.

Oliver, she thought wretchedly. How long would the pain of being without him continue?

'It's wonderful to have you here,' Marguerite said. 'And you're looking so much better than last time I saw you.'

Which was during the extended period when the two of them had been arguing themselves into stubborn, stalemated exhaustion. How much did Marguerite know of the reasons behind the break-up of her son's marriage? Perhaps she was glad that Oliver had been the chance of a fresh start. Maybe she even preferred Annabel Black to Flora.

Flora said: 'Living in the country is supposed to be less stressful—'

'And Oliver tells me you're making quite a name for yourself as an illustrator. He's absolutely delighted that you're doing so well.'

'He always used to be rather contemptuous of my drawing.'

'You sound rather bitter.'

'I didn't mean to. But he and I haven't spoken since we . . . How does he know what I'm doing?'

Marguerite tried not show surprise at Flora's tone. 'I expect you still have friends in common whom he asks for news of you. I've no doubt he needs to know that you're all right. You were married a long time and I know he misses you.'

'Not that much. He's married again.'

'He and Annabel haven't formalised it yet.'

From Marguerite's tone, Flora guessed that she did not entirely approve of the new woman in her son's life. 'I've heard that she's a wonderful actress,' she said, guilty pleasure making her generous.

'Did you by any chance see her in *Medea*?'

'Not yet.'

Marguerite carefully put down her mug and turned to face her former daughter-in-law. 'Flora. This is a question I've sworn to myself that I would never ask you. But now you're here, and obviously troubled, I can't hold back. It's unforgivably impertinent of me to ask, I know, but why did you leave him? Why? How could you break it up? Theo and I have never understood. Although Oliver is the light of our eyes, we're both aware that we spoiled him and are prepared to believe he might be difficult to live with. But you always seemed so happy together, so absolutely two halves of a whole.'

'We were.'

'Was it another man? Another woman? Annabel Black, maybe?'

'No.' Flora shook her head. 'No.'

'Was it . . . sex? Had it stopped being exciting? I know that can happen, but in a good marriage, other things can compensate.'

'It was always wonderful with Oliver,' Flora said. Always.

'Then *why*?' The misery in Marguerite's voice made Flora feel ashamed.

'Surely he told you?'

'Never. Even though Theo and I pressed him, he's always been absolutely loyal to you. Said it was none of our business. Which, of course, it's not.'

Oliver. My darling . . . Feeling that if Marguerite and Theo had not had an explanation yet, then they were owed one now, Flora said: 'It was to do with children. We disagreed about it. Once we settled in London, Oliver desperately wanted to start a family. And I—'

'—Wanted to wait? Surely that's—'

'I didn't want children at all. Ever.'

'Why not? If it's any of my business, which it's not.'

'For all sorts of reasons. Mostly to do with my own upbringing. Oliver couldn't accept that, though, and in the end it was easier to split up than go on torturing each other.'

'Poor Oliver. He's longing to be a father.'

'Yes.'

The two women were silent for a moment. Then Marguerite said, with a pretence of briskness. 'But I don't suppose that's the reason you came to see me. So what was?'

'It's about my father,' said Flora.

'Rupert Flynn.'

'As you know, my sister and I were told years ago that he was dead. We accepted that – children do. Maybe if we'd had a different kind of mother we would have asked for more details when we got older, but we never did. But recently my sister told me that she'd seen him two years ago.'

'That must have been a shock.'

'It was for me. Georgie's been pretending she didn't really care.'

'Where did she see him?'

'The Ragbags – the band she sings with – were playing in Dublin. He was in a play there.'

'The Frank McGuiness,' Marguerite said. 'I read about it though I didn't manage to see it myself.'

'You knew my father was in it?'

'Not at the time. Not consciously. But it just so happens I was looking through some of my files only last week and I saw the name R. Flynn. It didn't register: it's a very Irish name, he could have been a newcomer, someone whose work I wasn't familiar with. But now you've brought it up, yes, I can see that the part was one he would have taken.'

'Have you seen him in anything else recently?'

'I'd tell you if I had.'

'Would you?'

Marguerite hesitated. 'I *think* I would,' she conceded. 'I'd have to give it some thought first. But this is the first time I've seen his name for years. He completely dropped out of sight. And when you and Oliver started going out, and you told me your father was dead, I simply accepted it. Though, come to think of it, he could have changed his name. That's perfectly possible. Very possible, indeed. Because surely the name Rupert Flynn – or even R. Flynn – would have made some impact on me.' She considered the problem, head on one side. 'How very interesting.'

'I'd like to try and find him.'

'Is that wise? He seems to have gone to a lot of trouble not to impinge on your lives.'

'But he's obviously regretting it now. After all, he sought out my sister. Introduced himself to her. She'd never have known about him if he hadn't. She was only two when he left. And of all the people I could think of, you seemed the most likely to be able to help me. You know so much about the theatre, actors, what's playing where and so on. I wouldn't recognise him if I saw him. I haven't seen him since I was six.'

Marguerite closed her eyes, as though in pain. 'Oh dear. Poor Rupert. Though of course, he's seen you.' She opened her eyes again. 'But you couldn't have known that.'

'When did he see me?'

'Now you've told me he's alive, I'm perfectly certain he was at your wedding. I saw him there.' Marguerite got up and walked about, the brilliant colours of her clothes making her look like an exotic flower. 'This is most interesting. I saw this man and thought: Oh, look, there's Rupert Flynn. And then remembered that it couldn't be because he was dead, so I forgot about it. But I'm sure he was there.'

Flora's hands jumped in her lap. She pressed them firmly together, hoping to hide how much this information hurt her. She was going to have to sort out a number of things when she was alone again, not least the way so many people around had seemed to have been conspiring to keep information from her. Especially Georgie. And now, it appeared, Marguerite. Who else knew that Rupert Flynn was still alive? Besides her mother, who had deliberately hidden the truth, even after her daughters were grown up. She bit her lip to stop it trembling and stared at Marguerite, her eyes welling with tears. 'Why didn't he speak to me? That's so cruel, not to let me know.'

'His reasons for not doing so must have been very compelling.' Marguerite sat down beside Flora and drew the younger woman's head towards her. 'Cry, Flora. Cry if you want to. Even if we don't know why, it can't have been from lack of interest in you.'

'My sister, Georgina, is going to have a baby,' Flora said, sniffing back the tears, searching for a handkerchief. 'It's due in July or August and now that I know he's alive, I thought it might . . . He would want to . . . I don't know what I thought really, except that he might be pleased to know. That he ought to be told. But after all these years, I suppose it's a bit pointless. He obviously doesn't give a damn about either of us.'

'Don't you agree that he might have had good reason to stay out of your lives?'

'What reason could justify such a thing? Except, possibly, prison? Sometimes, I've decided that must have been what happened: he was sent to prison. Maybe he was gay: it was still illegal in those days, wasn't it?' The thought of prison, when it had first come to her, had hit her like a flung stone. Once lodged in her mind, it had provided a clear and simple explanation of why, after he had gone, he had never been mentioned. Why her mother might have preferred that her children should think him dead.

'Twenty-five years ago? I don't think—'

'Prison would at least explain why he never contacted us.'

'The theatrical world is quite small. We'd have known.' Marguerite sighed and shook her head. 'In fact, I can't understand why nobody knew that he was still alive. He must have gone abroad—'

'But even so—'

'People weave such complicated lives for themselves,' Marguerite said. 'And often it's only when it's too late to change the pattern they've started that they can see they've chosen the wrong one.'

'Sometimes they never do. Which is why I'd like to try to find him. If he's begun acting again under his own name, it shouldn't be all that difficult.'

'Is there an element of playground punishment in this wish, Flora?'

'In what sense?'

'Perhaps you want to confront him with your problems, blame them on him. Or thumb your nose, show him that you've managed perfectly well without him all this time, thank you.'

'No.' But though she protested, Flora wondered if she was being entirely truthful to herself. 'It's not that at all.'

'Or do you hope that by finding Rupert Flynn, you'll be able to change the direction your life has taken, switch it back on track, make good the damage that has been done? Because if you do, then I'm not prepared to help you.' Marguerite gathered up the trailing strands of her hair with one hand and skewered them with a wooden pin. 'And anyway, as you said, it should be a relatively easy task. You don't really need my help. If you set your mind to it, you could find him yourself.'

'You're right.' Flora stood up. 'I shouldn't have bothered you with what is a personal matter.'

'Sit down, Flora.' Marguerite spoke sharply and Flora, inured to obedience, did so. '*Is* that why you want to find your father? In the hope that he can somehow make things come right again for you?'

'Now I know he's alive, I thought that perhaps my father might want to know about my sister's baby. That's all.' Was it really, Flora wondered, glancing away from the upright figure of the woman seated opposite her, letting her gaze stray towards the far end of the room where windows looked out over the long, narrow garden. Thin-leafed branches patterned the sky. 'I thought that if he should turn out to be in the least bit interested, it might be a way for him to . . . I don't know . . . find his way back to us again. If he wants to.'

'And suppose he doesn't? Won't that be even worse than the first betrayal?'

'That's a risk I'm willing to take.'

'Of course I'll help you find him,' Marguerite said. She moved her head so that light from the window behind Flora turned both the lenses of her gold-rimmed spectacles blank, so that for a moment her face took on the aspect of some alien monster. 'Give me a few days. If he's playing in something somewhere, anywhere, I'm sure I can find him. What a blessing the computer is, don't you find?'

'I haven't got one,' Flora said.

'But, my dear, you must buy one immediately. It makes

everything so very simple. And the Internet! I simply love it. Quite apart from the professional advantages, it enables me to keep up a daily correspondence with theatrical friends and colleagues all over the world.'

'At the moment I don't have any use for one.' Flora felt left behind. Marguerite was the older by at least forty years and yet here she was, embracing the new technology with the fervour of a teenager. She stood again. 'I'd better go.'

'Theo will be so disappointed not to see you.' Marguerite smiled at the slippers on the hearth, ornate symbols both of Theo's scholarship and the devotion he inspired among those who had met him face to face. 'You'll come again, soon, won't you?'

Flora promised she would, not knowing whether she intended to keep her word. Looked at logically, it would be better not to. Being back here after so long had wrenched her emotions, and as she walked away down the North London street, she reflected that an organ as fragile as the heart can only suffer a certain measure of damage before it will cease to function.

Near the tube station, she was accosted by a red-faced man brandishing a bottle. 'Who d'ye think ye are?' he roared. 'Think ye're feckin' superior, feckin' bitch.' She sidestepped, determinedly ignoring him, and his cries followed her down the street on a waft of food smells: frying chicken, garlic, curry. 'Feckin' better than everyone else. Feckin' bitch.'

Good question. Who *did* she think she was? Nothing; nobody. She partook in none of the usual female roles. Not really a daughter, no longer a wife, an unsatisfactory sister, never a mother. Perhaps she'd never find out who she really was. She took the tube down to Pimlico and walked through Georgian streets towards the Tate Gallery. For a long while, she stood in front of the block of stone which was Epstein's version of Jacob wrestling with the angel of God. The angel was unwinged, the manifestation of spiritual struggle. The two beings fused into one embodied the mysterious strength of man against the invisible forces which surround him. Looking at the huge carving, monumental and significant, she was more than ever conscious of inadequacy; her own drawings of angels seemed no more than chocolate-box images. Pretty little paintings, as Georgie had said.

Gran had talked about angels one afternoon. Georgie had got into a fight with some kids on the beach and come running back to the house with tears streaming down her face. Gran had checked her for bruises and then said: 'Trust you to get into trouble the minute your guardian angel pops out for a pee.'

Georgie had stopped snivelling and stared open-mouthed. 'Have I really got a guardian angel, Gran?'

'Course you have. Everyone does.'

'Is he all my very own?'

'That's right, darling. Always there to look after you, keep you out of mischief.'

'Why can't I see him, then?'

'Oh no.' Gran had shaken her head. 'You can only see your guardian angel if you really really need to.'

'Why?'

'Why? Because if you could see him, you'd be wasting his time asking all sorts of stupid questions, wouldn't you?'

'How often do guardian angels have to pee, Gran?'

'See what I mean?' Gran had said. 'If that's not a stupid question, I don't know what is.'

Sometimes Flora felt there were times when she really could have done with a guardian angel. Perhaps she could draw herself one.

On the other side of the gallery, a man in a long black coat studied the Eric Gill carvings and Flora remembered Georgie's description of their father in Dublin and wondered where Rupert Flynn was, whether he had ever come here, as she did, to offer the fettered spirit a temporary soar. Although she would never admit as much to Georgie, she still had the painbox he had given her, some of the colours no more than smudges in the corners of the plastic squares. Were their tastes similar, she wondered too; was he overwhelmed by the same paintings as those which delighted and overwhelmed her? There was so much she wanted to know about him, so much they could have shared. So many years had been wasted by her mother's cruel lie, so many experiences lost. Except, a small, cold voice pointed out, it appeared he had not wanted to share them. Not with her. Or with Georgie. He could so easily have contacted them if he'd wanted to. Was there another Flynn wife, more children? Was that why he had kept away? Unable to stop thinking of him, she almost wished that Georgie had not told her he was still alive.

Down the long gallery, through the doors, she could see daylight fading across the Embankment, the lights coming on in buildings across the river, the geometric lines of the MI6 building white in the blue (was it, she wondered, Oxford blue? Indigo?) dusk. Walking down the steps into the chill evening, shrugging further inside her coat as she joined the people streaming towards the Tube station, jostled towards Paddington and found her train, she tried not to mind that she would be going home alone to an empty house. It was by her own choice that she did so.

Her car waited for her at the station. A layer of frost obscured the windscreen and she scraped at it tiredly, exhaust fumes rising around her. She drove slowly. As she bumped down the lane towards home, her headlights caught a figure moving down the middle of the road, not so much walking as propelled towards her by some invisible backlit force. A woman, she thought, as she slowed down, then realised that the sternly beautiful face caught briefly in the headlights belonged not to a woman but a man. He stepped quickly to one side to allow her to pass, not blinking though the beam must have been blinding, nor turning his head aside, his eyes curiously blank, like those of a blind man, his cheeks glistening as though wet with tears. No: not with tears, more as though the skin glowed from within. He wore hiking boots and, as far as she could tell, was carrying something one his back. Mildly intrigued, Flora speculated as to what he was doing out so late in the evening, and where he could be heading. Behind him, beyond her own cottage, there were half a dozen more houses, after which the lane ended in a gate which led into a field. Perhaps he had been visiting friends and was now striding on to wherever he was staying overnight.

Flora hesitated. It was a bitterly cold night: his breath had plumed into the air, solidified by the beams from her headlights. Although he carried no stick, the notion that he might be blind returned. Did he have far to go? Should she wind down the window and call back, offering a lift? She slowed down, searching in her rear-view mirror, but the man had disappeared, swallowed up in the darkness behind her. An owl swooped above the frost-thickened beams of her light and for a brief moment flew silently towards her, eyes glowing, white-winged, a creature fashioned from the elements, from snow and ice.

In the house, as close to the Aga as she could get, a mug of coffee in her hands, she reached for the phone and dialled Eithne Pascoe's number. Eithne was a couple of years older than Flora but still looked as she had in her early twenties. She attributed this fact to men. More specifically to sleeping with them. Often and energetically. Her pale skin and blazing red hair ensured that she was never short of supplies, all much younger than she was. She didn't discriminate: all she required was that they were gifted, young and good-looking. It was almost a rite of passage for the aspiring young artist, lawyer, writer, poet, anything, to have an affair with Eithne Pascoe. Last year she had let her flat in Dulwich for a year and moved to Cornwall, declaring it was time she got back to at least half of her roots, and besides, Cornishmen were so much better lovers than the English, a statement Flora had derided.

'Eithne, it's Flo,' she said when the receiver was picked up.

'And how are you, Flora, my darling?' There was nothing you could really put your finger on, say this way of pronouncing a syllable or that particular inflection was Celtic rather than Anglo-Saxon. Yet Eithne's voice was not and never could be, English.

'Upset.'

'And why is that? Are you missing Oliver?'

'I miss him all the time. If it wasn't such a cliché—'

'Nothing wrong with clichés.'

'—I'd say it was like toothache. Always there, always painful. You get used to it, but that doesn't make it any more bearable.'

'You could always go back to him.'

'Even if I wanted to, he's got a new woman.'

'Get away with you,' Eithne said. 'He loves you, just as you love him. This is the silliest thing I ever heard of.'

'I thought you understood why I went.'

'I never did that. Sorry for your troubles, yes, but understand them, no. And aren't you horny for him, after all this time? Aren't you fed up with sleeping alone – or are you not doing that? Is there a new man in your bed?'

'If there were, you'd be the first to know.'

'I'd like to believe that, I really would.'

'When are you coming up to London? It seems ages since we last met.'

'It'll be soon, I promise. Very soon. If only because someone's got to talk sense into the pair of you, and since nobody else seems to have taken the responsibility, I'll do it myself. I'd come up right now if it weren't that I'm rather occupied.'

'Oh sorry. Are you in the middle of—'

'Bonking? Yes. And he's away out of here in the morning, aren't you, my darling? So we have to make it a night to remember, isn't that right?'

An enthusiastic male murmur came down the line. Eithne laughed softly and put down the phone, leaving Flora not only sexually deprived, but lonelier than ever. Needier.

Angels covered the walls of Flora's studio. She had recently added an older pair. One had grey hair and a sad face, its wings grey, too, and drooping, its robe well cut but shabby; the other was sharp-faced, with long trailing hair and spiky wings that looked as though they were cut out of tin. She was working on a new angel, whose stern, still features were ageless, whose cotton robe had Save the Owl written across the chest. She put that aside and started to draw a different one, which wore a long black coat. There was a brassbound copy of the works of William Shakespeare under its arm, with the name of the author painted on the cover in elaborately mediaeval script. The wings which sprouted from the back of the coat were flamboyant, made from chamois leather to match the angel's elegant, actorish gloves. She studied the other drawings. Chocolate-box, she had thought them in the Tate. Perhaps if she drew them without wings . . . but that would defeat the purpose. Their wings were what made them different, angelic, something above the mortal. Besides, they needed wings to cover the long distances between man's spiritual side and his coarser, basic instincts.

Is there a new man in your bed? Although it might have been expected, she wished Eithne had not asked the question. There was no new man, nor ever likely to be, though Angus was more than willing to assume the responsibility. On one level, the recent trip to Madrid had been wonderful. She had wandered round the galleries, with Angus when his schedule permitted it, not minding when she was alone, since Madrid was familiar territory and she spoke good Spanish from her au pairing days. In the evening, they dined out, drank the soft local wines, walked hand in hand through streets of gentle evening air. It was only when they returned to the hotel room that it fell apart. Appreciative of what he offered her, she had determined not to let Angus know that sleeping with him would be an ordeal, aware that she would be looking for another passion, a different caress. He sensed her reluctance, and after attempting to rouse her, whispered that it didn't matter and held her instead. She was so grateful to him for not forcing the issue that she almost felt desire.

Oh, God. What was she to do? She closed her eyes and loneliness invaded her heart. It was impossible to rid herself of Oliver's presence. He was the first man she had slept with; she very much feared that he would be the last. Which showed what a sham her new independence really was.

6

The little shop was dominated by a wall of racked magazines which hung above a shelf of flat-laid newspapers. Even though they had been placed upside down to discourage customers to read without buying, Flora could see that the headlines were still dominated by the most recent murder. But it was the magazines which claimed her attention. Hundreds of them, it appeared at first glance; every possible interest group, from new mothers to campanologists, tiddleywinks to gastronomy, was not only represented but seemed to generate two or three publications a week. Yet, out of the whole array, one magazine in particular demanded her attention from the moment she pushed open the shop door. She went across and took it down from its place.

Birdwatchers' Review: it was not a magazine she had lingered over in the past. The cover of this month's issue showed a barn owl coming in to perch on the branch of a tree, snowy-white wings lifting behind and above the curving white body, benign gaze turned towards the camera. The captured instant possessed such delicate power that the hair lifted along the back of Flora's neck. Yes, she thought, without the least idea of what she meant. That is exactly how it is.

The moment of epiphany was too fleeting to be translated into anything more than a conviction of . . . of what, exactly? The pages were silky under her fingertips. Certainly, what she was experiencing as she stood there, jostled by a fat woman in a red jacket, was not anything she could have put into words. It was a conviction, none the less, that here, in the cramped and stuffy premises of Messrs Barker, Newsagent & Tobacconist, on a Thursday afternoon, she had not only found something for which she had long been searching, but had also reached a defining moment in her life.

Forgetting to purchase whatever it was that she had originally gone in for, she paid for the magazine and went outside into the familiar street of the little market town, while the bell attached to the top of the shop door juddered to a halt behind her. Oblivious to her surroundings, she started walking in the direction of the carpark, full of an incomprehensible excitement. When somebody called her name, she had to think for a moment where she was.

'Oh, Phil,' she said to the man who was waving at her as he crossed the street, dodging between a tractor and a horse-van, to fetch up at her side. 'How are you?'

Phil Chapman gave her a swift hug. 'Wonderful. And you yourself?'

'Fine.'

'You look well.' He smiled down at her; the business suit teamed with a silk tie told her he was on his way either to or from London.

'You too. Extremely prosperous.'

'Got time for a drink?'

Inwardly she shrugged. 'Lovely.' Whatever revelation she anticipated from the magazine would wait another half-hour or so.

In the George & Dragon, a Tudor building which had existed as a hostelry for over six hundred years, she watched Phil as he stood at the bar. In their shared youth, he had been broomstick thin, with a tangle of unkempt curls which matched his unvarying wardrobe: black polo-necked sweater and skin-tight black jeans tucked into shabby aviator boots. He was still tall, still lanky, despite the overlay of good living and the beginnings of a paunch. She remembered how subversive, how excitingly innovative a painter he had been then, regularly attracting West End dealers to his end-of-term shows. A great future had been promised for him. But fashions change; dealers can be fickle. Perhaps the fact that he had seduced and then refused to marry the daughter of a senior Bond Street gallery owner had something to do with their subsequent unwillingness to show his paintings. Or perhaps he felt he had worked through his rebellions, and accepted the wealthy, middle-class background from which he came, for suddenly, without the slightest apparent regret, he had gone into advertising, though he continued to maintain a studio at his home in commuter country. It was the proximity to Phil and his then wife which had prompted Oliver and Flora to buy the cottage; now that Flora lived there permanently, he had become a near-neighbour and friend, though if choices had to be made, she would always expect him to line up alongside Oliver rather than herself.

'So,' he said. 'Everything's good, is it? Not missing the dear boy too much?'

'Oliver, do you mean?' The younger Phil would sooner have submitted to the Chinese water torture than utter a bourgeois phrase like 'dear boy', despite – or perhaps because of – his public-school upbringing.

'The very one.'

'I don't hear from him, really,' Flora said. 'Not at all, actually.'

'Cut you off, has he? Always was a tad naughty about keeping in touch. As a matter of fact, we don't hear from him much either, apart from a bit of scribble on a Christmas card. But when we do, he always asks after you, regular as clockwork.'

And probably with as much feeling, thought Flora, wondering whom 'we' comprised at the moment – since his divorce, Phil had been going through women with dizzying speed. 'I don't even get a card.'

'What? After twelve – wasn't it? – years of marriage? Shame on him.'

'Right.'

'Incidentally, what's with that gorgeous sister of yours? We went to hear her singing somewhere a month or two ago. She looked terrifically well. Blooming, in fact.'

'That's probably because she's pregnant.'

'Really?' Phil gazed down into his drink. 'Never thought she was the type.'

'Nor did she.'

'Any – er – idea who the – uh – lucky man is?'

'None at all.'

'So has she decided to go the whole hog?'

'Which whole hog? What *do* you mean, Phil?'

'Get married, dear heart. Give up her independence and tie the knot.'

'That's not Georgie's style.'

'She's going to bring the sprog up on her own, is she?'

'That's the idea at the moment.'

'And she hasn't said who the father is?'

'You sound as if you're afraid it might be you, Phil.'

'*Me*?'

'Why not?' Flora had been joking, but from Phil's reaction she wondered whether she was closer to the truth than she had imagined. Or that Phil, at least, thought she might be.

'Ridiculous,' he said, laughing uneasily. 'By the way, if you ever get the cold sweats, do come and stay with us.'

'Cold sweats? What about?'

'This maniac who's going round ripping women to pieces.'

'I don't really think I'm his style,' Flora said, smiling.

'Come on, Flo. I mean it. This last one's getting a bit close to home, frankly. She lives – *lived*, poor creature – on the same housing estate as our daily. Single mother struggling to bring up a kid on her own. Makes you think.'

'What of?'

'You're determined not to take it seriously, but just remember, there's always a bed for you if you want it, until they've caught the bastard. Glad to have you.'

'Thanks, Phil.'

'You wouldn't be any bother, my dear. We've got that guest cottage at the end of the garden: you could stay there as long as you like.' He picked up their glasses. 'Another?'

'Not for me, thanks.'

'Nor me. Business meetings all afternoon.' He rubbed his hands together. 'So,' he said jovially, 'young Georgie's pregnant. That's really wonderful.'

'She took some persuading to see it that way.' Flora stared at him covertly. Surely Phil couldn't be the father of Georgie's child? Surely Georgie couldn't have been so asinine? On the other hand, women seemed to find him attractive, and he had known Georgie for years, ever since Oliver and Flora had started going out together.

'Wanted to get rid of it, did she?' he said now. 'I can see her point. Her profession and all. Singing with a group doesn't exactly make for ideal nappy-changing conditions and so forth.'

'I told her I'd help when it arrived,' said Flora, wondering why she was telling him this. And even more, why he was asking.

'And you've never felt the urge yourself?'

'Urge?'

'To produce a . . . um . . . sproglet?'

'No.'

'Not likely to change your mind, either, from your voice.'

The reason for his interest became suddenly clear. Talking about Georgie was only a clumsy detour into what he really wanted to know. She put her drink firmly down on the low, oak table in front of them. 'Have you been discussing me with Oliver?'

'Absolutely not.' He raised his hands, palms towards her, in protest. 'Not in the slightest. Always mentions you, of course, when we get together. But like I said, the lines of communication have closed down somewhat. Annabel doesn't seem to care for me much.'

'I wonder why.'

Phil leaned forward confidentially. 'Tell you one thing, old girl. It's always a bad sign when a girl tries to prevent a chap from keeping up with his old mates. Nine times out of ten, if push comes to shove, the chap'll choose the mates over the girl. Not that it's ever expressed in those terms.'

'So you think his current relationship might not last?' Lightness flowered under Flora's ribs.

'Convinced of it, m'dear. The woman's poison, for a start. Pure poison. I never thought to see Oliver looking henpecked . . . And he never did with you, not for so much as a second. You always took bloody good care of him. I bet he misses you.'

'Has he ever said so?'

Phil looked slightly embarrassed. 'Not in so many words. But chaps can always tell these things about other chaps, believe me.'

'And he hasn't asked you to check up on me, see if I've changed my mind about having his babies?'

'God, no. I only brought it up in the first place because we – Dodie and I, that is – rather gathered from something the lad said last time we got together – he's always refused to talk about it in the past – that it was the vexed question of offspring which'd led to the split between you two.'

'You could say that.' Flora smiled. 'Have I met Dodie?'

'Not yet. But you will. Love of my life, dear heart. The real one. I tell you, she's been well worth waiting for.'

'I'm glad.' He'd said the same thing about the last woman who shared his life. And the one before. She got up. 'I've got to get moving.'

Phil, too, rose to his feet. 'Look, sorry if you thought I was shoving my nose in, but we hate to see you and Oliver like this. Always thought yours was one which would last. I know he's taken up with this female thesp, but I bet if you gave him the nod, he'd be down here like a shot.'

'I don't want to give him the nod, Phil. We're divorced. It's over. Finished.'

'Shame.' His voice followed her across the low, dark room. 'You two were damn good together. A real shame.'

At the kitchen table, she sat down, refusing to consider the conversation she'd just had with Phil, or the implications it might have. Instead, heart percussive, she began to wade through the magazine she had bought, hoping for some explanation of why she should have been drawn into buying it. The articles were of no particular interest to her, though the one on the barn owl was well written and the pictures of the birds – as white and soft as goosefeather pillows – were full of beauty. There was another item about the behaviour of sea-birds in differing coastal environments which, in some indeterminate way, she found significant. But neither evoked even an echo of the excitement that had first gripped her, although she knew it had to be there somewhere, waiting between the pages for her to find it.

Starting again from the beginning, this time she read each feature with slow thoroughness; still her pulses did not quicken. Eventually she reached the small ads, where high-powered binoculars and canvas-patched jerseys in pure new wool competed for attention with photographers' tripods and country hotels.

She was wondering what could have induced her to buy a specialist magazine about a subject in which she had no interest whatsoever, when she found what she had been searching for. A bordered box, set among similar boxes, in which the advertiser offered a course on birdwatching and suggested that interested persons write for a brochure. She could not have said how she knew that it was this particular advertisement for which she had been looking. No name was given. No telephone number. Compelled despite herself, she cut it out immediately and sent off a letter asking for further details. Though not given to fanciful thought, as she dropped the envelope into the postbox she could not help feeling that she was about to set sail upon a choppy sea.

There were a couple of messages on her answering machine. When she pressed the replay button, Eithne's rich voice danced into the sitting room. 'Flora, darling. Look, it's about my visit at the end of the month. Wouldn't you know it, I've this friend who wants to come and see me and the only time he can make it is the week I was coming to you. Can you ever forgive me if I cry off?'

The second message was also from Eithne. 'The thing of it is, Flora my angel, that he's not only gorgeous but eager. And when you get to my age, believe me, eager is more important than gorgeous. I'll call you.'

Uplifted, Flora laughed.

Georgie was apprehensively navigating her passage through the mine-strewn waters of advancing motherhood. Sometimes she sailed serenely; at other times, convinced she had made the wrong decision to have the baby, it took the combined efforts of Flora and any number of her friends to keep her on course. Even Oliver had been called on to encourage and inspire. Georgie, telephoning Flora to thank her for writing to him to instigate his support, said he was being wonderful.

'As you know, he's never been my favourite man, but he was round here within five minutes of getting your letter,' she said.

'He shouldn't have told you I'd written.'

'I'm glad you did. Especially since Annabel Black is spitting mad at the way he's been rallying round a former sister-in-law. She'd keep him locked in a box, if she could. Only let him out on Sundays. Anything rather than him being in contact with his ex-wife.'

'He hasn't been, apart from my letter.'

'No, but she's so insecure that she's convinced he'll come back to you if he once sets eyes on you again.'

'Who says I want him back? It was me who left in the first place.'

'She's obviously jealous as hell of you.'

'I can't think why. Oliver and I have barely spoken to each other for nearly two years.'

'I bet he calls out your name sometimes, when he's screwing her.'

Flora did not answer. At the thought of Annabel Black making love to Oliver, the woman's hand on his flat stomach, her mouth tasting his skin, her body opening to welcome him inside her, a mixture of anger and pain flushed through her with the corrosive effect of acid.

'Oops,' added Georgie. 'I shouldn't have said that, should I?'

'Not if you had any taste or sensitivity.'

'Which I haven't, right?'

'Right.'

'Flo,' Georgie said. 'I wish you and Ol—'

'So how are things?' asked Flora, cutting across whatever Georgie had been going to say, not wanting to hear it, knowing it would echo a longing in herself which she was still trying to eradicate.

'Everyone's being so sweet to me. Especially Oliver. Always propping me up with cushions and bringing me things to eat which he's read will be good for the baby. He'd make a simply wonderful fa—'

'And you, Georgina. How are *you*?'

'Actually, things are pretty good except I'm getting the most awful heartburn. And the backache! You wouldn't believe it. Every single time I—' And for the next five minutes, Georgie was deep into the subject which currently absorbed all her energies: The Baby. It was as though she were trying to compensate for her initial rejection of the foetus in her womb. She wound down by saying: '—And then yesterday I went to a craft fair and found —'

'You went to a what?'

'Craft fair – you know, where you can buy pottery and wooden bowls, and silk cushions and so on.'

'I know perfectly well what a craft fair is – I've sold paintings at them often enough. I just never thought to hear that my little sister had started going to them.'

'Yeah, well, people change.'

Though seldom, Flora thought, as much as Georgie.

'Anyway, I found this gorgeous coverlet thing for the baby's cot, handmade patchwork in the most beautiful pieces of coloured silk, and then quilted. Like a miniature cider-down. It's just so *cute*.'

'Good.'

'You don't sound terribly thrilled.'

'I'm absolutely delighted that you're getting on OK, despite the heartburn and the backache. Asking me to show enthusiasm for cute little quilts is expecting a bit too much. And what happens to the coloured silk when the baby spews up all over it?'

'You're jealous. Just because I'm pregnant and you're not.'

'Yesterday you were weeping and snorting disgustingly on the phone for at least an hour, saying you were going to give it up for adoption.'

'It was one of the bad days.'

'And last week, if I remember correctly, you were going to end it all with an overdose.'

'That was a bad day too. We do have them, you know, Flo.' Georgie sounded infuriatingly smug. 'It's all very well you sitting down there in your cottage, being superior.'

'Is that what I'm doing?'

'You don't seem to realise that our hormones are all out of kilter. We can't help it. You ought to be more sympathetic to us.'

'Who's this us?'

'Pregnant women in general. And this pregnant woman in particular.'

'I'll try to remember that,' said Flora. 'I'll write out a hundred times, 'I must be more sympathetic' and stick it up on my notice-board.'

'God, you're bitter, Flo. Has anyone ever told you that before?'

'Never. And they'd better not start now. Especially not if they're some woman with unkiltered hormones.'

'When are you coming up to London again?'

'Why?'

'Because I'm thinking of moving from this place to something more suitable for a baby. In fact, I've seen somewhere and I'd like your opinion.'

'That's got to be a first.'

'Not only bitter,' said Georgie, 'But also incredibly twisted.'

I have a lot to be bitter about, thought Flora, as she put down the phone.

The new flat was in Hampstead, on the ground floor of a big house near the Heath. 'Two bedrooms, you see, so one can be a nursery to start with, until the baby's old enough to want a proper bedroom,' said Georgie. 'But it's the access to the garden that's really good. Kids need somewhere to run about in, so this is perfect.'

Flora walked through the empty rooms. A good, high sitting room, a kitchen big enough to eat in, a decent bathroom: French windows opened into a small town garden where, sheltered from the fierce winds of late spring, summer flowers were already in bloom. The place reminded her very much of the first flat that she and Oliver had bought. She did not comment on the fact that the house which he now shared with Annabel Black was only a ten-minute walk away, on the other side of the Health. Georgie would otherwise have wondered how she knew, with sororal percipience would have inferred a continuing interest which Flora was not prepared to admit.

Georgie, however, mentioned the proximity. 'I hope I don't bump into him sometime. Or, God forbid, into her. Snotty bitch.'

'You've met her, then?'

'Several times, unfortunately. The band was doing some work with some production she was in, and it was difficult to avoid her. Oliver must be off his nut, frankly, to prefer her to you.'

Flora did not say that she had come up to London only a week ago, to take in a matinée performance of *Medea*, and been stunned by Annabel Black's playing of the title role. By turns raging, demonic, tragic, she had dominated the stage, had even managed to make acceptable – or at least, comprehensible – the murder of her own children. At the end, wrung by catastrophe, Flora had humbly left the theatre. Anyone capable of producing such strength and fire, of carrying an audience along with her through the most harrowing of experiences and none the less managing to retain its sympathy, was a far more fitting partner for Oliver than she herself could ever have been. And what rapport there must have been between them, for the director to have drawn such a performance from his leading actress.

'The flat's lovely,' she said. 'By the way—'

'What?'

'Have you told *her* about it?'

Between the Flynn sisters, 'her' could only mean one person. 'No,' Georgie said.

'Will you?'

'Before it's born? Probably. But definitely after. It seems only fair.'

'Will she be interested?' Flora asked.

'Of course she will.'

'*He* certainly would be.'

'What the hell makes you think that? He's not got in touch with either of us since I saw him in Dublin.' Georgie looked at her sister pityingly. 'I know you've got this hang-up about him, but what good would it do for him to try to get back into our lives at this stage? I've long ago made all the necessary adjustments, even if you haven't.'

'Haven't I?' Flora changed the subject. 'When you move in, would you like me to come up and help with decorating the place?'

'Thanks awfully, but not really.'

'Are you having painters in?'

'God, no. I can't afford that sort of luxury. But the guys won't be leaving for the States until just before the baby comes and they've all offered to pitch in with paint-brushes, provided there's free beer. And several other people have volunteered. I thought we'd have a real blitz on the place, get it all done at once, and then order in takeaways and things. Have a pizza picnic among the paint pots.'

'So you won't be needing me.'

'Darling Flo, don't look so hurt. Of course you'd be terribly welcome if you want to come and join in. Personally, I should avoid it like the plague if I were you: a lot of musicians getting drunk on beer and splashing paint all over the place.'

It sounds fun, Flora thought enviously, driving back to her cottage. And she seems so happy, she has so many people around her. Whereas I . . . I have no one.

Acquaintances, yes. She had plenty of those. But apart from Angus and Eithne, and her once close but now rarely seen school friend, Katie Vernon, her circle of intimates was small. Oliver had always been all the friend she had ever needed: it was not until now that she realised how isolated she had been and still was, how alienated she had become from the rest of the world. How fragile were the bonds which anchored her.

Lying on the doormat was an envelope. As soon as she saw it, she knew it was from the birdwatching place. In the kitchen, she used a long, narrow-bladed knife to open it; tearing seemed a defilement, a destruction.

Dear Mrs Treffyn, she read.

Thank you for your letter.

There is a vacancy in two weeks' time, and I am delighted that you are free to come.

My terms and conditions, plus instructions for getting here, are enclosed. If you would like me to meet your train, please let me know, otherwise I shall expect you not later than 7 o'clock in the evening of the Friday.

I look forward with much pleasure to seeing you then.

Yours,

The signature was illegible.

It seemed sparse, to say the least. If not decidedly unprofessional. There appeared to be no possibility in the writer's mind that she would not attend the course, though at no point had she said she was available at the time stated. As it happened, she was, now that Eithne had cancelled her visit, but the course organiser had no way of knowing that. She read the letter several times, trying to get a take on the kind of person who had written it. It was obviously a one-man (or was it a one-woman?) show: the details given contained none of the usual 'we', none of the usual hyperbole, either. In fact, no description of the place at all, nor anything about what she might expect when she got there in the way of birds, or scenery, or accommodation. The instructions were equally cursory: nothing more than a list of equipment to bring with her, and some advice about transportation. The usual information such courses provided – amenities, telephone numbers, local attractions – had been entirely omitted, though in the original advertisement there had been mention of a brochure. It appeared there was only one train a day and no other means of getting there unless she drove, which, once she had calculated the distances, Flora decided quite definitely not to do.

She wondered how many other people would be there, what they would be like, whether she might even find someone to be friends with. For a moment she quailed. Excessive shyness, coupled with a sense of unworthiness, had always made it an ordeal for her to thrust her company upon others. Suppose all the people on the course knew each other, had been going on such weeks together for years, were experienced ornithologists? Suppose no one invited her into the circle and she had to spend the week miserably sitting on her own, leafing through bird magazines and pretending to enjoy herself?

If a telephone number had been provided, she would have been able to ring up and establish some sort of preliminary bridgehead. Or say that she couldn't come. As it was, she contemplated simply not answering the letter. After all, by making enquiries, she had not committed herself in any way. If the organiser (male or female) had bothered to enclose the promised brochure, she might at least have obtained some feel for the place. She visualised wildness, loneliness: whitewashed cottages, low hills on the horizon, acid-green bogs masquerading as fields, a donkey or two. And birds – screeching overhead, clustered on rocks, in flight, calling across wide skies, secretive among foliage. Names she had not realised she knew crowded her mind: a litany of guillemots, skuas, redshanks and ptarmigan, hoopoes, hoot owls, shearwaters, gyrfalcons. During this week, would she be watching seabirds or waterfowl, raptors or gamebirds? Was the place she was going to a bird sanctuary or just an unspoiled area where birds congregated? Would there be lectures and slide shows? Would it be fielded and wooded, or bare and lonely? Coastal? Or mountainous? The lack of information intrigued rather than irritated her. At the very least it would be a change of scene, might even generate a few new ideas, and if she took her sketchbook, she could always spend the evenings drawing, while the others went down to the local pub or pulled their excluding chairs closer to the fire to talk about mutual interests, mutual friends.

She wrote a letter confirming that she would take up the vacancy mentioned, that she did not wish to share a room with anyone, that she would be on the train mentioned and that she would indeed like to be met. She sent it off immediately, before she could change her mind.

'I'm going away,' she said to Georgie on the telephone.

'Why?'

Flora was not sure she herself knew exactly why. 'For a short holiday.' She could have said that she wanted to learn about the sinewy movements of birds in flight, the ripple of power through the shoulderblades, the swing of the hips on coming into land. That she wanted to see for herself how the wings furled and unfurled, to observe the minute manipulations of bone and feather, the tiny adjustments necessary to accommodate the invisible cross-currents, the curving cup of the air, in order to achieve maximum aerodynamic efficiency. But after Georgie's comments on her work, she kept such thoughts to herself.

'But you can't.'

'Who says?'

'Me. Suppose the baby comes early – I can't possibly have it without you there.'

'It won't come early – you've still got weeks to go.' Flora resisted the temptation to add that, in any case, Georgie had so much back-up support that an elder sister was more or less redundant.

'Suppose there's an emergency—'

'If there is, I'll come back. I'm only going for a week.'

'What are you going for, anyway?'

'To look at birds.'

'You mean, like blackbirds and seagulls, that kind of thing?'

'I think so.'

'Don't you know?'

'As a matter of fact, I don't.'

'I never knew you were interested in birds.'

'I'm not. At least – I haven't been until now.' Flora was not going to submit her angels to Georgie's telephonic scrutiny. 'But I will be when I get back, I expect.'

'You'll leave a phone number, won't you? Just in case.'

'Of course I will,' said Flora, even though there was no telephone number to leave.

It was warm enough now to have the windows wide open. She sat with a glass of wine in her hand and looked out over the garden already beginning to jungle with summer growth, though the last daffodils still starred the grass under the apple trees. Herbaceous borders and rosebushes were all very well, but she had always preferred the more unemphatic plants with their surprising names – toadflax, dog's mercury, yellow archangel – and encouraged them to proliferate as they pleased. It was soothing to sit quietly for a while before completing her final preparation for her journey tomorrow.

For some reason, she found herself recalling the summers

she and Georgie used to spend with her grandmother, though she had not thought of them for years. Perhaps she was subconsciously hoping that during the birdwatching week, she might find again the uncluttered peace which she had known then. The house where they stayed for a month each summer sat under a chalk cliff, separated from the sea only by a sandy, rutted path and a line of dunes. The two girls had shared a double bed, sleeping uneasily together, waking in salty darkness to find themselves entangled with each other: Georgie's arm across Flora's chest, Flora's foot caught in the hem of her sister's pyjamas. Vividly, she recalled the feel of Georgie's sleep-moist skin, the bony roundness of a shoulder, the particular scent of her, female and innocent.

Wakened by the sun outside uncurtained windows, they would leap out of bed, work their feet into damp tennis shoes, race out into the pale morning and across the path. In a scatter of pebbles, they would half run, half tumble down the dunes to where the water waited unmoving, absolutely still except for the wavelets breaking flatly over each other at the edge, clear as tapwater. If it were early enough for the tide to be right out, the shingle would have given way to mud; men would be moving slowly across the salt flats, digging for bait, each one bent double, carrying his own reflection across the black shine of the sand. And birds would be there, too, screaming round them, herring gulls, kittiwakes, their streamlined bodies endlessly circling and landing and taking off again as they watched for opportunities to snatch at food.

She would have said she had forgotten them or fused the several summers into a single composite, but now she discovered to her surprise that each one had been retained in her memory, separate and entire. The year she started her periods and thought she was going to bleed to death. The time Georgie fell and cut her knee so deeply that it left a scar. The time Gran drove them all the way to Liverpool to see *Hamlet*, for Flora's birthday treat, and they'd stopped overnight in a hotel before driving back the next day.

At the time, it had seemed normal enough that they should

have been alone with their grandmother. Now, looking back, she wondered where their mother went while they were away, and why their father, always believed dead but apparently very much alive, had never taken the opportunity, even for a weekend, to be with his own mother and his daughters.

She poured another glass of wine. She and Georgie had quickly realised that to ask about him was to trigger outbursts of hysterical or sullen rage from their mother, which usually ended in fierce slaps and door slammings, even for Georgie, and worse, much worse, for Flora. Poor mother, grown-up Flora thought, without compassion. How ably, with how much commitment, she had played the role of tragic heroine. She might have made an even finer Medea than Annabel Black. For an actress, it must have been the worst of thespian nightmares to find herself with an audience consisting of no one except two uncomprehending daughters who were unable to appreciate the nuances of despair and angst which she brought to the part. Time had not mellowed Flora's loathing for what she perceived as her mother's self-indulgences, nor for the casual physical mistreatment which had accompanied them. She felt now as she had always felt then: that no parent should make her children pay for the penalties inflicted on her by fate.

Sand used to sift into the beach house when the wind blew off the sea, feathering across the wooden floor, piling up against the furniture, filling the cracks between the bare wooden boards. Since the house was set on short stilts buried in the sand, footsteps always sounded hollow across the floors. There was no larder in the kitchen, just a root cellar set into the floor, a metal-lined recess where potatoes, parsnips, carrots used to be stored for the winter and which Gran used as a primitive refrigerator. On the wall of the all-purpose main room, there had been a framed picture formed from pieces of coloured paper cut into shapes and stuck onto a black background to suggest a farming scene. Staring at it, she and Georgie had played endless games of I Spy as they ate meals which their grandmother prepared in the unmodernised kitchen, proper meals with proper names, beef stew and macaroni cheese, shepherd's pie with the ridged lines of mashed potato dark brown from the grill, roast chicken whose herb-flecked skin had cooked to a crisp. Their mother did not cook: most of the time she produced indeterminate meals of which the elements were meat – grey mince fried with onions – potatoes and a green vegetable. There was something solid and satisfying about Gran's food, about knowing that tonight it would be spaghetti bolognese for supper, or Lancashire hotpot or toad-in-the-hole, though, as Georgie pointed out each time, toads weren't a bit like sausages. The best treat of all was when Gran let them walk into town to buy fish and chips which they would carry back, running with the paper-wrapped packages clutched to their jerseys to keep them warm, to find a big brown teapot ready on the table and bottles of malt vinegar and sticky red ketchup.

Their mother shuddered when they told her about it. 'That any daughter of mine should be seen queuing up to buy fish and chips,' she said. 'So vulgar – but typical of your grandmother. It really doesn't bear thinking about.' But Georgie and Flora thought about it often, longing to be back there. Their years were broken up into segments of which the summer month with their grandmother always shone the brightest. The rest of the time, Gran lived in the tall house in Northampton which had belonged to her parents and where she had been born. The rooms were hung with photographs of people in goat carts, of stern-looking men and wide-hatted women, of smooth-faced children in jerseys. In the bedroom which was called Flora's, there was a gold-framed engraving of trees standing on either side of a rather grand house with formal gardens in front of it. Underneath the picture, written in elaborate copperplate, was a verse which began: *When lovely Woman stoops to folly, And finds too late that Men betray . . .*

The Northampton house smelled of grandfather's pipe and the chutney which Gran made every year from basketfuls of green tomatoes. Nobody ever ate the chutney, and every year, more and more jars of it gathered on the pantry shelves, the labels growing fainter, the contents more disgusting. The two girls were allowed to visit her in Northampton for a week at Easter and Christmas, and occasionally at half-terms. Even in winter, the smell of chutney permeated the old house. The one punishment her mother had never inflicted on Flora was forbidding her to go to Gran's. Perhaps there were things she wanted to do by herself during those weeks; perhaps she was glad to have some time alone, without the two girls in tow. The rest of the time Gran was not permitted to figure largely in their lives, especially after the departure of their father.

Gran had a hunchback. The lump of it sat soft and solid between her shoulders and pushed out her cardigans so that they hung short at the back. Long ago, aged four, before Georgie had come, Flora asked: 'What's it for?'

'It's like a special kind of rucksack,' Gran said. 'Where I keep my wings.'

'What wings?'

'My angel wings, of course.'

It had seemed a logical explanation, even though she could never persuade her grandmother to take out the wings and display them for her. 'Have they got rainbows on the edges?' she asked. 'Like in paintings?'

'Sometimes.'

'Where did it come from, Gran?' Georgie asked once, later, touching the hump with tiny fingers.

'I was born with it.'

'Can't I have one?'

'Oh no, dear. Only lucky people have humps.'

'Is it heavy? Does it get in the way?'

'Never in mine, dear.'

'Did you have lots of boyfriends, Gran?'

'Lots and lots.'

'Did they mind your hump?'

'Loved it,' Gran said.

She had been a renowned singer in her youth, much in demand as a soloist with local choral groups. *Elijah. Israel in Egypt*. The requiems of Mozart and Verdi. Haydn's *Creation* . . . And every Christmas, without fail, *Messiah*. Not just once or twice, but all over the county. In the Northampton house there were books of cuttings: '*Christmas would not be Christmas without Miss Ashby's singing* . . .' they said. 'Once again, Miss Ashby's divine voice lent grace to the proceedings . . .' And the one which Flora liked best: '*The fabulous Miss Ashby* . . .' There were pictures of Gran in a middy blouse and long skirt, with a thick plait hanging over one shoulder. In some photographs she wore a boater.

'I snared 'em with my voice, do you see,' she said. 'Roped 'em in.'

'Like a cowboy, Gran?'

'Exactly like that. Lassoed 'em, tied 'em to my saddle.' It was a picture Flora carried in her head for years, Gran with a Stetson covering her plait and a spotted kerchief round her neck, whirling a lariot above her head as she rounded up the boyfriends.

'Did you snare Grandpa with your voice, Gran?'

'We were doing the *Creation*,' Gran said. 'He was the baritone. I was singing Gabriel and he was Uriel.'

'Those are angel names,' Flora said.

'I know that, darling. And didn't he just sing like an angel, too? Anway, they'd had to hire him up from London, d'you see, because the local man went down with the influenza. As soon as I opened my mouth, he fell head over heels in love.' Her voice still pure, she clasped her hands in front of her as she must have done so many times as a girl and sang: '*Mit staunen sieht das Wunderwerk* . . . That's German. It's about the angels looking at the new world God has just created and singing their tiny hearts out with the joy of it.'

'I wish I could sing,' Georgie said.

'You can, darling. Everyone can sing.'

'Could I be a singer when I grow up?'

'You can be anything you want, anything at all.'

'Did Grandfather carry you back to London with him, Gran?' asked Flora. 'Did he sweep you off your feet?'

'Oh no. I swept him off his. Right off.'

'The fabulous Miss Ashby . . .'

'We were married six months later, even though they said I'd never find a husband. Not the way I am.'

'Who said?'

'My mother, mostly,' Gran said. 'But she always talked a lot of nonsense, did Mother.' She smiled at Flora and nodded. 'Mothers often do.'

Knowing that Gran knew made it a little easier to bear.

When she died, the Northampton house was sold, the good furniture put into store; the beach house had been left to the two girls jointly. For the first few years after their marriage, Flora and Oliver had often gone to stay there, sometimes alone, sometimes with a couple of carloads of friends. They had been wonderful weekends, full of music and laughter, stupid games of French cricket on the beach, long summer days on the dunes. She told herself she must get out the photographs and look at them again. After a while, as Oliver's reputation grew and they were more often abroad than in England, there simply hadn't been the time to go to Norfolk, and gradually they had lost the habit. Georgie had taken men there occasionally, but recently they had left the old house alone. Thinking of it now, Flora remembered how those mother-free days had been her absolute guarantee that somewhere happiness did exist.

When the fabulous Miss Ashby died, the year Flora turned sixteen, her mother had prevented her from attending the funeral. That was the summer that Flora announced she was leaving school and going to art college. The summer that her mother told her that her father was not just elsewhere, but dead, before picking up a kitchen knife and cutting Flora's left arm open from the shoulder to just above the elbow.

7

Darkness was falling across a landscape which seemed only now to be greening into spring, although down in the south of the country summer was already well established. Above the low hills which for the last couple of hours had lined the horizon to her left, the sky had widened, indicating that somewhere beyond them lay the sea. Pressing her face against the window, she could make out very little except vague landmarks and a fading line of daylight, though she had a definite impression of the lowering temperatures outside in the gathering dark, and of bracing winds blowing in from the coast.

She was quite prepared to be braced. Two winters in the cottage had taught her to accept the cold with fortitude, if not with pleasure, but she hoped that the birdwatchers were not expected to be too hardy. Although there was thermal underwear in her suitcase, and some thick jerseys, she had none the less imagined herself in a short-sleeved shirt looking up into a blue sky and listening to larks and peewits. Now she saw this for the fantasy it was; she had not possessed a map detailed enough to enable her to pinpoint the exact whereabouts of the place to which she journeyed, but this close to the sea, it was bound to be colder and wilder than further inland.

Over the train's intercom, a voice announced the name of the station which they were approaching, reminded travellers to take all their luggage with them and told them of other destinations for which they should change here. Flora gathered her bags together and got off. There was a thirty-five-minute wait before she was able to get onto a local three-coach shuttle. Settling into a seat, while the train waited to begin its slow wind towards the coast, she felt a certain anticipation rising. Anyone else travelling on the train might well be attending the same course as herself. She imagined striking up a conversation with them, perhaps finding out something more about the place to which they were making their conjoined ways, and the people with whom they would be spending the coming week.

But once the train had jerked again into motion, she discovered that she was alone. Nor, when she peered through the interconnecting doors at each end, could she see anyone else in the carriages on either side of hers. Surely this entire train was not hurrying through what, by now, had become a definite darkness, just for her?

What past can be yours, O journeying boy, towards a world unknown? Though not thought about for years, the lines suddenly leaped into her mind. She had been ill, feverish with flu and her father, deputed to look after her one morning, had sat by her bed, reading aloud from a volume of poems by Thomas Hardy. As his fine voice declaimed the lines, the journeying boy, with his pale face and the key on a string round his neck, had come to life. Where was he going? she asked. Why did he travel alone? Had his father been sad to put him on the train, had he reminded him about the ticket stuck in the band of his hat? Her father had not known the answers. Years later she had painted a picture of the boy, a slight figure with hollow eyes and a thin unformed body, his inner trepidation reflected in the way he hovered on the edge of his seat.

Where had her father been all these years? If he was alive after all, why had he ignored them? There had to be a reason. It was inconceivable that he should have simply abandoned them.

Now that her own journey was nearly over, she realised, uncomfortably, that she too had undertaken a plunge into the unknown. How ill-conceived it was, to be hurrying through the night into a void where she knew nothing and nobody. Until now, she had always been put onto planes and been met at the other end, she had always known precisely where she was headed and who would be there to welcome her at her journey's end. Now, each mile they covered seemed to be taking her further from the familiar and known: she saw her former life tumbling away from her, twisting and turning like a skydiver launching himself backwards into space. The mere fact that she, usually so cautious, could have set off like this, with virtually no information to hand, seemed like the act of a lunatic. If no one arrived to meet her at the station, she had neither a telephone number, nor a name to contact. Not even an address, she now realised, since her two letters had been dispatched to a post office box number. She reassured herself that the place was probably so small that as soon as she mentioned a birdwatching holiday, they would know where she meant, and the name of the person in charge, though who this 'they' might be she did not really know. If this was an old movie, there would have been an elderly porter leaning on a broom, an eccentric taxi driver waiting on the station forecourt, friendly cottages clustered round a pub. But these were the days of unmanned halts and ticket machines, and if the place was too small to be found on an ordinary map, there probably was no village pub. Suppose she got out and found that there was nobody about? No houses anywhere. No lights glinting in the hills towards which she could start walking. Nothing.

She attempted insouciance. At the very worst, she might end up spending an uncomfortable night huddled in a station waiting room. She had enough clothes to keep her warm and there was bound to be another train the next day. Wasn't there? It depended how isolated the place was. With the closing down of uneconomic lines, the railway system was considerably less reliable than it used to be. There were certainly places where trains might not stop more than a couple of times a week. She felt that she should begin panicking, that she ought to feel some anxiety, but was disinclined to do so. It would all turn out all right. Probably. There was a bar of chocolate in her backpack, and a couple of apples.

Although she was feeling fairly hungry, she could survive until daylight on those. This was the British Isles, after all, not the Amazon jungle; she couldn't possibly be that far from civilisation.

Outside the window, something flared briefly in the dark and was gone before she could properly identify it. Fireworks? Sparks from the wheels? One or two lights now shone dimly in the thick blackness on the other side of the window so obviously the area could not be entirely uninhabited. The train began to jerk, preparatory to slowing down. She stood up, put on the thick, lined jacket she had brought with her, slung round her neck the green cashmere scarf which had been her last present from Oliver before they split up. Had he already started an affair with Annabel Black by the time he gave it to her? And was that affair now on the verge of breaking up? Poor Oliver: what had she done to him by leaving? His desires were so simple: a marriage as stable and long-lasting as that of his parents, children, fulfilment in his career. For years she had shared two of those goals, connived at them, indeed. But the third one had proved the stumbling point. She had never once doubted that he was faithful to her; now, looking back, she wondered why she should have remained so certain of him when his opportunities not to be so must have been numerous. He was good-looking, charismatic, renowned in his field. And the theatre was his life. She knew all about the heightened emotions that went with the job, the exhilaration that came with a shared goal achieved, the sense of existing together inside a closed environment which only its inhabitants could fully understand and appreciate.

Oliver had always dismissed it as a fickle, artificial world of quick loves, quick feuds and quick endings, yet – and she had not really admitted to herself how much this had hurt – it was only a few weeks after her departure from the London house that his name and Annabel's had begun to be linked.

The train pulled up. Flora stepped out into a wind which, after the heat of the carriage, seemed arctic. No one else got out and after a moment, the train dragged itself away into the darkness, leaving her there alone. Behind her stood a building, which must once have contained a ticket office and waiting rooms, but which was now deserted. At the far end of the platform there was a wicket gate; above it, a lamp shed a cone of weak yellow light. The chilly air was full of rain and, once the train had gone, silence. She waited. Surely someone would come for her? She listened for the sound of a car engine, even the sound of hooves, for in this rural remoteness, they might still be using the horse and cart as a means of transport.

Gradually the night sounds grew clearer: the rustle of leaves in the wind, the long wail of an owl, a barely audible murmur far away. The gate creaked faintly. Something flew through the lamp-glow, so that a flicker of light skittered along the platform. A bird? A bat? High overhead she could hear seagulls, their cries muted by the darkness. There was a sudden whoosh as though someone far away had sent a rocket lifting into the sky. She could be anywhere. Or nowhere.

She became aware of light shimmering somewhere at the edge of the building and as it grew stronger, saw that silhouetted against it was a figure. Man or woman? Standing against the light, it was anonymous, unfeatured, androgynous.

'Hello,' she called, uncertain if she could be seen in the darkness.

Someone said her name. 'Flora.' Although the voice was indeterminate, without gender, she decided it was male.

She moved towards him. Held out her hand. 'I'm Flora Treffyn. How do you do?'

He took her hand, holding it between both of his. Although a cold wind blew, tangy with the hidden sea, he wore no gloves. The initial touch of his fingers was cool yet, at the same time, a comforting warmth lay beneath the skin. After a moment, when he still had not spoken, flustered, she said: 'I was beginning to think I'd got the wrong day or something.'

'There are no wrong days,' he said.

'Do you think so?'

'Or perhaps all our days are wrong days.' He smiled. Despite the dark, she could see how the muscles of his smooth face lifted and his eyes crinkled. 'Let me take your bag.'

'Sorry,' she said, following him round the back of the building to a dim-lit, paved area in front of it. 'I don't know your name.'

'There's no need to apologise.'

'Well, I wasn't exactly—'

'We have more travelling to do,' he said.

Flora felt a squirm of anxiety. He seemed to be addressing someone else, not her at all. *There are no wrong days . . .* What did he mean by that? His method of conversation was eccentric, if not decidedly strange. And she was here alone with him, without anyone knowing her whereabouts or how to look for her if she did not return. Was it wise to set off into the darkness with him? For a moment she hesitated, even though some instinct told her that his odd manner was the result of a learned strength rather than of menace. Besides, at this stage, what alternative did she have?

The late-model Range Rover waiting in the station forecourt reassured her somewhat, being definitely contemporary, sturdily of the here and now. He slung her bag in the back and helped her up before swinging himself up into the driver's seat. Turning on the ignition, staring ahead of him, he said: 'You are troubled.'

She blushed, embarrassed that he had guessed what she was thinking. 'No, no,' she said. As they set off, she added awkwardly: 'I just thought there might be other people on the train who were also coming on this course.'

'Did you?'

'Until I realised that I was the only person still travelling on it, that is.'

'We make all our journeys alone,' he said.

'Yes, I suppose we do.' Flora hoped there was not going to

be too much of this heavily symbolic talk; it had been a long day and she was tired.

'Why don't you try to sleep?' her companion said. 'We have nearly an hour of driving before us.'

It would solve the problem of having to make conversation. She still didn't know his name, or even what he looked liked. It would all be easier when they reached the centre and she could blend in with the other people. Until then . . . 'Good idea,' she said and turned sideways, resting her head against a shawl of soft wool which was thrown over the back of her seat and closing her eyes.

Air pushed coldly past them, red light gleamed slickly on wind-ruffled waters. Through her mind rushed spaces of cerulean blue full of rainbow-tipped wings and crimson lakes crowded with scarlet bird life. Dozing, she recalled the day of her wedding, when everything had pointed towards perfection, and how primitive colours had glowed like underwater jewels in the subaqueous light of the marquee erected on the back lawn of Oliver's parents' house. The pure pink and silver of cold salmon, the cool citrus of lemon slices, blue dishes of yellow mayonnaise up and down the tables, platters of tiny new potatoes glistening like marbles with melted butter, the exquisite green of the parsley sliding down their greased sides. A brass ensemble, dressed in white flannels and striped blazers, had played in the garden, jerky 1930s tunes which mingled with the voices of the guests and imbued the occasion with the contented falsehoods of between the wars.

Even her mother had seemed less inimical than usual. There had been people there whom Flora had never heard of, and many she had, who seemed to be known to both Jessica and the two Treffyns. Newspaper names, theatrical names: had she given more thought to what was happening outside herself, she might have realised that for the first time in her life, she was seeing her mother in her natural element, recognised that her mother was beautiful and admired. She remembered half-caught phrases which spread like a fine mist around her as she passed, whose meaning she had not analysed: *Jessica, so wonderful . . . sacrificed . . . devoted herself . . . brilliant . . . Jessica . . . Rupert . . . such a pity . . .*

She had not been really listening. That day, she had been purely happy for the first time in her life, and known that from then on, she always would be, for she would have Oliver at her side. Oliver, her love, her rescuer, her escape. Oliver, who annihilated the hostility in her mother's eyes. She had a photograph of him at the wedding, posed in front of a tuba, his head brass-haloed by the great golden mouth of it. As she dozed, other voices rang through the caves of her mind, plangent against the walls of memory: I will love you for ever. For always All my life. I will always love you. For better, for worse.

Oh, Oliver . . . Only half-awake, she whimpered. Where did it go, all that brightness? Why did it go? Had it always been doomed, or had she, glimpsing Paradise and not daring to believe she would be allowed in, deliberately chosen to turn her back on it, pre-empting rejection?

And Jessica: why had she not ever before considered those faintly remembered voices and what they were saying? Clearly her mother had spread the myth of the Devoted Parent to good effect: what would have been said if they knew the truth?

The Range Rover jolted over a bump in the road, and she could feel, lying just below her surface, tears of loss and pain. About to weep, she felt the birdman's hand on her arm, soothing as a magic potion. The tension drained from her and she turned into the softness of the shawl on her seat, and slept.

She awoke as they rolled to a halt in front of a long, low building, lights showing behind drawn curtains. The air was cold, acid with frost, despite the time of year; she could smell the sea. Though she could see nothing, there was a sense of space all round her, and emptiness.

'Where are we?' she asked, made stupid with tiredness. It had been a long and exhausting day, and she felt she had already travelled further than she had expected.

'Where do you want to be?'

It was another of his enigmatic questions, too deep, or too pointless, she considered, to be worth answering. Or was he simply one of those people who had no time for small talk, for the little niceties of two strangers evaluating each other? She wanted to be at her journey's end, obviously. Warm by a fire. Friendly with others. A drink would not have come amiss, either, though she suspected that bird watchers might not be great imbibers, which was why she had packed among her sweaters a discreet bottle of whisky.

He opened a door, and light spilled out. For a moment she hesitated. Out here, in the vast darkness, it was peaceful; once she stepped through the doorway she would be entering another place, where more would be required of her than merely existence. Then, pulling back her shoulders, she went past him into the building. The room she entered was warm and wood-lined, with a shallow, open staircase in the middle of it, leading to an upper floor; the floor was sanded and sealed. To one side, under the open staircase, was a harpsichord made of some light-coloured wood, painted with cherubs entwined in faded blue ribbons. Logs burned in a generously large fireplace, there were two glasses and an open bottle of red wine on a table set between two comfortable armchairs arranged facing the fire.

'How nice,' Flora said, instinctively making for the hearth and warming her hands at the flames, although they were not cold. She could smell something cooking: a *boeuf bourgignon*, she thought. Hoped. 'What is this place: one of those purpose-built study centres or something?'

'No.'

'Is it yours? Your own place, I mean?'

'I built it.' He was bringing her bag in, a tall, blue-eyed man in a sweater and jeans, with a strong, ageless face. His hair might have been gold or grey: it was difficult to tell. Looking at him in the light, she was teased by familiarity.

'Alone?'

'How else?' He smiled faintly.

She was struck by the banister which guarded the open stairs and rose to the floor above. Each flat balustrade had been fashioned into the stylised likeness of an angel, dramatically winged. 'You carved those yourself?'

'Yes.'

'Do you live here all the time?' So many questions: she felt as though she were a child again, demanding to know more, wanting whole loaves of information rather than the crumbs she was being given.

'No.'

Flora looked round. There was no sign that anyone else was in residence. So who had opened the wine, who had cooked the meat? 'Where are the others?' she asked.

'Others?'

'Surely I'm not the only person on this course.' All her doubts came rushing back. He could be a murderer. A rapist who had enticed her to this lonely spot in order to indulge in his love for sadistic torture. Headliness raced through her mind: Woman's Mutilated Body Found . . . Brutal Sex Slaying . . . 'Isn't anyone else here?'

'Not at the moment.'

'But—'

'Your need was greater.' He smiled at her and began to climb the angled stairway with her bag.

She called after him, resolute. 'Excuse me.'

He turned. Looked down at her. 'Yes?'

'Could you tell me,' she said, wanting to know what he meant, determined to demand concrete details, to root herself somewhere. '. . . Am I . . . Are we here . . . Is it going to be just the two of us here tonight?'

'Would that bother you?'

Looking at the fine, strong planes of his face, she thought: Not really. What, in any case, would be the point in arguing about it? Even if it did bother her, he was not going to take her back to the train station and even if he did, what would she do there? Where would she go?

She thought: besides, I'm hungry, I'm tired. I'm here. And

I've paid for the week. Swallowing whatever else she might have replied, she said: 'Might I pour a glass of wine?'

'Pour two.'

His footsteps made no noise on the wooden boards. She supposed that quietness was something that birdwatchers cultivated. She sat down in front of the fire with the wine in her hands and stared at the flames. Later, she would make him tell her exactly what was expected, who else was coming, what the course consisted of. If she was to spend a week here alone with a man she had never seen before, in a place whose existence she had not even been able to establish, she ought at least to know his name.

He reappeared, sat down in the other armchair and lifted the glass she had poured for him. Crimson reflections fell onto his cheek. On her father's desk had stood a brass lampstand with a Tiffany shade, brilliant pieces of glass making up a border of flowers and leaves which glowed like rubies, emeralds, sapphires, when the light was switched on.

'Am I alone on this course? The only one?' she said, knowing suddenly that she was.

'Not alone, while I am with you.'

That was not quite what she had meant. She stared again into the fire. Little turquoise flames flickered along the logs; tiny spirals of smoke hissed suddenly upwards from minute cracks and crevices hidden in the soft surface. Sea wood, driftwood, rescued from the waves. Sometimes she and Georgie had walked along the shoreline gathering branches smooth as bones, and stacked them by the empty grate in Gran's summer cottage until an evening came cold enough to burn them.

'I don't even know your name,' she said.

'Names signify nothing.'

'Maybe not,' she said, irritated by his games. 'But they're useful none the less. You called me Flora. What can I call you?' She lifted a hand. 'And please don't tell me I can call you whatever I want to. Which is what I suspect you were about to say.'

He laughed. 'So, you know me already.'

This time, she was not to be deflected so easily. 'What do I call you?'

He hesitated. Looked at her and then into the fire. His mouth tightened for a moment, as though he were taking some decision, then he said: 'Gregor.'

She looked at the angel balustrades. 'Gregor,' she said. 'That's Scottish.' She did not ask if that was his first name or his last.

'Is it?'

'It's a good name.'

'In what sense?'

'It's . . . I think *solid* is the word I'm looking for.'

He shrugged. His expression moved her with its sadness. 'A label, merely.'

'Labels identify.'

'I should be the same whether you labelled me or not.' His accent was not so much regional as faintly remote, as though English were not a language he was accustomed to, but from what area, what country, he came from she could not have said.

'What do you do when you're not here?' she asked.

'Does it matter?'

She could not decide whether the question was intended to be offputting, or simply posed out of interest in her answer – or whether either mattered. 'Perhaps not,' she said cautiously. 'But—'

'It's so unimportant.' He interrupted her vigorously. 'All that nonsense: the stuff of cocktail parties and dinner-table conversations. Why do you want to know what I do – by which you mean, how do I earn my living – or where I live, or what kind of background I come from? What matters is who I am, inside, and how I came to be that person, and the things which have happened to change or not to change me, and those are things nobody but I myself can ever know. All the rest is nothing but superficial detail.'

'I'm an artist,' she said with an equanimity which surprised her. She had never described herself in such terms before. Had never presumed to. 'And when I paint, it's precisely by the building up of superficial detail, stroke by stroke, colour by colour, that I eventually produce a finished picture. And that's how people who look at it know what went into its making.'

'That presupposes that you want them to know. But *I*—' His fingers gripped his glass and for a moment she thought he was going to smash it on the hearth. '— I don't want others to know the person I am inside.'

'Why not? Are you frightened of what they'll see?'

He smiled a little grimly. 'Or am I simply frightened of what I'll see? I don't know the answer to that.'

'Are you married?' She was curious as to whether his inner solitude had ever been breached.

He breathed sharply in, as though it pained him, then said: 'Not in your sense.'

'What is my sense?'

'With papers and rings and meaningless promises.'

Meaningless promises . . . Was that all there had been between her and Oliver? Angered at his presumption, she sipped her wine and did not reply. If he wished to obfuscate, fine. She was not going to pander to his determination to give nothing of himself away.

After a while, he said: 'You're hungry.'

'Yes.'

He got up. 'In five minutes we shall eat.'

Instead of standing too, of moving into bustle mode, of being helpful, she stayed where she was. Just as the prickled shell of a chestnut splits to reveal the glossy nut within, so she felt as though the protective layer which had enclosed her for so long had at last split to reveal a newer, shinier Flora. A Mary who let others, the Marthas, get on with things. She smiled into the fire. 'That would be good.'

Afterwards, when Georgie asked her what the week had been like, she was not immediately able to answer. In the end, she could only say: 'It was peaceful.'

'Is that all?'

'Not all. But a lot.'

There had been birds, too, of course. Ordinary birds who did not excite much curiosity, most of them looking like the sort of thing she saw out of her window at home. The seabirds were more interesting: riding the heaving water which surrounded them, soaring, gliding, diving like dropped stones into the waves, coming in to land. 'It's the wings,' she explained to Gregor, in one of the rare moments when they spoke. 'I'm not really interested in birds so much as in the way they fly.'

'The wings?' The wind was strong that day, blowing in from the sea, so that he had to cup his hand round his mouth and speak into her ear in order to be heard.

'That's right.' She did the same, feeling the warmth of his skin against her wind-chilled face. 'I want to know how they use their wings to balance, to soar. How they fold them, the way they tuck them in around their bodies.'

'Ah,' he said, his lips as close to her as a kiss. 'Look at that cormorant: see how it settles after a long glide, how it rears up with its feet thrust forward, how its wings beat as it drops?'

'Just like swans.'

'Yes. But different.'

'Because they're built differently, with different body parts to manage?'

'Exactly.'

Would angels fly like swans, she wondered, with that measured, singing beat, or would they be quicker in flight, and finer, like gulls, like thrushes or mallards? Would Gregor know, if she asked him? She thought of humming-birds, tiny and brilliant, and the massive muscle movements involved in keeping them in the air while they fed on honeydew.

'And look at the shags,' he went on. 'Although they're related to the cormorant, you can see that they don't glide nearly so much, they skim rather than coming down in a long single movement.'

'Yes.'

* * *

It rained a lot during the week. Sometimes the two of them tramped inland, away from the sea, pushing through knee-high wet grass, along bramble hedges, stumbling over the thick, rough clods at the edges of ploughed fields. They would lie on their stomachs, watching through glasses as some nondescript bird perched and fluttered among thorny branches only just beginning to show bud, jerked its head this way and that, pecked, started. As they gazed, Gregor would speak quietly, his mouth at her ear, telling her about the bird, its preferred habitat, its song, the colour of its eggs. Each day, he packed sandwiches for them which he carried in a small pack on his back, along with a thermos. They would eat together, leaning against a tree or sitting on a cliff, with the wind roaring round their ears. They seldom spoke directly to each other. Sometimes he would say quietly: 'See that? Over there?' He would stand behind her, his body close-packed with hers, his arms round her holding the glasses steadily to her eyes. Sometimes his face touched hers and she was aware of the curiously chill warmth of it against her cheek.

One morning she looked out of her window and saw only greyness. Sea and sky were continuous, without demarcation; long lines of rain beat heavily at the sodden earth. At the breakfast table, she said: 'So we shan't be going out this morning,' as though he had spoken, had explained that the birds would not be easy to spot on a day like this. This was not the first time she had felt his thoughts projected into her mind.

'I think not. So what will you do?'

'Draw.' The spareness of his conversation had become pleasing to her, was even infectious.

'It will be good.'

'What will?'

'Your book about angels.'

She stared at him. 'How did you know?'

He looked away. 'You said.'

With pretended nonchalance, she said: 'Did I?' Certain she had not.

The rain did not let up all day. Towards the early evening,

she went up to her room to change out of her jeans and sweater. She rarely heard any sound from below, but to-day, she heard music. Very quietly, she crept across the floor of her room and opened her door. Gregor must be playing a tape as he prepared the supper. She listened for a minute or two, entranced. The sound was like nothing she had heard before, unearthly, somewhere between tenor and soprano. She could not even tell whether it was a male or a female voice. She would like to have known what the tape was but because she didn't want him to think she had been spying on him, she did not, later, ask.

He dealt with all domestic matters. Flora felt no obligation to do anything more than help to clear away their dishes after a meal. It was the first time in her life that she had allowed herself to be waited on; she sloughed off a lifetime's habit of serving as easily as an unnecessary coat. Lying in bed in the early mornings, watching the play of sea-shadows on the ceiling and listening to Gregor in the kitchen below, she felt as though her limbs were elongating, her soul was being stretched and moulded. She wondered how it was that although the two of them spent many hours a day together, she did not find him in the least erotic. He was good-looking, strong, infinitely patient, yet he roused nothing more in her than a desire to nestle into the quietude with which he surrounded himself. Was it because he himself felt no sexual need? No desire? Sometimes, half-asleep under the creaking roof, she was aware that something of him had trespassed into her dreams. A brightness. A sorrow.

Once, she might have felt it incumbent on her to be busy with conversation or personal enquiry but since he did not attempt to invade her own quiet, she was glad to leave his untouched. None the less, she sensed in him a tragedy, a loss so overwhelming that it could never be articulated. She guessed that in the open air, enclosed by wind and rain and sun, he found a healing which momentarily set him free from his grief, whatever its cause might have been.

One afternoon she walked without him along the cliff and

down to the beach. Gulls, between which she was now able to differentiate – herring, common, black-headed – wheeled noisily overhead, as she followed the chalk path which led towards the sea. A few holiday chalets sat above the dunes, though it was still too early in the season for them to be occupied. An estate agent's board had been attached to the peeling wooden railing which bordered one nominal garden – a patch of sandy grass scattered with sea holly and the dried stalks of mayweed – otherwise there was no indication that anyone ever came here. The little houses were shuttered: thin sand lay on their frail, windswept verandahs. She was reminded of the summer holidays of childhood. Of Gran.

Gregor had told her that this was Rhannan Head, a small promontory, a semi-island, which jutted out from the mainland and was sometimes cut off during the high spring tides. To her left was the purple-hazed outline of the coast; to her right, only the sea. Where was she? Intellectually she knew that on a map she could have put her finger on her approximate whereabouts but all the same she felt that she had strayed into a limbo where concepts such as time or place had no meaning. She could have been here weeks or only minutes; she could remain here for the rest of her life and still feel that she had arrived only yesterday.

Peace . . . It amazed her that she could have reached this moment and not realised before how profoundly it had been lacking in her life, how deep was her need. All this time, she had been confusing it with solitude, equating the two, though they were not the same at all. Her cold cottage with its wild garden was lonely but not peaceful, she saw that now. Oliver prowled there still; although Jessica had never visited the cottage, her unfriendly spirit hung about the rooms. When she returned, Flora determined she would purge the place of them both. Get rid of Oliver's old coat, pass on to Georgie the Coalport tea service which Jessica had given her on her marriage to Oliver, even though she loved its navy blues and thick golds, the tiny hand-painted flowers. And thinking this, she realised that she would achieve nothing by such sacrifices; if she wanted peace, she must find it in herself rather than in her surroundings.

Gregor, she saw, as the breakers crashed higher up the beach and the agent's board banged against the railing of the house behind her, was not at peace. What could he have done, what had been done to him, that he should be filled with such pain? It was unlikely that she would ever find out; certainly she would never ask him for she had now learned that he avoided answering personal questions. Besides, there was no necessity for her to know.

Climbing back up the precipitous path between the grass laced with sea campion and spurges, she watched the sea slide and tilt as her perspective changed. By the time she was on the cliff top again, panting slightly, it had settled to its accustomed place, flat on the rim of the sky. There were no boats, no ships, no lights beginning to show as evening gathered, no sign of other humans. Just the birds, diving and skimming, or screaming in the vague air. She walked to the very edge and looked down at the sea, curling and creaming far below. The desire to throw herself over into the shrill spaces seized her. For a moment, she contemplated the possibility, then she stepped back. The brief, exhilarating moment of free-falling semi-flight would inevitably be overtaken and consumed by terror, by the realisation that this was now the end, and there could be no going back.

At the house, there was no sign of Gregor, though the fire was burning and there was wine on the table, the smell of something cooking in the kitchen. She went up the stairs and along the gallery which spread across one wall. As she reached her room, Gregor appeared at the door of his.

She gasped. His eyes appeared blue-blazing, blind and pupilless, as though he was two-dimensional, his face a paper-cutout held against a summer sky. 'Gregor!' she said. She realised that she had never addressed him by name before.

'Flora.' He blinked and she saw that it was simply a trick of the light which had made his eyes seem no more than holes in his face. He appeared to have just stepped out of the shower;

his face seemed to shine although his skin was not wet. He was bare-chested. 'For a moment, I thought you were—' There was such profound longing in his voice that she lowered her eyes, embarrassed.

'I was only—' she began.

He groaned, looking beyond her. Or through. 'Do you know what it is to be cast out?'

'Yes,' Flora said.

'Such pain—'

Behind him, his room was filled with clear sea-light. The windows must have been open, the breeze catching at the curtains, for as she stared something behind him slowly fanned the air. What held her attention, however, were the striations which lay across his body, not on the surface, like tattoos or scars, but lying under the skin, glistening slightly, as though they were streaks of ore in a piece of rock. They formed a pattern which was distantly familiar, though she could not imagine where she might have seen them before. In a book? A picture? In the newspaper?

She was overwhelmed by the strength of her desire to touch them. Nothing more than that. Simply to lay her fingers over the marks. The silver stripes. They would pulse beneath his soft-fledged skin, be cold within his warm flesh. She pressed her hand against her throat; the air seemed to have been sucked out of the passage and it was difficult to breathe. She turned the handle of her door, fumbling as she tried to push it open, half-falling into her room.

He turned away from her, his expression bleak.

'I'll be down soon,' she said, and closed the door behind her, firmly setting a barrier between them. Standing at the window, she watched the sky flood with orange light as the sun sank into the sea, and wondered why the look on his face as he emerged from his room had been one of expectation, rather than of surprise. In such wild and isolated country, who had he hoped she might be? Whose arrival had he looked for with such fearful anticipation?

* * *

On the day of her departure, he drove her to the station and waited in silence until they saw the little local train rounding the bend.

He touched her shoulder and said, as he had done the night of her arrival: 'Flora. You are troubled.'

This time, she was strong enough to answer: 'So are you.'

8

The door stood open to the green garden and sunshine flooded her studio. When she had more money, she might replace the present tiny windows and turn the end wall into a sheet of glass. And money, it seemed, might be on the way. She had spoken tentatively to Antonia, her agent, about the book of angels, shown her some of the preliminary drawings, and been quietly pleased at the enthusiasm with which they had been greeted. As yet, she had no linking storyline — or any text to add to the pictures; there was still too much missing, too much that she had not yet tapped into. But she sensed that soon she would do so, and then, Antonia insisted, her book could be up there with other children's classics like *Alice in Wonderland* or *Charlie and the Chocolate Factory*.

However, that was still in the future. For the moment, there were her bread-and-butter commissions to work on, more than a year's work in themselves, with the likelihood of others long before they were completed. She took a stool outside and planted it among a riot of hogweed and bronze fennel. She was finding it unusually difficult to reproduce the feathery fronds on paper, and knew that lately she had not been concentrating. Georgie's baby would be born any day now, which was distraction enough. In addition, there were the periodic telephone calls from Marguerite Treffyn. Rupert Flynn was proving unexpectedly difficult to track down.

'It must have been deliberate,' she had said, shortly after Flora's visit. 'Unless he simply took up some other profession.'

'But he was an actor. What else could he have done?'

'Teaching drama, perhaps. Or writing – under another name, of course. Lots of actors turn into novelists – look at Dirk Bogarde. Or Anthony Sher. And a very fine fist they make of it, too. Or he could even have got himself work of some kind, to tide him over between parts, and found that what started out as short term and temporary became permanent and then long term. It's easily done.'

'No,' Flora said. She did not want to think of Rupert Flynn working behind a bar, waiting tables, taking some ignominious job in order to make ends meet. 'He was a fine actor. He wouldn't have thrown up a successful career just like that.'

'He might, if the reasons for him to do so were strong enough.'

Then, two or three weeks ago, Marguerite had rung in some excitement. 'I think I can explain why he didn't get in touch with you,' she said.

'What could be so compelling that he would abandon two little girls?' Flora spoke coldly: she was less convinced about the wisdom of finding her father than she had originally been, putting this down to fear that even if she found him, he might none the less reject her a second time.

'He went to the States. To New York, initially, and then to California.'

'That needn't have stopped him contacting us.'

'Did you know he had a cousin living on the West Coast?'

'I don't know anything about my family, apart from my grandmother, his mother. I've always wondered why she at least didn't say anything about him. If you think about it, he must have been in touch with her.'

'Perhaps he asked her not to. Perhaps he thought it would be too painful for you if she talked about him but he never saw you.'

Sitting in her garden, the boundary-making hedges thick with elderberries turning from green to purple, Flora recollects that there were always postcards on Gran's green-painted dresser, photographs of cacti blooming in deserts, of snow-capped mountains, of cities at night. Some, blue as swimming pools behind the teapot shaped like a hen, and the four Clarice Cliff saucers, showed several small photos, four or even six instead of one single large one, with their location printed across the bottom in red or black lettering. The Empire State Building, the Golden Gate Bridge: now they have been recalled to her attention, she remembers them perfectly, as out of place in the linoleumed kitchen of her grandmother's house as ostrich eggs or incense. Boston, Atlanta, Seattle, Dallas, the names had been planted in her mind and remained there, unsprouted, like seeds which had never been watered. There were letters, too, airmail letters of flimsy blue paper, piled into the brass-fronted letter holder on the mantelpiece above the coke-burning boiler. If she thought about them at all, she assumed they were from holidaying friends, or admirers of the fabulous Miss Ashby. Why had she never asked where the postcards came from? Why had Gran never referred to them? It makes obvious sense now to assume that they had come from her father. And thinking further, she remembers that trip to Liverpool, the performance of *Hamlet*. Did Gran take them because Rupert Flynn was in it? If so, what part had he played, what name had he used? Why has she thought so little about any of this before?

While Marguerite spoke of tracks which were lost and ends which were dead, Flora was back in the house in Northampton, the smell of chutney rimming her eyes with vinegary irritation, wishing that the past were not so irremediable; that second chances could be granted.

'Why didn't my grandmother ever say anything about him?' she asked, as though Marguerite could possibly know.

'Perhaps he'd asked her not to. Or perhaps she was afraid of your mother.'

'That's another mystery: my mother. Why did she never get back into the profession? Why did she throw it up completely?'

'She might have found it too difficult to work with two young children to care for.'

'She could have had an au pair. A housekeeper. There never seemed to be a shortage of money.'

'Maybe.' Marguerite lingered over a pause. 'How old is she now?'

'In her late fifties.'

'How often do you see her?'

'Never.'

There was a heavy pause. Then Marguerite said, 'You never see your own mother?'

'No.'

'Don't you feel you should?'

'As you know, we've never had much of a relationship.' I hate her, Flora wanted to say. But Marguerite, though aware of fondness lacking, had no idea of how much Flora disliked her mother, nor the extent of the aversion which could exist between people so closely linked. Even less would she have been able to understand the violence which occasionally raged beneath Flora's quiet exterior: it alarmed Flora herself.

'She could probably tell you more about your father than anyone else.'

The thought had already occurred to Flora. 'There has to be another way to find out what I want to know.'

'Surely, at your age, you could start building bridges with her? To her.'

'You have no idea of the way she treated me when we were children.'

'After all this time, can't you forgive her?'

'I could, but I don't want to.'

'She's your mother, Flora.'

'She means nothing to me.'

Another pause. Then Marguerite said: 'I think she does.'

But she does not.

Turning over a fresh page of her sketch-block, Flora starts again to draw the bronze fennel, aware that where filial affection should be, there is simply a space. Perhaps not even that. The scars have healed and grown over. She has survived her childhood, and that is enough.

When the phone rings, she runs, hoping to hear the news she has waited for so long.

'What are you going to call her?' she said.

'I don't know.' Lying back in bed, Georgie sounded both exhausted and as though she were high on something. 'I thought Beatrice, at first, much ado about nothing and all that, but she doesn't really look like a Beatrice, does she?'

'Does anyone?'

'Her name ought to be something exotic. Something . . . powerful. Look at that nose: she's going to be somebody when she's grown up, I can just feel it.'

'What sort of somebody?' Flora examined the cards accompanying the flowers which already half filled the private room Georgie had booked into for the birth of her daughter. So many of them. Written with such affection. Were she the one sitting crooning to a new baby, how many people would be celebrating on her behalf? Many fewer than this, of that she was sure.

'I don't know. Not a politician. A writer, maybe. Or even an actor.'

'Like—'

'Yes. Like him.'

'And her, don't forget.'

'How could I possibly? The entire time I was pregnant, I was terrified in case it was a girl. But now she's here—' Georgie turned fond eyes to the bassinet which stood beside her bed.

Not the entire time, Flora thought. To begin with, you wanted to jettison the tiny, slit-eyed creature with the milky-blue eyes who lies so docilely in your arms and drinks from your breast. To Flora's dismay, and in spite of the efforts she had made to rescue this baby from the fate decided for it, now that she was face to face with the crumpled nose, the spotty cheeks, the frail skull which almost invited violence, she felt antipathy, dislike. Certainly no feeling of love.

Yet Georgie was able to gaze down at the rash-covered face and reiterate, each time with absolute conviction: 'Isn't she gorgeous? Isn't she heavenly?'

Holding the child, Flora was aware of an alien force. When it fixed her with its unfeeling, lizard-like gaze, she wondered: 'What have I done?' For without any doubt, this creature owed its life to her. In what relationship did that place them to each other?

'I like those Victorian names,' Georgie said. 'Emmeline and Henrietta. Strong names like that.'

Flora bent over the crib and gazed into the pale blue eyes, as fogged as those of an nonagenarian. 'She's not a Victoria,' she said slowly. 'Nor a Christabel. Do you know what she looks like to me?'

'What?'

'A Matilda.'

'Matilda?' Georgie pushed the name around her mouth and frowned. 'Don't like it. Too wimpish.'

'She was a queen of England,' said Flora. 'You can't get much more powerful than that.'

'I remember: didn't she escape through the snow in her nightdress or something?' Georgie leaned over and scooped the baby into her arms. 'Actually, Matilda's not bad.' She yawned. 'I'm tired. You've no idea how exhausting this motherhood thing is.'

Flora wanted to say that this aunt thing wasn't exactly a good night's sleep, but refrained, knowing how scornful Georgie would be. It was true, however: an immense weariness had overtaken her since the baby's birth, as though the pregnancy, the labour, the final delivery, had all been as a result of her own efforts. Only now that they were successfully ended did she realise how stressful the past months had been. Although, after the night they had wrestled in the snow, Georgie had accepted that she would keep the child, there had still been endless moments of doubt, endless despairs, requiring constant reassurance. Flora stared again at the baby, and wished she could share that undemanding love which had instantly enveloped her sister. 'Matilda,' she said, and heard her own voice soften, as though giving the baby a name had removed one of the barriers to intimacy.

'I'll think about it,' Georgie said, over another yawn.

Flora had been staying in her sister's flat for the past few days. When she arrived back, it was to find several messages on the answering machine. Most were from well wishers whose names she did not recognise, but one of them was from Oliver. 'Watch Channel 4 at ten-thirty tonight,' his electronically mutated voice said. 'You'll find it interesting.' Was he speaking to Georgie? Or was he aware that she herself was staying there? It sounded as though he didn't yet know that the baby had arrived.

For a moment, she hesitated, urged by the temptation of a proper excuse to ring him, to hear his voice on the line, to talk to him in circumstances where bitterness would have been out of place. She told herself that it would hardly be tactful to discuss the birth of a new child with the man whose children she had not had, despite his desire that she should do so. But why not? He and Georgie were neighbours, after all. Did one stop being a sister-in-law when one's sister's marriage ended? It was one of those situations which the etiquette books had not really tackled.

At ten twenty-five, she was seated in front of the television set, a drink in her hand. The movie Oliver had spoken of was foreign, its incomprehensible title translating as *Smoke and Roses*, and directed by a man with a multi-consonanted name. Subtitles and significance: it was the last thing she felt like watching. Tonight, she was up for something frothy and undemanding, washed down, perhaps, by a couple more drinks. Why had Oliver urged Georgie – or herself – to watch it? Perhaps he was responsible for the sets. She watched closely as the titles flowed past, arranged on a background of rosebuds tumbling away into blue air on plumes of smoke. This was a joint production by a company called USlav but she recognised none of the names which followed.

The action made no sense to her tired brain. An old man

walked in a park with a small boy. A young woman passed, looked back over her shoulder at the pair then continued on her way. A old lady in a fur coat took the child somewhere. There were shots of the city skyline, dominated by statues on top of buildings: civic dignitaries, saints, angels with spread wings. Then a shot of the young woman, naked, dead, in a hotel room. A man in a raincoat and a hat appeared and went about his business with some determination. The boy's face featured frequently, showing signs of terror. There were a lot of gritty angle shots and chiaroscuro; everybody smoked heavily, all the time. Although it made little sense to her, Flora decided *Smoke and Roses* must be some arty *film noir* of which she ought to have heard, and that the man in the raincoat was the detective solving the murder of the young woman. Why was it being shown on English television? Oliver had always enjoyed such films but why did he want Georgie – or possibly her – to watch this particular one? The final sequences featured close-ups of the detective being quietly efficient, walking through the same park as was shown at the beginning, holding the hand of the child. The titles rolled. She leaned forward, waiting for Oliver's name to scroll past, unable to work out which character was which. Again, she recognised none of the names.

As she used the remote control to switch off the set, the telephone rang. 'Well?' said Oliver, without preamble. 'What did you think?'

The sound of that well-known, much-loved voice disturbed and exhilarated her. As in the worse kind of romantic novel, pulses thrummed, the heart beat suddenly faster. She pushed air from her lungs, feeling almost unable to breathe and said: 'It's not Georgie here, it's Flora.'

'I know who it is. That's why I left the message about watching.'

'How did you know I was here?'

'I know where you are most of the time.'

Hadn't Marguerite said something rather similar? 'That sounds vaguely sinister,' she said lightly.

'It's not meant to. Anyway, Ma told me you were staying there. So what did you think?'

'What about?'

'The man in the film. The detective,' Oliver said impatiently. 'Didn't you recognise him?'

'No.' But as soon as he said the words, she knew who she had been staring at blankly for the better part of ninety minutes. 'Was that . . . it can't have been—'

'Marguerite told me you were looking for your father. That was him.'

'That was—' She broke off to clear a throat which had gone husky.

'Rupert Flynn. Yes.'

'Oh, Oliver,' wailed Flora. 'Why didn't you tell me?'

'I thought you'd recognise him.'

'Of course I didn't. I haven't seen him since I was six. Besides, he was speaking Serbo-Croat or something.'

'Czech, actually. Except his voice was dubbcd.'

'If only I'd realised.' Flora tried to recall the detective's features, review the film, capture again the face in close-up under the snap-brimmed hat. Rupert Flynn. My father. Long lost. Sadly missed. 'Marguerite said she thought he'd gone to the States. Did he go to Europe after that?'

'Looks like it. They have a thriving film industry over there.'

'When was that film made?'

'A couple of years ago, I think, but only released a few months ago. It shouldn't be too difficult for us to contact the production company. USlav or whatever. Find out exactly.'

Us? she thought. 'I wish you'd told me beforehand that it was him,' she said again.

'Tell you what, darling, I'll see if I can get hold of a print of the movie.'

'Could you?' Had the endearment just slipped out, Flora wondered, or did he really still think of her as his darling? 'But, Oliver: how did you know it was him? I didn't see the name in the titles.'

'My mother's been asking people about him for weeks. Someone from the National Film Institute rang and told her he was in the film that was going to be showing on Channel 4 tonight.'

'But was he acting under another name? Rupert Flynn wasn't in the titles.'

'It was probably a Czech version of his name. Rupotsky Flincik or something.'

'So that's what he looks like now?' Flora could hardly believe that she had stared for the length of the film at that handsome, dissolute face and not recognised her own father. There was something so disturbing about this that it seemed easier to change the subject. 'Did you know that Georgie's baby's arrived?'

'Only the bare fact that she'd had it. Tell me about it. Everything.'

Flora did so.

'Great. Terrific. What's her name?'

'Georgie wants to call her something powerful. I suggested Matilda.'

'Good, good. I like Matilda. In fact, I love it. Now tell me, Flo, are you sitting there all alone in Georgie's flat?'

'As it happens, yes.'

'Right. I have to go now. Talk to you soon, yes?'

'Yes.' Putting down the phone, she felt deflated. For a moment there, talking, it was as if they had never parted. And then, she imagined, he must have heard a key in the door as Annabel Black came home, shaking raindrops from her vivid hair, perhaps, or removing a scarf, calling out some small piece of news as she hung up her coat. After the divorce, he had let the house he had shared with Flo and moved in with Annabel. This was the first time they had spoken to each other on the phone for over two years, yet he had sounded so much her husband that for a moment she had difficulty in remembering the coldness of his voice when asking for a divorce.

She poured another glass of wine, and forced herself to

think about Rupert Flynn rather than Oliver. If the film had been released only a few months ago, it must be a fairly accurate portrait of how her father looked at the moment. Georgie had said he was pathetic: on the screen he had seemed strong, though a little melancholy. Unable to sit still, Flora swallowed the rest of the wine in her glass and launched herself out of the chair. Striding across the room, she twitched Georgie's curtains, straightened the cushions, rearranged some scarlet roses which stood in a vase on a sidetable. Dammit. *Fuck* it. If Oliver had only said, she would have been able to concentrate on the detective, search his face for familiar expressions, relearn it. As it was, the filmic images had passed before her and made no special impact: she had not been conscious of any rapport, no particular feeling had leaped electrically from the screen. It had been the face of a stranger.

What else had she expected? They *were* strangers, she and Rupert Flynn. They could be nothing else. Searching for him was a futile exercise: after so long, there was nothing they could say to each other to bridge the years. She had half known that already: her lack of instinctive empathy at the sight of him on the screen merely confirmed it. Tomorrow she would ring up Marguerite and say she was no longer interested in finding her father.

The downstairs bell rang.

She stood still in the middle of the room, already knowing who waited on the doorstep. She pressed the buzzer which would release the lock, then opened the door of Georgie's flat and waited. He came bounding up the stairs towards her, then stopped at the sight of her, his face alight. 'Flora,' he said. He took her into his arms, pulling her against him as though he wanted to cram her into his own body and make them one element again. 'My darling, my love,' he murmured. 'Oh Flora, Flora.'

'Hello, Oliver.' Without letting him go, she drew him into the flat and he kicked the door shut behind him.

'Flora. I've missed you so. It's been so long—'

Her eyes were closed as his mouth lingered on hers. He was so dear, so . . . *known*. He moved her into the big sitting room and to the sofa, drawing her down beneath him. 'I love you,' he said. 'What else is there to say?'

'That'll do,' she murmured. 'That's all I need.'

He was undoing her clothes, uncovering her as he had so many times before. She pulled at his. They were not urgent, they had done this so often that it was merely the following of a deliciously familiar routine. When he came into her, they both gasped softly with the pleasure of rediscovering their own secret landscape. They lay there together for long minutes, fused, absorbing the tiny, hidden pulses and throbs of the other's body. Only their hands moved, circling, stroking, checking over the minute details, making sure that something dearly loved and believed lost had not changed. 'Ahhh,' they murmured. 'Ohhh.' 'My darling.' 'My sweet love.'

The rhythm of their stillness changed. His mouth roamed her face, pressing down on jaw and eyebrow, hovering beneath her ear, at the base of her neck, above a nipple, across her belly. 'My Flora,' he said.

'My angel love.' She shifted under him, and as though it were a signal, he began to move inside her. She groaned, needing him now more than she would have believed possible. She had believed she was beginning to erase him from her heart. She had never thought to smell his skin again, or feel the way the sinews moved beneath his shoulders, never thought to clutch his buttocks tight in her hands again or feel him strain inside her towards his climax, or move herself towards her own, wanting to share, wanting to give, urging him onwards, arching under him, gasping, tears running from her eyes.

'My God,' he said. 'Oh, God—'

'I love you, I love you—' Even at the moment of coming, she was aware of her indiscretion; he would go back to Annabel knowing what she had sought to hide from him. For the moment, however, nothing mattered but now.

'You have no idea—' he said softly. She could feel the

words as well as hear them, vibrating against her breast. 'Not the least notion—'

'Of what?'

'How I've missed you, Flora. How I love you. How I've ached for you. Not a day's gone by when I haven't wanted you. Not an hour.'

'Me too.'

'Do you love me?'

'Truly.'

'For ever?'

'And ever.'

'Till death do us part.'

It was true. And yet together they had come to this separateness. Somewhere beyond them, a chilly wind blew. She thought of Gregor and his tough solitariness. Could she be as strong, or as alone? For without Oliver, she feared that was all she could hope for. She pressed his back as though hoping to find the soft nub of wings sprouting there, the swing and waft of feathery love. Nothing, she told herself, had changed. Nor could it ever do so. He wanted her: perhaps she had always known that. Just as she wanted him. But there could be no going back. If they tried, the arguments would not change, his desire for children would be just as strong. And she would continue to be unable to give him what he wanted.

His mouth moved again and she knew what he would say. 'Come back to me, Flora, let's try again.'

It was no good. It could never be any good. She said nothing. It would be so easy to agree. It was what she wanted above everything else. Inside her head, the bright, harsh figure of Medea moved across a bare stage with blood upon her breast while behind her stirred the shadows of her murdered children.

'Flora?'

Loving him, she none the less forced herself to sound a cautionary note. 'Annabel.'

'What about her?'

'What would she think if she could hear you? See you here with me?'

He moved slightly, setting distance between them. 'How can you bring her into it? As if she matters now, when we're together again.'

'Of course she matters. Presumably she loves you. She must think you love her.'

It was his turn to remain silent. She could feel his hurt. She longed to tell him the truth but feared his anger if she did so. 'Oliver. Darling. I can't give you what you want. You know that.'

'I know you've got some damn silly theory about being afraid of acting towards your own children the way your mother behaved to you. I know you've broken up our marriage because of it,' he burst out, his voice bitter. He raised his head and looked down at her. There were lines on his face she did not recognise. The black hair had more silver in it than formerly. Frowning, he kissed the tip of her nose.

'It's the old thing about an immovable object and an irresistible force,' she said. 'If I – if we tried again, nothing would change.'

'All right. I'll accept what you say. But, Flora, I need you. You can't imagine how much. Come back to me, for God's sake. Even if we don't have children. Ever since you left I've felt as if I was slowly drowning.'

She hated herself for the exultation she felt. 'Doesn't she arrange things the way you like? Doesn't she keep your life as well ordered as I did?' she asked, mocking him.

'Since you ask, no, she bloody well does not. She's too busy being an *act*-aw—' He gave the word its full derisive weighting. 'And when she's not doing that, she's either staring into the mirror and moaning about how old she's getting, or else having fits of temperament.' He kissed her again. 'Never marry a woman with a career.'

'I've got a career, Oliver.'

'Your drawing. Of course you have. But you'd never let it interfere, the way Annabel does.'

'You don't know that. Things have changed. My agent thinks the book I'm working on could be a terrific success.'

'But you'd always have room for me and my concerns, wouldn't you? I'd always come first.' He covered her breast with his hand and squeezed it gently.

'I wouldn't count on it. I'm not the little sweetheart-wife you used to know.'

He was growing inside her. She breathed through her mouth, staring into his eyes, lost again as he moved his hips against her. 'Flora,' he whispered. 'Come back to me.'

'Don't,' she said. 'Or I just might.'

And if I did, she thought, falling again into the enchantment of the two of them together, whatever we think now, as the long, delicious thrusts grew harder and longer, it still, it still – oh darling, Oh God, oh yes! – wouldn't, couldn't work.

When Matty was six months old, Georgie rang in a state of high excitement. 'The band's just told me that they've been booked for a tour up north in two months' time. Leeds, York, Darlington, Newcastle, a couple of other places. Nine gigs in twelve days. And guess what! They want me to go with them.'

'Sounds good.' Flora was abstracted, angels occupying her attention, the soft sound of wings sweeping across the conundrum she had set herself: if angels truly were the manifestation of some blinding insight, how did they fit in with a dreadlocked character in torn denims, or a fairy-like creature with gauzy rainbow skirts? What insight were they displaying, if any? And how could all her angels be bonded together into a single story?

'Good? What're you talking about? It sounds bloody marvellous! I've been dying to get back into the biz, and this looks like the perfect way to do it. It'll give me chance to see how I manage, without having to make too much commitment.'

'Mmm.' Haloes: what about haloes? Should the angels have them and if so, would the publishers agree or would it prove to be too prohibitively expensive to have real gold on the pages? Or even just on a few – the title pages, for instance?

'—Don't you agree?' Georgie was saying.

'Definitely.'

'I mean, even if it doesn't work out, it's some money coming in and after all, I haven't earned a penny over the last few months.'

'Quite.'

'You're not listening to a damn thing I say, Flora.'

'Of course I am. I . . . um . . . just wondered about the baby. Will you take her with you?'

'Frankie's sister's said she'd have her and I think I'll take her up on the offer. It's only for twelve days and she's into all that baby stuff.'

'Will Matty mind?'

'I hope not. She's such a *good* baby, never seems to cry and adores being with people. I've been weaning her for the past month, so she should be fine.'

There was a pause which Flora tried to see simply as a pause rather than a chance for her to rush in herself, offer to take care of her niece while Georgie was gone. Was that the expected thing? She didn't want to. From time spent with Georgie in London, she had seen how overwhelming was the amount of paraphernalia a baby required; there just wasn't room in the cottage for all the cots and pushchairs and changing tables that went with one small human being. Besides, in two months' time it would barely be April, and the weather would still be cold, not at all suitable. As she thought up her objections to the unasked-for favour, she realised that she could easily move into Georgie's flat. But that, too, was out of the question. Not at this particular moment, when she was spending so much time in her studio.

The truth was – and she was perfectly willing to acknowledge it – that this book, her first venture into a truly adult world, was far more important to her than Matty. Which was not to say that she felt any animosity towards the child. Far from it. Her initial instincts of dislike, and even fear, had transmuted over the months since Matty was born into what she supposed was as close to fondness as she was likely to get. Matty was a pretty little creature and, as her doting mother said, she was good. Sometimes, with the tiny fingers holding one of hers, the deep wallflower-brown eyes staring fixedly at her until the sudden widening of the little face heralded Matty's smile, Flora felt something deeper than mere auntly approval, something fiercely wistful, the shadow of an unappeasable ache. Then she would remind herself that she had chosen her own path, and must tread it without faltering.

And for now, the book had to come first. Stifling her feelings of guilt at her lack of familial support, she merely said: 'If you're sure Frankie's sister can cope—' and left it at that. If Georgie wanted help, she would ask for it, as she had always done.

Georgie returned from her tour of the northeast on a Sunday, but it was not until the following weekend that she contacted her sister.

'How did it go?' Flora asked, her head full of feathers, soft as duck down, quilled and jagged, her fingers rainbowed with ochre and gold, viridian and coral.

'Brilliant. Fantastic. We got rave notices everywhere we went. And the best thing is that Matty doesn't seem to have missed me at all.'

'That's supposed to be good?'

'You know what I mean. I was a bit narked at first, but it's actually a real plus if she's going to be so good about me going away. It gives me much more freedom to do another tour.'

'Does it?' Flora could already guess what Georgie was about to say.

'As a matter of fact, the guys were talking about the possibility of an American tour next year. Remember the first one, which I couldn't go on?'

'Clearly.'

'Another chance has come up, and they've already asked if I'm likely to be free to go.'

'When next year?'

'Sometime in the late spring, early summer.'

'And for how long?'

'They were talking about, like, six weeks?' Georgie's voice rose interrogatively, as though expecting Flora to comment.

Instead, she asked: 'What about Matilda? Are you going to take her with you?'

'Hardly.' Georgie laughed heartily, as though the idea were

perversely idiotic. 'It'd be terribly unsettling for a child of that age – she'd be nearly two by the time we came home – to be travelling around in a bus with a randy bunch of pot-smoking, boozy musicians, staying in a different hotel room every night. Don't forget she'll be walking and everything.'

'It's not me who's forgetting anything,' Flora said.

'What's that supposed to mean?'

'I thought you were going to be the perfect mother, devoting yourself to your child until such time as she no longer needed you. And here you are, planning to abandon her for weeks at a time when the poor little thing's scarcely out of the womb.'

'That's damned unfair. If I remember it right, it was you who talked me into having darling Matty in the first place, and though I wouldn't change anything, being a mum has kind of limited my horizons. And you promised all kinds of help and support, which I can't exactly say you've been doing. And I've got a right to have a life too, you know.'

'Of *course* you have.'

'And the trip up north was marvellous. I'd forgotten just how much I enjoyed all that, the audiences and the music and the late nights and and the fan mail.'

'You said just the opposite when you were thinking about having an abortion,' muttered Flora.

'Let's face it, right from the start, I knew I'd have to be a working mother. The breadwinner and so on. And singing is how I win my bread. *Matty's* bread. Not that I'd give the States a second thought if it hadn't been that Matty was so good with Denise – that's Frankie's sister. So don't give me any crap about me neglecting her.'

'All right. I didn't mean that.'

'It's not going to happen for at least a year.'

'Even so, she'll still be awfully young.'

'Well, thanks a lot for all your support, Flora. I ought to have known I wouldn't be able to rely on you.'

'That's damned unfair. Why don't we discuss it nearer the time?'

'Or not at all.' Georgie slammed the phone down.

Despite the rapport created by Georgie's pregnancy, the relationship between the two sisters was sometimes distinctly edgy. Flora still found it difficult to forgive Georgie not only for allowing their father to walk out of her life as casually as he had walked back in, but also for trying to keep her sister ignorant of the encounter. If it hadn't been for the whisky they had drunk, the intimacy of the shared bath that evening when Matty's fate was decided, she would never even have known that Rupert Flynn was still alive.

They had quarrelled about it at intervals since then. It was hard to understand why he should have surfaced in Ireland, only to vanish again, unless the lack of response from his younger daughter had made him decide it was futile to try to take up a relationship which had withered before it had been given a chance to flourish. Flora blamed Georgie for this.

'Did he say anything about the two of you meeting again?' she had demanded hostilely during a recent visit to Georgie in Hampstead, returning yet again to the subject.

'How many times do we have to go over this, for God's sake? I've already said he didn't.'

'Why didn't you suggest it yourself, then?'

'Jesus. I wish I'd never told you about it.' Georgie poured another gin into her glass. 'Why didn't I suggest it? Because it just didn't occur to me.'

'He probably thought you didn't give a damn,' Flora said angrily.

'Too right. I don't.'

'You may not, but *I* certainly do. A lot more than just a damn. Did you explain that she'd told us he was dead?'

'No, Flora, I did not. I've told you a thousand times that I didn't.'

'Georgie, for God's sake. Don't you think it's important?'

'No, I bloody don't.' Georgie scowled. 'If he was that concerned about us, he could have got in touch years ago. He'd have known how to do that, through Gran.'

'Did I tell you that Oliver's mother says he was at my wedding?'

Georgie rolled her eyes. 'Only about twenty times a week.'

'He took the trouble to come to my wedding. So he must have kept tabs on us, followed what we were doing, at least for a while.'

'Big fucking deal. He didn't make himself known, did he? He didn't come up and kiss you, did he, or give you a hug. Why should his being there make any difference?'

'But don't you see, it shows that he *did* care?'

'Oh, sure he did. You know as well as I do, although you just won't admit it, that probably what *really* happened was that he buggered off with someone younger than Jessica, and left her to bring us up as best she could. It's just a sodding shame that her best wasn't better than it was.' Georgie cocked her head and looked up at her sister, who was standing over her with clenched fists. 'You know, now I'm bringing Matty up on my own, I'm beginning to feel a certain sympathy for poor old Jessica. I bet dear Rupert Flynn didn't contribute a penny towards our upkeep.'

'Don't talk about him like that.' Choking with anger, Flora turned away before she hit her sister. She was alarmed at the ferocity which seemed to have been released in her since the break-up of her marriage. For most of her life it had lain dormant: now, the placid docility with which she had always faced the world was providing to be no more than a sham.

'Come off it, Flora,' Georgie said. 'He had plenty of opportunity to get in touch before I went to Dublin. You seem to think he might have been living abroad, but even if he was, he'd have had to come back after Gran died. Don't tell me Jessica cleared out the Northampton house herself: she'd have summoned him to do it. Gran was his mother, after all.'

'It was probably *her* fault he didn't see us. She probably refused to let him have any access.'

'We don't even know that they're divorced, if you think about it,' Georgie said, and the thought had lodged in Flora's mind. It wouldn't help in the search for Flynn, but at the moment, every scrap of information she could get hold of, however irrelevant, seemed important, if only because it would help to round out the picture of the man she wanted, despite her hesitations and vacillations, so much to know. At thirty-four, divorced and childless, she could see all too clearly the march of time: she wanted to know him before it was too late. She wanted his approval for what she had done, what she would become: as all parents must, she wanted him to validate her. And more than that: deeper down, she knew that part of finding him was the chance it would give her to triumph at last, for once and for all, over her mother.

None the less, she had told Marguerite to drop her search, saying she was having second thoughts about the wisdom of confronting her father after so much time. Marguerite was too tactful to say so, but she clearly felt this was the most sensible course to take. But not before she had telephoned with more information. Despite the Czech film, it was proving difficult to discover Flynn's current whereabouts.

'He could be deliberately covering his tracks,' Marguerite said.

'Why would he want to do that?'

'Non-payment of taxes? Vengeful women?'

'Do you mean my mother?'

'I was thinking more on the lines of women with whom he might have established a relationship and then moved on from. Dumped, in other words. Your mother and he split up an awfully long time ago: I can't believe that after all this time he's still too scared of her to come out into the open.'

'You don't know my mother.'

'True.'

'But if he really was hiding from something or someone, why would he bother to contact Georgie in Dublin?'

'Impulse, perhaps. Or curiosity. It would be a natural urge to want to know how his own daughter had turned out.'

'He could have done that years ago.'

'Yes.' Marguerite's voice was soft with sympathy. Now, as always, Flora wished fiercely that the vagaries of birth and encounter had landed her with Marguerite as a parent rather than Jessica.

'He doesn't sound like a very admirable character, does he?' she said sadly.

'I wouldn't say that. We don't know what confusions and problems he's had to contend with.'

Flora had not seen Oliver since the night he had spent with her at Georgie's flat when, slippery with mutual craving, they had stumbled from the sofa to the bed, clutched together as though they could never have enough of each other. Had that long, long night of passionate lovemaking really happened? Sometimes Flora wondered if she had imagined it, whether it had been merely an hallucination born out of her deep yearning.

For weeks afterwards, lying in the big double bed in her white-painted bedroom limboed between sleep and the new day, she could conjure him up again beside her, so real, so loved that she grew wet with desire. But reality asserted itself. Whatever she felt, until she could throw off her infatuation for him, there could be no real progression. She knew, too, that it would be impossible to continue much longer in this state. She must purge herself. She must come to terms with Oliver's permanent absence. Even though he had evidently wanted her as much as she wanted him, he still lived with Annabel Black, and was likely to continue doing so, whatever Phil Chapman might have hinted about the relationship. He must be cleared from the attics of her mind.

He had begun to ring her, but after the first three or four times, she had left her answering machine on and only picked up the receiver after checking that the caller was not him. However much he haunted her, she knew that it could come to nothing. As much as the need to meet her deadlines, this was why she spent so much of her time on the angel book now, getting up early, going to bed long after midnight. One way or another, she absolutely had to disburden herself of Oliver.

* * *

Antonia, Flora's agent, telephoned to say that she had been talking up the angel book to such good effect that she was going to set up an auction for the rights between interested publishers.

'But it's not ready,' Flora protested.

'It can't hurt to start generating interest, darling,' said Antonia.

'I haven't even got a story, yet. Just the pictures.'

Antonia ignored her. 'There's one place in particular that I hope'll go for it. They might not pay as much as some but they do take such tremendous care over getting the design and graphics right.'

'When you say they might not pay as much, what sort of money are we talking about?' Flora asked, with as much nonchalance as she could manage.

Antonia told her. 'But that's just the ballpark figure.'

Flora gasped. '*How* much?' she said.

Antonia repeated the sum.

'But that's—' Flora couldn't think what word would adequately describe her feelings of amazement, of awe, of complete incredulity that any of this could really be happening. And to her, Flora Treffyn. Horizons expanded in front of her interior gaze: new worlds glimmered. Unlike Georgie, she had married too young to have developed a career, would have said that she had not needed one: now, she felt a space inside herself being plugged, a space of which she had only really become aware since Matilda Flynn was born.

'Isn't it, though?' Even Antonia, who worked at a level of professional fervour which Flora often thought must be exhausting, sounded truly enthusiastic. 'The only snag is, you might have to deliver the finished manuscript no later than the end of next June. The publishers will want to get it into production in time to hit the Christmas market.'

'Next June? I don't think I can be ready by then.'

'Of course you can, darling. And even if you can't, you'd damn well better be. It's a terrific deal for you.'

'I realise that.' Flora knew that she would do her very best to meet the deadline, even if it meant she had to incarcerate herself in her studio between now and then. Despite Antonia's ever-expanding sales forecasts, her talk of spin-offs and film deals, subsidiary rights and Japanese markets, it wasn't the money which mattered. Far more important to Flora was what the book symbolised. Entirely her own creation, conceived and carried through without help from anyone else, it represented her first real steps towards an independence she had never known.

As the weeks of hard, exhilarating work went by, she sometimes panicked. She wanted the printed pages of the book to appear to be handwritten, like an illuminated manuscript, and, as in those monastic archetypes, the script to flow in and out of the marginal decorations which would embellish each sheet. It all involved much more work than she had originally intended. In addition, there were the full-page illustrations to complete and the storyline, which still didn't link her various angels in the integrated way she had at first hoped, to work on. But what had once been a vague dream was now well on the way to attaining a life of its own, a reality she was determined to realise.

The only time she allowed herself away from her studio was spent with Georgie and Matty. Together they marvelled at each new and precious stage in the baby's development. The first staggering steps, the first sound vaguely resembling a word, the first hardness of tooth in the soft gums, the way she laughed, turning her head from side to side as though in disbelief, whenever Flora said something she considered amusing. Often Flora remembered the first days after her birth and wondered how she could have felt so cold, so indifferent, to the little body in her arms. Sometimes, staring at her reflection in the mirror, she would think: this is the portrait of a Doting Aunt.

The telephone broke into her thoughts. It was Georgie, ringing for a gossip though she did this so seldom now that Flora instantly suspected she wanted something. What that was became apparent when she said casually: 'By the way, the tour's definitely on for next year, next May.'

'Really?'

'They've extended it, too. Terrific news, isn't it?'

'Absolutely.'

'They want us for nearly three months now. Starting in Boston and moving across the continent via Atlanta to California. Should be great.' Yet Georgie didn't sound as over-the-top excited as she should have.

'And you want me to have Matty?'

'I know how you feel about young children,' Georgie said humbly. 'And I don't want you to feel you must. But if you could, it would be so much better all round than farming her out with strangers.'

'The only problem is that I'll be up to my ears getting my book ready for the publishers.'

'Oh yes, your book. I'd forgotten about that.'

'No reason why you should remember,' Flora said stiffly. She bit her lip, wondering what to do. There was nothing she would have liked more than to have Matty with her, but the book, the angel book, was so important to her, so precious . . .

'Let's play it by ear,' said Georgie. 'At least you're not saying no.'

Flora would have pointed out that she wasn't saying yes, either, but something in her sister's voice – a weariness, a sense of disengagement – made her feel guilty. Georgie was right: all those months ago, as snow covered the fields outside the cottage and the two of them had wrestled for Matty's life, she had promised to help take care of the baby when it came. Indeed, she wanted to. More than anything. Just not then, not when she would be working flat out to finish what she had started. 'Of course I'll have her,' she said, as warmly as she could.

'Oh, Flo. It would be such a help to know she's with someone like you, rather than a stranger.'

Georgie sounded so defeated that Flora forced her worries to the back of her mind. 'Don't worry. We'll work something out.'

'OK.'

'Are you all right, Georgie? You sound tired.' Again guilt smote Flora: she should have been more sensitive to the stresses of bringing up a child alone. 'Is anything worrying you? Money? I've got some if you need it.'

'It's not that. I'm just a bit depressed. I mean, I'm used to getting dirty letters from my fans, but recently I've had some . . . This real weirdo keeps on writing to me. One of those religious nutters, calling me the whore of Babylon, seduced by glitter and baubles. With extensive quotes from the Bible to prove that a woman's place is in the home. I seem to be tired all the time these days, otherwise I wouldn't be letting his stupid letters get to me.' Georgie produced a laugh which sounded more like a sob.

'Do you mean the sort of letters made up from words cut out of newspapers, that sort of thing?'

'Nothing as stylish as that. Not even green ink and pink writing paper. Just ordinary writing on ordinary paper.

'This guy – I presume it's a man—'

'Isn't it always?'

'—He's not threatening you, is he?'

'Not really.'

'I don't think I'd like that much. Shouldn't you go to the police?'

'They'd probably laugh. If you set yourself up the way I do, singing on a stage in front of a lot of drunk wankers fingering themselves in the dark, I'm only getting what I deserve – that's the way they think. At least he's not masturbating into a tissue and sending me the results.'

'Georgie! That's disgusting!'

Georgie sighed heavily. 'Tell me about about it. Stuff like that goes with the territory, I'm afraid. I usually just chuck them in the bin and forget about it, but I guess I'm a bit vulnerable at the moment and it's getting me down more than it ought to. Funny how nutters like that don't seem to see the contradiction between the names they call me and the fact that they're out in the audience watching me and getting their sordid little rocks off. Typical of the patriarchal society – and talking of patriarchs, how's dear Oliver?'

'If that's supposed to be a dig of some kind, I'm going to pretend I didn't hear it.'

'Come on, Flo. I know you're besotted with him, God knows why, and always have been. But surely even you can see how manipulative he is with you. Or was.'

'Then why do you bother to ask about him?'

'Because I heard that he and the lovely Annabel are definitely on the outs.'

'I didn't know that,' Flora said slowly.

'I wondered if he'd come running back to you.'

'Perhaps he's—' Flora wished she were strong enough not to care. '—Got someone else.'

'I'm sure I'd have heard, if he had. But hey: I've got better things to do with my time than check up on the Sainted Oliver.'

Forgetting her guilt and reluctant empathy with her sister, Flora said coldly: 'You really are a first-class bitch sometimes,' and put down the telephone, her mind churning.

If it was true that Oliver and Annabel Black were having problems, why hadn't he mentioned it to her? Admittedly she hadn't given him much chance to talk on the phone, but he could have written. Surely after that night, just after Matty's birth . . . Or had it been no more to him than a fuck for old time's sake, nothing more? She refused to believe that. Nobody could have been so tender, so loving, so *intimate*, with someone they didn't care for deeply. But if Georgie was right, it raised another question: would he come back to her – or ask her to come back to him? And if he did, would she go?

Hoping that it wouldn't arise, or at least, not yet, and worrying about her sister, Flora went back to her easel. She listened to the news, most of which she seemed to have heard a dozen times before. An oil crisis. A hurricane crisis. An African crisis. Mass graves unearthed in one place, a single body found in another. 'Police are not ruling out the possibility of links with other murders which have occurred in the same area over the past two or three years,' a grave voice announced. 'Meanwhile, women in the area are advised to take extra security precautions, and to report anything out of the ordinary which they may notice. Even small details may be of significance—'

Which area was it this time? Flora hadn't been listening closely enough, and in any case, she wasn't particularly frightened to be living on her own. But suppose it had been a local murder? There had been several around here, she remembered. Glancing over at the door of the studio, noting the heavy key unturned in the lock, she walked across and shot the bolts. Gran had a nightly routine at the house in Northampton, walking in her dressing-gown from room to room, one of Grandad's golfclubs in her hand, testing the window locks, putting up the chain on the front door, turning keys, while the two girls followed behind, each holding a cast-iron frying pan, half-giggling, half-fearful, nudging each other behind Gran's back, rolling their eyes at the foolishness of it yet at the same time not sure that it was entirely a game.

'What would we actually do if somebody broke in, Gran?' Flora asked once.

'Three strong women like us? We'd clout him with the pans and then sit on his head until the police came,' Gran declared.

'But why would he break in here? We've got nothing valuable.'

'Don't you be too sure, my girl.'

'What, Gran?' Georgie tugged at Gran's sleeve. 'What've you got? Jewels, have you? Diamonds and rubies and pearls?'

'Never you mind what I've got.'

'Go on, Miss Ashby, tell us,' coaxed Flora. 'Is it tiaras and brooches and emerald bracelets? A gift from a former lover, a world-famous opera singer whose name you cannot reveal?'

'You've been reading too many of those trashy novelettes,' said Gran.

'Or love letters. Is that what it is? Love letters which could bring down the government?'

'Dear, oh dear,' sighed Gran, looking pleased. 'I don't know where you get such ideas, really I don't.'

Thinking about it now, Flora wondered if there ever had been anything worth stealing in the house or whether Gran had just been injecting some drama to their lives. Not diamond tiaras, perhaps, but one or two good pieces of jewellery, bits of antique furniture, stocks and bonds. As well as being a popular amateur tenor, her husband had been a prosperous grocer in Hackney and must have left her well provided for. Just before he died, they had sold up their London house and moved back to Northampton, where Gran lived the life of a reasonably well-off widow, unostentatious but comfortable. So where had the money, her assets, gone after her death? As well as the beach house, which was left to them jointly, there had been legacies for her two granddaughters: the rest must presumably have been left to Rupert Flynn, her only child. Perhaps Gran's solicitor knew of his whereabouts – or another partner in the firm, more likely, since the person who had originally handled her affairs might well be dead by now. When – if – she decided to take up the search for her father again, the solicitor would certainly be worth checking up on.

Except . . . The thought made her pause, paint-brush in hand . . . She hadn't the faintest idea who they were. And there was only one obvious way to find out: through Jessica Glanville.

Was she ready for that?

Would she ever be?

'How're we going to get there?' Flora asked. She stood in the drawing room, twisting a handkerchief in her hands, and tried to keep her voice from trembling.

'Where?' Her mother raised indifferent eyebrows, indicating her unwillingness to talk to her daughter by marking with her finger the place she'd reached in her book before Flora had interrupted her.

'To Northampton, of course.'

'Northampton?'

'Yes. For the funeral. How are we getting there.'

'We?' Her mother's manner was hostile; as so often, her face was averted, her body half-turned away from her elder daughter. Jessica hated the sight of her, Flora knew that, and in addition, could not bear to see her red-rimmed eyes and shiny nose, evidences of an unshared grief. Had Flora been wiser or more sympathetic, she might have wondered whether there was not something defensive in that posture, something, perhaps, even pathetic.

'Me and Georgie. And you, I suppose, if you're going.'

'If you're referring to your grandmother's funeral, none of us are.' Jessica bent her head and looked down at her reading. Not a book, a play, Flora noted, scanning it upside down.

'What?'

'I'm sure you heard me the first time, Flora. But in case you didn't, I'll repeat what I said: we shan't be going to your grandmother's funeral.'

'Why not?'

'Because I say so, that's why.'

Stunned, Flora said: 'That's not a proper reason.' She

avoided glancing at the gold-framed oil of her mother which hung above the marble mantel. Jessica Glanville as Rosalind, in *As You Like It*. A special light with a rectangular gold shade was fixed above it.

'It's all the reason you're going to get.'

'But—'

'That's that, all right? I'm not prepared to discuss it any further.' Jessica flipped over a page and found a place halfway down the righthand side.

'What about what *I* want? I've got rights, too. And I want to go to Gran's funeral.'

'While you live under my roof, you have no rights,' Jessica said, not raising her head. 'You'd do well to remember that. Until you're earning your own living, you're dependent on me. And that means you do what I say.'

'*Why* can't we go to Gran's funeral?' repeated Flora.

'I've already told you. Because I don't choose to.'

'But Gran's our family.' Flora hated the way her voice had risen in a squeak of indignation.

'Yours, perhaps. But certainly not mine. A vulgar little . . . *cripple* like that?'

'She can't help being a . . . having a . . . being the way she is. And she's not vulgar. She's *not*.'

'Whether she is or not, she's nothing whatsoever to do with us.'

Flora stiffened. 'I can't believe you really said that. Gran only died three days ago.'

'Believe it, my dear.'

Everything rose inside her like a gigantic bubble, like the mudpools of Rotarua, the hot springs of Icleand, all the misery and loss, all the pain suffered over the years. Emotions long suppressed suddenly surfaced. All this time, for reasons she had never examined too closely, she had subjugated her feelings about her mother, tried to placate rather than confront. Now, she found herself giving expression to thoughts which had festered inside her for years.

'I hate you,' she said, her voice throbbing with loathing and contempt. 'I *loathe* you.'

'Really?'

'You're utterly disg*us*ting. You had no right to have children. No real mother would treat her children the way you treat us.'

Jessica's face twisted. 'Don't speak to me like that.'

'I want you to know, that's all,' Flora said. She had always been aware that one day she would give voice to these feelings, had always thought that when the time came, she would tremble and hesitate. Instead, it was as though, beneath the soft skin-surface, her body had turned to steel. 'I don't want there to be any mistakes about it. I *hate* you.'

Jessica's hands were trembling. She gripped the covers of her book. 'If I've been so terrible to you, why didn't you go and sneak on me? Tell someone at school? Was it because you were too scared? Is that the reason? Or was it because you thought they wouldn't believe you?' A tic started up by the side of her mouth, as thought some small buried creature was dragging at the skin, trying to get out. 'It wasn't by any chance because you were afraid that they'd see through you, see what a disruptive little liar you've always been?'

Flora couldn't remember a time when her mother's antipathy had not been a factor in her understanding of the world she inhabited. None the less, it had never before been so clearly and unequivocally articulated.

'You know that's not true,' she said. Her mother's accusations stung. Was she really disruptive, did she tell lies? Perhaps she did occasionally tinker with the facts, bend them slightly one way or another, but it was only in defence of herself or her little sister. 'Anyway, even if it is, that's not what we're talking about. Just tell me why we can't go to Gran's funeral.'

'I've already told you, you wretched girl, that I don't want to discuss it further.'

Flora shook her head. The contempt she had never shown before twisted her features. 'Jesus, I can see why he left you,' she said.

Jessica moved threateningly to the edge of the sofa, as though poised for attack. 'I do hope you're not referring to your father.'

'It must have been sheer bloody hell for him, being your husband. Even worse than it's been for me, being your child.'

'Your father—' Jessica began, teeth gritted, eyes fierce. Then she stopped, as though forcing back down her throat the words she wanted to say, and resumed her nonchalant posture.

Flora pushed. 'What I don't understand is why he ever married you in the first place.'

'You never will know, either,' Jessica said. 'A cold fish like you, without a heart or a feeling in your entire body, what'll you ever know about love and desire? About men and women and the ways they come together? No man in his right mind is going to give *you* so much as a first glance, let alone a second.'

The accusation was horrifying. 'That's not true,' Flora screamed.

'Oh, my dear,' said Jessica, smiling terribly. 'We both know it is. You've only got to look into the mirror each morning and see that ugly little face of yours, stare into those cold eyes, to see that there's nothing behind them, to know that it's true. Men want something warm, something responsive. Not someone who insists on being in control, not an ice maiden who's never felt anything for anyone else in her entire life.'

'That's not true, it's not *true*.'

'Isn't it? I don't suppose you've ever even been kissed and here you are, almost sixteen. It's abnormal, really, a girl of your age, but I suppose the boys are put off by your manner.'

'Whatever I'm like is because you've made me that way.'

'Ah, so it's my fault, is it?' said Jessica. 'You admit that you're some kind of freak, but insist that it's *my* fault. How very typical of my darling daughter—'

'I'm *not* your darling daughter.'

'—Always blaming someone else for her own shortcomings, never taking responsibility for herself.'

'You horrible bitch.' Despite her determination not to let

her mother's cruelty affect her, tears started in Flora's eyes. She blinked them away, but more came and more, tumbling down her face while Jessica looked at her coolly.

'No, I don't think so.' Again came the awful smile. 'Though, of course, you would know all about horrible bitches, wouldn't you, being one yourself?'

'I don't care what you say, I'm going to Gran's funeral.' Flora turned towards the door.

Jessica leaped up and grabbed her shoulders so hard that the fingers felt as if they had sunk half an inch into Flora's flesh. 'No, you are not.' Her breath, hot against Flora's cheek, was crabapple-bitter.

'Is it because my father will be there?'

'Your father—' Jessica let her go and turned away. 'Your father is dead.'

The words fell into Flora's heart like drops of frozen lead. 'Dead?' she finally managed. 'Since when?'

Jessica hesitated. 'For ages.'

'I don't believe you. Why haven't you told us this before, if it's true? Why didn't Gran say anything?'

'We . . . we didn't want to upset you.'

'Oh, like I really believe that. When have you ever cared what I felt about *any*thing?' Flora's sense of disorientation was profound. All this time she'd been hoping that one day her father would comc to her rescue, she'd dreamed of riding off with him into the future, leaving her mother behind. And now she was told that her dreams had no substance: he was dead. She was determined not to let Jessica see how distraught the news had made her. 'All the more reason for me to go to the funeral, then,' she said, as firmly as she could.

'I don't think so, Flora.'

'Try and stop me.'

'Don't worry, my dear. I shall.'

And she had.

Wrenching herself free, Flora had run up to her room, and flung herself onto her bed, sobbing with rage and hurt. All these years, some small tender part of her had still hoped that deep down, her mother really loved her. Hope had at last died. Nobody could speak to their own child with such cold loathing unless it was an expression of their true feeling. As she had so many times before, she wished that Jessica would die, that she would fall under a bus or drive over a cliff, be murdered by muggers or locked into a cold-storage depot and freeze to death. She thought of Gran's bent little figure lying in her coffin, the angel wings now folded for eternity inside her hump, her sweet voice forever silent. And Dad: Dad was dead. That was a grief she was not yet ready to think about. Meanwhile, she and Georgie were all the family Gran had left. Which made it all the more important that someone was there tomorrow to do the right thing. To show respect. To show that the fabulous Miss Ashby had been loved.

She finally wiped away her tears and splashed cold water onto her face from the basin in her room. She made her plans carefully: later in the evening, when her mother had calmed down and was watching television, she would go over to Katie Vernon's house. Katie was her best friend and Mrs Vernon would take her in for the night, Flora was sure. She packed an overnight bag for herself and checked the amount in her savings book, the product of Saturday morning work at the local supermarket checkouts, and babysitting jobs. It was more than enough to buy a train ticket to Northampton, or even two, if Georgie was brave enough to defy their mother and come too. Katie's mother would lend her the cash until she could draw some out of the post office and pay her back. Georgie could slip out of the house tomorrow morning, meet her at the station and catch the train, then take a taxi to Gran's house. Someone would be there, surely. Someone would tell them where to go.

When she was ready, she picked up the bag and tried to open the door. At first she thought it was merely stuck until it became obvious, after frantic pulling, that it was locked. Jessica must have come upstairs and quietly turned the key before removing it. Flora's first reaction was a desire to scream, to kick at the door panels, but she realised that by behaving in such an undisciplined and ultimately pointless way, she would be giving Jessica the advantage. She knew that the window offered no escape: she was on the fourth floor of the house and it was a sheer drop to the narrow front garden. Since she had no choice, it would be much better not to give her mother the satisfaction of hysteria but to wait with dignity until such time as Jessica chose to let her out, which would not be, she realised, until there was no possibility of her getting to Northampton in time for Gran's funeral.

'I hate you,' Flora repeated dispassionately. She sat on a stool at the kitchen counter. The door of her bedroom had finally been unlocked at one o'clock that afternoon, when Jessica had told her to come down for lunch. Despite the hunger she felt, not having eaten since the evening before, Flora had refused to join her mother at the table.

'You've already said that.' Jessica sounded as though she couldn't give a damn.

'I'll never forgive you for the rest of my life, for stopping me from going to Gran's funeral.'

'Oh dear.'

'What does it feel like to have your own child detest you so much that even being in the same room as you makes her feel sick?'

'I can't say it affects me much, one way or the other.' Jessica Glanville went on polishing the wine glass she had just washed, twisting the tea towel round and round inside it, over and over again, until the cloth squeaked against the glass.

'You must be the cruellest, most neglectful mother in the world.'

'What makes you say that? You've never gone hungry, you've been denied nothing, you've grown up in a nice house, been cared for—'

'Cared for? Is the way you've treated me what you call being *cared for*?' Flora curled her lip in direct imitation of her mother's sneer. Behind her mother's head, she could see the garden and the big mulberry tree, abundantly leafed, green against the blue sky. Outside existed a normal world: inside, there was only this space where hatred thick as treacle had coagulated, forcing out the breathable air. As though to emphasise the feeling, a couple of flies dashed themselves at the window panes, buzzing furiously.

'What would *you* call it?' Jessica picked up the casserole which held the indeterminate dish she had served for lunch and set it down hard on the kitchen counter.

'I wonder what my father would say if he knew how you've treated me. I bet he'd think I should go to the funeral. I bet he'd agree that you're a—'

Jessica whirled. 'Leave your bloody father out of this.'

'Is that what you did – leave him out of everything? Or were you as vile to him as you've always been to me, until he finally couldn't stand another moment of you and left? I wish he hadn't gone—' Flora looked down at her feet, '— but I can't say I blame him for not being able to stomach you.

Jessica moved towards her, face twisted in anger, hand outstretched to wrench and pinch. 'Don't speak to me like that.'

Flora was grown now, too big for physical bullying. She slipped off the stool and stood her ground, no longer afraid to confront her mother. 'What's the matter, Jessica? Can't you face the truth?'

Jessica moved again, her hand closing round a knife which lay on the counter. 'You know absolutely nothing about 'the truth'. Nor about the relationship between your father and me,' she said. 'You're a pig-ignorant, self-satisfied little shit, and until you know what you're talking about, I suggest you keep your mouth shut.'

Flora smiled, sensing that for once she had managed to stir her mother into real anger. 'Don't worry,' she said. 'Whether I keep it shut or open, you're not going to have to put up with me much longer.'

'Flora Flynn, the drama queen, eh? Don't tell me you're threatening to do us all a favour and kill yourself.'

'No, I'm not.'

'What *are* you threatening, then?'

'I've had plenty of time – all night long, in fact – to think about it. And I've decided that I'm going to leave school at the end of the term.'

'You can't. You've got your 'A' Levels to do.'

'Fuck my 'A' Levels,' Flora said. She loved the feel of the strong, bad word and, even more, the way it made Jessica's eyes go momentarily blank. 'I'm sixteen. Legally I could leave school today and you wouldn't be able to stop me.'

'Don't be ridiculous, Flora. You need 'A' Levels to get into university. What kind of life do you think you'll have if you leave school without any qualifications? If you don't get a degree?'

'I don't want to go to university. All I've ever wanted to do is draw and paint. It's what I'm best at. So I've decided to go to art college.'

'You ignorant little fool.'

'It's absolutely pointless staying on at school for another two years when I could be getting on with my real life.'

'You'll still need 'A' Levels, even for art college.' Jessica's hand unclenched and the knife she had been holding fell with a little clatter onto the tiled surface.

Flora said firmly: 'I can do them somewhere else if I have to. I'm not going back to school in September.'

'I think you are.'

'And I'm moving out of here, so you needn't try to threaten me with cutting me off without a penny. I'll find somewhere to live.'

'You haven't the faintest—' For a moment Jessica stared speechlessly at her belligerent daughter, then said, as though defeated, 'I give up. Have it your own way.' She turned away, shoulders bowed.

'What a relief. You'll never have to worry about me again, will you? Not,' added Flora, pushing home the advantage, 'that you ever have.'

Except for the faint electrical hum of the refrigerator, and the frantic buzz of a fly worrying at the window, the kitchen was suddenly still. Then Jessica snatched up the knife again and faced Flora, her cheeks blotched with red. 'You know nothing, you little fool, *nothing* . . . Of course I've worried about you, almost from the day you were born, as any mother would. You've never understood . . . You probably never will . . . Oh, fuck it, what's the bloody point talking to you, you stupid, pointless, ungrateful creature?'

'Ungrateful? Jesus.' Flora shook her head disbelievingly. 'You seriously think I should be *grateful* to you?'

A strange expression crossed Jessica's face, almost as if she were amused. 'I sometimes wish I'd drowned you at birth,' she said.

'Why didn't you?'

'Because you were—'

'Oh please,' said Flora, scathing. 'You and Lady Macbeth. Don't give me any crap about how vulnerable I looked, my tiny head nestling against you, in that first moment before I began to suck the poison from your breast. I don't suppose you've ever had a tender thought in your life.'

'You really are a vile little—' Jessica left the phrase unfinished, as though the effort of finding a word bad enough for her daughter was simply not worth the trouble.

Flora had no such problem. 'I couldn't help noticing you were reading *Medea* yesterday,' she said. 'It's a pity you're way too old for the part, otherwise it'd be perfect typecasting.'

'That's enough, Flora.'

'Bitch mothers, the pair of—' Before she could complete the sentence, Jessica had lunged at her in rage. The knife she was holding caught Flora at the top of the shoulder and as she pulled away, terrified, from the blaze in her mother's eyes, cut down the length of her arm, ripping open the flesh until it hit the bone of her elbow.

Remembering, Flora shudders. From this vantage point, nearly twenty years on, she can see how antagonistic she had been, how horribly adolescent. The hot, tinny smell of her own blood rises in her nostrils again. The flies caught against a window pane buzz frantically once more, greenbottles, iridescent, like jewels in the innocent light from the garden. The kitchen cupboards are the white of feathers, their slim silver handles gleam like sword-strokes. Like knife slashes.

Mother . . . Medea. That it has come to this.

Blood and flies fuse.

Stomach churning, she gets up from her easel. Runs water into a glass. Rinses her mouth.

Ice maiden. Cold fish. The insults wound her still, the more so because she now knows them to be true. Only someone without emotion could have left Oliver. *What'll you ever know about love and desire*? her mother screams again, but there she is wrong. *About men and women and the ways they come together*? Flora knows all about that. Knows all she wants to about that.

By early afternoon, feet tired and calf muscles aching, Flora found herself in a hamlet containing no more than a dozen lichened stone houses, a church and, blessedly, a pub. It was a long time since she had had leisure or inclination for walking like this. Her thoughts at first were caught up in that far-off time when she and Oliver used to tramp for miles at weekends, he talking, gesturing, throwing out ideas as they went like a firework, she listening, smiling, offering alternatives, agreeing. Doing it alone was a new experience, unexpectedly more rewarding than she had thought it would be and gradually, as the miles peeled away behind her, she was able, even if only temporarily, to relinquish the past.

This tiny place was new to her: she had expected to have to make her way back to her car and drive before she would find anywhere to have lunch, but the Swinford Arms, already three-quarters full, was still serving food and she went gratefully into the warm fug of wood smoke and damp wool and wine-based casserole which filled its tiny rooms. Fires burned in the grates, there was an atmosphere of Sunday contentment, people on their day off relaxing, wearing casual clothes, enjoying a pint without office stress.

Surprisingly, she found that she was happy. Spring was well advanced. Warmer weather lurked behind the cold winds which curled over the low Cotswold hills, the seasons progressed and the shape of her life was changing. It was already April, soon it would be May and time for Georgie to leave for the States. Then Matty, darling Matty, would be entirely hers for a precious few weeks. 'I'm a sucker,' she thought, smiling to herself. 'I'll spoil her rotten. But when she looks at me with those enormous brown eyes, when the dimple shows in her cheek, I would give her anything, anything at all.' The pleasure she took in the child was so intense that sometimes it almost seemed orgasmic.

She had spent Christmas with her sister and Matty, and various friends of Georgie's who had come and gone, sometimes without even identifying themselves. Some of the Ragbags had appeared on the afternoon of Boxing Day, clutching six-packs of Newcastle Brown, and more and more people had arrived, turning the flat into an impromptu concert which only ended when the police, summoned by a neighbour, turned up at the door. Georgie's busy, happy life: once Flora would have been envious, but the paintings for her book were progressing so well, that she barely had time to feel lonely. She was still looking for a firm storyline: so far she had begun and rejected at least three, but she felt confident that the right one would eventually come to her.

Ordering a sandwich and a half of lager, she carried them into a further room with a stone-flagged floor where another log fire crackled in a smoke-blackened fireplace. Someone let her squeeze in beside them and she was happy to sit in silence, boots stretched towards the fire, listening to scraps of the conversations going on around her like a modern Greek chorus.

'Bloody government—'

'Even stole the children's teddy bears—'

'—These days they don't get married—'

'—Made redundant at forty-four—'

'—We're inviting absolutely everybody we know—'

'—Blame the government.'

She had been looking at birds, studying the different ways they moved, the differences between the wing-lifts of the little birds like wren and the bigger wood pigeons, the top-heavy flight of pheasants, the flutter of robin or tit. She had even seen a couple of hawks hanging above her head, wings scarcely moving as they waited to pounce, folding their wings in to their bodies as they fell head first towards the ground. The view towards the west – cold blue sky, pale hills, winter-green fields – had, as always, lifted her spirits. Full of angels, she had scarcely thought of Oliver over the past few hours, still less of Rupert Flynn.

Half-asleep, she at first barely registered the man who paused briefly at the door of the crowded room, looking for a place to sit. He had a pint of beer in his hand, wore comfortable clothes – fawn sweater, dark corduroys – and walking boots. There was a stillness about him, an apartness, which made her look again just as he turned and moved into the next room. Surely that was – she got up, apologising to the man whose elbow she jogged, picked up her binoculars and pushed her way to the second room. He wasn't in there, but in a further tiny place which must once have been a cowshed, she saw him sitting on a wooden pew set sideways on to the fire, which had been lit here too, watching the door.

'Gregor.'

'Hello, Flora.'

'Did you see me in there?' She knew he had, had taken note of the way his eyes had widened briefly before he turned and went away.

'Of course.'

'Why didn't you—' She smiled. 'But what's the use asking you questions like that? You never answer them.'

'You have your own answers,' he said. He too smiled. Put down his pint on the table in front of him. Leaned towards her. 'You're happier than you were.'

'I believe I am.' She gestured towards the place beside him. 'Can I join you?' And, as he opened his mouth to speak, added: 'Please don't tell me that two individuals can never be joined, must always remain separate.'

'I wasn't going to say that,' he said mildly. 'I was going to say I'd be delighted if you would.'

She felt absurdly pleased. 'Good.' It was the first unloaded remark she had heard him make. Sitting down opposite him, she said: 'I hadn't realised you were from round here. How are things with you?'

He nodded at her field glasses which she had brought with her. 'You've been birdwatching.'

'Yes.'

'And you're still drawing angels.'

'That's why I'm looking at birds. I'm still having trouble with the wings. I don't think tiny little fairylike angels would use their wings in the same way as bigger heftier ones.'

'They would not.'

'And like me—' she nodded at his muddy boots, '—you've been hiking.'

'It eases my soul.'

'Mine too.' There was a long pause before she asked: 'Have you come far?'

He sighed. 'An unimaginable distance.'

Once again, he was answering questions which had not been asked, rather than those which had. They sat in silence. Flora told herself that when there were words to say, they would be spoken. Otherwise, there was no need to say anything. Gregor's ability to feel comfortable in the midst of conversational gaps was the exact opposite of her own compulsion to rush in with social banalities. She had forgotten how earthbound and lumpen he could sometimes make her feel. She finished her lager and looked at her watch. 'I'd better get going.' It would take her a couple of hours to tramp back to where she had parked her car.

'I passed your house the other day,' Gregor said.

'Why didn't you come in?'

'I wasn't ready,' he said.

'For what, exactly?'

'Intrusion.'

She smiled. 'It wouldn't have been that, Gregor. I'd have been glad to see you.'

He turned his water-clear gaze on her. 'You don't know that. Besides, you didn't need me.'

'Need?'

'You had other occupations.'

'I repeat, whatever I was doing, I'd have been so happy to see you.' She got up. 'Next time, please do knock at the door.'

'Flora,' he said.

'What?'

'It's a good name for you.'

'As Gregor is for you.'

'Don't go yet. Sit down.'

Obediently, she did so. As when they had met before, she felt no sexual pull towards him, yet she was as reluctant to move out of the circle of peace around him as he seemed to see her go. He gestured at her empty glass. 'Do you want something?'

'If you mean another lager, the answer's no.'

'What do you want, Flora?'

'Many things. Doesn't everyone, even you?'

'I want only one thing.'

'And you wouldn't tell me what that is, even if I asked.'

'I might.'

'So tell me.'

He looked at the window. 'Return,' he said.

'To where?'

'Where I once was.'

'Can you explain?'

He shook his head slightly. 'I will. But not today.'

Small muscles in her neck relaxed. So even if she went away from him now, he would make contact again. The thought made her happy. 'In the end, what does anyone want except to survive unscathed?'

'Which means uninjured. None of us can ever hope to be that.'

'All right. Then, to reach a measure of contentment.'

'Not happiness?'

'That doesn't last. By its nature, it can't last.'

'It's human nature to challenge God.'

She was beginning to get something of his thought patterns. 'You mean, like the angels who were flung out of heaven?'

Again he stared at the sky beyond the window. 'How they must long to get back,' he said. 'Imagine the loneliness.' He brought his gaze back to her. 'What most people do not realise is that happiness is dangerous.'

She thought of Oliver. They had been happy. And by hoping to maintain their happiness, she had destroyed it. She wondered what had happened to Gregor's. Perhaps one day he would tell her that, too. 'You're right,' she said.

The night was darkening by the time she got back, the sun sinking in a vast, iron-red ball into the hills. None the less, as soon as she turned into the unmade-up road which led past her house, she could see a car waiting outside, a car she recognised immediately.

He was waiting for her inside the house. 'I hope you don't mind, darling,' he said. 'But it was cold outside and since I still had my key—'

'I do mind,' she said. 'We agreed that this was to be my place. You ought to respect my rights. Technically, you're trespassing.'

'Are you going to throw me out?'

'Possibly. Depends how you behave.'

'How do you want me to behave?' He came closer, took her into his arms, kissed her hard.

'Oh, Oliver,' she said. A sigh began somewhere deep inside her, and died. Why didn't she simply admit that for her, there could never be anyone else but him? Why not go back to him – if he still wanted her to? She pulled back against the circle of his embrace, wanting to say more but he stopped her.

'Don't say anything now. Just get in the car and we'll talk then.'

'What?' She tried to pull away. 'I can't—'

'The Consort of Ancient Musicke is playing at the Sheldonian in Oxford. I thought you'd like to go so I got tickets. But we'll have to hurry to get there in time.'

'I can't go like this.' She looked down at her walking boots. 'I'm not—'

'Who's going to notice what you'rc wcaring?'

'Me, for a start.'

'Run up and get your concert-going shoes and change them in the car. I've made smoked salmon sandwiches and there's a bottle of wine in the fridge.' He hopped about impatiently. 'Come on, come on, let's go.'

Later, in the car, with a Bach prelude drifting from the car radio, she said: 'How are things? I heard that you and Annabel—'

'Over,' he said. 'Finished. It was madness from the start to think that I'd get over you by trying to make a life with someone else. Unfair to you. And damned unfair to Annabel. I feel bad about it. She kept telling me I was using her, and she was right.'

'She probably used you too. You must have been a good career move for her.'

'For an ambitious lady, that's forgivable. Not that she needs it, since she's got a great future in her own right. But using someone for emotional ends, the way I did, isn't.'

Flora leaned against his shoulder. 'Are you miserable?'

'Not nearly as much as I thought I'd be.' He leaned over and planted an awkward kiss on the top of her head. 'And not at all now I'm with you.'

'We haven't even spoken for—'

'Whose fault is that? Not mine. I came because . . . because I needed to see you. It's selfish of me to burst into your new life, I know that. And you've made it pretty clear that you don't want me around. But—'

'That's not true.'

'Refusing to speak to me seems a fairly solid message.'

'It's just – Oliver, whatever I feel about you, whatever we feel about each other, I can't give you the one thing you want more than anything else in the world.'

'You, you mean?'

'Children.'

'I already said, if I have to choose, I'll take you over all the fecund, big-breasted earth mothers in the world.'

'You think my breasts are too small?'

'Let me refresh my memory later and I'll tell you.'

She laughed. It was the way it had always been. The way it was meant to be.

He drove up to London the next morning. He had not asked her again to come back to him, but eventually he would. And when he did, would she go? She was not sure. Perhaps. On certain terms. They knew each other too well to be able to tolerate the whims and foibles of someone else. Oliver had tried and found it not possible. Last night she had sat in bed, drinking the champagne he had brought with him, helpless with laughter that she knew she ought not to be enjoying, as he demonstrated Annabel Black's hen-like pecking at her food, her nightly routine in front of the mirror, the grim passion with which she attacked routine household tasks. 'It's truly frightening,' he said, collapsing onto the bed and holding Flora tightly. 'If I were a broom, I'd run a mile.'

'But it's that intensity which makes her such a brilliant actress, isn't it?'

'Which is fine when she's giving us her Medea, or her Cordelia or her Mother Courage. But over the cornflakes every morning, or buying a pair of tights, it's a bit bloody much.'

She giggled. She had missed the laughter he so easily generated almost as much as she had missed the sex. 'What an intolerant beast you are.'

'And what an adorable one *you* are.'

Before he left, he said, looking shy, 'I ran into Georgie at the supermarket the other day and she told me that you'll be looking after Matty while she's in the States.'

'Maybe. Why do you bring it up?'

'I was thinking that maybe the two of us could play Mummies and Daddies.'

She kissed him. 'I love you, Oliver,' she said softly.

'And I you. Always. Always.'

Later, working in her studio, she heard Angus's voice outside the door, heard his knock and pulled back the bolts to let him in.

'I was driving by,' he said. 'With this madman loose, I thought I'd better stop in and check up on you.'

'Madman?'

'Didn't you hear it on the news yesterday?' He paced about impatiently, stopping to look at the drawings pinned up on the wall, picking up things and putting them down again.

'I must have missed it. What happened?'

'Another poor woman murdered yesterday. Over towards Cheltenham, this time. They're definitely linking this with the murders of the other women in the area.'

'Oh, God,' Flora whispered.

'He slashed her to pieces and left her on the floor of her kitchen for her kids to find when they came down in the morning.'

Flora stared at him, seeing blood. Blood, darkly crimson on the tiles, red as anger, thick as hate. That summer afternoon, blood had poured from the wound in her arm, splashing onto the kitchen floor, soaking Flora's cotton dress, while she and her mother stared at the deep gash in horror. Then Jessica, snatching up the tea towel she had been drying the dishes with, tied it tightly about Flora's upper arm, pulled another from a drawer, bound it below the elbow in an effort to keep the two cut edges together.

At the hospital, the nurses had looked oddly at the pair of them, whispered, heads together, while Flora, teeth chattering with shock, insisted it was an accident, a matter of carelessness on her part. Afterwards, she had understood that instead of denouncing her mother as she might so easily have done, she had protected Jessica because she recognised her own accountability. She was as much to blame for what had happened. The moment, briefly, had drawn them together.

'Look, Flo,' said Angus. 'Why don't you move in with me until they've found him? I promise not to make any . . . demands on you. You can have your own room and everything. But I shall worry myself sick about you if I think you're here alone and might find yourself at the mercy of this psychopath.'

'Dear Angus.' Flora tried to smile reassuringly. She knew she ought to tell him about Oliver, but this didn't seem the right moment. 'I had all the windows fitted with locks after the last murder. I even had the police come out and check the security for me. There's a peephole in the front door now, and I'm not stupid enough to open up to a stranger after dark. Besides, as far as I remember, if the same man's responsible, hasn't he killed most of his victims during the day?'

'Precisely.'

'So moving in with you won't make a lot of difference, will it? I mean, you're gone most days.'

'But there seems to be some evidence that he's watched these poor women for a while, stalked them or whatever they call it, before he kills them. There's even a theory that he knows them already: so far the police haven't found any sign of a break-in, as if the women let him in quite willingly. Maybe he gets acquainted with them first, chats them up in pubs or in the supermarket checkout queue or on the train or whatever, susses them out. And it's almost *got* to be someone who lives locally or at least has reason to spend a considerable amount of time in the area.'

'That's only a theory.'

'But it's one which fits the facts.'

'I haven't chatted up any homicidal maniacs in the supermarket recently, I promise you, Angus.'

'The point is, if he decides on you and then discovers that you're living with a man, especially one with irregular working hours, he'd probably not risk it. He'd look elsewhere.'

'So my gain would be someone else's loss – of life? What a dreadful way to put it.'

Flora knew she was ignoring obvious facts. She lived alone, in relative isolation. She was a woman at home much of the day. If it was the same man as before, the police had almost no leads on him: he could be anyone, anywhere. He could be local and already know about her accessibility. She remembered the man coming from nowhere whom she had passed in her car one night, and the man who had come to the door onc afternoon, saying that he was looking for Mrs Baker, the woman from whom she and Oliver had originally bought the house. Both could have been perfectly innocent incidents – almost certainly were. On the other hand, they might not.

However, she had a book to finish. There were angels who needed the attention that only she could give them. Leaving her work space would be a complete distraction. She would disturb the delicate filaments of association and inspiration which filled the studio like invisible spider webs. Ideas hung from the beamed roof, possibilities clung to the walls. Moving out would destroy all those fine creative threads.

'I'm too involved at the moment,' she said.

'This is with the angel book?'

And Oliver. 'Yes. If I moved to your place, it'll completely ruin things.' It was impossible to describe her feelings to him.

'Would it help if I moved in here with you instead? I wouldn't bother you. I could—' his glance swept round the studio '—set my computers and drawing boards up somewhere, work here.'

'I wouldn't dream of letting you disrupt your life just for me.'

He grabbed her hands tightly in both of his. 'Flora,' he said forcefully, 'I can't tell you what it would do to me if anything happened to you.'

'I'm terribly grateful.'

'You know I love you, don't you?'

'Oh, Angus. *Dear* Angus.' She looked away from the emotion in his eyes, not wanting to get caught up in it, take responsibility for it. *Ice maiden, cold fish.* 'And I promise that if I feel in the slightest danger – strange men wandering down the lane outside, or following me in their car – I'll move in immediately. All right?'

'No, it's not all right,' he said. His kind face was creased with anxiety. 'And I've got to go to the States next month. I shall worry myself sick about you.'

'You mustn't.'

'I wish I had some authority, some kind of influence over you, so I could persuade you to do what I want.'

'But you haven't. Nobody has.'

Not any more.

Not even Oliver.

'Look at vis,' Matty said.

'Do I have to?'

'It's pretty.'

'It's revolting, Matty. Take it away at once.'

Instead, Matty dropped the snail onto Flora's arm. 'It's *pretty*,' she repeated.

Her mouth twisted with disgust, Flora none the less had to admit that the whorled shell, striped in bands of coffee and cream, was pretty. The snails were a feature of this part of the world and Matty was entranced by them; it seemed that snails in Hampstead were of a different breed altogether. 'I agree that the shell's pretty,' she said. 'It's what's inside I don't like.'

'Silver,' Matty said. 'Like Christmas.' She indicated the long ribbon of snail slime which ran along the paved terrace towards the hostas which Flo had planted two years ago.

'Christmas decorations,' agreed Flora. There was a certain similarity, she supposed, between the snail trail and the tinsel strands which she had hung over the branches of last Christmas's tree. She picked her niece up and sat her on her knee. 'Can you really remember that far back?'

'Ess.'

'It's more than a quarter of your lifetime ago,' Flora said. She kissed the little button of a nose, breathed in the odour of clean infant hair.

'I found vis, too,' Matty said. She breathed deeply and held out her other hand.

Flora screamed. 'Oh God, Matty.' The slug on Matty's hand was brown and fringed with orange.

'Don't you like it?'

'No. I *hate* it. I *loathe* slugs.'

'It's intressin'.'

'It's not.' Flora set the child on her feet and led her outside the back door where she lifted the lid of the dustbin. 'Now, drop it in there.'

'Why?'

'Because I say so.'

'It's my friend.' Matty stuck out her lower lip.

'Slugs don't have friends. Especially not cute little girls.'

'Vis one does.'

'It does not. Besides, it chews up all my plants. Now drop the ghastly thing, and don't bring any more into the house. Ever.' Flora looked at her watch. 'How would you like to watch television for a bit?' She despised herself for succumbing to the temptation of the electronic babysitter, but she desperately needed some time to herself: her book, which ought to be finished by now, was well past its deadline and still nowhere near completion.

'All right.'

'But let's wash your hands first, shall we? I don't want slug all over the sitting room.'

'Why not?'

'I just don't, all right?'

Flora lifted the firm little body onto the draining board and ran water into the kitchen sink. Matty, she thought. What a miracle. Sometimes she thought she could kiss the child to death, so intensely did she love her, so delicious was the feel of her. To think how nearly she had never been . . .

Five minutes after she had settled Matty in front of the television, the phone rang.

'Hi. It's me!' Georgie's voice had an edge of excitement to it, a deep throb of happiness: hearing it, Flora braced herself for unwelcome news.

'Hello,' she said cautiously.

'How's Matty?'

'In great form. She's accumulating a vocabulary Shakespeare would be proud of. As for her ability to commune with nature, I'm afraid words fail me.'

'Is she missing me?'

'Absolutely not. Doesn't mention you more than a couple of hundred times a day. In fact, she said only yesterday that if I wanted her candid opinion, I was much more fun than you and infinitely more tolerant in the matter of bedtimes and eating up what's on her plate, and she'd much prefer it if you never came back to collect her.'

'She did not.'

'Of course she didn't. We talk about you all the time, and look at the pictures you send and I barrel out some of your songs and she laughs her little head off and says you're much better at singing than I am.'

'A wise child, obviously.'

'Like aunt, like niece.'

'You're enjoying having her, then?'

Enjoying? Flora closed her eyes. What she felt was so far beyond enjoyment that there was simply no way to express it. 'Of course I am,' she said. You know perfectly well I'm the most besotted aunt on the planet. I adore her, as you know. And if you're calling to ask if it's all right to stay over there for longer than you planned, there's only one answer: yes.'

'Oh dear.'

'Why do you say that?'

'Has it changed your mind at all? About . . . you know . . . having children yourself?'

'Is this just a routine check-in call, Georgina,' Flora asked, her tone tart. 'I thought there might be something particular you wanted to discuss.'

'How can you tell?'

'I'm your sister.'

'As it happens, there is something . . . You'll never guess what! Never.'

'So don't keep me in suspense.'

'Remember me telling you about Jerry Long? The bass player?'

Why did Flora's heart sink, drop, plummet? Why did images of death multiply inside her head: skeletons carrying scythes, dark-cowled figures, tolling bells, graves and coffins and white lilies blowing? Could love and dread have enabled her, in that moment, to foresee something of what was to come? 'Yes,' she said.

'You sound very wary, Flora.'

'I'm waiting for the rest of it.'

Georgie took a deep breath. 'Well . . . We're engaged!'

'A gig, do you mean?' Flora tried to imagine Georgie singing while some T-shirted ponytailed bassist thrummed and thumped an accompaniment.

'No, dummy. We're getting married!'

'Married?' Flora felt stupid with surprise and already-anticipated loss.

'You could try and sound enthusiastic.'

'I am. I'm . . . I'm absolutely delighted for you, love.' Flora pressed a hand against her chest in an effort to relieve the tension she could feel building up inside her. 'What about Matty?'

'Jerry's thrilled at the idea of a ready-made daughter, and since he comes from a huge family himself, he wants more children right away.'

'Wonderful,' Flora got out. 'Where will you live, here or there?'

'In California to start with, I guess, though we might move to New York eventually. Oh, Flo, you can't imagine how happy I feel! It's like all my dreams come true. Christmas and Valentine's Day and winning the lottery and fantastic sex and a joint all rolled into one.'

Flora struggled. Managed to say, again: 'I'm so pleased for you.' And all she could think, as Georgie babbled incoherently about nightclubs and chance phone calls and coincidences, was that Matty would be going. Not just from the cottage, from Flora's care, but from England, too. Miles away. Out of reach. Lost. 'It sounds so exciting.'

'I know. I'll be flying back in two weeks' time, as soon as

the tenant moves out of my flat. Then I'll have to organise getting my stuff sent over to Jerry's place, and after that's dealt with, Matty and I'll fly back here and Jerry and I'll get married in San Francisco.'

'I'm delighted. I'll miss Matty terribly, of course, but—' There were no 'buts' about it. 'Buts' were redundant. She would miss Matty terribly. Her absence would be a gaping and unfillable wound.

Oh, Matty. Lost. Lost, too, the delicate line of her dark eyebrows, the fragile neck . . .

'I was worried about that, but as Jerry pointed out, the States isn't that far away any more. And fares are coming down all the time. There are special flights and all that.'

'Two weeks?' Flora said bleakly. Matty laughing . . .

'Look, I know it's a bit much to ask, with your book and everything – how's it coming along, by the way? – but is there any chance of you coming back with me, being my bridesmaid . . . matron of honour or whatever? As I said, Jerry's got a big family and it would be nice to have someone from my side. And in any case, he's dying to meet you.'

'I'll come,' Flora said slowly. 'Of course I will.' She cleared her throat. 'What about Jessica? Have you told her yet?'

'You were at the top of the list to tell. Has she been down to the cottage to see Matty while I've been gone?'

'No.'

'Did you invite her?'

'No, I—'

'You should have done, Flo. She's Matty's grandmother. She has rights too.'

'Pity she didn't think about my rights when I was little.'

'Flora, for heaven's sake. You've got to let the past go. Put it behind you. We've all moved on from then. We're adults now. Can't you see how it's eating you up? Hatred's so corrosive.'

'Excuse me, is this Mother Teresa I'm talking to here?'

'I mean it, Flo. You can't let something which might or might not have happened years ago ruin your life.'

'What's this "might or might not" business? It *did* happen.'

'At some time or other, you're going to have to start taking responsibility for yourself, instead of blaming everything on Jessica.'

'What do you mean: "blaming everything"? What everything are you talking about?'

'She did the best she could in difficult circumstances and—'

'The hell she did! And where do you get off, anyway, telling me my life is ruined?'

'Isn't it? Isn't the fact that you're on your own at least partly because you don't want children in case you turn out to be like her?'

'Not in the least. And it may interest you to know that far from allowing Jessica to "ruin" my life, I never give her a thought from one end of the year to the other.'

'Which probably amounts to much the same thing.'

'It certainly does not.'

'Flora, I'm not going to quarrel with you,' Georgie said, her voice taking on a creamily self-righteous note which made Flora want to scream. 'For one thing, I'm much too happy, and for another it's mind-bogglingly expensive to telephone from here at this time of day. So tell me more about Matty, why don't you? I'm just longing to see her again, after all this time.'

Later, putting down the phone, Flora stared at the angels lining the studio walls, not really seeing them. All this time, she had been wrong to believe that she would not enjoy motherhood. The surrogate parenting that Georgie's absence had forced on her had given her a fulfilment that she would not have believed possible. Happily she had altered her routines to accommodate Matty's, happily given herself over to the demands of childrearing. And found, to her astonishment, that she was still able to work, that time stretched, that the mental muscles could be trained. 'I can see now,' she said to Oliver, on one of his many visits, 'how useful all those years with you really were. I got accustomed to domestic tyranny.'

'What're you talking about? Tyranny? I'm the mildest,

sweetest of men. Aren't I, Matilda?' He picked up the little girl and sat her on his knee. 'Aren't I the sweetest man you've ever met?'

'Are you the Man in the Moon?' she said.

'Yes,' he told her. 'Which is why, thank God, I never have to eat cold pease porridge.'

'Why not?'

'Because it would burn my mouth, of course.'

Matty touched his cheek with awe, not sure if he was teasing her. She was currently fascinated by the moon, the way it spread from a fingernail to a beach-ball, then shrank again in the night sky.

Oh, God: try not to think of Matty staring round-eyed up at the stars, Matty staggering across the grass, arms outstretched for balance like a plump little bird, Matty holding a silver balloon on a glittery string.

Oliver would be devastated at the loss of Matty. At the news that she would no longer be an eighty-minute drive from London, but oceans away. And that even when they had been traversed, she would still be separated from him by a whole continent of prairie and mountain and desert. Lost. Irretrievable. As for herself, she did not know how she was going to bear this snatching away of something which had taken such hold of her heart. Flora bowed her shoulders and gave way to tears, feeling such a rending of the spirit that she wondered if she would ever be free of it again. Was this pain what mothers who bore children for other people experienced at the moment of giving up, of passing over to a stranger the responsibility for a creature which had been nourished by their own body? Was this how it felt to hand a baby to adoptive parents, or to have a child die? She reminded herself, banging her palms hard against the counter, that Matty did not belong to her but to Georgie. She told herself how despicable was her inability to feel anything but hatred for the absent Jerry Long, the soon-to-be brother-in-law who was causing her this grief. It changed nothing.

She breathed deeply, willing herself into a state of calm so that Matty, with her sensitive child's antennae, should not realise that there was anything wrong when she was wakened from her nap. It's not fair . . . The thought, preserved from childhood, carried with it a heavy overlay of remembered sadnesses. It's not fair that just when I've found something to cherish unreservedly without any of the accretions of rivalry or loyalty or longing that cling to the others I love, the object of my adoration is going to be snatched away from me, and I shall have no right to protest, no say in the matter, can do nothing except resign myself to a life from which Matty is absent.

And even as she thought this, the elusive storyline for which she had been searching came into her head. It could concern a child, lost or removed in some way, the subsequent search for it, the happy ending. It would provide the gravitas she needed to make her angels meaningful, the focal link. It would pass on the message that if things were often far from satisfactory, even for angels, whatever they might mean, how much more so must they be, then, for fallible unwinged human beings? Immediately, objections began in her brain. Was the whole idea too saccharine? How would she reconcile all her angels, bring them into line with the idea? She examined the drawing of the angel in Doc Martens and ripped jeans. Where would it fit in? It seemed so long ago that she had painted it; so much had changed since then.

And was about to change still further. Resolutely she thrust the thought of Matty aside to concentrate on her fictional lost child. Should it be an angel? And if so, should it have wings? Which raised another question: were her angels fundamentally different from the humans she would need to include? They had to be. The whole point about angels was the wings which lifted them nearer God, making them better than men. Her mind was busy as she reached for the bottle of Indian ink which stood on the work table in the centre of the room. Recently she had been studying calligraphy, in preparation for producing the finished pages of her book, but had not yet written any text with them. She was going to work hard and fast if she was not to go well over her deadline: to her surprise, the thought exhilarated rather than frightened her.

Using a broad-nibbed pen, she began writing, painstakingly limning out the strokes and curves of the letters in the same way as a mediaeval chronicler might have done, knowing that once the ink had marked the vellum, there could be no going back. She didn't mind the leisurely pace of the process; she remembered what she had said to Gregor, about building up a picture line by line, detail by detail, and how people who eventually saw the finished picture were aware, without knowing how, of the layers from which it was constructed.

She would not speak to Oliver about Matty's departure until they were next together. If she were with him, she could comfort him, though God knew she was as much in need of solace as he would be. Determinedly, she laid down her pen and went to the phone. She would ask him to come down as soon as he could, tonight if possible, and tell him then.

Sitting at her easel, she is unwinged; she is fallible. She is aware of her weaknesses. Her tamped-down rages. Her stubbornness. Her lack of charity. Georgie is right: she ought to have asked Jessica down to visit Matty and has not done so. She works with one ear listening for the sounds of Matty's stirring in the house. Oliver has fixed up a system by which she can hear the child while she is working, which enables her to relax when she is over here in the studio.

She knows what Oliver's response to Georgie's news will be. His face will grow pale, his body will sag. For Oliver hates flying. Oliver, who used once to fly everywhere as easily as he took a bus, has developed a phobia. He is afraid of travelling by plane. If he were an angel, she thinks, he could fly there under his own power. She sees him, lonely in the vast American skies, his great wings beating above the powerful domes of Washington, above the hazy hills of Tennessee; she sees him buffeted by winds over the Grand Canyon, scorched by the hot dry airs of Nevada.

And will he then say: 'Come back to me'? They have discussed this question a hundred times in recent weeks. She had been content with things as they have been. If she takes up life once more as Oliver's wife, it will all start over again. With Matty gone, would it be different? She has changed. Or, if not changed, then at least she has begun to venture into the landscapes of herself, round which she has hitherto only skirted. She has discovered that she is capable of living with a child and not treating it as she herself had been treated. She has discovered a whole passionate conduit into love. So what will she to say to him when, inevitably, he asks the old questions? How far towards the truth is she prepared to go? Will she dare return to Paradise, risk another expulsion?

Lucifer comes into her head. Morning star, Light Giver, the brightest angel, the child of light. Imagine, she thinks, being flung out into space, disgraced. Imagine falling into infinity, the dark air rushing, streaming behind you. She envisages herself as a comet, sparks fizzing in her wake, and the huge void below, her terror changing to exhilaration and then to ecstasy as she spins and turns, buoyed in nothingness by the cushions of emptiness which check her fall.

Imagine being the deviser of your own destiny, spreading your wings, a butterfly, a bird, an angel plunging through the immensity of nothing. After the initial seconds, even as the lights of paradise fade, there would be no fear. Fear would only exist if the fall was limited by its already-imagined ending, finished almost before begun.

Staring at the blank paper on her easel, she thinks again: I need an angel of my own. A guardian angel. She imagines it, her personal angel, falling towards her through epochs, through millennia, wings spread, or folded round itself, plunging through the immensities of space. Stars rushing by: Arcturus and Lucifer, Polaris and Sirius. Solitary planets rocking in the darkness. Moons lingering, suns burning and then gone. Streams of matter, debris aeons old, stirred up by her passing. Galaxies scintillating in the darkness, melting, exploding, reforming.

Imagine the power of it.
Imagine the loneliness.

'She wants to take Matty to live in the States?' Oliver repeated desolately. 'To San Francisco? How shall I be able to see her?'

'It's terrible, I know, but you can manage to fly if you absolutely have to. You went to New York last month without too much problem.'

'Yes, but I was in a panic the entire time. I looked like a melted jelly when we touched down at JFK.'

'There are courses you can take, to try and overcome the fear. Or hypnosis. You never used to worry about it, so you might be a good subject.'

'I know.'

The two of them sat silently, side by side on the sofa, staring at nothing. Then Flora said: 'There's nothing we can do about it, Oliver. We should be thankful that this Jerry seems to be happy to take Matty on as well.'

'I wouldn't think much of him if he wasn't.'

'Actively happy, I mean, not simply resigned to the fact that Georgie comes with baggage – not that Matty is baggage.'

He sighed. 'I shouldn't mind so much, I know. It's just that over the past few weeks, it's been as though we were . . . a proper family. You know?'

'Of course I know.'

'Will we ever be again?'

'Darling Oliver, how can I say? I'm sure we will.'

She had waited to tell him the news until they had put Matty to bed and had dinner. Now they sat on either end of one of the comfortable sofas, with the curtains drawn and a glass of whisky each. As she had expected, he had gone white when she told him, his nostrils pinching together, his mouth tightening, but he relaxed as she pointed out that San Francisco was not all that far away, any more, had told him – lying – that he would be able to see Matty more or less as often as he wished to, that in any case, whatever they felt, it was their duty to be pleased about Georgie's happiness, and the fact that Matty would have a father now, and probably siblings too.

'Not that it matters, but has Georgie ever given any hint as to who the father is?' Oliver said.

'Never. I've asked her, but she so obviously has no intention of telling me that it seems pointless to keep on questioning her about it.' Flora laughed. 'I have wondered sometimes if it was Phil.'

'Phil Chapman? You can't be serious.'

'He seemed awfully interested when Georgie first got pregnant, much more interested than you'd have expected in the circumstances, and definitely edgy, as well.'

'But he's got that sculptress woman, hasn't he? Dodie Something.'

'Having one woman's never stopped Phil from having another.'

'I suppose it's possible. Matty's dark, like he is. But I can't say I've ever seen any likeness to him. Have you?'

'Not so far.'

Oliver frowned. 'He's never tried anything on with you, has he?'

'Of course not. I'd imagine even Phil would draw the line at that, you and he being best friends and all that. Why, would you mind?'

'Of course I'd mind.' He reached for her and drew her alongside him. 'You're mine.'

'Oh, really? That didn't stop you moving in with a certain famous actress. Or do I mean *act*-aw?'

'I told you before, that was a stupid mistake. I've tried to put it right.'

'She's doing very well, isn't she? Every time I open the paper the critics seem to be raving about her in that new production of *Hedda Gabler*.'

'Just shows that what a brilliant actor she is, whatever failings she might have as a person. It's damned difficult to make Hedda sympathetic: the character's so obdurate, there's so little self-discovery, so little acceptance when she finally realises how she's trapped herself. Annabel keeps ringing me up and reading me her reviews, as if I wouldn't have read them anyway. She's hugely talented.' His face suddenly brightened. 'God, I completely forgot to tell you . . . All this business about Matty and Georgie put it right out of my mind, and I've been thinking of nothing else all the way down here.'

'What?'

'I had a call yesterday from the choreographer of the Moscow Opera Company. He wants to discuss the possibility of me designing sets for their next European touring season.'

'That's wonderful.'

'It could be. He's talking about sets *and* costumes. The whole works. It would be a hell of a challenge for me: I've never done opera before and it's so much more of a spectacle than straight theatre.' The words came tumbling from his mouth as they used to long ago, in another life.

'You did do that musical in New York.'

'It's because of that that the Moscow man thought of me when he was casting about for a designer. They've signed up some spectacular counter-tenor – Grigori Something—'

'I think I heard him sing in a Prom last year.'

'—For the season and they want to make full use of him. Showcase him. The director wants a completely new look for the company, says they've been tied by Kremlinesque directives for far too long and it's high time they got into the twentieth century. I didn't like to point out that by the time his European tour starts, we'll practically be in the twenty-first.' Oliver took Flora's hands in his and squeezed them tightly. 'Listen, my darling. I had this really fantastic idea, coming down in the car—'

'What was that?'

'I don't know why I never thought of it before, but . . . Would you help me? Would you work with me? It'd be right up your street: think of the ballet in *Sleeping Beauty*, for instance, or *Nutcracker*. And this guy's choreographing a whole new ballet, too, based on Russian folktales. There're always masses of animals in those, and I can't think of anyone as good at that sort of thing as you.'

'What sort of animals?'

'Wolves and bears and . . . um . . . boars? I don't know what they have in Russian forests. Badgers? Elk?' He looked so helpless that she laughed.

'*Elk*? It's a wonderful idea, darling. And I'd love to help.'

'Not *help*, that's the wrong word. 'Assist-design' they call it. It would look great on your CV.'

'As long as the angel book is finished.'

'I'd forgotten the book.' He looked dejected for a moment. 'But there's plenty of time to do both. Wouldn't it be exciting, though? We've never worked together on a project – it would be wonderful if it all pans out, don't you think?'

At least the loss of Matty had been offset a little by the possible commission from Russia, and in an attempt to keep the evening positive, she demanded more details and asked what ideas he'd already thought of, until it was time for bed.

Lying awake after he had fallen asleep, her body curved into his, one hand holding her breast, his knees paralleling the V of her own, she recalled his question about Philip Chapman. If Phil wasn't Matty's father, who was? There had been a moment when she'd wondered if it could have been Angus, who had obviously crossed Georgie's musical path at some point, and possibly – though she had never asked him – shared her bed. Because of Oliver's more frequent visits, she had seen less of Angus since Matty had come to stay, though he too was enchanted by the little girl, and liked nothing better than to sit reading to her while she cuddled in close to his side. Until now, she had assumed that in Matty he found some balm for the aching wound of his own lost daughters but perhaps she had been wrong about that, as about so many things.

She tried to bring his face to mind and juxtapose it with Matty's but all she could manage was a torturing mental image of Matty last Christmas, plumped out with warm clothes against the cold, wearing an absurd hat of floppy black velvet with its brim pinned back against the crown by a pink velvet rose. It was too big for her and every time it fell down to the end of her little snub nose she would push it back up – and suddenly Flora was crying again. Her face streaming with tears, she tried carefully to extricate herself from Oliver's sleeping embrace without waking him, but his arms tightened around her and he held her closer, murmuring into her neck.

Because of him, she had thought she had become something of an expert in love; now, facing the loss of Matty, she realised that hitherto she had been a novice, merely. An apprentice. A tenderfoot.

Georgie arrived back in England ten days later. She had put on weight. Not a lot but enough to fill out the hollows in her face and remove the angularity from her body. Watching her emerge from customs into the airport concourse, Flora was struck again with how beautiful she was; Jerry Long was a wise man not to have wasted any more time before securing her sister for good.

'Darling!' Georgie cried, catching sight of her. 'You're looking fabulous.'

'You too.' They brushed cheeks then, both moved by sudden emotion, hugged each other tightly, not speaking.

Breaking away at last, Georgie cried: 'Isn't it all exciting and thrilling and fantastic?' Heads turned at the pure delight in her voice. 'I can't wait for you to meet Jerry—' Then, as a shy Matty emerged from behind Flora, she swept the child up into her arms and smothered her with kisses. 'Darling! Baby! My honey-bun!'

Don't overdo it, Flora wanted to say. She hasn't seen you for three months and she gets a bit overwhelmed – and sure enough, Matty's face was turning red, her eyes were filling with tears and her lower lip was beginning to protrude. But Flora had no rights, and kept silent, even when Matty, not entirely sure who this semi-stranger was, put out her arms towards her, begging to be carried.

In the car, driving back to the cottage, Georgie chattered on, telling Matty about Jerry's apartment and its view across the bay, about the Golden Gate Bridge and the sunshine and how there was an orange tree in front of Jerry's building from which you could pick real live oranges and squeeze them for breakfast. 'It'll be such fun,' she kept saying. 'You wait and see.'

After a while, she became aware of Flora's silence. 'What's the matter?' she asked.

'Guess.'

She lowered her voice. 'Losing Matty? Is that it?'

'Yes. I'm – we're devastated.'

'We?'

'Me and Oliver. Since Matty's been staying. I've seen much more of him than I used to. You know how he's always wanted children: he's been able to pretend that we're a family unit. When Matty goes, so will a lot of other things.'

'Well, there's an easy way to put things right,' Georgie said briskly. 'Have a couple of your own.'

'Don't think we haven't discussed it.'

'Great.' Understandably, Georgie's mind was far more on her own affairs than on those of her sister. 'Now listen, I hope it'll be all right me using your cottage like a hotel until I can get back into my flat.'

'I told you, I'm absolutely at your disposal. As long as you're free for the Big Day?'

'Which day is that?'

'Somebody will be celebrating their second b-i-r-t-hday next week.'

'God, I almost forgot!. I can hardly believe it.' Georgie put her hand on her sister's knee. 'Flo, have I ever thanked you for stopping me when I was so determined to—' She broke off and glanced over her shoulder at Matty in the back seat. 'How I could for a single minute have contemplated having an . . . She's the absolute light of my life.'

Mine too, thought Flora. The icing on my cake, the apple of my eye, the be-all, the end-all. 'I only helped you to make up your mind,' she said. 'You were never really going to . . . You know.'

'Maybe.' Georgie sighed. 'Anyway, if we can continue to stay with you, it'll be much better for Matty not to be disturbed again before the big move.'

'Big move,' Matty said.

'Yes, darling. Enormous move. And I've got lots of pictures to show you of your new daddy and we've had your bedroom decorated with a special picture which goes all round the wall: it's got Humpty Dumpty and Jack and Jill and Little Red Riding Hood – all sorts of people.

'Has it got the Man in the Moon?' asked Matty.

'Maybe. If not, we'll put him in too – Jerry's sister is a painter, like you,' Georgie added to Flora.

'I'm sure she'll be happy, once she's settled in.' Flora was aware of anxiety for Matty, a desire to be there to ease her into her new life, above all, of a temptation to tell Georgie how to handle her own daughter. It took all her willpower to bite back the words: less than three weeks from now, Matty would be gone, and no longer her responsibility, in even the most superficial way.

As though sensing a rebuke, Georgie said defensively: 'I know it'll take a bit of time. I'm removing her from everything she's accustomed to. I know that. In some ways. I almost wish I hadn't – but then Jerry and I wouldn't have . . . But don't you think that a happy mother means a happy child? And I'm going to be so terribly happy, we all are, me and Jerry and Matty.'

'I'm not. Nor is Oliver.'

'Darling Flo. I'm sorry. Really I am. But we've got terrific plans. Jerry's putting a new group together – and you wouldn't believe how sweet Frankie and the boys have been. They all knew Jerry from when we were over there before, and they're thrilled that we've got it together this time.'

Flora tried to smile. It was wonderful to see Georgie on so much of a high, but it was no consolation for the loss of Matty.

'Now—' she said, turning into the drive in front of the house, parking, leaning into the car to unbuckle Matty from her car seat while Georgie extracted her suitcases from the boot. '— Arrangements for the next few days. You'll tell me what you want me to do, won't you?'

'Basically, keep on telling me how lucky I am, and looking after Matty for me. I'm going to have to go up to London a lot – you wouldn't believe the amount of paperwork involved in taking up residency in the States. Plus getting married to a United States citizen. And there's the flat, and selling it, or leasing it out on a temporary long-term basis, till Jerry and I see what our plans are likely to be. I mean, we might come over here for a while, you never know. Jerry says that the best session musicians live in London, and it might suit us to have a place we can move into.'

'I've only got one engagement which I can't get out of,' Flora said later, as they sat over a cup of tea in the kitchen. 'I have to go up to London myself next week, to meet the publishers and my agent. And then I'm going to the theatre, so I'll be stopping over that night.'

'Fine. What're you going to see?'

'*Hedda Gabler*. It's had some good reviews.'

'And Annabel Black's playing the lead.'

'As it happens, yes.' Flora didn't add that that was the reason she and Oliver were going to see it.

Georgie picked up a spoon and kapped it gently on the table. 'From what I've heard, you'll find it a bit of a surprise.'

'In what sense?'

'Wait and see.'

Flora stared at her, comprehension slowly dawning. 'You don't mean Rupert Flynn's in it, do you?'

'Christ, Flo. You're not still banging on about him, are you?'

'Not really. I decided you were probably right and it was better to let sleeping dads lie. But that doesn't mean I'm not interested. Anyway, how do you know who is or isn't playing in a London production? You've been out of the country for the past three months.'

'They're not entirely lacking any culture in the States, you know. The *New York Times* and the *San Francisco Chronicle* have both had long articles on the current state of British theatre and the best plays on. And they also have these useful gadgets called telephones.' She stretched deliciously. 'God, I'm exhausted. The flight was an absolute nightmare. I had Mrs Michelin sitting next to me, taking up at least half my seat as well as her own. And there was a kid in the row behind who kept kicking the seats in front. And I'd already seen the movie, which was pretty lousy anyway, and on top of that, a couple of hours before we were due to land, we got into some real bad turbulence and all I could think of was that I wasn't going to make it safely home. Luckily, by the time I'd run through the funeral service you'd have for me, and pictured my family and friends weeping at their sad loss and beating their breasts and eulogising me from the pulpit—'

'You'll be lucky.'

'—We'd got through it and were practically at Heathrow. Which reminds me, I don't want any prayers at my funeral or sadnesses, just a whole lot of my favourite hymns and maybe at the end, Frankie and the band playing something that everyone can have a good old sing to.'

'How about *"Falling Angel"*?'

'It's difficult to sing. And too sad.'

'It's your *funeral*, Georgie. It's *supposed* to be sad. Anything else, while you're at it?'

'You can have the first part in a church, if you like, a nice old-fashioned one with stained-glass windows. There's one near the flat, actually, that I've been to a couple of times. After that, cremation, for God's sake, not burial. I can't bear the thought of spending eternity lying next to a bunch of other dead bodies.'

'I'll try and remember that.' The notion of Georgie going to church seemed singularly inappropriate, given her lifestyle, but Flora didn't say so.

'And champagne all round afterwards.'

'Yes, ma'am. Though isn't this a little macabre, practically on the eve of your wedding day?'

'Actually,' Georgie said seriously. 'I've thought a lot about death since I had Matty. Mostly in terms of wills and things.

Worrying about her, who'd look after her if I wasn't around, how I want her educated.'

'Would you want me to bring her up, or Jerry?'

'I've specified you in my will. But if we're talking ten years down the line, with other kids and so on, I suppose it'd be best to leave her there with him.'

'Talking of that, what're you going to do about your half of the beach house? If anything happens to me, I've left mine to you, so it would be all yours.'

'As it happens, I've done the same. Presumably you'd see that it eventually got back to Matty, or half of it would.'

'I don't know why you think you're going to die before me. I'm older than you.'

'I just like to be prepared.' Georgie laughed. 'Lord, it's all such fun, isn't it? I'd never have believed that me and Jerry would . . . Did I tell you how we actually got together again? It was the most amazing coincidence you ever heard—'

'Yes. But tell me again.' Flora let her rattle on, although she had heard about the amazing coincidence at least four times before. When Georgie had fallen silent, except for a series of massive yawns, she said: 'Did you get any more of those anonymous letters?'

'Funny you should ask.' Georgie sat up straight. 'As a matter of fact I did.'

'How did whoever it was know where you'd be playing? Or staying, come to that?'

'I don't know. In England's one thing: it's a small country. But that he should have known so much about the band's itinerary in the States . . . It was really quite weird.' For a moment she looked serious. 'I hope it's the band he's following, not me personally. I mean, I hope the letters are addressed to me because I sing with the Ragbags, rather than because I'm Georgie Flynn.'

'Were the letters harmless?'

'Mostly. One or two implied that we'd got a relationship going before I left England, and said how angry he was at my behaviour, but I think that's kind of par for the course with these sickos.'

'I hope so.' Flora didn't say that there had been a spate of stalking cases while Georgie had been away, or that she had read of the disruption such behaviour had caused to the lives of the women involved. Once Georgie quit the Ragbags, moved to San Francisco, married Jerry Long, the letters would come to an end. It was usually women living on their own who were persecuted in this way, rather than those who were married.

'And what about the local murderer?' Georgie asked, her eyes beginning to glaze. 'Have they caught him yet?'

'Not yet. But at least there haven't been any more victims for a while. The police thought he might be a sales rep of some kind, or a long-distance lorry driver who had to make regular deliveries to this part of the country, but now they're wondering whether he's in prison for some other offence. Or even that he's a foreigner who's returned to his own country.'

'Aren't you scared, living here on your own?'

'I suppose I ought to be, but actually I'm not. And what with Matty, and my work reaching a critical stage. I couldn't really move out anyway, so I just have to tell myself I'm not in any danger.'

'Mmm.' Georgie's eyes closed. 'Sorry,' she said, forcing them open. 'Jet lag.'

Flora stood up. 'Come on,' she said. 'You go upstairs and crash out while I take Matty for a walk so's not to disturb you. All right?'

'Lovely,' said Georgie drowsily. 'Sounds wonderful.' She caught hold of Flora's hand as shegot up. 'In case I've haven't mentioned it before, Flo, I do love you. Lots.'

'And I you.'

A week later, Flora kissed Matty, hugged Georgie and drove the twelve miles to the nearest mainline station. Leaving her car there all day, a hostage to fortune, or vandals, was always a bit of a risk, but there was no other way to catch a direct train to London, apart from an expensive and often inefficient taxi service which operated idiosyncratically out of the village pub. She hated to miss so much time with Matty, with so few days left, but she had no choice. She was alone on the platform; although the station was in the heart of the town, roses hung over a white picket fence, and the scent of lavender floated from nearby back gardens. In her briefcase were some new pictures, and a piece of revised text for the book which, thanks to intensive hard work on Flora's part, had been completed only a week after the deadline. Georgie and Matty would be gone in a week's time, and if there were further changes, she would then be able to concentrate fully on any last-minute details. It would be one way to deaden the pain of Matty's departure.

The yellow front of the train from London rounded the bend beyond the railway bridge and crept towards the platform opposite her, like a large caterpillar. She watched without much interest as it drew to a halt and people got out, slamming doors behind them before making for the iron-latticed footbridge which straddled the rails and surging across. As they stamped down the wooden steps on her side of the station, the silver-blond hair and pared-down face of one of the passengers caught her eye. He saw her at the same time, and his austere features lightened.

'Flora!'

'Hello, Gregor. I didn't realise this was your local station.'

'It isn't. Where are you going?'

'Up to London, to see my publishers.'

'The angel book. I'm pleased for you.' He looked down the line. 'Will you be back this afternoon? Maybe we could—' The possible invitation was too tentative to assume any real form.

'I'm staying in town overnight.'

'A pity. Otherwise—'

'Yes.'

By now the other passengers had gone and they were alone. He bent his head towards her. She watched the glow of the late summer sun behind him turn his fair hair into a nimbus of light. 'You're in need again, Flora.' Did she imagine the word 'my' before her name, lighter than a whisper?

'As a matter of fact, yes.' How did he know? Were her feelings so transparent? 'My sister's staying with me at the moment, but any minute now she's flying off to San Francisco to marry an American, and live out there permanently.'

'A long-term parting, then.'

'And made much worse by the fact that she'll be taking her daughter, my niece, with her.'

'It's always hard to lose what we love.'

'Matty's been living with me for the past months, you see,' Flora said, embarrassed by the way her eyes had filled with tears, 'while her mother was in the States. I shall miss her horribly.'

'So it will be an especially difficult leave-taking.'

'Yes.' Flora took a deep breath. 'Yes, it will.'

He put his arms lightly around her and the warm familiar chill of his skin seemed as peaceful as an old sweater. *All sorrow and sighing shall flee away*: the words came into her head, though she could not place them. The Bible? A hymn from her school days? She wanted to put her arms around him too, and hug him close, but simply stood within the unthreatening circle of his embrace until he pulled away and said quietly: 'You'll be strong, Flora. I know you will.'

Hearing the conviction in his voice, she believed him.

'Here's your train,' he said.

Lifting her head from his heart, she could hear the rails singing.

'You *are* strong,' he said.

'I know.'

'Flora, remember—'

'What?'

'You are not alone. And you can endure.'

'I shall.' Because one does, always. Whatever happens, one

endures. She stayed looking back towards him long after the train had taken the curve away from the town and was swaying through the countryside towards London. If she were to have described her own personal angel, he might look very like Gregor. His conversational technique was undoubtedly odd, but he also possessed the gift of extracting stress as though it were nothing more than a beesting. The going of Matty seemed less unbearable now: as Jerry Long said, flights were cheap and easy, and in any case, if he and Georgie had not met up again, Georgie would have returned to London and resumed her maternal responsibilities. How much of Matty would Flora have seen then?

The play was not one Flora had ever much enjoyed. The character of Hedda was too unsubtle for her liking. Even Annabel Black had to struggle to make her appear anything more than boorish and ill-mannered, though she did succeed in injecting enough emotion into the role to enable the audience to feel a certain measure of pity for her dilemma. But what really caught and held Flora's attention was the actress playing the part of Miss Teksman. Oliver must have known who was in the cast, so why had he not prepared her for the surprise of watching, for the very first time, her own mother performing on stage? It was a small and undemanding role but Jessica Glanville managed to imbue it with both pathos and dignity. During the interval, she flicked through the CVs at the back of the programme, and discovered just how much theatre work Jessica had undertaken in the past few years. She was surprised, and ashamed for being so. She ought at least to have been aware of what her mother was doing; she ought by now to have learned to make some accommodations.

But why? She had no cause to love her mother. Even if she accepted that Jessica's life had been difficult after her husband walked out on her, that could never make her into someone for whom Flora felt any warmth. Even if, as Jessica had once pointed out, she had provided her daughters with a materially comfortable life, she had done little else for her eldest daughter.

'Are we going backstage?' Oliver asked, as they made their way out into the Haymarket.

'Why should we?'

'Come on, Flo. You know perfectly well why.'

'I don't want to.'

'You can't go for the rest of your life without seeing her.'

'I can't see why not.' She knew she sounded both childish and petulant.

He slipped his hand under her arm. 'If you can't face her tonight, that's fine by me. I'm not going to force you into something you don't wish to do. But one of these days—' They turned the corner into Trafalgar Square, where the fountains fell in cascades of glittering white light. '—You might find it'll be too late.'

'For what, exactly?'

'To make up whatever it is that's between you.'

'You know what that is.'

'Darling Flora, have you ever wondered if you've exaggerated the past? Rewritten it in blacker letters than it was?'

'No.'

'She might not have been the easiest of parents, but she wasn't exactly the wicked step-mother out of *Snow White*.'

'She didn't love me.' Down the Mall, she could see the moonface of the clock on Big Ben against the blue-orange glow of the night sky. Pigeons drowsed along the ledges of the buildings around the square and beneath the figure of Nelson on his column. 'That's the one thing parents are supposed to do: love their children.'

'Perhaps you weren't very lovable.'

'I was only a child,' she said. 'I thought of myself as weak and timid, terrified most of the time, constantly trying to do the right thing in order to escape her violence.'

'How violent was that. Really, how violent?'

'She whipped me with a belt once.' Or was it a stick, a bamboo stick? Memory slid around her mind, elusive as water.

'Just once? For no reason?'

Flora tried to think. That afternoon, the smooth-branched tree, green leaves against the sun, the crunch of beech nuts beneath her sandals: why had they stuck in her mind so clearly? Was it because the beating was in fact so out of character? Surely not.

'Not being able to demonstrate her affection for you, I can see that that's violence of a sort. Being mean to you – and I'm sure she was. But actual physical violence . . .?'

'No,' she said slowly. 'Perhaps not as much as I think. But you've never been anything but loved. Adored. You can't imagine the bleakness of it.' And as so often, she visualised those early years like an Arctic landscape, towering cliffs of ice under a grim, grey sky, snowy wastes stretching to infinity with nothing of comfort or warmth anywhere, and only the cruel sound of the icebergs, cracking and moaning in the howling wind.

'Oh, darling Flora.' He took her into his arms, laid her head against his chest. 'Sweetheart. Don't think I'm not aware of the damage done. But we all have to grow up eventually.'

'I know. And I promise I'm trying.'

'We'll eat, and then I'll drop you off at your hotel. Are you sure you won't change your mind about staying with me?'

'Yes. Antonia's set up this really early working breakfast with the publicity people and so on, and obviously it'd be more professional in a hotel dining room than in your flat. Especially if you start wandering in and out in that short dressing-gown of yours.'

'What's wrong with it?'

'Apart from the fact that Annabel gave it to you? It's indecent, that's what wrong. It shows just about everything you've got.'

'I can't help it if I'm well hung.'

'You don't have to wave it at anyone who passes by.'

'I don't know about that: it could help your meeting. The publishers might even push up the ante.'

'In your dreams. My agent's a radical lesbian.'

* * *

The train next day was delayed outside Oxford. She sat looking out at meadows, distant trees, blue ridges, a river winding. The end of summer was apparent in the tired green of the trees, the occasional yellow-beige of leaves already turning. It was a pastoral landscape, a vista of comforting certainty. But she herself was falling apart. She needed to talk to someone about her mother, unpack her psychological baggage and see how much she could leave behind. Had she been misjudging Jessica all this time? Bearing grudges which had no foundation? If she could only pour it all out to someone, she might be able to put the past into better perspective.

Gregor came to mind: how soothing it would be if she could sit with him, tell him how it had been. She was beginning to accept that perhaps her stored-up resentment had caused her to over-emphasise her mother's cruelty, that it might not have been as terrible as she had always believed. She tried to remember what else she had done, that summer afternoon. There might have been other reasons why Jessica should have beaten her, though nothing occurred to her. But it wasn't all her imagination, she knew that.

She wished the train would start again. Georgie would be someone she could talk to. lovely, open, generous-hearted Georgie. These last few days with her sister had only made her imminent loss all the more poignant. How much she would miss her. How wise she was, too. Judgemental, perhaps, and more on Jessica's side than was helpful, but she'd been there, she'd experienced it along with her. She would understand. And after that, maybe she could find Gregor again, talk to him, who knew nothing of anybody involved except her. Perhaps she should attend another of his bird watching courses. The thought lay lightly within her, smooth and rich as a golden egg.

Interval

Blood everywhere.

It was a phrase often heard or read. People said, after cutting themselves with a knife or describing the scene of an accident, something like that. 'It was dreadful: there was blood absolutely everywhere.' They didn't mean literally, they didn't really mean that it was *every*where. But that morning, after opening the front door which Georgie hadn't bothered to lock last night, standing in the hall, calling out that she was back – although it was almost midday Georgie was obviously still in bed – then stepping into the sitting room, that was what she saw.

Blood everywhere.

The sofa covers were stiff; blood had soaked into the cushions and then dried. The walls were thickly splattered; the curtains, still closed from last night, were blackened where blood had saturated them. The glass on the pictures, the books on the shelves, the silver, the Coalport tea service, the white parchment lampshades – Georgie had left the lights on – sprayed with drops of it, dried now, brown as gravy.

For a moment, she stood unsure, wondering if somehow she had walked into the wrong house, or the band had been down for the evening and she had blundered into a background set-up for one of their new songs. Or even if Georgie was playing some weird joke. Then, upstairs, Matty shrieked her name, and she was jolted back into reality.

Moving further into the room she saw that in front of the dead-embered hearth (the white chimney breast blotched and smeared with blood) lay something hideously unrecognisable yet, at the same time, all too instantly identifiable. Trying not to breathe the brassy-smelling air, she took in the horror of it – clothes hacked away, clotted slashes of flesh, a hand lying parallel to the arm from which it hung by a ribbon of skin.

But reaction had temporarily to be shelved by the urgency of the now-screaming child. Overhead, light footsteps ran across the floor and she heard Matty begin her laborious backward clamber down the stairs. Stepping, nauseated, over blood-soaked rugs, Flora hurried back to the hall, her hand at her mouth. The child must see none of this.

Before closing the door, she turned, steeling herself, to look at the . . . What was the best word: object? thing? shape? . . . To look at what lay on the floor between the comfortable sofas. It was Georgie. Her sister. Her – despite everything – dearest friend. Matty's mother. There could be no doubt about it. No pushing away the evidence. Her eyes accepted details which her brain tried forcibly to reject. The bright, blood-stiffened hair. The generous mouth, slack in hideous death. Teeth gleaming. Long-legged jeans stretching across the hearthrug, the denim showing blue between the streaks and gobbets of dried blood which stained it.

Oh, God. Oh, Jesus. Nausea pushed at the back of her throat. Terror suddenly overcame her. 'Matty,' she screamed, pulling the sitting-room door shut behind her.

Already halfway down the stairs, Matty choked on Flora's name, pausing to draw fresh reinforcements of air into her lungs. Her bottom was bare under her tiny nightdress, and looking up at it. Flora felt such a rush of love and grief that she too choked as she ran up the stairs and swept the child into her arms. 'Oh, Matty.'

She trying to reassure, to comfort, knowing as she did so that there could be no comfort for this child – nor for herself – ever again. She could not banish the image of those blood-stained walls, the body on the floor. Had she really seen it, all that blood? Georgie's blood? She knew she had. Imagination is never that cruel. Worst, most horrible of all, was the knowledge that this was her fault. Directly. Incontrovertibly. Her grievous fault.

If she had not insisted that Georgie kept the baby inside her, Matty would not now be facing the worst bereavement of all. By insisting that Matty must live, she had ensured that her life would be permanently damaged.

'Matty,' she cried. 'Matty.'

The little girl sobbed against her shoulder. 'I didn't know where you was,' she said. 'You didn't came.'

'I'm here now,' Flora said. She breathed in the soft, sleepy smell of the child. How long had she been alone while her mother lay dead on the floor? Had she heard anything? Seen something? It was unthinkable. Impossible. Unbearable. None of this could be true. Yet her mind was working again now, accepting that it was. There were things to do: above all, Matty must be protected, but then the police had to be called, the emergency services alerted. Not that they could do anything now. The multilated body had surrendered hours ago to death.

Only the blood remained.

Everywhere.

Act Two

'I still don't know when,' said Flora wearily. 'At the moment, I simply want to be on my own, with Matty.'

'I understand,' Oliver said humbly. 'Will you mind if I keep ringing?'

In the weeks which had followed Georgie's murder, Flora had found herself retreating further and further from the world, from reality (whatever that might mean), into a small, dark place where there was no room for anyone but Matty and herself. Outside, she knew, the cold winds howled and wild creatures threatened her sanctuary, but if she could only keep the two of them huddled together, Matty enfolded within the circle of her arms, they might – just – survive. There was no way she could explain this to Oliver. 'Of course not.' She tried to soften her tone, knowing he did not understand her current eremitical impulses.

'I just want to see how you two are getting on, to check up.'

'It's sweet of you. As long as you understand that it's nothing personal. I can't bear the thought of seeing anyone at all at the moment. It's all been so dreadful – and on top of everything else, Matty's suddenly started having nightmares. I suppose she's been repressing it and now it's all coming out.'

'Does she dream about Georgie dying?'

'Not specifically, as far as I can make out. She's still too young to have the vocabulary to describe it for me, poor little thing. I think she's accepted that her mother's not coming back. In one sense, it was a good thing that Georgie died so soon after she got back from the tour of the States . . . I mean, if she had to – to die at all. At least Matty had got used to being with me.'

'That's true.'

'So if you can just go on being there for us both, Oliver.'

'Whenever you need me. You know that.'

Upstairs, she heard Matty whimper and knew it was only the prelude to the wracking shrieks which had begun to terrorise them both. 'I've got to go,' she said, and put down the phone.

Matty was sitting up in bed, her eyes blank and terrified, her mouth wide. Whatever it was that frightened her, she could not or did not articulate it, simply gave vent to a wild, forlorn screaming. It was as if, even at her young age, she was able to conceive of such bleaknesses as loss and chaos, and the irretrievability of death.

Flora picked her up and held her. 'Oh, Matty,' she said. 'Matty, darling.' Her own bereavement seemed almost trivial when compared to the child's.

Matty sobbed and shuddered against Flora's shoulder. 'I wan' . . . I wan'—'

'What do you want, darling?'

But Matty couldn't say. She had never spoken of Georgie, never mentioned her sudden vanishing after her almost as sudden reappearance. The cornucopia of delights she promised Matty were not referred to; instead, Matty clung to Flora and the small, soft koala bear which Angus had given her, and tried to deal with the demons which threatened her.

Flora could only hope that the unthinkable had not happened, that Matty had not been wakened by the sounds of her mother being killed and come down to investigate. By the time she had returned to the cottage, Matty must have been alone for several hours. Flora's deepest and most fervent hope was that Matty had spent them asleep.

Death lies in her bed. Death is irremediable. Clocks cannot now be put back, bridges never be built. Sometimes she imagines she is still a child and all of this is still to come, has never happened. But not today. Nor yesterday, nor tomorrow. She cannot pretend that Georgie will be alive once more, that the husky, gin-hoarse voice will ever again drift across smoke-filled rooms in a spray of notes . . . *falling angel, darling angel* . . . piercing the heart with its wry sweet cadences, singing of lost love and melancholy . . . *do you know, do you care, how lonely you are*? . . . and all the doomed endeavours of the human soul.

Jessica had came down from London as soon as she heard the news. She went with Flora to the mortuary and stared dry-eyed at the dead, wounded face of her younger daughter. They had tried to repair some of the damage inflicted by her murderer, but the scars and contusions were still plain to see, long cuts and purple-brown bruises against the candled flesh. Jessica had lifted one of the broken hands and held it against her cheek before leaning forward to kiss the cold lips. She stayed for the rest of the day, sitting unspeaking in the kitchen of Philip Chapman's house, where Flora and Matty were staying. One thin arm was clutched across her chest, holding the elbow of the other, while in her hand she held an unlit cigarette. Her eyes had met Flora's only once, and then briefly. They had been hostile, dark with accusation. She looked older than her years, her strong beauty diminished by her mourning, as though she had covered it with a veil. Just before she left, she turned and said: 'Well, Flora. Now there's just the two of us.'

No, Flora wanted to say. There's also Rupert Flynn, but before she had nerved herself to say the words, Jessica was gone, back to the Haymarket for the evening's performance of *Hedda Gabler*.

'Darling,' Oliver had said, when Flora criticised this behaviour. 'You know as well as I do that the show must go on.'

'Two days after your daughter's been murdered?'

'Work helps to keeps her mind off it. Don't forget she's lost Georgie too.'

The media had left Jessica alone for some reason. Flora had not been so lucky. The police had determined that Georgie was another victim in the lengthening series of Cotswold killings. In addition, she had been young, attractive, a show-biz professional with a reputation that made her more news-worthy than just another single mum on a housing estate. Furthermore, she was the former sister-in-law of good-looking theatre director Oliver Treffyn, and they were determined to make the most of it. Following police advice, and much against her own inclinations, Flora had appeared in front of TV cameras to issue a public statement of the usual kind, saying that someone must know who he was, someone must be sheltering him, for the sake of other vulnerable women, he must be found quickly, please please if you have any information however insignificant it may sound, call this number . . . And so on. After that, she had refused point-blank to talk to the press, begging Angus to handle it for her. 'Why do they ask such stupid questions?' she raged, once. 'Why do they ask me how I feel? How do they bloody well *think* I feel?'

'It's their job.' Angus was patient when her frayed nerves caused her to snap at him, a constant, loving presence when she needed him. Always there, yet never intrusive. Oliver would have been, which was one of the reasons why she didn't want him to come down; Oliver would not have been unobtrusive. Angus was an oasis of calm.

'Who says?' demanded Flora angrily. 'What use can me telling them I'm devastated, distraught, all the rest of it, possibly be? Anyone reading the story who's got an ounce of imagination knows how I feel. And the rest . . . Who cares about them? What difference does it make to them whether I'm devastated, or I'm delighted?'

Devastated came nowhere near describing how she felt. Devastation was light years away from the emptiness which filled vein and artery, and punctured the heart. Her fault. She could think of nothing else. If she had not gone to London, if she had taken more precautions, if she had not been so wrapped up her book, so consumed with misery at the thought of losing Matty, then none of this might have happened. Georgie's picture had appeared on the front page of most of the national dailies; one of the Sundays had produced yet another detailed résumé of the murders so far attributed to the man they were calling the Cotswold Killer, with ringed circles marking the previous murder sites. Georgie was the seventh victim: Flora could not bear to read about it, nor to see her sister's photograph among that gallery of brutalised women.

The whole process which had linked Georgie into the list of earlier victims had been a long nightmare. From the arrival of a uniformed officer in answer to Flora's first anguished telephone call, the machinery of investigation had swung into leviathanic action. They had their routines; their own esoteric language: 'Let the room know.' 'SOCOs.' 'Suiting-up.' 'Exit and entry points.' Georgie became merely dead flesh, lit briefly by photo flashlights, caught on video, swabbed and bagged and combed and vacuumed, before being trundled away by the undertaker's men. The two CID men leading this part of the investigation, Detective Chief Superintendent Prince and Detective Superintendent Martyn, had explained the need to collect everything, fibres, alien hairs, semen samples, saliva, fingerprints, bite marks, anything at all which might eventually lead the police to the right man.

Prince and Martyn had called in Scene of Crime officers, who were, in fact, not police officers but civilians, two sensibly dressed young women in trousers and neat shirts.

'We're working on the theory that he's a travelling man of some kind,' Det. Chief Supt David Prince said. 'Sees his opportunity, gets into the house, does his number and is off again before anyone knows what's happened.' He and his CID colleague had been kind but brisk, sympathetic but impersonal. They had a job to do and kindness, sympathy, was one of the tools with which they hoped to draw enough details from Flora to enable them to do it.

But Flora could tell them nothing. 'I was away that night. If only I'd been here, I could have protected her, stopped him somehow.'

'If you'd been here, he wouldn't have tried it,' Prince said, and she felt even more responsible for her sister's death.

'Since there was no sign of a break-in,' said Martyn, 'it might have been someone she was already acquainted with. It's long odds that she knew someone that one of the other victims also knew, but we can't afford to overlook even the vaguest leads.'

But when they went through the names in the address book found in Georgie's handbag, Flora had been of little help. Most meant nothing to her, another cause for shame. Although they were sisters, Georgie's life had been virtually unknown to her.

There had been no sign of forced entry at the houses of the other victims, either. Prince and Martyn had theories. 'He could have been selling something door-to-door. Or a man picked up at the local pub. Someone she met out walking?' They stared at her with avid eyes, their faces full of the hope that she might be the one to provide the vital clue which would lead to their man. She knew nothing.

She offered them the anonymous letter writer. 'He'd even written while she was in the States,' she said. 'Perhaps it was a personal thing, she was specifically targeted, rather than being just a random victim. Perhaps she wasn't one of the Cotswold murderer's victims after all,' and wondered why she would find that possible specificity marginally easier to bear than the arbitrary truth, as though it would lift her dead sister out of a common rut, make her special, significant, remove Flora's last view of her as so much butchered meat carried out of the house on a stretcher.

'Do you have any of the letters in your possession?'

She shook her head. 'I think my sister burned them. But I know he tracked her all the way to the States, because he wrote several to her there, so maybe he also knew that she was staying with me, and then, when he found out that she was alone in the house that night—'

But the eyes of the CID men showed their lack of interest. 'We'll look into it, but it doesn't fit the pattern as we know it,' Prince said.

'You could ask the other Ragbags – that's the band she sang with – because I know she talked to them about him.' But it was a long shot, and the information the members of the group could offer was minimal. Without any further evidence, there was little the police could or wanted to do about finding the man who had written the letters.

She went round the house with them, but apart from the mayhem in the sitting room, nothing seemed to have been disturbed, nothing removed. They had even questioned Matty, in as unthreatening a way as they could, but the little girl clung to Flora's hand and shook her head, the elastic-banded bunches on either side of her head quivering with the violence of her unspoken denial.

'The trouble is that this bastard seems to have a one hundred percent hit rate,' Martyn said dispiritedly. 'When they go out stalking, prossies or whatever, they usually have one or two false starts, misses, the victim gets away or survives an attack and gives us a description, tells us something useful about him: he's got a tattoo on his arm, blue eyes, brown hair, he's black or Asian, that sort of thing. But so far nobody's come forward to say that a man they'd asked into the house had then tried to hack them to pieces. Nothing like that. No mentions of men met at the pub who've turned violent, no casual pick-ups brought home for a bevvy, nothing like that at all. Somehow he's managing to make his kill and leave, without anyone the wiser.'

'Georgie wouldn't have been at the pub,' protested Flora. 'She had her little girl here.'

'That's about the only thing we've found common to all the murders, apart from the locality,' said Prince. 'They've all been respectable single women, living on their own with their kids.'

'And nobody's ever seen anything? The neighbours or whatever?' asked Flora.

'He's too smart for that. Or else just damned lucky.'

'But since all the . . . um . . . murders have been in a smallish area, wouldn't that make him someone local?'

'It might. Or else so obvious that nobody's notices him. Like the postman. But believe me, we've been into all that with a fine-toothed comb. Can't find a thing. Which is why we're betting it's someone who lives a distance away whose job brings him this way in a regular cycle, perhaps during the summer.'

'Why do you say that?'

'Most of the murders have been committed between the months of April and August. If he was local, someone, somewhere would have noticed. Surely they would.' The two officers looked at each other with defeated eyes.

'Nobody can go on being that lucky,' one of them said.

'Which is why we'll get him in the end.'

Telling Jerry Long had been another difficult hurdle to climb over. Flora had found his telephone number in Georgie's address book and called him. Hearing her English accent and voice asking his name, he had, in the first few dreadful seconds, taken her for Georgie. 'Hi, hon,' he said, and the warmth of his greeting made it even worse to have to flounder through an explanation of who she was, and why she was ringing. Nobody, Flora thought, should have to impart such irrevocable and painful information. He had broken down on learning what had happened. 'And it's all my fucking fault,' he had added, speaking through gritted teeth. 'My stupid fucking fault. If I hadn't let her go before . . . If I'd been less of a dickhead and more of a man . . . My fault, all of it.'

'No,' said Flora. 'You can't blame yourself.'

'If we'd gotten married when she wanted to, first time around . . . But I was too fucking . . . Oh, my God, this is . . . I don't know what to—' His broken cries continued while Flora could do nothing but listen, and hope that it helped.

Finally, partially pulling himself together, he had asked when the funeral would take place. 'The police haven't yet released the . . . haven't . . . The body isn't . . . I don't know yet.' Flora had stumbled over the words, unable to see her sister as that: simply a body, lying in the morgue, blue-white, cold, a toe-tag all that was left to identify her as the unique, unrepeatable, distinctive and singular person who had been Georgie Flynn.

'You'll let me know, won't you?'

'Of course.'

'I want to be there. I *have* to be there. And . . . to meet . . . little Matty—' His voice dropped. 'I'd wanted—' He began to weep again. 'Shit. I'm sorry. But we were going to be so happy. I promise you, we were . . . I was going to take such good—'

'I know.' Flora was crying too. 'She told me. She was so excited, so happy about the future.'

'And now—'

Now nothing.

For the past month, Flora had been living in the guest cottage at the end of the Chapmans' large garden. 'I can't go on living in the cottage,' she said. 'In my own house, I mean. Not after what's—'

'Nobody's asked you to. Or expects it,' said Oliver.

'And you know you can stay here as long as you like, dear heart. Dodie and I love having company, don't we?' Phil looked across the table at his current partner. The four of them were sitting in his technologically advanced kitchen, which looked as though no one had ever so much as buttered a slice of bread in it, let alone cooked a meal.

'Of course we do,' Dodie said. 'And Matty's an absolute sweetheart, poor little thing.' Dodie was a tiny bird-like creature, in a striped sweater which seemed too small for her, and doll-sized jeans.

'We know what it's like,' Phil added. 'Remember me telling you that our cleaning lady knew one of the victims?'

'You can't possibly know,' objected Oliver, who had come down the previous evening.

'Well, of course not *exactly* what it's like. The grief and so on. But the outrage . . . the pity of it all—' His voice died away. What, after all, is there to say in such circumstances? What do comforting words mean, how does sympathy help?

Even Oliver seemed distanced from her, Flora thought. Her sense of alienation seemed to be increasing as the days dragged by, as though she was cut off from the rest of the world by an invisible glass barrier. She had read that this was how parents who had lost children felt: as if they were imprisoned behind a wall which no kind heart could scale, banished to a place to which only the similarly bereaved had the key. None of them could really know what she was going through. Looking round at their concerned faces, she wondered dully if Rupert Flynn had read about the death of his younger daughter. She knew, too, that whatever her hesitations, she would have to find her mother and speak to her. No one should have to suffer this grief alone. Not that Jessica would be burdened in the same way as Flora, who was responsible, who had left her sister alone with Matty. Who had, in a sense, allowed this desecration to happen. She would never be free of that, never.

'I'll have to go to London,' she announced abruptly.

'When?'

'As soon as possible. May I leave Matty with you?'

Dodie nodded her cochineal-coloured hair. 'Any time. Will she mind being left with us?'

'I hope not.'

'Let me drive you up,' Oliver said.

On the journey, they talked little, and then of insignificances. Flora had found it difficult to resume the relationship with Oliver which had, for a while, seemed to be resurgent. Partly this was because of the load of guilt she now carried; being with Oliver might lead her back to happiness, which was something to which she now felt that she had no right. Then, too, Georgie had always treated Oliver with a kind of amused cynicism, had wondered aloud why Flora was so loyal to him, had pointed out how he had held her back. Looking at him with new clarity, she could not help wondering whether there had been some truth in what her sister said. And yet, she told herself, she herself had changed. She no longer followed his opinions slavishly; she had too many of her own. She questioned.

Oliver dropped her at the top of Baker Street. She did not intend to tell him why she had wanted to come to London, had implied that she had a meeting with her publisher. She took the Underground to Piccadilly Circus and walked down Haymarket. *Hedda Gabler* played two matinées a week, and this afternoon was one of them. When the performance was over, she would go backstage and talk to her mother, however difficult it might seem. It was something Georgie had advised, had clearly wished she would do, and in the aftermath of her sister's death, she was inclined to do anything which could bring Georgie nearer.

She reached the theatre halfway through the show and asked one of the attendants what time it finished. Ten minutes after the curtain came down, she went round to the stage door and asked to see Jessica Glanville. Before she could explain that she was the actress's daughter, the doorman shook his head.

'Sorry, madam. Miss Glanville's part is being played by an understudy for the rest of the week.'

'Oh. I see.' Slowly the adrenalin drained from her body, leaving her cold and a little empty. Having steeled herself for this meeting, it was a considerable anticlimax to find that she was unable to accomplish what she had set out to do. 'Do you know where she is?'

'I'm afraid I don't. She's been bereaved recently – you might have read about it in the papers – her daughter was murdered not long ago and as you can imagine, she hasn't felt up to working just yet.'

Flora turned away. What now? She could go back to the Chapmans'. She could telephone Oliver. Or she could begin a task she had been putting off: the sorting out of Georgie's flat. She had been there once since the murder, with Det. Supt Martyn and a uniformed officer from the local station, though it had been a fruitless exercise. The tenant – a Japanese businessman – had moved out only a couple of days before Georgie's death, and left it looking uncharacteristically neat. Even so, she had not been familiar enough with the place to be able to say with any certainty whether anything had been removed, and the police had been more interested in finding the killer than in examining the unnecessary details of his latest victim's private life. She had seen then that Georgie's interest for them lay more in the chances she afforded them of success in the hunt, than in her own unique personality. They were only concerned with her insofar as she connected with her killer. Since the murder had taken place elsewhere, and any clues they might find resided in Flora's cottage rather than the victim's surroundings, where, in any case, she had not been living at the time of her death, their examination of the place had been fairly cursory.

Nor had Flora had any wish at that time to linger. The flat had still been too full of Georgie and the gaiety which had been snuffed out by a madman's whim. For he must be mad, must he not, this monster who preyed on women? Did he simply kill for the pleasure of it, the thrill, or did he have some crazy justification for what he did?

'A lot of work's been done on serial killers,' Martyn told her. 'Particularly in America. Seems that often they're motivated more by the desire for power than by sexual needs. Your sister – and the other victims – weren't raped, or sexually abused, though there was evidence of sexual activity in some of the cases.'

'You mean he masturbated over the bodies? Or even—' dreadful thought, that someone wanted to, that someone could, '—came inside them? Something like that?'

'Not always.' Flora was aware that they had particular reasons to suspect that Georgie had been killed by the man which they were not going to divulge. 'The point is that in the case of the man we're currently looking for, the perpetrator is first of all a killing machine seeking power over an individual he perceives as deserving punishment, and only secondly a sexual animal. In other words, the need to get even, to punish, far outweighs the need for sex. Some of these killers even say that the rape part was the bit they least enjoyed, that it was the stalking, the thrill of the chase, the thought of eventual punishment which motivated them.' He glanced at his colleague. 'Not that it pertains in these particular killings.'

'You said these people – these killers – want to get even: with what? *For* what?'

'Who knows? Mother, perhaps. Childhood. Nearly always, when they're finally caught, these people have a history of unstable and abusive upbringing, grossly inadequate parenting, hostile relationships with one or other parent.'

'Not to mention,' added the local officer, 'sexual abuse of some kind, often committed by a family member. Isn't that right, sir?'

'I should have taken more notice,' Flora said helplessly. 'But . . . apart from the way she was attacked, what other similarities were there between the other victims and my sister?'

'And thc fact that she was alone with a child and no husband? Well, the other women were all physically similar, and all had light hair. Your sister's was more . . . dark and coppery, I think you'd say. But otherwise, she was the same build as the others: tall and thin.'

'But I understood the man you're looking for probably selected the victim and then watched her for a while before—'

'That's what we thought originally. Now we're not so sure.'

'I see. Because I was going to say that my sister had only been in my cottage for a week before he . . . And a lot of the time she was in London. So he can't have had time to watch her. Quite apart from the fact that I was in the house all the time, as well.'

'Have you considered the possibility, Mrs Treffyn, that you were his original target?'

'Me?' No, she had not. Which made her all the more culpable, didn't it, if he'd come looking for her and found Georgie instead? 'But I'm small, not the same build as my sister. Surely if he was after me, once he'd seen her he'd have realised he'd made a mistake and left.'

'Perhaps it wasn't until he got into the house that he realised this wasn't the woman he'd been stalking but by then it was too late. Perhaps he's beginning to change the physical look he looks for in his victims. Even serial killers develop different tastes, different requirements – the Boston Strangler is a case in point. Perhaps he *had* been stalking your sister: she was with you for a week, after all, before he killed her.'

Her mouth was dry as she asked: 'Does that mean he might keep on trying?' My fault, my stupid careless fault, she moaned inwardly. If I had only listened to Angus, to Oliver, taken better precautions, Georgie would still be alive. Part of her almost wished that the killer *would* return: it would be a kind of atonement for Georgie's death.

'It's unlikely. He's kept to the same area, but never struck more than once in the same place.' Martyn spread his hands. 'I'm sorry to be talking like this to you. Everything at the moment is conjecture: we shan't know the truth, what really motivates this man, until we find him.'

She had recently listened to a radio item in which an eminent psychologist had profiled him: 'He'll be something of a loner,' he had said, 'but none the less a man who functions adequately within his own society. He will almost certainly have lacked parental affection in childhood and have grown up as an introverted and lonely child who was never able to fit in. None the less, he may still be living with his parent or parents, or with a wife who is not too involved in his life, who is used to his absences without finding them particularly remarkable. He will be intelligent, certainly able to hide his perversions from those around him. One thing is certain: when he is finally caught, most people will be astonished that he could have committed such crimes, having accepted him for what he appears to be.'

Queried on this by the interviewer, who had mentioned Hungerford and Dunblane, and how many people had regarded the perpetrators in both those massacres as walking time bombs, the psychologist had explained further: 'This is not a man with a burning resentment against society as a whole, who desires to make his mark upon a society which has so far ignored him, as occurred in both those cases. Nor is it a man wishes to destroy innocence because he himself is no longer innocent, or was never allowed to be. This is a man with a specific grudge against specific types of women, a man who, from the evidence so far, is willing to take his time, to prepare the ground before he moves in for the kill. Rather than being an elephant running amok, he is a tiger, able to wait for the right moment, lying unseen in the long grass, picking out the woman who will be his next victim. He won't stand out: if he did, he would be noticed and that would spoil his plans. So he blends in, he's one of us, the man standing next to you in the pub, the man reading his newspaper on the tube, the man who does his job efficiently and without fuss and goes back to his home at the end of the working day.'

The flat was cold. She stood in the middle of the big sitting room, hearing again Georgie's voice as she talked of the garden where Matty could play, and the room which would be Matty's nursery. She thought of the child's bedroom in San Francisco and the painted frieze which Matty would now never see. Her mouth trembled and, as so often these days, she felt the choke of tears rising in her throat.

Such thoughts, she told herself, achieve nothing. She went into the kitchen to make herself a cup of tea. While the kettle boiled, she picked up the wooden coffee grinder and turned the handle slowly, remembering all the times she had seen Georgie doing the same thing. Forcing herself, she walked down the short hall to Matty's room. The Japanese businessman had been agreeable to Georgie's personal possessions being stowed there, since he would only need one bedroom.

The key to the padlocked room was on her ring; grudgingly, wishing she could leave it untouched, she opened it. A scent of orange blossom greeted her, Georgie's scent, and as though she was watching a film being fast-forwarded she saw Georgie again, a child in the tree-house, running along the seashore, touching Gran's hump with her starfish fingers. She remembered the giggly afternoons in Georgie's bedroom, with herself and Katie and Gemma Craig, Georgie's best friend ever since kindergarten, the four of them screaming with laughter while Georgie sang, holding a hockey stick as a pretend mike. And Sisters In Crime, the all-girl band Georgie had formed with friends in her class, all of them dressed in black with hideous gothic make-up. She remembered Georgie's ever-changing hair: punk, long, tied back, chicly sheared, red, purple, bronze, blonde. She remembered her own shame at not knowing of her sister's broken heart, she remembered the kindness, the coarseness, the caustic sense of humour, the weaknesses. Above all, the strengths. Georgie had always known who she was and where she was headed. If she had hesitations, she rarely showed them. And now . . .

It would have been easy to break down yet again, to fling herself onto the sofa and weep away the pain until the next time it grew too much to handle. Instead, Flora set her mouth and began the task of sorting out her sister's life.

'I don't know if they're any help at all,' she said to Det. Chief Supt Prince. 'But I thought you ought to have them.' She handed him the envelope containing five of the anonymous letters which had been sent to Georgie. They were all crumpled, as though Georgie had screwed them up and thrown them into the bin and then had second thoughts, had smoothed them out again, realising they might be useful in finding the identity of the person who'd written them.

'They might be.' Prince looked through them, turning them over with a pencil. 'But so far we have no reason to believe that your sister wasn't killed by the same man who killed the other women in the area. Which would make these a bit redundant.'

'Unless you've found other anonymous letters in the homes of the others.'

He shook his head. 'We haven't. I'm sorry. But we'll certainly hang on to them for the moment, if we may. You never know what the computers will turn up, do you? And when we finally get the bastard . . . Well, like I said, you never know.'

'I suppose not.' Flora turned away. For a moment, she had felt convinced that the killer and the letter-writer were one and the same, that if they could trace the latter, they would have the former. But even if they did, nothing was going to bring Georgie back. And that was what mattered, and would matter for the rest of her life.

Death lies beside her in the thick night. When she sleeps, she dreams of angels. Clouds of them, and one among all the rest who has Gregor's face, and tears of ice lying on his cheeks.

She dreams of blood.

14

Georgie haunted her. Now that there was no future, Flora found herself obsessively reviewing her own behaviour in the past. Moments when she had been dismissive of Georgie's enthusiasms. Times she had not listened. Her aloofness. Her indifference. All their joint lives, she had envied her sister's apparent gaiety and freedom: she began to wonder just how dearly they had been bought, how much of a front they had been. *If onlys* crowded in on her; she faced the fact that for much of her life she had not behaved generously to those about her. She did not like herself.

Increasingly she found herself clinging to Matty, drawing strength from the little girl who seemed at times to be so much more able to deal with emotional turmoil than she herself was. The nightmares gradually reduced; Matty appeared to be almost back to her old self. But for Flora, peace was ever more elusive.

There were so many phone calls, most of them from appalled friends of Georgie's, but several for herself. One came from Katie Vernon, now married to a doctor and living in Cheltenham. 'I'd no idea we were living so close to each other,' she kept saying. 'Oh please, Flora, come and see us as soon as you can. My husband's sister was killed in a car crash not long ago, and it helped him so much to talk about her with people who'd known them both as children. They're quite different from the friends you make when you're an adult.'

'I'll come,' promised Flora. 'Just as soon as I can.'

Another of the calls came from Gemma Craig. 'I can't believe it,' she repeated, over and over again. 'I just can't believe it. Not Georgie. Not lovely Georgie, always so alive, so . . . joyful.'

'I know, I know.' Flora wept openly into the telephone. 'I know.'

'We must meet up again,' Gemma said. 'We must, we will,' and putting down the phone, Flora felt sure that they would, and was comforted.

Eithne came, holding Flora against her soft bosom as Flora held Matty. Only with Eithne did she feel entirely free to break down, to sob and scream, endlessly going over that terrible discovery in the sitting room. 'Flora, darling,' Eithne said, soothing, repetitive. 'My poor sweetheart. Dearest Flora. Don't be blaming yourself, it wasn't your fault, it's not you were the one responsible.' And though Flora dared not believe her, the constricting walls behind which she was imprisoned seemed for a while to be less impenetrable.

She had tried several times to get in touch with her mother but without success. The home telephone number she called was either not answered or was picked up by an answering machine; eventually a computerised voice told her that the number was no longer in service. Letters explaining her desire to meet had been ignored and then began to be returned by the post office. A small notice outside the theatre announced simply that the part of Miss Teksman had been taken over by Andrea Turpin; enquiries at the stage door and box office received such a stony response that she wondered whether Jessica had given instructions that no details as to her whereabouts were to be passed on to anyone. Until her mother resurfaced, there was little further she could do. As once she had hoped to find her father – and still did – so now it grew increasingly important that she find her mother. At night she lay awake, hoping that she had not left it too late. They would probably never become friends, but a rapport might be established, if only through the ghost of the Georgie they had both loved.

Leaving the Chapmans', she moved into Georgie's flat with Matty and put her cottage on the market, with a view to buying something similar when it sold. Local gossip made it inevitable that few buyers came forward, reluctant to purchase a house where a woman had been brutally done to death.

She rang her publishers to say that she was finding it impossible to work on the last-minute revisions they had asked for, and was given sympathetic encouragement. 'If you can't do it, don't worry,' her editor said. 'If we have to delay the project, so be it. I still think it would do brilliantly if it's out in time for the Christmas markets, but who says it's got to be *this* Christmas?'

'You'd be willing to wait?'

'Projects like your don't come along every day of the week. And the longer lead time we have, the more we can hype it. And though I hate to say it, the reasons for the delay won't exactly do the book any harm.'

It took Flora a moment to work this out. She said: 'That's outrageous.'

'I agree, but we're running a business here, whether we like it or not.'

'You can't seriously imagine I'm going to cash in on my sister's death.'

'No. But the fact remains—'

'Would it be better if I returned the advance?' Flora said coldly.

'Flora, my dear. I sound hard, I know, but publishing is no longer simply a gentleman's game. Selling books has to be conducted on a commercial basis these days, like everything else and if there's a USP, we'll use it.'

'USP?'

'Unique selling point. Which you have. You've got to face facts.'

'Some facts shouldn't have to be faced.'

'Sorry, Flora, but that's the way it is.'

It was not until after Christmas that Frankie came round to the flat with Dave and Spick, two of the other guys in the band. Flora's sense of self-abasement was increased by the fact that she had never met any of them before now, that it had taken Georgie's death to bring them together. They sat about on Georgie's floor, drinking beer from bottles they'd brought with them, and playing with Matty. 'We were just gutted about Georgie,' Spick said softly. At first sight, Flora would have taken him for a prize fighter, given his brutally cropped head and broken nose, but she had quickly realised that behind the tough face was the gentlest of personalities. 'Of all the people—'

'She was a real mate,' said Dave.

'Can't tell you how much we're gonna miss her.' Spick swallowed, his mouth turning down like a child's. His eyes were red-rimmed and haunted.

'You'll be lost, I shouldn't wonder,' Frankie said. Frankie was a surprise, a big, balding, worried-looking man who looked as if he should be working in a local government office.

'Us, too,' said Dave.

'Something's Burning and I think it's love,' sang Spick into Matty's hair. She was sitting on the floor inside the space created by his spread knees. 'On a good night, even Dolly Parton couldn't give it what Georgie did.' Tears came out of his eyes and he wiped them away with the back of his hand.

'She often told us how close you two were,' Frankie said to Flora.

'She told you that?'

'Said you'd protected her, looked after her from the day she was born. Said when you were growing up, you were more of a mother to her than her real mum.'

'Is that what she really said, Frankie?' The burden Flora had been carrying suddenly seemed a little lighter.

'Honest.' He glanced at the others, who nodded. 'When you're on the road, once you've done a gig, there's not much else to do except sit round with a bottle and get sloshed. So she knew all about our sorry lives, and we knew about hers. And the way she talked, she couldn't have gotten along without you.'

Tears stung Flora's eyes. Georgie, she thought. My sister. My friend. 'It was a case of mutual support when we were children. When we got older, it was different. But if we weren't close, it was my fault, not hers.'

Frankie nodded sympathetically. 'She said you'd got . . . well, problems. Told me about your mum and dad. He sounded a right plonker, if you ask me.'

'I don't think he—'

'Behaved like one, too,' Dave put in, 'if you don't mind me saying so.'

'I haven't seen him since I was six.'

'No loss there,' Frankie said. 'When he came up, spoke to Georgie like that, me and the boys couldn't believe it, could we, lads?'

The other two shook their heads. 'Rat-arsed,' Spick said.

'Runs out on his daughter when she's still a kid and the first time he sees her again, tries to touch her for fifty quid.' Dave tutted disapprovingly. 'Leave it out.'

'I'm not sure what you . . . Georgie didn't tell me all the details, apart from the fact that she met him in Dublin.'

'Yeah. He, like, staggers into this hotel where we're staying, stinking of booze, yeah? Says, hey, I'm your long-lost dad, and before Georgie can blink, adds: and by the way, since you look like you're doing OK, how about a handout for the old man? That's more or less how it went, wasn't it, Spick?'

'Yeah. Poor old George. You could have knocked her over with a wet tissue when he told her who he was.'

'She didn't tell me that.'

'Didn't want you to know,' Frankie said. 'She knew you'd be upset. Said you had a bit of a fixation, despite him buggering off like that.'

Oh, Georgie: trying to preserve my illusions for me . . . 'He was drunk?'

'Well lit up, I'd say.'

'Definitely rat-arsed,' repeated Spick.

'She told me he wasn't.'

The men looked at each other. 'Wanted to spare you, I expect,' Frankie said.

'He was in a play at the theatre there, wasn't he?'

'He was, yes. She showed us his picture outside when we walked past the next day.'

'She said he looked distinguished.'

'Distinguished but rat—'

'—arsed,' said Matty.

'Here,' Spick said, putting his large hands round her small body and setting her on her feet in front of him so that their eyes were on the same level. 'There's some words only big people can use, yeah? And that's one of 'em. So don't let me hear you say that again, right, or Frankie'll come round and give you a right bollo – he'll have your guts for garters, he will.'

'Will you, Frankie?' Matty didn't seem at all worried about it. She leaned against Spick, one hand on his shoulder.

'You bet I will, cookie.'

'Who's the prettiest little girl in London?' Spick said.

'I'm not little.'

'Aren't you?'

'Soon I'll be two and a half,' Matty said carefully; she found the words difficult to pronounce.

'Two and a half!' exclaimed Spick. 'Hey, that's really *old*.' He drew Matty towards him and kissed the top of her hair with a look on his face that sent a pang through Flora's heart.

'It'll be Zimmer frames all round before we know where we are,' said Dave.

Flora realised that these men had been as much Georgie's family as she herself had. More so, perhaps. She wanted to squeeze every last detail from them about the encounter with Rupert Flynn. Lowering her voice, she said to Frankie: 'If you wouldn't mind, I'd like to hear more about my – my father, and about Georgie. Perhaps when Matty's not around.'

'Got it.'

'There's so much I didn't realise.'

He patted her hand. 'I understand. Give me a call – or any of us – and we'll pop round for a natter.'

Lying in bed, she remembered an occasion when Matty was about six months old. Flora had turned up at Georgie's flat at a time earlier than they had arranged. She let herself into the building with the key which Georgie had given her months ago and went up the stairs. Inside the flat she could hear someone moving around. She pressed the bell.

When the door was opened, she thought for a moment that she must have come to the wrong flat. Frowning, she had opened her mouth to murmur an apology before reality reasserted itself. And asked rudely: 'What are you doing here?' struggling to come to terms with the fact that she was standing face to face with Jessica Glanville. Her mother. Then Georgie had appeared, wearing a tatty old dressing-gown and looking distinctly the worse for wear.

'You weren't supposed to arrive until later,' she said ungraciously.

'I know. But I got a lift up with Angus Macfarlane.' Why is *she* here? Flora wanted to scream. Why didn't you tell me? I'd never have come if I'd known she'd be here. I didn't realise you'd been seeing her.

'I'll put the kettle on,' Jessica said. Normal words to ease what should not have been but was an abnormal situation. She and her elder daughter had not been as physically close to each other as this since the day of Flora's wedding, when they had posed together for photographs and then not spoken again until it was time for the bridal couple to leave.

The two younger women stood in the hall, waiting for the sound of water running as Jessica filled the kettle from the tap. Then Georgie said, her voice low and fierce: 'Don't blame me.'

'I'm not.'

'You should have rung. I could have put you off.'

'How often does she come here?'

'About once a month. To see Matty.'

'You never told me.'

'What would've been the point?'

'You should have said.'

'If I had, you'd have kicked up a fuss, as usual.'

'I would *not*.'

'She's not the arch-fiend you seem to imagine.'

'I'm not imagining anything.' Flora said angrily, strained by the need to keep her voice low. 'I'm remembering what actually happened. It's not the same thing at all.'

'She's getting older.'

'So am I.'

'And mellower.'

'So fucking what?' demanded Flora.

'Don't start. Please don't start.'

'Me start? *Me*?'

Georgie clutched at her forehead with one hand. 'Matty's kept me up half the night and I'm just not up to a fight this early in the morning.'

In the kitchen, the kettle started the run-up to its whistle and then died away into a gurgle. They heard a cupboard open, the rattle of cups, the slam of the refrigerator door.

'Who's fighting?' Flora demanded. 'You think I'm about to start a fight?'

'Yes,' hissed Georgie. 'You're always fighting. You were bloody *born* fighting.'

'I was *not*.'

'For God's sake, don't wake the baby. I've only just got her down. Besides, babies are very sensitive to atmosphere and I don't want Matty upset.'

'Tea's ready,' their mother called.

'If you think I'm going to sit and sip tea with that woman, you're wrong,' Flora said. 'I'm going. I'll ring you later.' She had turned and left the flat.

Why had she done that? How could she have been so . . . so *cold*?

Remembering the incident, she was filled with excoriating shame. It was clear that Georgie was expecting her to make some kind of hostile fuss, that she always did. *Born fighting*, Georgie had said. Looking back, she could remember animosities of various sorts. A number of them. Yet she had always envisaged herself as a mild, even timid person. She would have said that the anger which had so often filled her over the past few years had been the result of recent circumstances: was it, instead, how she had always been? Was that why Jessica had always seemed so antagonistic?

Outside in the street, a car horn hooted, an ice-cream cart sounded its sing-song chimes, someone called a dog to heel. Did everyone see her as hostile, confrontational?

Did Oliver? Since Matty's birth, she had grown accustomed to having him back in her life, had begun to accept that he loved her still. But recently, even he had begun to show signs of impatience with her intransigent attitude to her mother. She hadn't told him about her efforts to contact Jessica Glanville. Maybe she should. He'd see then that she had at least tried.

Nearly six months after the murder, the police rang to say that they were finally ready to release Georgie's body. *Release Georgie's body* . . . Once, such words would have sounded bizarre, macabre. Now, they were simply the stuff of the everyday that her life had become. As she chose hymns, ordered champagne, called the band to ask them to play, rang Oliver for help with sorting out a crematorium, telephoned Jerry Long in California, she thought how morbidly prophetic it was that Georgie should have discussed the details of her own funeral only a week before she died. She rang the theatre and left word for Jessica, begging them to pass on the information about the funeral: there was no other way she could think of to let her mother know.

Eithne came up from Cornwall again. Draped in extravagant layers of cloth, she enveloped Flora in a swirling, perfumed hug. 'Isn't this more than anyone should have to bear?' She shed her cloak and poured herself a drink. 'But there's no use in looking back. Tell me what it is you want me to do, and I'll do it.'

'Just your being here is enough,' Flora said. Eithne's exuberance was exactly what she needed at this point: she was a healthy reminder of the way the life force ran and bubbled and flowed, inextinguishable. Ever since Georgie's death, she had subconsciously feared that everything had now come to a halt. By her presence alone, Eithne confirmed that it continued.

Jerry Long telephoned to say he would be flying in to Heathrow the following day. Eithne volunteered to go and meet him. 'The poor man can't be arriving at the airport like that, alone and grieving,' she said. 'I'll take Miss Matty with me, give you an hour to yourself.'

'I could do with it,' Flora said. 'Thank you.'

Jerry turned out to be short and plump, older than she had expected him to be, with kind brown eyes. Eithne said to Flora in the kitchen: 'Is he gorgeous, or what?'

'I don't know: is he?'

'Those eyes! They look right into the very heart of a woman.'

'I don't even know if I've got a heart any more.'

'Sure you have, darling. You may not believe it, you might not even want to think it, but these troubles will pass.' She drew vigorously on a cigarette. 'Everything passes. You'll find your heart's still functioning. I promise you.'

Jerry put up at a nearby hotel, but came round frequently. 'It helps to see where she lived,' he said, the evening before Georgie's funeral, sitting opposite Flora and Eithne with a martini in his hand. 'At least I can picture her here.'

'I feel so helpless,' Flora said. 'There were so many things I didn't do when she was alive, words I didn't say.'

'Me too, hon.' Jerry put an arm around her shoulder. 'I'll never forgive myself for letting her go the first time. Back then, I thought I had more important things to do than be with her. Thought there were stars to follow. Only to find she was the star I wanted.'

'There's nothing either of us can do to change that. I'd give anything if I could only . . . but I can't. Why didn't I see this when she was alive?'

'Everyone feels that way when they lose someone loved,' Eithne said, patting Flora's hand.

'But the things that were wrong were my fault, not hers. Mine.' Flora wrapped her arms around herself as though for hot-water-bottle comfort.

'Regret. Guilt. It's the natural order of things,' said Jerry. 'It's why we ought to learn to do and say the things you're talking about while we still can.'

'Georgie said that about me and my mother. But ever since she died, I've been trying to get hold of Jessica – my mother. She seems to have gone into hiding.'

'Maybe she needs some time on her own,' said Eithne. 'Don't forget the poor woman's lost a daughter.'

'Oh, God,' Flora said, wrenched by many things. Above all, by her own failures. Her grief and guilt seemed to be increasing rather than growing less as Georgie's murder receded into the past. Why had it taken her death to realise just how much she had meant?

'You're no better and no worse than a million other people on God's earth, darling. So don't go thinking you are.'

'I hope you get to make it up with your mom,' Jerry said. 'At least you've been making the effort.'

They sat in silence for a moment. Then Flora said: 'Did she ever tell you who Matty's father was?'

'She never did say.'

'Would it, by any chance, have been yourself?' asked Eithne.

'It could have been.' Jerry looked awkward. 'I mean, the timing's right. We'd seen each other . . . But she said it wasn't. And if I had been Matty's dad, once we'd decided to get married, there'd have been no reason for her not to tell me.'

'I hope that you – when this is all over, that you'll still think of Matty and me as part of your life,' said Flora.

'I appreciate you saying that.'

'Not that this can ever really be over.'

Eithne said, 'That's no excuse for giving up.'

'Matty'll see that I don't.'

'Are the cops any further forward with their investigations?' Jerry asked.

'Not that I'm aware. One of them told me the other day that they might have to wait for another murder, or even two, before they got him.'

'What a truly appalling thought that is.' Eithne shuddered largely, then poured them all another drink.

At the funeral ceremony, they sang some robust hymns. Frankie spoke of Georgie as friend and workmate; Jerry Long stood to speak but could only manage a few sentences before breaking down. At the end, when the vicar had said a blessing – Flora decided it didn't count as a prayer – Jerry, Frankie and the rest of the band picked up guitars. 'OK,' Frankie called out. He struck a chord, and another. 'Tune up.'

Turning, looking back into the body of the church, Flora saw that half the congregation seemed to have brought an instrument with them Slowly, Frankie swung into *'Falling Angel*', Georgie's song, and all the other musicians began to play along. Guitars, saxophones, flutes, fiddles. Somewhere, she knew, Angus would be playing his trombone. *Falling angel, dropping past a star* . . . The rest of the congregation hummed along to the haunting melody, some of them clapping softly in time. *You'll always be my shining one* . . . Frankie and Spick were openly weeping, Jerry Long played with bent head, while Dave pranced before the altar with his guitar. *Sad angel, lost angel, come back to me* . . . Had Georgie known, had some intimation of how short a time she had left?

Oliver took Flora's hand and she turned to him, her vision blurred by tears. Coloured sunshine streamed through the stained-glass windows and aureoled his hair with gold so that for a bewildering fraction of a moment he did not look like himself but like some fiery angel. *Remember angel*, sang the congregation, *remember* . . . Flora also tried to sing, her voice breaking, bitterly aware of her loss, not just of Georgie but of all the opportunities she had never seized, all the words left unspoken . . . *you have my heart, you'll always have my heart.*

When the time of dying is appropriate to the life lived, then there is occasion to celebrate that life, as well as mourn the death, which is why funerals often turn into a party. Georgie's did not. Despite the music and the champagne, everyone who came back to the flat after the ceremony was conscious that hers was a life untimely cut short, that future happiness had been denied by events, that there was a little girl left parentless. For Flora, it was made the more painful by the fact that neither of Georgie's parents were present. They should have been here to say goodbye to their daughter. And then she saw her mother. How long had she been in the room? She stood by the windows, looking out at the garden where Georgie had hoped Matty would someday play.

'Mother.' Flora stood next to her. 'I'm so glad you were able to come.'

'Glad?' Jessica's eyes were, as they had always been when they lighted upon her elder daughter, stony. And yet, beneath the hostility lay vulnerability. Looking at Jessica as a person rather than as her mother, for the first time she saw how fragile she was. Had she always been that frail or had she been embrittled by the circumstances of her life? 'An odd word, given the circumstances.'

'Glad to see you.'

'Really?'

For a moment, Flora hesitated. Then, knowing that she must make an effort, however difficult, she said firmly: 'Yes.'

Jessica stared at her for a long moment, while Flora quailed at the possibility that Jessica might publicly reject her, might turn on her heel, walk past her to greet someone else. But she did none of those things. Instead, she moved closer and put her arms about her daughter. She said: 'I'm sorry.'

Much later, alone in bed, for though Oliver had wanted to stay, she had told him that she needed to be by herself, Fiona had time to go over the encounter. She felt again her mother's insubstantial bones between her hands, and saw the sadness in her dark eyes. Was Jessica merely saying she was sorry about Georgie's death? Or was there more to it: was she apologising for Flora's childhood, acknowledging blame, sharing it, asking that her own pain be shared?

Georgie's song echoed in Flora's head: *do you know, do you care how lonely you are*?

Maybe the words applied as much to her mother as they did to herself.

Act Three

'Have you listened to the news this morning?'

'No.'

'Read the papers?'

'I haven't had time, Oliver.' Flora was sharp. It was nearly nine o'clock, and Matty, having kicked and screamed while getting dressed, was now refusing to eat her cereal, despite the fact that it was the same one she had willingly eaten every morning since Georgie's death, that she had even chosen it herself in the supermarket. 'Why?'

'It looks as though they've got him at last.'

'Got who? Look, I can't talk – I'm trying to get Matty ready for play group. Can I call you back?'

'Do that.' Oliver put down the phone without saying goodbye.

But as she was walking back from dropping off Matty, Flora realised, with a great whoomph of the heart, to which 'him' he must have been referring. She turned back towards the village and went into the newsagent.

COTSWOLD KILLER CAUGHT, the tabloids blared. MAN HELD OVER DEATHS, the broadsheets declared more decorously.

Muted elation filled her. At last. At bloody *last*! She had not been able to bring herself to read details of the subsequent murders, or, indeed, the preceding ones, but she knew that two more women had died after Georgie, both with the trademark pieces of evidence which convinced the police that the same man was responsible. Two young women, single parents, hacked to pieces in their own homes. Now there was one more. More orphaned children, more circles of grief rippling from the flung stone of violent murder. Parents, lovers, siblings, friends, all caught up as though in a giant net before being dashed down and left to swim for the shore as best they might.

The terror had been going on now for five years. There had been ten victims in all. Thousands of men interviewed. Hundreds of thousands of man hours spent on eliminating cars and suspects, collating evidence, making house-to-house enquiries, following up leads provided by the public. Even with the help of computers, the police were constantly in danger of being swamped by the deluge of information. Det. Chief Supt Prince told her once that the police forces involved were desperate to avoid getting so bogged down with information that they missed vital clues and overlooked important evidence.

'That's what happened with the West Yorkshire police when they were looking for the Yorkshire Ripper,' he said. 'But I'm sure we haven't come across our man yet. I know George Oldfield said the same thing about Peter Sutcliffe, even though by then he'd already been interviewed several times and they should have—' He shrugged.

'But we've so much less to go on than they had,' Det. Supt Martyn added. 'No sightings, no suspects, no photofits to jog people's memories, nothing. I just don't think we've met him yet.'

'What we don't want,' said Prince, 'is to come out of this feeling that more women died because we missed something we shouldn't have.'

The case had aged them both. In the nearly two years since Georgie's death, they had kept in constant touch with Flora. She knew that, like the rest of the enquiry team, they were working flat out to find the man responsible before he killed again. Yet, despite the huge team of policemen working on the case – a hundred and twenty at one point, she had read somewhere – until now, they had been no nearer to finding him than they had been after the third body had been discovered and it finally became clear there was a multiple murderer on the loose.

Now it was June once more, and he had begun to kill again.

Flora no longer had a paper delivered each morning since she found there was so much to be dealt with that at the end of the day, it was still unread. Accepting the inevitable, she had given herself over to child-orientated domesticity; in two months, Matty would start at the little local private school, and she had promised herself that then she would begin again to concentrate on the inessentials of the spinning world: war, famine, oil spills, politics, art, literature. For the moment, her next angel book was on hold. Following the success of the first, the second one would be out in time for the Christmas market and already, so Antonia informed her, had been subbed in at a spectacular rate, so much so that the publishers had been forced to reprint twice.

It was over a year since Flora had finally sold the cottage where Georgie had died and had moved herself and Matty into this one, ten miles or so away. She had considered moving somewhere else completely, perhaps to the beach house in Norfolk, or to the West Country, nearer Eithne, but had decided against it for the sake of Matty's play group and the friends she had made in the area. And Angus. Oliver had tried to persuade her to live with him in London, or allow him to live with her, but she had refused to do either. She felt sure that eventually the three of them would become a family unit, but Matty needed some kind of stability to overcome the trauma of losing Georgie, and until that was achieved, she did not wish to jeopardise the little girl's peace of mind.

'It's not going to damaged by having me around,' Oliver had protested, 'She knows me by now.'

Flora had been adamant. 'She's too vulnerable. Quite apart from anything else, she's having nightmares again, which shows how upsetting it's all been for her, even though she doesn't say much about it.'

'She'll probably have those for the rest of her life, poor little girl.'

'You could be right. And there's no question that they're worse after we've had visitors – or even varied her routine significantly. At the moment, she needs as much peace and security as I can provide for her. And continuity.'

'That more than anything, I suppose.'

Yes, above all, Matty needed the reassurance that things would go on as they had been. And that kind of certainty would take time. Poor defenceless Matty, bewildered by events which were so far out of her control as to be incomprehensible. In some corner of her mind, Flora had settled on the closing of the police investigation as a suitable moment to set up the new family unit which could offer Matty the security she needed.

Since her sister's death, she had avoided any discussion of the killings. Even when the first and then the second succeeding victim had been discovered, causing headlines and enquiries and editorials, she had refused to read or listen. Now, she poured over the papers she had carried home with her. The front pages of the tabloids showed a close-up of a man staring expressionlessly out of a car, with beside him, beyond him, some indeterminate figure, its head shielded from the media cameras by a covering blanket. The broadsheets merely showed a police van turning in at authoritarian gates. Flora learned that Don Blackett (32), of Darlington, had been helping police with their enquiries for the last two days and had now been charged with the murder of Monica Fairholme, the most recent victim, with further charges still outstanding. They seemed such prosaic formulations for so momentous an event as the arrest of the man who had been making headlines for five years.

She read the story, filling in gaps from one paper's coverage with details from another. Blackett's car – a white Granada – had, it seemed, been noticed but not particularly remarked upon by a neighbour of the victim, Mr Reginald Parsons, who saw it parked beside the wall of the local church. He would have paid little attention, had it not been for the fact that he was a member of the parish council which had been debating for some time the question of double yellow lines in that same spot beneath the churchyard wall. The matter had been held over until the next monthly meeting, since the council had been hotly divided on the issue, some maintaining that double yellows would disfigure the quaint street on which the church stood, others insisting that cars parked there were a traffic hazard and, in any case, just as disfiguring as yellow lines would be. On returning from walking his dog, forty minutes later, Mr Parsons, one of those who favoured the lines, saw the car still in the same position and noted down its make, description and number plate, intending to use it as fuel for the next parish council meeting. Later, he went to call on Mrs Fairholme to discuss a matter of parish business and was surprised to find the very same car parked in front of her house, even more so to discover the front door ajar. Stepping into the house, he encountered a young man in the hall.

'I knew there was something up, the minute I saw him,' he told the reporters. 'He was all over blood, and holding this long knife, looked like a bread knife to me. So naturally I asked him what he was doing there.'

The man had apparently mumbled something unintelligible and when Mr Parsons had asked – bravely or stupidly? – about the blood, had said he'd been helping Mrs Fairholme in the kitchen and had cut himself.

'He was well spoken,' Parsons was quoted as saying. 'Quiet-like. Never occurred to me who he was.' He had then enquired where Mrs Fairholme might be and been told that she was in the sitting room. Pushing open the door of the room, Parsons had discovered a scene which, Flora thought, gritting her teeth, must have been very similar to one she had seen for herself. 'It was horrific. There was blood everywhere,' Parsons said. 'Everywhere. It was unbelievable. I fought in the last war, but I've never seen anything like it. Sheer butchery.'

By the time he had registered that the bloodstained heap lying on the carpet was Mrs Fairholme's mutilated body, the young man had gone. 'That poor woman,' Parsons said. 'She was only young, too. All her life before her. And the little kiddy upstairs the whole time. It's unbelievable . . . I'll have nightmares about this for the rest of my life. She hadn't been living there more than a year, either. Recently divorced, she was, and hoping to start a new life.'

He had been able to give a full description of both the car and its driver, and later that same day, Mrs Fairholme's murderer had been apprehended by traffic policemen who found his car parked in a lay-by while he drank coffee from a mobile tea-stall. One of the tabloids had unearthed a blurred photograph of Don Blackett in younger days, playing football for an amateur side, grinning at the camera in a striped shirt. Another had interviewed a former girlfriend, whose shock was easily apparent through the conventional phrases of horror which she used. The broadsheets made up for their own lack of a photograph with fewer references to monsters and beasts who preyed upon helpless women, and more diagrams of murder scenes and pictures of the previous victims, including – Flora looked round and past and over it, anything rather than at it – one of Georgie's publicity stills. Blackett had put up no resistance when the police picked him up, swallowing the last of his coffee and putting the polystyrene cup tidily into the litter bin provided before stepping calmly into the waiting police car.

That was all the media had for the moment. Although she listened to the news bulletins at lunchtime, kept the television switched on, no further detail was given about the arrest. The police, perhaps wanting to avoid the unseemly gloating which had accompanied the capture of the Yorkshire Ripper, had decided against any kind of press conference beyond an announcement of the bare facts that a man had been charged in connection with the crime and no further details were being issued for the moment. Tomorrow, there would be headlines across the globe. Everyone who'd ever known Blackett would have been tied into exclusive and lucrative deals by the Fleet Street buy-up men. The whole intrusive business would start again, the rehashing of the victims' lives, the circumstances of their deaths, the speculation and morbid excitement, the media people and their equipment, the desperate racing after any detail, however trivial, which would titillate the British reading or viewing public. Flora herself would inevitably be caught up in the media frenzy, try as she might to avoid it. The police would again be part of her life as they sought to make the case absolutely watertight against Blackett.

She had believed that when the man responsible for killing her sister was finally brought to book, she would experience some degree of peace; instead, she found herself deeply disturbed by the fact that he had at last stepped out of the shadows which had concealed him. Before, he had been a faceless, nameless entity out there in the dark, unimaginable, incorporeal. Now, he had a name, an age, a presence. Paradoxically, this made him more terrifying than when he was simply a concept. The Cotswold Killer. It was impossible to rid her mind of him. Don Blackett. Thirty-two years old. From Darlington. She and Oliver had once bypassed the town on their way to the Edinburgh Festival, seeing the name on gantries which urged them to turn off the motorway in diminishing slices of distance – three-quarters of a mile, half a mile, a hundred yards – if Darlington, amid other destinations, was where they wished to go. She wondered what Darlington was like. And Blackett. Was he a newcomer to the town or had he lived there all his life? Was he known to many or to no one, was he a local hero for his football prowess, was he liked by those who knew him, or was he a man people crossed streets to avoid? Was he a member of his local church choir, a darts player, married or single? Did he drink in the local pubs? Did he have siblings, parents, children, a home?

The papers said he was a salesman but did not explain what he sold: that too occupied her mind. Itinerant salesmen came occasionally to the door, as did collectors for charity and representatives of organisations holding jumble sales. She could not imagine letting them into the house nor what kind of product would persuade women on their own to do so. Why would Georgie have allowed a vacuum cleaner salesman, a seller of dusters and cleaning products, even a census worker, into the cottage? She was not even the occupier, she was on her way to live in the States, what possible interest could she have had in anything being sold at the door?

During the morning, Flora developed a tremor. Whether it was due to remembered shock or to stress, she found she was shaking as though she were stricken by ague. It was impossible to concentrate, impossible to work at her easel. She would have telephoned Oliver but found herself rejecting, in advance, his sympathy and understanding. She needed something more bracing, less involved. She rang the number which Prince and Martyn had given her but was told that neither of them was available. Restless, she telephoned Eithne, but got only the answering machine. Standing irresolute with her hand on the receiver while she wondered whether to call Katie Vernon, she felt the handset vibrate beneath her palm. Lifting it, she heard a voice which instantly calmed her.

'Flora.' It was Gregor.

'Hello.' Had he somehow sensed her need? The jitteriness which had been jumping round her mind since she had learned of Blackett's arrest drained away.

'You must be happy.'

She didn't need to ask what he meant. 'Not really. Not at all.'

'Happy was the wrong word,' he said. 'Relieved would be better.'

'I thought I would be, but I'm not.'

'I know how you feel.'

'Giving him a name, catching him, proving that he's real: somehow it's made it all worse, rather than better. It's almost as if I preferred it when they were still trying to hunt him down. Now that I know he really exists—'

'I can understand that.' Silence stretched, until he said, hesitantly: 'Flora—'

'Yes?'

'Are you alone?'

'Except for my little niece – my sister's child—'

'Matilda.'

'Yes.' Flora could not remember telling him Matty's name. 'Except for her, I am.'

'Would you like me to—' The break in his sentence hung between them.

'What?' Flora said softly.

'If it would help, I could—' Again the incomplete sentence was left to drift along the silences.

'Could what, Gregor?'

Flora wished he would say what he meant. Her body felt heated, as though she had stepped under a hot shower. She was acutely aware of herself, of skin and hair, tiny pulses flickering deep inside her, mysterious flowing of blood through vein and artery, breath moving in and out of lungs, heart beating under breast. If he were to visit, she knew how she would settle into his serenity as into a feather mattress, could feel already the pulling round herself the comfort of his tranquillity. If he came . . . She was startled by the sudden realisation of how powerfully she wanted him to. That she was excited by the thought of him.

'Flora—'

'I'm here.'

Each listened to the other's breathing. She thought of space, time wheeling, an infinity of black sky filled with stars. The movement of her blood sounded like a rush of wings. This was, she knew, ridiculous. Gregor was a man of remoteness, a man aloof, not to be desired. None the less, she desired him.

Finally, he gave a small sigh. 'If you need me—' he said.

I do, she thought. More than you can know. 'I've always needed you,' she said and replaced the handset.

Gregor. Where had her feelings for him come from? They had met only three times. Admittedly they had spent a week together, but until now, she would not have said she felt anything more for him than liking, than an appreciation of his emotional strength. And now? She groaned. Longing demolished her, enfevered her. In the hearth, flames flickered, licking at the logs she had put on the fire earlier. She remembered the first time she had seen Oliver, in the art school cafeteria. Remembered the frantic, pulse-beating, feverish, overwhelming and not fully understood desire which made the body sing. How could it have happened that she was racked by the same half-formulated but specific desires now as she had been then? 'Gregor,' she said aloud. Ridiculous. She didn't even know if it was a first or a last name. 'Gregor.'

This was probably nothing more than a natural response to long-pent emotion being allowed at last to flow free. She went over the conversation again: *I can understand that* . . . he had said, *I know how you feel* . . . More than anyone she had ever met, Gregor knew exactly how she felt, about everything. The degree of empathy between them was remarkable. Almost uncanny. Should she ring him back? What would she say when he answered? What *was* there to say? She could ask him over for supper one evening. She could say she would like to talk to him. There was nothing to prevent her, they were both adults. Yet still she hesitated. Their relationship, long-drawn out as it was, rested on so few encounters.

None the less . . . She dialled 1471, and was almost relieved when the mechanical voice told her that they did not have the caller's number to return the call. As she replaced the receiver, the phone rang again. Gregor's voice said: 'Flora.'

She didn't pause. 'Will you come here?' she said.

'When?'

'Tomorrow? Sevenish?'

'Yes. Or—' The space between them vibrated with words not spoken. Then he added: '—I could come now.'

'Yes.'

It was adolescent, she told herself. Foolish in a woman of thirty-eight. This sense of anticipation, this wild thumping of the heart, this silvery tingle in the throat. She loved Oliver, she was perfectly well aware of that. There had never been anyone else for her: never so much as a meaningful brush of the hand or a flirtatious look at another man. Until an hour ago, she had scarcely given Gregor a thought, certainly not a thought of this kind. Yet here she was, breathlessly waiting for him to arrive. And when he did, what then? The flames threw a soft, warm light round the sitting room. They could sit opposite each other, drink a glass or two of wine, talk of this and that, two rational adults brought together by nothing more than cruel circumstance. Then what? She closed her hands tightly into her palms. Then he would drive home again. That would be all. That would be that.

When she heard the knock at the door, she forced herself to get up slowly, taking a deep breath as she opened the front door. He stepped into the house and looked down at her. He had always been beautiful, she thought. Luminous.

He put his arms around her. 'Flora.'

'Gregor.' He was tall, much taller than she remembered. Looking up, his face seemed to shine against the stars. With her face pressed against his chest, once again she felt the tension and the longing drain away. 'It's late.'

'But not too late.'

Flora did not ask for what. When she pulled away from his embrace to fetch wine and glasses, she discovered that the ferment in her blood had eased. She poured him some wine and they sat beside the fire, looking at each other. For a long time, neither spoke. Gregor's presence had provided sufficient healing; the sexual *frisson* had been engendered simply by the circumstances. The feelings which had flooded her earlier were aberrational, nothing more than the need to know that life continued even when death seemed to have conquered. Besides, Gregor stood apart from other men, he belonged elsewhere, he should not be the recipient of such base emotions. He urged her quietly in directions she knew she ought to go, and helped her to work out for herself the things which only she could decide upon.

As he left, he smiled at her. 'I'll come again, when you need me.'

'If I do.' She felt immeasurably strengthened.

'You will.'

She smiled back. 'Perhaps.'

The trial of Don Blackett began in September, two and a half months later. The task of the police in bringing the case to court had been made easier by the fact that he had made no attempt to deny his crimes. He had pleaded guilty to the murder of Claire Marie Fairholme at his preliminary court appearance, and done the same when later charged with the murders of seven other women. Of the ten murders attributed to him, two – those of a woman in Lydney, and of Georgina Flynn – had been left to lie on the files for consideration at a later stage.

'The CPS – the Crown Prosecution Service – isn't too keen on pressing charges in either of these two cases,' Martyn, who had been promoted to the position of Detective Chief Superintendent during the years of Blackett's activities, told Flora, calling at the house to inform her that a date had been set for the trial. 'Although we know he did them both, there's just not enough conclusive evidence for them to be absolutely certain of pinning the deaths on him. And given the cost of a trial—' He spread his hands.

Flora was outraged. 'Cost? But there are two dead women involved.'

'Yes. But since we know he did it, and he's admitted to all the others, the CPS doesn't want to waste time and money on providing evidence when we've got so much on Blackett already. Obviously, if new evidence comes to light later—'

'What exactly is it about Georgie's death that makes them hesitate?'

'We think he might have been interrupted.' Martyn looked away briefly, then met her eyes once more.

'Who by? Matty? You don't mean by Matty, do you?'

'Maybe.'

'I hope not.' Dear God, if the poor child had stumbled into the scene of her mother's murder, no wonder she was troubled by such terrible nightmares.

'It's hard to say. Something certainly stopped him from going the whole ho—' Martyn broke off, recognising that the phrase was inappropriate. 'He certainly didn't have time to leave all his usual trademarks, complete his usual rituals, so it'd take longer to find the evidence to support a not-guilty plea on that one, which is what Blackett's trying to pull.' As he left, he reached into his breast pocket and produced an envelope. 'I don't suppose you want this, but I brought it just in case.'

'What it is?'

'The pathologist's report on your sister. And don't worry about the fact that Blackett's not been charged with her murder: we've got more than enough evidence in the other cases to put him away.'

Flora was satisfied by this. As long as no other women suffered the way Georgie had done, it didn't seem to matter a great deal whether he was tried for her murder or for someone else's.

While Blackett had killed few, judged by the standards of a Ted Bundy or the infamous South American killer, Pedro Alonzo Lopez, the ferocity of his attacks and the growing fear as his reign of terror lengthened without a single clue as to his identity being discovered, were enough to bring print and television reporters flying in from all over the world. Two renowned true-crime writers, one from New York, one from London, had already been assigned to produce books about Blackett. The case took precedence over other news for the entire length of the trial, and Don Blackett's life and circumstances became for a short time as well known to the public at large as that of their own families.

Oliver attended court every day of the two-week trial but Flora could not bear to listen to or read about the ugly and ultimately repetitive details of how each woman was murdered. The cataloguing of wounds sustained, the weapons used, the points at which blades entered bodies, the mutilations, sickened her. The police had offered her a reserved seat in Number One Court at the Old Bailey, where the trial was being held, but she turned it down. Even though Georgie's murder was not going to be specifically addressed during the trial, whatever had been done to the eight victims on the charge sheet had also been done to her sister. If she listened to the forensic evidence, she would never be able to dislodge the details from her mind. She'd seen the room in which Georgie had died. She'd seen Georgie's body. That was more than enough, more than anyone should have to undergo. There was nothing further about the murders she wished to know. Women who should have been alive no longer were; children had been left orphaned, parents childless. The inventory of sorrow was enough epitaph for the needless dead without further gawping by those outside the hideously charmed circle of the bereaved and those responsible for bringing the killer to justice.

'What I can't get a grip on is his psychology.' Flora and Angus were sitting by the fire in her new house, while Matty slept upstairs. '*Why* did he do it? What drove him to kill with such hatred? We're hearing all about the how, and nothing about the why.'

'You have to wait until after the trial, when the books appear and the articles are written,' Angus said.

'But I want to know *now*.'

'I'm not an expert, Flora, though since your sister was killed, I've done some reading up about it.'

'Tell me.'

'Brooding about it probably isn't terribly helpful.'

'It would help to know what lies behind her death. Otherwise, it all seems so pointless.'

'As far as I can tell,' Angus said quietly, 'Blackett seems to fit the profiles they drew up before they caught him. Youngish and white, with a domineering mother and absent father, a sexually abusive upbringing, feelings of inadequacy towards women, unresolved anger because of early rejection, all the stuff that leads to this kind of murder.'

'But what triggers such abnormal behaviour? If he's thirty-two now, and he started murdering people five years ago, what happened at the age of twenty-seven to set him off on a killing spree?' She had already asked Oliver the same questions but received no real answer. She suspected that the truth was that nobody knew why some men's minds twisted out of true whereas others, experiencing the same disadvantages and influences, remained unaffected by them.

'We'll have to wait to find that out. The psychiatrists suggested during the trial that it might be linked to the fact that his wife walked out on him about then. According to the books I read, these killers have a highly developed sense of their own superiority over ordinary people, so when something goes wrong, like the wife leaving, showing that he's not the all-powerful superman he likes to think he was, he takes his revenge.'

'And how did he choose his victims?'

'Darling Flo,' Angus said gently, 'I know it's a difficult time for you—'

'I need to sort it out in my own mind.'

'All right, then. We already know from the evidence produced so far in court how he chose them and what triggered each of the murders.'

'I don't. I can't bear to read the reports. I've tried to. But every time I pick up a paper it seems to be an endless list of the things he did to those women and then I think of Georgie and how terrified she must have been and I . . . I—'

'Blackett's some sort of missionary,' said Angus. 'Works for one of these agencies who try to help subsistence farmers in Pakistan or something similar. There are teams of them. They spend eight months of the year in Asia, then come back to England for four months in order to raise funds. Knocking on people's doors, asking for aid. He usually came back in the summer, which is why most of the murders were committed between May and August. He covered the whole of the south of England but for some reason, he only seems to have killed women in your area. We'll probably find later that he spent his early years there or something similar.'

'How'd he get into the houses? If he came to my door, I'd have found some money to drop in his collecting tin and then closed the door on him.'

'He wanted more than a contribution. That's how he got inside. He wanted commitment. People were asked to sign a covenant for three years. And that involved coming into the house, signing forms, banker's orders, showing the prospective convenanter where and how the money would be used. People *would* invite someone like that in: it wouldn't occur to you that he might be a psychopath. Apparently he'd ask if the husband would be home later, so he could talk to him as well, and if the woman said she didn't have a husband, she was living on her own with children, it drove him crazy. He seems to have told the police that he heard voices telling him to kill these women to make sure that the children didn't suffer the way he had. And once he'd . . . done what he'd come to do, he was gone, off in his car, back to his cheap hotel, until the next time the compulsion came over him.'

'There was so much blood,' Flora said, biting her lip, remembering the scene she had walked into, the horror of it. 'He must have had some on him. He must have been covered in it. How'd he explain that?'

'He's a bachelor. And autonomous. The charity gave him a free hand to work the system whatever hours and whichever way suited him best. He wasn't answerable to anyone except once a year, when he had to report to the head office in London before he went back to Pakistan. He usually chose isolated houses, like your cottage was, or places where he could park right up close. So he was able to cover himself up once he got back to his car, and then dispose of his blood-stained clothes at his own convenience. The police found some of them in a plastic bag, after the fifth murder, but there wasn't anybody to link them to at that point, though they were able to at the trial. And his car was a different one each time, hired from different agencies and then returned before he'd vanish again for eight months. They found forensic evidence in the last car, the white Granada, but all the others he used are long gone.'

'Oh, God,' whispered Flora. How would she ever be able to forget the image of the knife, slashing and cutting; the blood? One morning during the trial, she had actually opened the pathologist's report which the police had brought her and glanced down the close-typed forms. Words had leaped into her brain and clung there like a plague of fleas, phrases glimpsed before she could turn her eyes away. '. . . Massive haemorrhage . . . antemortem wounding . . . vascular organ . . . traumatic shock . . .' There had been nearly thirty separate wounds of which at least five were fatal, producing words which she did not wish to know but which she read with horrified fascination. She learned that Georgie could have died of aeroembolism, cadaveric spasm or exsanguination; according to the autopsy, the wounds had been so severe that she had lost nearly ninety percent of the blood in her body. Differentiations were made between the various categories of wounds: stabs and punctures, incisions and cuts.

As though sensing her pain, Angus pulled her closer. 'Flo, you can't change any of it. It happened. I know it sounds brutal, but you've just got to accept it and get on with life. Matty's still alive, even if Georgie isn't, and you've got to do the best you can for her sake.'

'I know that. And I try to. Matty's the most important thing in my life.' She laid her head on his shoulder, wondering if any of the women had ever understood why Blackett had begun slashing at them with his knife. The attacks must have come shrieking at them out of the blue, while they examined photographs of irrigation projects and self-help plans, but had he said anything, told them, as they lay dying, what had driven him, sought to justify himself, given them a reason?

The horror of it engulfed her yet again. Endlessly, she saw

herself in Georgie's place. How would she have coped if the man calmly discussing covenants had suddenly pulled out a knife, begun raging, cursing, accusing her of sins which had nothing to do with her? Would she have tried to save herself or would she have been paralysed by fear, by the scent of madness? Some of the women had fought strenuously for their lives. Georgie was one, which accounted for the severity of her wounds. There had been twenty-seven stab wounds on her body. Several of her fingers had been severed completely. Other victims seemed, from the little she had read or heard, to have put up no fight at all. Or had they died almost before they realised what was happening to them?

With Angus's heart beating steadily against her ear, she visualised how it must have happened, how Georgie, euphoric with happiness, had invited Blackett in, leafed enthusiastically through the brochures showing the benefits of earlier projects, promised him enough money for half a dozen wells. She would have said that yes, she was a single mother and then, before she could explain further, before she could offer the appeasing information that she was about to marry and set things right, the knife would have appeared in his hand. Which of the twenty-seven blows had killed her? How many times had she felt the pain of that knife piercing her flesh before she finally succumbed? Flora groaned. The breath stuttered in her throat, and she wept, turning into Angus's shoulder.

'Oh, Flora. If only I could take some of the pain away,' he murmured. He kissed her wet face as she burrowed against him.

'Nobody can,' she gasped. 'Nobody. Not ever. I'll live with it for the rest of my life, always, it's my fault, it's—'

He pressed his mouth onto hers. His jaw rasped against her cheek. He smelled male; he smelled kind. When his hand closed over her breast, she moaned, moving to make it easier for him, wanting him to make love to her even though it wouldn't change anything. In the hearth, the logs crumbled and hissed as Angus eased her onto her back on the carpet.

'I love you, Flora.'

'I know. I'm sorry. I've taken advantage of it, let you help me and given you nothing in return.'

'Oh, Flo.' He laughed unsteadily. 'If you only knew what you've given me. You and Matty. So much. Such . . . comfort.'

His hand was under her skirt, his finger probing into the soft, wet places between her legs. She raised her hips and let him slip off her pants. 'Angus,' she said, her eyes still streaming with tears. 'Come inside me.'

'Flora. My darling.' He parted her. He was long and elegant; as he moved into her she shuddered with delight. Neither of them spoke after that. She cried out when he came, and again as she reached her own climax, but even as she did so, she thought of the knife again, and Georgie's body as it plunged into her. How long had she remained conscious? How long did it take before terror provided its own anaesthetic?

In the small hours of the night, Flora wondered about this with an anguish which no amount of Prozac or Temazepam could diminish.

On the final day of the trial, at Oliver's insistence, Flora went to London to stay with him in the house they had once shared, first dropping Matty off with Marguerite Treffyn. Oliver told her that the judge had completed his summing up that morning and the jury had been sent out, only to return just before the end of the day's proceedings to say they were finding it impossible to produce a unanimous verdict. 'He's told them he'd accept a majority verdict,' Oliver said. He was excited and restless, pacing about the room, picking things up and putting them down again. 'He's ordered that the court reconvene tomorrow. We should have a verdict, thank God.'

'Is that why you're so keyed up?'

'Of course,' He poured whisky lavishly. 'Once this is over, we can all get on with our lives again.'

'Can we? I wonder.'

'Nothing's ever going to be the way it was, of course. But we'll be released from at least some of the tension. The number of times I've wondered where that bastard was, whether I might be brushing up against him in the street, or standing behind him in a queue.' He gulped at his glass; his hand was trembling.

The doorbell pealed and he went to answer it, returning shortly with Chief Supt Martyn. 'Sorry to bother you good folks,' the policeman said. 'But the chances are that they'll come up with a verdict tomorrow. So I've come to say that we can reserve a seat for you in the court if you want to hear sentence passed.

'No,' said Flora. 'Absolutely not.'

'Go.' Oliver urged. 'Get it out of your system.'

'I can't. I couldn't bear to look at him.'

'He's just a man,' Martyn told her. 'In spite of what he's done, he's just a man.'

'He's a monster,' said Flora.

'Inside he's a monster, but outside – you've blown him up in your mind,' Oliver said. 'If you see him, it'll cut him down to size.'

'I've heard other bereaved families say that facing up to the person who'd killed their loved ones was important,' Martyn said. 'That it helped to see him sentenced and to know that he was behind bars and the nightmare was over. That's why I came.'

'The nightmare will never be over.'

'It'll be the same for you, I'm convinced of it.'

Flora shook her head. She was touched by the policeman's obvious concern, but it was impossible to explain the dread she felt at being in the same room as the man who had murdered her sister.

'If you don't want to do it for your own sake, go for Georgie's,' Oliver said.

For Georgie's sake . . . the words touched something in her which nothing else had done. Like water poured onto a fiercely burning fire, it wouldn't reduce the heat, but it might help to extinguish the flame. And if she was there, if she looked at him, she would at least know what Georgie had seen in those last few minutes before she died.

'Will you be there too?' she asked.

Oliver nodded. 'Of course I will.'

They sat in the seats reserved for VIPs and members of the victims' families, immediately below the public gallery. The court room was smaller than Flora had envisaged, too small for the recounting of such violent deeds, for so much emotion. So many violent crimes had been tried in this room, so much evidence handed round: photographs of mutilated bodies, weapons of torture and destruction, pictures of waste ground and deserted alleyways, pictures of blood. So many horrible deeds had been recounted here, the deaths of so many innocent victims described: she imagined she could see all the words fluttering at the high windows, hundreds of thousands of them, like a flock of dark butterflies, desperate to escape. Pain had soaked into the wooden benches, the long oak evidence table, the leather chair where the presiding judge sat gazing down at his papers. Pain coated everything in the room.

The clerk of the court rose and called for silence and a hush fell over the court. Someone in the gallery above Flora was shuffling their shoes on the wooden floor, but that didn't prevent the sound of feet mounting the stairs from the cells. Two uniformed officers appeared, then came Blackett himself.

What had she expected? Rationally, she knew he did not possess leathery wings and devil's horns. She had told herself repeatedly that he was going to be like any other man she might pass on the street. Seeing him for the first time, she was unprepared for just how ordinary he seemed, a slight man with a pale face haloed in curly hair. He kept his gaze straight ahead, staring above the judge's head at a sword which hung on the wall. So ordinary; so normal. So absolutely unmonstrous. Flora felt faint. She knew that she would have let him into the house, just as Georgie and all those other women had done. She dimly saw the clerk turn and ask the foreman of the jury to stand and deliver their verdict, watched as the foreman, a black woman in a severe, navy blue suit and white blouse, read out the charges one at a time, and after each one, pronounced the word 'Guilty.'

The first time, there was a sigh, a choking sound from someone further along the benches, a hushed cry. After that, there was complete silence until the foreman had sat down again. Blackett himself appeared impassive. Could he have been? Or had he had time, between his arrest and his trial, to accept the inevitable, to comprehend that if he ever walked as a free man again, he would be old, his life gone from him? She understood then what a life sentence could mean. To what extent was it better to be Georgie and those others, suddenly, if cruelly dead, than to watch life slowly slip away, knowing that this was all there would be, these bars, this bunk, the company of other men with unspeakable crimes to their names?

She stared at him. His slight figure had made no move as sentence was handed down. She heard the clank of metal and realised that he must be handcuffed to the officer who sat so close to him. He had risen to hear the verdict pronounced. Now he was led away. Before he went, resisting the pressure of the officers on either side of him, he turned and surveyed the court. His eyes rested on the dark panelling, the jury: he nodded slightly at the foreman, as though thanking her, then turned again. His eye caught Flora's for a second and she felt the small hairs prickle the back of her neck. He might look normal but this was no ordinary man. This man had killed. The word drummed inside her head, heavy as lead. *Killed.* His hands had been covered with Georgie's blood, had slipped inside the wounds inflicted on her body; he had looked at her severed veins and sliced muscle, had listened to her dying pleas. She wanted to scream at him, to curse, but all she could see was Georgie lying on the carpet, her hand almost cut from the body, her open eye staring through the bloodstained—

Hurriedly she got up and pushed her way past obstructing knees, over bags and coats. She felt cold and sick. *Sick unto death* . . . Outside in the corridor, she leaned her head against the wall, eyes tight shut, taking deep breaths in the hope of stamping down the rebellion in her stomach. Oh, God. Oh, *God* . . .

'Flora. My dear.' It was Gregor. 'I saw you rush out. I was sitting behind you.'

'I didn't see you.'

'I was there, none the less.'

Oliver appeared, shrugging into his coat. 'Are you all right, darling?' he said. 'Let's go and find some brandy or something.'

Flora smiled weakly. 'I'm all right. It was just . . . seeing him there—'

Oliver put his arm round her, staring enquiringly at Gregor, evidently taking him for the bereaved relative of another victim. 'I'm sorry,' he said. 'So sorry.' He pressed Flora closer. 'Would you like to join us? There's a pub round the corner.'

'I won't, thank you.' Gregor took Flora's hand and pressed it. 'Goodbye for now.'

'Goodbye,' she whispered, her voice not under control.

'Be strong, Flora. Maybe things will get better now.'

'And maybe they won't.'

'There is something I must tell you, Flora.'

'What's that?'

'We are many.'

What did he mean? Why did she find the simple words so comforting? 'Thank you,' she said.

In the pub, Oliver asked: 'How come he knows your name?'

'We've met before,' she said tiredly.

'Where?'

'Does it matter?'

'Not really, I suppose. Why did he tell you to be strong?'

'It's something he says.' Flora wanted to go home. She wanted to sleep for a year and a day, the way people did in fairy stories. When Oliver steered her towards the street, she said: 'Would you mind awfully if I went home?'

'Of course not. I'll call a taxi.'

'Home to my own house, I mean.'

'We'll have to pick up Matty first, and pack up your stuff.'

'I want to be by myself. Just me.' She saw the look on his face, and put a hand pleadingly on his arm. 'Please, Oliver. Just me. I'll drive down and come up again tomorrow. Matty'll be fine with your mother or you until then.' If he didn't agree, then she would break away, run down the street into the Underground, make her way home on her own. Or find a hotel. Somewhere impersonal where nobody knew or cared who she was. She longed to be anonymous, nothing, nobody, just for a while. When Oliver remained silent, she said again: 'Please.'

'Are you fit to drive?'

'Yes. Absolutely.'

'I don't like it.'

'Oliver. I need to be alone.' It came out harshly. Spacing the words to gve them greater emphasis, she said. 'Let me be alone. Please.'

'If that's what you want.'

'I'll be back to normal tomorrow.'

But she knew she would not. Could never be. Blackett had seen to that.

'You have an art school training, I believe?'

'Yes.'

'Have you always been artistic, even as a child?'

'I suppose I have.' This was the last of several interviews and Flora was becoming practised at imparting the kind of information which features writers liked. 'I used to love painting, splashing all that wonderful blue and red powder paint about. Drawing things. Drawing my family.' The line of her father's overcoat, the curve of Gran's hump, the glorious feeling of seeing them translated onto paper, absolutely right.

'What sort of age was that?'

'Five or so. And on my sixth birthday, my father gave me a paint-box. I can still remember the sense of power it gave me to know that I had all those colours at my command,' Flora said. The reporter fiddled with her tape recorder. 'Not just ordinary colours, but gold and copper and wonderful purples and grey and turquoises. It made me want to go out and paint the entire world in all those brilliant shades.'

'And where did the angels come from?' The young woman, who had introduced herself as Jane Something, widened her eyes. She had done this several times already.

Flora looked away, hoping that her irritation at the mannerism didn't show. The lobby of this big hotel behind Oxford Street was packed. Between palm trees planted in ceramic pots were tourists, businessmen and women shoppers surrounded by department store bags drinking coffee and chatting. The journalist was one of several Flora had been interviewed by in the week following the publication of her second angel book.

'Divine inspiration, perhaps?' she said, with a smile. 'I was perfectly happy illustrating children's books, mostly drawing animals and plants, and then one morning the first of them just appeared from under my brush. I hadn't consciously thought of painting an angel standing on a jam spoon in the middle of breakfast clutter, but that's what happened.' She tried to think what she'd told the last woman, who was representing a West Country weekly. She had a dislike of repeating herself, of sounding rehearsed or jaded, but when it came right down to it, the story couldn't be radically changed. What she dreaded was when they got onto the subject of Georgie, as so many of them did, briefed by the press release put out by her publishers.

'You come from an artistic family,' this one said, looking down at her papers. 'Mother and father both actors, you yourself formerly married to Oliver Treffyn, who's made such a successful transition from theatrical design to directing, and your sister, Georgie Flynn, who used to sing with the Ragbags?'

'That's right,' Flora said brusquely, waiting for the loaded question to which this recitation of known fact was leading. She hated talking like this about Georgie, using her death to sell books, even though she had been persuaded by the publishers that it was a necessary sales tool.

'And your sister was a victim of the Cotswold Killer?'

'Yes.'

'I'd just like to say that I really do know how you feel.' The journalist was about the same age as Flora, maybe a few years younger. She did the trick with her eyes again, but this time they were filled with tears. 'My sister was murdered, too, a few years ago. Not by him. Someone broke into her flat in South Kensington one night. Raped her and then strangled her.'

'Oh, God. That's awful.' Flora was appalled. She had thought that murder was rare, remote, that in any population, only a few would ever be brushed by violent death. Increasingly she was made aware that murder lurked only just around the corner of everyone's life. She still vividly recalled the relatives of those killed by Donald Blackett, after sentence had been passed. Twenty-five or thirty of them were in court though there were many others who had not been present that day. Their faces had shown incomprehension, pain, bitterness. They belonged to people who were marked out from everyone else by the extent of their loss. Here was another victim, of another killer.

'They got the man who did it,' Jane whatever-she-was said. 'But it didn't make any difference to us, her family.'

'It doesn't, does it?'

'My father had a heart attack a year after it happened, and died. He was only fifty-six,' the young woman said. 'He didn't just rape her, he tied her up and did the most—' She stared at Flora. 'Sometimes I dream of having him at my mercy, torturing him the way he tortured Lynn, listening to him plead for mercy. A life behind bars isn't enough to atone for what he did, especially when, with time off for remission, they'll probably let him out on parole in another ten years or so.'

'That's understandable.'

'When you hear these people who've had husbands murdered, or children, saying that they feel sorry for the person who did it, I can't understand that at all. I don't feel sorry for the man who killed my sister, I hate him. I loathe him.'

'Does loathing do any good?'

'Probably not. Trouble is, it's not just the ones who're killed who are affected, is it?'

Flora examined the journalist more closely. There was something vaguely manic about her, as though she was not quite plugged in to the rest of the world. Perhaps others had noticed the same about herself. Perhaps it was part of belonging to the confederation of the bereaved.

'I'm really sorry—'

'They should be castrated,' Jane said flatly. 'And then hanged. I'd like him to suffer the same way we all have.'

'That's a point of view, certainly, but—' Revenge was something Flora had not considered, the ancient primitive justice of eye for eye, tooth for tooth. If Blackett had to suffer as Georgie had, would it help, would it make anything better, or even different?

'Sometimes I fantasise about killing the man myself, when he gets out of prison.' The young woman gave a little shake of the shoulders. 'But we're supposed to be talking about you, not me.' Unexpectedly, she smiled. 'I saw Jessica Glanville – your mother – once, playing Lady Macbeth. She was very good. You must be proud of her.'

'I am.'

'And is she equally proud of you?'

'I'm sure . . . Yes, I expect she—' Flora stumbled around the answer. It was almost impossible for her to tell a direct lie, but the truth was, she had no idea whether Jessica was proud of her, or indeed whether she even knew about the publication of the book. Flora had sent her a copy, via her theatrical agent, but had heard nothing. The moment of rapproachement at Georgie's funeral had not been followed up by any further meeting. Jessica had not been in touch since, and Flora had not had time to search seriously for her. She had mentioned it to Margaret Treffyn and discovered through her that Jessica was currently touring Scotland. It was supremely ironic that having ignored her mother for so long, now that she wanted to approach her, it was proving so difficult. 'We don't see a great deal of each other.'

'Why not?' Jane's face acquired an expression similar to that of a fox espying an inattentive chicken. 'A family squabble?'

'Not at all, nothing like that. We're both busy people, and my mother's work necessarily takes her all over the place. Sometimes it's hard to find time to meet.'

'Your father was an actor, wasn't he?'

'Yes.'

'What does he think of your achievement?'

'Um—'

'Or is he involved in this family squabble too?' Jane Something widened her eyes again.

Flora had been warned about these journalists: if she denied it, the woman would only probe further: 'Piranhas, the lot of them,' Antonia had cautioned. 'Don't tell them anything you wouldn't want to see in print. They'll act like your best friend, then pull all sorts of personal information out of you without you realising.'

'I believe this interview is supposed to be about my book, not my personal life,' she said sharply.

'Of course it is,' said Jane, 'but naturally our readers are interested in anything we can tell them about the lives of the people we feature, as well as in what they do. And everybody has disputes with their parents. The more our readers can relate to you, the more likely they are to go out and buy your book. Which is presumably the reason why you and I are sitting together today.' Once again she widened her eyes.

'I suppose it is.' Flora could feel irritation building up inside her, though she was careful not to show it.

As though sensing this, nonetheless, the interviewer changed tack, asked a few more conventional questions and then wound up the meeting. 'I'm grateful for your time,' she said, standing up. 'Here's my card, in case you want to get in touch.'

Flora considered the possibility remote, but took the card anyway. The woman was called Jane Glass, she saw, and lived in Bayswater. 'Thank you.'

'And I'm truly sorry about your sister,' Jane said, as they stood on the steps of the hotel.

'As I am about yours.' The two women smiled without warmth at each other before going their separate ways.

Anxious to get home to Matty, Flora caught the next train back to the country. Her publisher's publicity department had set up a number of media interviews for her and for the past five days she had been staying in Oliver's house in order to fit in them all in. Oliver, meanwhile, was staying at the cottage to look after Matty. The little girl was causing Flora a great deal of concern. Having started at the small private school in September, for a while she had appeared calmer. The number of wrenching nightmares had lessened, and her behaviour had become less antisocial. But in the past two or three weeks, she had reverted to her unsettled ways.

Oliver had begun to come down from London more often, in order to give Flora a chance to catch up on the sleep she had been missing; the reports he had been giving her over the phone in the past five days had not been encouraging. 'She's sleeping very badly,' he had said last night.

'We may to have to get someone professional to see her,' Flora had said worriedly.

'I don't like the idea much.'

'Is it Georgie's death, do you suppose, or something else?'

'Who knows? I'd have thought by now she would have accustomed herself to being with you—'

'And you.'

'—But perhaps not. Children are supposed to be infinitely adaptable, aren't they? To accept changes of circumstance because they assume that's the way things are meant to be. Maybe Matty's just taking a little longer.'

'You don't think it could be physical in some way, do you?' Flora said. It would almost be a relief to have an objective reason for Matty's outbursts of wild and hysterical behaviour. Then something might be done to help her.

Oliver met her off the train. In the car, he said: 'The headmistress wants us to go in and see her this afternoon. She's worried about Matty too.'

'Oh, God.' Flora clenched her fists in her lap. 'How many terrible things do we have to suffer? All three of us. Georgie being murdered was bad enough, but this—'

Oliver took his hand off the steering wheel and rested it on her sleeve. 'We'll get through it somehow. Most of the time she's perfectly ordinary, excited about Christmas. And of course you don't know about yesterday's big news because I was saving it up for her to tell you herself: she's been chosen to be an angel in the Nativity play. Everybody in the whole school gets a part, of course, but at least she's not going to be sixteenth sheep from the left.'

For a moment, ordinariness filled the car. 'An angel,' Flora said. 'She'll be *so* adorable.'

The two of them looked at each other with identical expressions of cherishing soppiness and then burst out laughing. 'That it should come to this,' Flora said.

'If we can't dote on our little girl, who can?' said Oliver.

'How true.'

'By the way, I've got to leave for London earlier this evening than I thought,' he said.

Flora switched off from worrying about Matty. 'You're off to Moscow tomorrow. I'd forgotten.'

'While I'm gone, you're not to brood. Things will turn out all right in the end. It just takes time.'

'Yes.'

At the school, Anne Barker, Matty's head teacher, sat them down in her office. 'Matty is a very bright child,' she said. 'She's already showing a number of aptitudes, not just intellectual, but artistic as well. What she's less good at is her social skills.'

'In what sense?' said Flora.

'I do understand the trauma the poor child has had to suffer, and believe me, everyone here is trying to make every allowance possible.'

'What's she done?' Oliver asked bluntly.

'It's more a question of what she doesn't do. She seems to lack the ability to mix with her peer group.'

'She went to play school,' Flora said defensively.

'We have a lot of children in our care, and we simply cannot jeopardise their well being for the sake of a single individual.'

'The greatest good of the greatest number, eh, Miss Barker?'

'That's right, Mr Treffyn.' The headmistress gave him a bright smile. 'And do please call me Anne. We try to keep formality to a minimum here.'

'What exactly is Matty doing wrong?' Flora asked. 'How is she jeopardising anything?'

'It's not that she does anything exactly wrong. She won't

mix with the others. She won't share with them, and becomes quite . . . um . . . agitated if forced to do so. And quite a number of the children in her class are saying that she . . . *looks* at them. Some of them find it disturbing.'

'She *looks*, Miss Barker – Anne?' Oliver said. 'Since when did looking become a hanging offence?'

'I quite appreciate what you're saying, Mr Treffyn. But if it's making the other children uncomfortable, then obviously I have to see what I can do to ameliorate the situation. For Matilda's sake as well as for theirs.'

'Let me see if I've got this right,' said Oliver. 'You've asked us – or at least, my former wife, Matty's guardian – to come in because Matty is, firstly, not good at mixing with her peer group and secondly, she *looks* at them. Is that it?'

Anne Barker laughed uncomfortably. 'It sounds ridiculous put like that, I know. But her class teacher has asked me to speak to you.'

'Why don't we discuss it with Matty at home?' Flora said. 'See if she has anything to say.'

'An excellent idea, Mrs Treffyn. And if we can't work something out, perhaps we should seek professional advice. I can recommend a number of educational psychologists who are extremely experienced in dealing with disturbed children.'

'You think Matty's disturbed?'

'I'm wondering whether the – um – circumstances of her mother's death have caused deeper problems that we at first thought.'

'No,' Oliver said forthrightly. 'We're not putting her through something like that. If anything's guaranteed to make things worse, it's the so-called professionals.'

Flora could say nothing. In her heart she agreed with Oliver, but was Anne Barker hinting at something really seriously wrong with Matty? Tears came into her eyes. Blindly, she reached out for Oliver and found his hand. Thank God he was there. Thank God that their relationship had survived the divorce. Perhaps she had been wrong to think that Matty needed calm isolation and it was now time for the three of them to form an official family unit.

Matty was waiting for them in the navy duffle coat and blue beret which was the school uniform. All the way home she babbled about the Christmas play and the wings she would be wearing for her part, singing the first lines of Christmas carols, pointing out a rabbit which darted into the road right in front of the wheels. She sounded so . . . so *normal* . . . It was impossible to believe that this was a child with psychological problems.

A car was parked in the lane beside the hedge which ran in front of Flora's house. As they turned in between the white gates and parked, a car door slammed and Det. Chief Supt Martyn walked towards them.

'Mrs Treffyn . . . Flora. Could I have a word?'

'Hello, Bob.' He was almost a friend by now. 'Come in.'

While Oliver gave Matty tea in the kitchen, Martyn stayed with Flora in the sitting room. 'This letter was passed on to us, and I undertook to see that it got to you,' he said, holding out an envelope.

'Oh?' She looked down at it. Her name was neatly printed by hand; there was a Home Office stamp in one corner. 'What is it?'

'I ought to warn you that it's from Don Blackett.'

'Blackett.' The letter in her hand seemed suddenly obscene, as disgusting as a piece of used lavatory paper. His fingers had touched it, just as they had touched Georgie's blood-slippery body, his eyes had read these words just as they had gazed pitilessly at his dying victims. Her mouth was dry. 'I don't want to read it.'

'I think you should.'

She held the letter by a corner, between thumb and fingertip, as though it would otherwise contaminate her. 'What can he possibly have to say to me?'

'Read it and find out.'

'Do you know what it says?'

'I do indeed. His letters are read as a matter of course, and this was passed on to us from Gartree, where he's currently being held. As you know, there are still two cases lying on the files. We haven't given up hope of charging him with your sister's murder.'

Flora sat down and slowly opened the folded pages. There were several of them, each one covered in neat blue-biro writing which spread from one side of the page to the other without benefit of a margin. She was deeply reluctant to start reading it. To do so would be to link herself with him at some level; if whatever he had written was allowed into her brain, the two of them would then be joined in some unspoken but none the less clearly defined pact.

Martyn sensed her reluctance. 'It's not *him*,' he said quietly. '*He's* safely locked up. That letter is nothing more than paper and ink and words.'

'But what words?'

'That's why I wanted to be with you when you read it.'

She looked down at the words travelling so inexorably across the pages.

Dear Mrs Treffyn, she read.

I hope you will not mind me writing to you. As you know, because you were in court when I was sentenced, or so I was informed, I have not tried to pretend I did not do what I did, which is why I pleaded guilty as charged. There is not much point in me trying to persuade you that I was justified in what I did. I am not trying to excuse myself. Someone like you would not have any experience of what it is like to grow up in a house where there was no warmth and the light of love never shined.

I know perfectly well that although I was sexually mistreated by both my father and my mother, and also constantly beaten by the latter after my father disappeared from our lives, there is no excuse for what I did. There is never any excuse for taking another person's life, even though at the time of committing the crimes I was concerned that the children involved would never have to undergo the suffering which has blighted my life.

As I have previously said, I have never attempted to deny my crimes. I understand that there are two outstanding charges left on the police files, one of them being your sister, Miss Georgina Flynn. Whatever the police say, I had nothing to do with the woman in Lydney. I also want to say to you personally that I was not responsible for the murder of your sister, whatever the police may say to you. Yes, I was in your house that day, which is why the police found my fingerprints there, but I did not kill her. I do not expect you to believe me, but I would like my conscience to be cleared of this crime which I did not commit.

Yours sincerely,
Donald Blackett.

Flora read this and then turned back to the beginning and read it again before handing it over to Bob Martyn. 'Is he telling the truth?' she asked.

'About which bit?'

'He says he was in my house—'

'We found all kinds of evidence to support that, yes.'

'—But that he didn't kill her.'

'Of course he did,' Martyn said. 'As you know, the evidence was never as clear cut as in the other cases, and rather than weaken our submittal, we preferred to keep the case on file. But there's no question that he killed her. We found traces of him all over the place.'

'He admits that. But denies the murder. He seems rather anxious that I should believe him.'

'Flora, they always do this. I've seen it many times before, and so have my colleagues. You'll get a chap clearly convicted of the most bloodthirsty killings and he'll spend hours assuring you that OK, yes, he did the murders but it definitely wasn't him who stole the victim's car or took a bottle of beer from the fridge. No way. He's innocent. Must have been someone else entirely.'

'Why would they bother to do that?'

'Maybe it's need to prove to themselves that though they're wicked, they're not as wicked as everyone thinks. I suppose it's better than the other kind, the ones who claim that they've done fifty other murders on top of the ones we've got them for, thus proving how smart they are and how thick we are.'

'Why does he deny the murder over in Lydney?'

Martyn looked embarrassed. 'We may have slipped up there: the MO was pretty similar to Blackett's and we assumed at the time he did it. The case is under review.'

'If he's right in denying that he murdered her, why can't he right about my sister?'

'Because we know he's as guilty as sin. His fingerprints are all over the place, for one thing.'

'But he admits that.'

Martyn shrugged.

Flora held out the letter. 'So what am I supposed to do about this?'

'If you want my advice, forget it. Put it out of your head.'

'I hope I can.'

'Do as I do when I'm handling a murder enquiry, Flora. I've seen scores of them in my times, scores of brutalised bodies – nearly all of them women. Some of the things I've had to look at you simply wouldn't believe. The only way I can handle it is to forget about the person who's been killed, and the effect it's had on the families, and concentrate on hunting down the animal who did the killing. It's the only way to remain even halfway sane.'

'I haven't got that satisfaction.'

Martyn's face sagged. For a moment he looked like a man whose dreams were as painful as Flora's own. 'It's not much of one, to tell you the truth.'

'This letter: should I do anything about it? Answer him, for instance?'

'No. Like I said, forget it.'

Easier said than done. She was able to put Blackett's letter out of her mind in the bustle of getting Oliver packed and on his way back to London ready to fly to Moscow the following day. There was also Matty to look after before she was free to relax from her own day. Wrapping her in a towel after the bath, holding her so tightly that Matty protested, Flora could not help wondering just what terrors were locked inside the little four-year-old head. Flora read from her first angel book while Matty snuggled into the crook of her arm, following the words along with one pudgy finger, as though she could read them.

'I'm going to be an angel, too,' she said importantly.

'I know you are, darling.'

'With wings and everything.'

'Will you have a halo?'

'What's a halo?'

Flora showed her the halo in one of the pictures.

'What does halo mean?'

'It's to show that you're very holy. Very good.'

Matty looked doubtful. She drew her feathered brows together in a frown. 'I'm not very good, I don't think.'

'Who says so?'

'Anne. And Jane.' Jane was the girl in charge of Matty's class. 'She says I mustn't look at people.' Matty raised herself up and stared into Flora's face from three inches away. 'The thing is, Flora, if you don't look at people, you can't see them, can you?'

'Not really.' Matty's eyes were as soft as flower petals.

'I think Jane's stupid.'

'I don't suppose she really is.'

None the less, tucking Matty up, kissing her goodnight, Flora wondered just what it was about Matty's looking that so upset the other children. She should have asked, should have demanded to know exactly what the child was doing. She'd sort it out tomorrow.

It was only when Flora was finally in her own bed that she could give further thought to Blackett's claim that he was not responsible for Georgie's death. Was Bob Martyn correct in saying that it was just an attempt on the murderer's part to seem less culpable in his own eyes? Should she brush the claim aside? Or was Blackett telling the truth? What worried her most of all was the fact that Martyn had told her months ago that he thought Blackett had been interrupted in his crime, which was why the usual evidence was lacking in this case.

'I'm not going to trouble or offend you with the details, unless you absolutely insist.' She could hear his voice in her head. 'But there were one or two reasons to believe he might have been distracted.'

He'd spoken of trademarks, of signatures. She had asked whether it could have been Matty who caused him to leave the scene prematurely, but Martyn had considered it unlikely. Now, in view of Matty's increasingly unsettled state, it was impossible not to conjecture that maybe the little girl had seen something that terrible night, had maybe even witnessed her own mother's murder. She longed to believe what the Detective Chief Superintendent had told her and to dismiss the letter. But doubt wove its way in and out of her wakeful brain. Why should Blackett deny responsibility for this one death? What could he possibly hope to gain? Just supposing he wasn't lying, just suppose he was innocent of Georgie's death: was there anyone else who could conceivably have wished her dead? And if so, why?

Rationally, she could tell herself that Blackett had to be the murderer. The chances of there having been a second homicidal maniac on the prowl in that area that night was too bizarre to be worth contemplating. Blackett had admitted to being in the house that day. Georgie fitted the profile of his other victims and had been killed in the same way as they. Blackett was responsible beyond all reasonable doubt, and Martyn's explanation for his denial, based on wide experience, was almost certainly one hundred percent correct.

None the less, the unreasonable one percent continued to nag at her.

Was there another explanation.

Had someone else wanted Georgie dead? And if so, who?

On New Year's Eve, Angus drove to her house, bringing half a litre of Johnny Walker and champagne in a silver bucket.

'Very grand,' she said. 'I've always wanted a silver bucket, but until recently, I could never afford champagne to put in it.'

'The champagne's mostly for you.'

'What about you?'

'I prefer Black Label,' Angus said. 'Though I only ever buy it duty free.' His eyes met hers. 'Maybe the new year will bring a change of fortune – for both of us.' He smiled in a way which made it clear that he hoped the two of them might one day end up together.

She ought to tell him about Oliver, she knew that, but somehow the time was never right; this evening was no exception. 'Here's to all of us,' she said.

As they sat waiting for the chimes of midnight to sound, Angus said diffidently: 'I hope you don't feel I'm invading your territory.'

'In what sense?'

'With Matty.'

'Of course you're not.'

'In some ways, she means more to me than my own daughters. You know that I haven't seen them for nearly a year, don't you?'

'I hadn't realised it was that long.' And I should have asked, Flora thought. I've been so taken up with my own affairs that I'm becoming distanced from other people's problems, even those of my friends. She thought of Eithne, to whom she had not spoken for weeks. Of Katie Vernon and Gemma Craig, who had offered her friendship which she had not availed herself of. And of her mother, from whom there had been total silence since Georgie's funeral. Did her own apparent indifference cause them to avoid her? She determined that she would telephone Eithne the next morning. Perhaps she should bring Angus and Eithne together; they might suit each other very well. Angus was not, admittedly, twenty years younger than Eithne, nor particularly handsome, but he had other charms which Eithne might enjoy, among them a career and an income. Contemplating this, she decided that on second thoughts, she would discard the idea. She told herself that it was to protect

Angus from Eithne's predatoriness but knew that it was something quite different, something more selfish and possessive which did not wish to see Angus with another woman. She took his hand. 'Not seeing them must be dreadfully sad for you.'

'You'd think so. In one sense it is. In one sense I am so . . . *wounded* by the spaces between them and me that I sometimes can scarcely breathe.' The whisky he had poured was trembling against the sides of the glass. 'And yet, in another sense, I feel almost indifferent. It's been so long since the girls and I have had any kind of meaningful association, and their mother has worked so hard to make me out as some kind of ogre, that when they're with me, we're embarrassed by each other. And I ask myself, what is the point of trying to keep alive a relationship like that?'

'How old are they now?'

'Emily's nearly ten, and Sophie's eight.'

'You just have to go on doing your best, Angus, however awkward and difficult it is. Because one day, they're going to be sixteen, eighteen, twenty, forming their own opinions, thinking for themselves, and if they know that you tried, that you didn't give up on them . . . Isn't that going to be better than the opposite?'

'I suppose you're right.'

'They're clever girls, from what you've said about them. They may listen to their mother at the moment, but the time will come when they judge for themselves.'

'And I mustn't be found wanting?' he said bitterly.

'Perhaps it's unfair, but that's more or less right. In their eyes, or in your own. It's the best you can do.'

Muffled by closed windows and drawn curtains, they heard the pealing of bells from the church at the end of the road. Flora got up and opened the door and the sound flooded in. It had rained earlier in the evening, but was not cold. As she looked up at the star-studded sky, a spray of sparks seem to swoosh past her like the tail of a rocket. At the same time, something brushed her face, swept her cheek with the lightness of a feather, so close that she jumped back in surprise.

'Goodness, what was that?' she asked.

'I didn't see anything, but it sound like a firework going off.'

'But it was just outside the front door.'

'Probably not as close as you thought.' Angus came to stand beside her, and put an arm across her shoulders as the bells reached a climax of joyful sound and gave way to a long, slow tolling of the last seconds of the year. 'Happy New Year, Flora,' he said softly.

'And to you?' She reached up and kissed him. 'Let's hope it's a good one for all of us.'

'Yes, indeed,' he said fervently, and turned away to wrestle the top off the waiting bottle of champagne.

Flora remained at the open door for a moment. She'd heard that strange noise before, somewhere, but she could not remember where. It had been dark then, too, and cold; the air had been damp, just like tonight, and she was alone, in a strange place. Where had it been? The memory eluded her and she shut the door in the end, and came inside to begin the new year with Angus.

What was Oliver doing, she wondered. Was he drinking vodka and eating caviar with a bunch of theatre people? He'd rung several times since his departure to exclaim over the Russian capacity for alcohol and she half expected him to telephone on the stroke of midnight, but he did not do so.

Angus put his arm around her shoulder. 'May I stay the night, Flora?'

'Of course.'

'I don't just mean in your house, but in your bed.'

Unaccountably, she blushed. 'Dear Angus. Darling Angus.'

'I want to make love to you.'

'Yes.' There was whisky on his breath, warming, celebratory. She took his hand and the two of them went upstairs to bed.

For Matty's sake, Flora lived uneventfully. Increasingly she found that the child was upset by any departure from their daily procedures, so reasoned that the duller the routine, the more chance she would have to settle. She had therefore tried to see to it that the events of Matty's life remained unchanged, day safely following day, and she was pleased to see that the regime seemed to be working. In the weeks around Christmas and the New Year, the nightmares grew less, and after the first week of the new term, Anne Barker telephoned to say there that had been a great improvement in Matty's behaviour and attitude. Putting aside the question of whether a child of four could have an attitude, Flora took this as confirmation that she was right in opting for dullness.

Since Matty did not like unexpected visitors, it was lucky that she was at school when three callers arrived at Flora's house in a single day.

The first rang the bell at eleven o'clock in the morning. A woman. 'Hi,' she said, smiling, extending a hand as soon as Flora opened the door. 'My name's Beth Harding.' She was shaggy haired, with a strong, bare face and vivid blue eyes; her smile was piercingly beautiful.

'Yes?' Flora said, unwelcomingly.

'I'd like to talk to you, if I might.'

'What about?'

'Your sister.'

Flora scowled. 'My sister's dead.'

'I know that.'

'What are you: a journalist? Looking for a sensationalist story, are you?'

'Nothing like that, I promise.' Seeing Flora's continued hesitation, Ms Harding said urgently: 'Please let me talk to you, Mrs Treffyn.'

'Why should I?'

'Because what I've got to say could be very important to you.' Again she flashed the brilliant smile. 'I'm not dangerous, I promise. You could pat me down to see that I'm not carrying a concealed weapon. Or you could check my credentials.' Reaching into her shapeless velvet bag, she handed over a laminated card.

Holding it, Flora assured herself that the woman looked harmless enough. What Oliver would have categorised as a do-gooder. Flowing Oxfam skirt, indeterminate coat, Timberlands and socks over thick black tights. And although women were constantly told not to let strangers into the house, it was male strangers they were warned against rather than female ones. 'I suppose it's all right.'

She took the visitor into the kitchen and offered coffee then sat down opposite her, still wary. 'What exactly do you want?'

'I'll come straight to the point.' Ms Harding said. 'I've misrepresented myself, in order to get inside your house.'

'What?' Flora half rose.

'I had to. If I'd told you I'd come on behalf of Don Blackett, would you have let me in?'

'Absolutely not. And now you *have* told me, I'd prefer it if you left right now.'

'See what I mean?'

'The man murdered my sister. Why should I listen to you or anyone else who claims to be speaking on his behalf?'

'That's precisely why I'm here. Don is absolutely insistent that he did not kill your sister.'

Flora knew she did not want to hear this. She had managed to accept the official explanation for Blackett's letter, and had pushed it to the back of her mind. 'And you believe him?' she asked.

'Let me tell you about Don.' Ms Harding placed both her forearms on the kitchen table and clasped her hands together.

'I've got no special axe to grind. I'm not related to him. I'm not his girlfriend or anything like that. I'm simply a colleague who's known and worked alongside him for many years, in Pakistan—' She nodded at the laminated card which Flora had put down on the table, '—who finds it difficult to visualise him as a monster. I know, I know—' She raised a hand as Flora opened her mouth. 'He's killed those women, I know that.'

'Killed them horribly. Viciously.'

'Yes. And yes, I suppose that does make him a monster. But what I'm saying is, even though I and my colleagues know what he did, we still find it difficult to reconcile the Don Blackett we knew with the bestial freak that he's been made out to be. So when we visit him in the prison and he tells us, over and over again, that he did not kill your sister, we're inclined to believe him.'

'Go on.'

'Somewhere inside him is the good man he used to be. I firmly believe that. He's sinned in the most appalling and unforgivable way. He's a murderer, yes. And I suppose he deserves to stay locked up for the rest of his life. But that doesn't make him – and I know this sounds ridiculous in view of what I've just said – that still doesn't make him a liar.'

'Oh, please,' Flora said wearily. 'Who cares whether he is a liar or not? He's a self-confessed murderer, isn't that enough?'

'Think about it for a moment, Mrs Treffyn. If he is telling the truth, you see what this means, don't you?'

'What's that?'

'That someone else killed your sister. Someone who is out there now, a free man. You may feel that because of what Don has done, it really doesn't matter whether he's innocent or not of killing Miss Flynn. But it does. If you think about it, you have to believe it just as much as I do. Because if he's telling the truth – and he is, I'm sure of it – then a murderer has got away with it, and may kill again. For your sister's sake, if not for Don's, at least accept that it's possible he didn't kill her.'

'Even if I believed it, what do you expect me to do about it?'

'I don't know why it's so important to me, really,' Ms Harding said. Her chin trembled. She lifted her hands to her face and rested her head on them. The shaggy ringlets of hair swept down on either side of her face. When she spoke again, her voice was choked with tears. 'You can't imagine the effect this has had on us. We were a team. We were doing good work. We were doing *good*. All of us. Including Don. This has – you can't believe what it's like to realise that the kind, gentle, caring man you've worked with for nearly ten years is a depraved maniac. And on top of that, that he should have been using the charity's work to find his victims.'

'You're just another casualty,' Flora said, and was surprised at the hardness in her voice, the indifference in her heart. 'Like me. Like the others. Don't expect me to feel particularly sorry for you.'

'I don't. I don't even know why it's so important to me to prove that Don Blackett isn't lying to us. But it would— ' she shook the wild hair again,' —it would make it that little bit less bad. Maybe restore some of the faith we always had in each other. Revalidate all that we've been trying to do.'

Flora gazed at the top of the other woman's head without sympathy. 'I'm sorry for you,' she said, knowing she did not sound it, 'but I feel sorrier for all the people who lost daughters and sisters and mothers because of your friend Mr Blackett. I feel a lot sorrier for myself, and for my sister's child, who is suffering badly from the loss of her mother and probably always will.'

Beth Harding lifted a wet face to Flora. 'I apologise for breaking down like that. But that's part of what I came here to say. If Don didn't kill your sister, who did? Isn't it worth at least wondering?'

'I repeat, what can I do about it?'

'You could go to the police.'

'They won't believe me. Your friend has already written to me, saying that he didn't do it, and they've seen his letter. They say he's behaving typically by denying responsibility for

Georgie – my sister. The most they'll concede is that he might have been interrupted after he'd murdered her, because some of the trademarks of his other killings were missing in her case.'

'Don't you see?' cried Beth.

'See what, exactly?'

'Doesn't that prove my point? It was different from the others. Surely you could find out exactly how. Surely it could be proved that he wasn't there the night she got killed.'

'He's already admitted he was in my house that day.'

'Yes, but not when she was was murdered. If we looked hard enough, surely we—'

'We?'

'You. Someone. *Any*one. The charity hasn't got much spare money, but we'd be willing to pay for a private detective if it would help.'

'I'm sure that won't be necessary.' But the idea took root in Flora's mind. Why not? At worst, it might prove that Blackett was lying when he said he was innocent of Georgie's death. At best . . . Except that in this sorry business there were no bests.

'Did they check his alibi?' asked Beth. 'I bet they didn't.'

'Did he offer one?' For the first time, Flora wished that she had followed the trial more closely.

'I've no idea. But since they weren't charging him with that crime, it probably never came up. And if it had, they wouldn't have bothered to waste time and money on it. But *we* could – you or me. Or a detective, if we went that way.'

'I don't know why you keep talking about "we". I can't see that you're involved in this at all.'

'You're absolutely right, Mrs Treffyn.' Beth Harding grimaced resignedly and pushed back her chair. 'It was stupid of me to come here hoping that you might listen to me sympathetically. And I can't really blame you for not doing so.' She levered herself upright. 'I'm on half-leave for the next three months, however, and I intend to do some investigating of my own. If only for the sake of the charity and Don's colleagues.'

'Fine,' Flora said.

'I'm going to leave you an address where you can reach me. If you should by any chance change your mind, or think of anything you'd like me to know, please call me. It means so much to us.'

'Right.'

'We feel in some way responsible. Perhaps if we'd talked to him more caringly after his wife walked out on him, picked up the signals, realised that he was troubled, we might have been able to help him before his compulsions grew too strong for him to control.'

'Perhaps you might.'

Glancing with compassion at Flora's stony face, Beth remarked: 'We can't bring them back, you know. None of them. And what Don has done is . . . unrecompensable. But we can at least try to put one small injustice right. You never know. It might illuminate something in ourselves which we aren't even aware is there.'

'I doubt it.'

But when she had closed the door behind her visitor, Flora sat down again at the kitchen table. What the woman had said was quite right: if Blackett was innocent of Georgie's murder, then someone else must be guilty.

And there was something else, something which she had tried hard to expunge but could not. She had feared that by reading his letter, she would find herself shackled to him in some way. She was right. He had written: *Someone like you would not have any experience of what it was like to grow up in a house where there was no warmth and the light of love never shined.* It was a sad phrase, one which found echoes in her own heart. The light of love had never shone in the house where she had grown up. Not on her. That lack had affected everything she did. Everything she was. It had obviously affected Blackett too, in the most terrible way. Did she – it was an unpalatable thought – *owe* him something for that, if for nothing else? Did he deserve a chance to prove his claim?

And even if he did not, surely she should at least do some

very elementary checking. Because, as Beth Harding had pointed out, if by any chance he was telling the truth, then there was a murderer on the loose. Free to kill again.

She stared at the walls around her. She didn't want this, any of it. She felt as though she were swimming in oily water and was about to drown.

Just after lunch, there was another knock on the front door. Her mind on other things, Flora opened it. The man standing on the step was vaguely familiar. She tried to remember where she had seen that handsome, raddled face before.

At the sight of her, he stepped back a pace and held out both hands. 'Flora, is it?' He had a rumbling bass voice which crunched like a steamroller across something which had been hidden inside her for years.

'Yes. And you are?' But, asking the question, she already knew the answer.

'My dearest girl,' he said.

She was wary. For a start, what did you call a man who was your father but whom you had not seen for nearly thirty years? Father? Dad? Mr Flynn? The etiquette books were silent on this as on so many other of the socially necessary rules of modern life.

Flora settled for: 'You're Rupert Flynn. Do you want to come in?' After so much wanting and hoping, to have him turn up like this should have been the answer to a prayer. Instead, her own almost neutral reaction surprised her.

'I'd hate to have travelled all the way here only to be turned away,' he said, smiling.

She stood aside without speaking and let him pass her and walk down the hall. Had he always had this faintly Irish lilt to his voice? She couldn't remember now. As he passed the sitting room, she watched him pause at the door, absorbing the pleasant, middle-class shabbiness, the Coalport tea service in the display cabinet, the good pieces of furniture which had come from Gran, the pictures on the wall, including the Jack Yeats drawing which had been a present from Oliver's parents.

'You've made it very nice,' he said.

Belligerence heaved like a seventh wave inside her. How patronising. How banal. One would have expected more from a long-lost father than these stilted phrases. Besides, since he'd not seen the room before, he couldn't have known what she had done to it.

'And isn't that my mother's Pembroke table?' he went on.

'It was Gran's, yes.' She wanted to insist that Gran had always been more her grandmother than his mother. 'So's that cabinet.'

'I'm glad to see them being looked after.'

'Come through.' Flora was reluctant to let him sit down on the sofa, or lean against her cushions. The hardness of kitchen chairs would retain less of him when he was gone than the soft furnishings. In the kitchen, she paused with her hand on the kettle. 'Would you like tea? Coffee?'

'Fine. Whichever you're having.' His eyes were darting about: was it curiosity only, or was he searching for something? She poured him a mug of coffee and sat down. It was bizarre to be in so familiar a setting with this man, this father, who ought not to be, but was, a stranger. What is a father, she wondered? Is it only a blood relationship, or is there more to it? And if so, could this man really be said to be her father? It was too late now for the lonely years of her childhood to be replaced. She could feel anger surging like a tide against the beach of her memory.

'I read about you in the paper,' he said. His own hands were beautiful, the fingers long and tapered, the nails professionally manicured. Staring at them, she could feel self-control slipping away, memory taking over. Or, rather, half-memory, impressions. His hands spread, skin wrinkling over the knuckles, the line of the bone, the splay of his thumb. Where had it been? Why should she remember it?

'Did you?'

'Where you told them about the paint-box you were given by your father.'

'Paint-box?' She stared at him. Was it for this man she had

yearned her way through childhood? She remembered Georgie saying that she felt sorry for Jessica, married to him. The painful tide inside her reached shore. 'You walked out of my life over thirty years ago, without a word,' she said angrily. 'I haven't seen you since then. And when you *do* show up, completely out of the blue, all you can talk about is a paint-box.'

He reached across and took hold of her hand. 'Think about it, Flora. What else can I talk about, with all those empty years between us?'

'Whose fault is that? You're the one who left. I didn't even know you were still alive until recently.'

'Jessica told you I wasn't.' It was a statement, not a question.

'Who else?'

'That didn't mean I was dead.' He attempted a joke. 'Though if wishing could make it so . . . Fortunately, even Jessica's not that powerful.'

Flora found herself resenting this sideways jeer at her mother. 'You might as well have been,' she said roughly. 'Why didn't you contact us? Why didn't you come and see us? We stayed with Gran often enough. You could have come then.'

He said nothing, looking at their two hands entwined.

She tried to pull hers away. 'Or, when we'd grown up, you could have got in touch. Why *didn't* you?' The retrospective rage swelled at the pit of her stomach. 'Someone told me you actually came to my wedding, but you didn't bother to speak to me. Why *not*?'

'Look at me Flora.' When she unwillingly did so, he said sympathetically: 'You have every right to be angry. But anger doesn't help much, does it?'

'It's all I've got.' If she closed her eyes, she could be back in the days before he went. *No, I am not Prince Hamlet, nor was meant to be . . .* The beautiful voice flowed through her mind with the richness of spilled syrup. 'You know that Georgie is dead.'

'I do.'

'But you didn't bother to come to her funeral.'

'I couldn't find out where it was, or when.'

'You could have, if you'd wanted to.'

'I didn't know who to ask or where to look for the information. I telephoned your mother, but was told that she'd moved recently and they didn't seem to know where she's living now.'

'You could have got in touch with me.'

'I could have.'

'Why didn't you?'

'Guilt, I suppose. You're the one who's suffered most.'

'How do you mean?' But Flora realised she did not want to hear the answer. Quickly she asked another question: 'Why have you come now, after ignoring us for so long?'

'Ignoring you is not what I've done.' He smiled slightly. 'I've kept an eye on you. You might not have seen me, but I've been there. Perhaps more often than you think.'

She'd known that. Been aware of someone. Not all the time, but often enough to have been made uneasy. Memory rushed into the voids and fissures of her mind. Someone there, on the periphery. Watching. Waiting.

'We'll have a sea fire tonight, girls,' Gran said.

'Lovely.'

'You'll have to collect some wood, though. Better go now, while the tide's out. And while you're gone, I'll make a nice shepherd's pie and we'll eat on our laps in front of the TV.'

'My favourite,' Georgie said. Eating in front of the TV wasn't allowed at home.

The beach was harsh under their feet; there was salt on their lips. Flora, ten years old, could hear the wind rattling the marram grass along the dunes and the strident gulls swooping through the clear air. She and Georgie piled their driftwood discoveries in a pile at the foot of the rough concrete steps which had almost disappeared under the shifting sand.

'That man's there again.' Georgie nudged Flora. They stooped to pick up the smooth, bleached bones of wood and Flora glanced sideways, shading her eyes to see him more clearly. He was only a silhouette, a flat black figure against the brightness of the sea.

'I saw him the other day when I went to post a letter for Gran,' Georgie said. 'He was on the other side of the road when I came out of the gate.'

'Were you frightened?'

'No.'

'Are you now?'

'No.'

'Nor me.' Surreptitiously Flora stared at the man again. He was walking towards them, and there was no one else on the beach. Gran said they weren't to talk to strange men: suppose he spoke to them? As he came nearer she could see that he was wearing an open-necked navy blue shirt, and white flannel trousers. He had a panama hat on, too, with a coloured ribbon round the crown, like the old men who sat in the shelters along the promenade and stared out to sea with milky eyes, though he was much younger than them.

'What'll we do if he offers us sweets?' Georgie said.

It was difficult. You were told not to accept sweets from strangers, but you were also told to be polite to people. No one ever said how you were supposed to do both. 'We say no thank you very much, we're just going home for our tea.'

She could see the marks of his feet stretching back behind him on the shingle, a double line of them like a neat row of stitching, shiny with sea water. He was nearer to them now. She hoped he would just pass by, that he wouldn't speak to them And yet she wanted him to. There was something about him which attracted her, something . . . something familiar, she could not have said how, exactly. In some undefined part of her brain she wondered if something she knew to be wrong could be right.

'What will happen if we do speak to him?' Georgie had asked Flora once, whispering when they were in their safe and salty bed one night. Not really sure, Flora had replied: 'It's something to do with babies.'

'I wouldn't mind a little baby,' Georgie had said thoughtfully. 'We could keep it in our bedroom, Flo. Save bits from supper for it.'

'Better not. What would happen if *she* found it?'

So Flora hoped he would not speak to them Not just in case of having a baby, but because of being rude, and the funny feelings he aroused in her. But as he approached them, he lifted his hat from his head and smiled – such a lovely smile. She wanted to ask him who he was. Why did she feel that she already knew him? Or had once? She longed to find out more about him. Although she would never in a million years have admitted as much to Georgie, he had sometimes appeared in her dreams, along with Paul McCartney and the boy who lived further down their street who was at Westminster and going to Cambridge in the autumn.

She straightened, face flushed from bending and shaded her eyes again against the sun. He came nearer. Then, instead of passing on, he stopped. 'You're Flora,' he said, that special particular afternoon.

'And I'm Georgina,' Georgie said.

'I know.'

'How do you know?' asked Flora.

'I'm . . . a friend of your grandmother's.' He hesitated, as though about to say more, then lifted his hat once more and passed on his way. She'd seen him before. She knew she'd seen him before, but where? She watched him go, wanting to run after him, take his hand, walk along the beach beside him and though she was much too young to be aware of what love really was, she knew that she had fallen in love with him.

'That was you,' she said softly, remembering it, reviewing it from the perspective of adulthood. 'On the beach. Watching us.'

'Yes.'

'And when Gran took us to Liverpool to the theatre . . . But you *were* Prince Hamlet.'

'That time, yes.'

'Why didn't I recognise you? On the beach, I mean?' And yet she almost had.

'You were so small when I was . . . When I went away. And for various reasons, I'd lost a lot of weight. And Jessica certainly didn't keep photographs of me about the house – at least, not where you two girls could see them.'

And at the theatre, they hadn't bought a programme: Gran had bustled them into their seats, saying they didn't need one, saying 'The play's the thing,' in a voice which meant she was making a special kind of grown-up joke. Obviously she hadn't wanted the two girls to read the list of players and discover that their own father was playing the title role. But why? Why such secrecy? Even Gran had been included in the conspiracy to keep them from their father.

'Your grandmother told me afterwards that you thought the play was a bit boring except when Hamlet was on stage,' Flynn said. 'It's a review I treasure beyond all others.' He laughed. 'Can't you just see it on the boards outside the theatre. *Boring except when Hamlet is on stage* . . . says Flora Flynn.'

It would have been too easy to succumb to his charm. He was very like Oliver, she recognised. Engaging. Amusing. Warm. Perhaps that was why she had fallen so instantly in love with Oliver, recognising those characteristics at some subconscious level. But that hadn't stopped Flynn from deserting – neglecting – his daughers.

'All right,' she said with impatience. 'So why have you broken cover now?' As a fox might, or a tiger.

'Look at me,' he said again. The dark eyes stared deep into hers. Hypnotic. Persuading her that things were other than she knew them to be. That wrong was right. Right wrong. Again she tried to pull her hand from his but he held it too tightly. 'Time is passing, Flora. Faster for me than for you. And when you start to realise just how few days you have left, you remember the things you've done wrong, or the things you wish you'd not done at all, and you tell yourself that maybe it's not too late, after all. That perhaps you can put a bit right here, a bit there.'

Despite herself she could feel herself believing it. She remembered looking into those eyes years ago, seeing questions there which she didn't want to answer. She remembered how much she had loved him.

'Why did you go away?' she said, her voice catching, snagged on old sorrows.

'I had no choice.'

'Why? Where were you? Were you . . . in prison?' She so desperately wanted to understand.

'Why do you ask that? Did your mother—'

'No. It was my own . . . She never talked about you. She'd be furious if we ever dared to ask.'

'She was a woman of violent passions.'

'Still is.'

Again he smiled. 'Which, in an actress, is no bad thing.'

'What did you *do*? What was so terrible that she wouldn't let you even see us?'

'I don't want to talk about it.'

'Surely you had a legal right to have access to your own children?' But asking the question, Flora remembered Angus's wife and the way she circumvented his paternal rights, and saw how Jessica could have done the same. 'So why have you come back now?'

'Because of Georgina's death. And because I think you're in trouble, Flora. The little girl, Matty – my granddaughter – is not happy.'

'Your granddaughter—' Yes, that was what Matty was, strange though it seemed. 'How do you know that she's unhappy?'

'I told you: I keep an eye on you.'

She said scornfully: 'I don't suppose you even know what Matty looks like.'

'You sound like your mother,' he said. 'Hard.'

'Like my *mother*.' Flora was outraged. 'If there's one thing in this world I do not resemble, it's her.' As she flung the rejecting words at him, however, she wondered if she was right. As a girl, she had been soft, pliable, afraid. Over the years, she had fabricated a carapace around herself, a crust which might well produce a likeness to her mother. But inside, she was still the vulnerable creature she had always been. And as the thought formed, she wondered about Jessica. What lay behind that glacial exterior crust: more ice, or the same shrinking uncertainty as Flora's? Was Jessica, too, vulnerable? Was her hardness not naturally come by but deliberately assumed?

'Georgie was different,' Flynn said. 'Softer. Sweeter. More like me.'

'Georgie was loved,' said Flora. 'It's easy to be soft and sweet. Not that Georgie was particularly sweet. Any more than *you* can be, or you wouldn't have ignored your daughters for the past thirty years.'

'Matty's so pretty,' Flynn said, disregarding that. 'The prettiest little girl in the world.'

She hated the way the words came out of his mouth. Long ago, his voice had pronounced the same phrase and she knew she had hated it then as well. She shivered. She was thirty-eight, aunt, guardian, author, yet at the same time she was four, five, six years old again, settling under the bedtime covers while her daddy tucked her up for sleep. There had been bears on her pyjamas. The buttons were made of plastic that looked like bone.

'And you're alone now,' he continued. 'I thought you might need someone to lean on.'

If he knew so much about her, why didn't he know that she and Oliver were more or less back together? 'And you seriously hoped it might be you?' she said.

'Like I said, I hoped I might be able to put some of that right. Make up a little of what I owed you.'

'Impossible.'

'Is it?' His brown eyes were sad.

When he left, she stood at the door and watched his car turn in front of the house and drive away. If only she dared to trust him. But she didn't. Not his charm. Not his words. All those years without a single attempt at connection. Did he honestly expect that he could turn up like this and she would play Cordelia, take him back into her heart? Yet, despite her mistrust of him, she was tempted. She longed beyond expressing to be loved as Georgie had been loved, and Oliver. As Matty was.

Her last visitor was Det. Chief Supt Martyn. 'I was just passing. Thought I'd see how you were.' He grinned at her. 'Maybe cadge a cuppa.'

'The kettle's on.' Flora led the way into the kitchen. Once there, with tea made, she said: 'Bob, I've got to go and see him.'

He didn't pretend not to know what she meant. 'Blackett.'

'I know you don't agree with me, but I feel I must talk to him.'

'I told you last time you brought this up to remember that even if, by some inconceivable chance, he didn't kill your sister, he's still responsible for the deaths of eight, probably nine, other women.'

'I know. But even so—'

'What's made you decide you want to see him now?'

'I had a Christmas card.'

'From him? I don't remember—'

'Via one of his regular visitors. A colleague.'

The card was blue, with a white dove of peace embossed on it. Inside, the man who sent it wrote that each time he visited Blackett, he insisted upon his innocence of Georgie's murder. *God knows the poor man deserves little compassion for what he has done*,' the sender had added. '*But on this one matter alone, could you not find it in your heart to give him the benefit of the doubt? Or even let him tell you about it himself?*'

'I can't recommend it,' Martyn said.

'I had a visitor this morning, too. A woman called Beth Harding.'

'Oh, yes. She's been onto us, too.'

'What do you think of her claims about Blackett?'

'The man's stood trial, he's behind bars. The best all of us can do is try to get on with our lives. Going to see him will revive things for you that you should be trying to put behind you.'

'If there's any shadow of doubt about—'

'There isn't.'

'But if there *is*, then I want to know. And the best way to do that is to talk to him. You said that the evidence against him wasn't as strong as in the other cases. You also said that he had been interrupted.'

'That's true.'

'Why did you say it?'

'I've told you: although we didn't emphasise it, there was some evidence of sexual interference in most, though not all, of the other murders. In your sister's case, there was none.' He pushed his teacup away from him and put both hands on the table. 'Flora, I can't advise you too strongly against going to see him.'

'Why? You were so insistent that I attend the final day of the trial, you said it would be therapeutic for me to see him in the flesh.'

'That was then, when everything was still raw and incomprehensible. I thought it would bring the death of your sister back into perspective for you – as far as that was possible. But there's been so much water under the bridge since then. Now, I think it would just disturb you, churn it all up again. It has nothing to do with me, I know that, but I *really* don't think you should go.' From his tone, she received the strong impression that he might also seek actively to prevent her; he probably had enough influence to do that.

Accordingly, she changed tack. Adopting a shamefaced expression, she said: 'It probably sounds rather vindictive, and perhaps it's natural, but I need to confront him.'

'Oh?'

This was an altogether more productive line to take. This,

she saw, the policeman could encompass. Years ago, when she first met Oliver, she had told him she couldn't act. She'd been wrong. 'I want to tell him just how much damage he's done. How his actions have affected my life. And Matty's.'

'I see.'

'I – I can't sleep at night. I keep seeing his expression, that last moment before he went down to the cells, after the jury had delivered its verdict.'

'And how do you think visiting him would help?'

'Perhaps it won't, but I just have this feeling that if I could sit opposite him, face to face, and tell him what I feel, it might ease something.'

Martyn considered. 'I'm quite certain it won't, but if you're determined—'

'I am.'

'—I'll see what I can do. It might take a while.'

'Thank you, Bob.'

'How's the little girl doing?'

'I think she's calming down a bit. The teachers at her school say she's been much more settled recently.'

'Enjoyed Christmas, did she?'

Flora saw wistfulness behind the question and wondered what Martyn's home life was like. Was there a wife? Children? Was he some family's favourite uncle? Or did he live alone, drinking a little too much, not taking enough exercise, wishing things had worked out differently? Too late, it occurred to her that she should at least have asked him if he was doing anything on Christmas Day and, if not, invited him to join her. Another lonely man – if that was what he was – wouldn't have made any difference, when she already had Angus at the table. 'Very much. You must come round for Sunday lunch sometime and see for yourself.'

His face lit up and she saw that her conjectures about his circumstances had probably been correct. 'I'd very much like that,' he said. 'Mr Treffyn still away?'

'He's in Moscow until at least the end of the month.'

'And does Matty miss him?'

'She doesn't seem to. I think keeping her routine exactly the same, day after day, is the best thing for her, so I don't talk about him, and she doesn't, either.'

In fact, Matty's favourite person at the moment seemed to be Angus, which inevitably meant that Flora was seeing him very frequently now. To hear Matty chuckling as he read her a story, to watch the two of them bent over a snail in the garden – Matty had lost none of her passion for snails – or discussing with frowning seriousness which television programme they wanted to watch, made her realise just how much normality Angus brought into the house. When Oliver returned, there was a danger that he would feel himself supplanted in both Matty's affections and in hers, but it was a risk she was prepared to take for Matty's peace of mind.

Now that the moment had come, Flora realised she was frightened. Intellectually she knew that there was nothing Blackett could do to harm her. A prison officer would remain in the room with them throughout the interview and there would be others within call. However, it was not physical attack she feared so much as emotional assault. She was, quite simply, afraid to sit at the same table with a self-confessed killer, afraid that some of the evil, or the madness, might leak out of him and, by osmosis, into her. She felt that she could not but be tainted by such proximity.

In one corner of the long, light room, children's toys spilled in an overflow of bright primary colours. There were a few much-thumbed copies of magazines on a plastic-topped table, and a couple of canvases on the walls which she assumed had been painted by inmates. On a window sill there was a clean-washed mustard jar with a bunch of snowdrops carelessly jammed into its narrow neck. Who could have put them there? Waiting for Blackett to be brought in so that the two of them could talk, she wondered whether, in this place without expectation, the chaste white flowers offered hope to those who noticed them, or merely increased despair.

The only thing she wanted to say to Blackett when she saw him, was: 'Did you kill my sister?'

He would deny it. She knew that already. None the less, the question had to be put, face to face; an answer had to be given. Her main concern was whether she was a sufficiently good judge to be able to determine if he was telling the truth. Only after that would she attempt to look at the complex issues which would be raised by that expected denial.

The door at the end of the room opened. Keys grated in locks, metal handles turned, a chain rattled. Two men came into the room. One was a prison officer, fiercely neat in clean white shirt, black tie and V-necked navy sweater. The other was Blackett, his blue-striped shirt worn open over a blue prison T-shirt. His face was familiar to her. She had seen him once, at the Old Bailey, but since then his features had melded and blurred into the photograph so familiar from the newspapers. His cheeks were plumper than when she had last seen him, his complexion paler. The curly hair which had framed his face like a halo was now long and wild; his small mouth smiled at her.

She didn't like that. She did not want to be smiled at by this killer of women. She wondered why the officer's tie was black, whether it was symbolic of some kind of mourning. If so, was it for the horrors the men locked up in here had inflicted on society, or for the way society had treated them?

'All right, Don?' the officer said. He nodded at Flora. A newspaper was folded under this arm.

'Yes, thanks, Ian.' Blackett pulled out the iron-and-canvas chair opposite Flora's and sat down at the small table. As though her sense had been sharpened by this proximity to the wilderness where men like him operated, she was acutely aware of his smell. The laundry scent of his shirt, the faint cling of institutional cooking, cigarette smoke.

The officer retreated to a chair against the wall at the side of the room, and unfolded his newspaper.

Blackett leaned towards Flora and she smelled, in addition, his aftershave lotion. There was something touching about the fact that he should have splashed himself with Old Spice before being led along the prison corridors to meet her. She studied his face in silence, looking for the marks of the beast and finding none. He was evil, she knew that. Pitiless, sadistic, cunning as a tiger. But she could see no traces of it in his guileless blue eyes, which matched almost exactly the blue shirt-stripes.

She cleared her throat, preparing to speak, to ask her

question, but he got in first. 'Thank you for coming, Mrs Treffyn,' he said. 'I'm grateful to you.'

She wanted to protest, demand that he not use her name, ask him what right he had to speak to her as though no darkness stretched between the two of them. 'I . . . uh—' She coughed a little. 'I came because of your letter. And because Beth Harding asked me to.'

'She told you exactly what *I* told you, I expect. That I didn't kill your sister.' Blackett's voice was neutral, not accented in any discernible way, soft and rather warm. She would not have placed him as a northerner if she hadn't known he came from Darlington.

'She said you were very insistent that you didn't.'

'That's right. And why should I lie?' He bent even further across the table towards her, his face so close that the officer snapped the pages of his newspaper in a manner they both took to be a warning. 'I've admitted the other murders. Except for the Lydney one. I've been tried and found guilty. I shan't be out of here for years, so I've got nothing to lose by telling the truth. Which is that I didn't – I did *not* – kill your sister.'

'Why should I believe you? They found your fingerprints in my house. In the kitchen, as well as in the sitting room. They found fibres which matched up with similar fibres on you.'

'I've never denied that I was there. Earlier that evening I was there. Georgie Flynn: I recognised her, soon as she opened the door. I'd heard her sing at Ronnie Scott's once. I'd got the Ragbags' tape: *'Falling Angel'* . . . I knew who she was. She invited me in, we started talking about Billie Holliday, she offered me a coffee. When she went into the kitchen to make it she asked me to come too, so I followed her.'

The image of them both in the kitchen cut across Flora's mind with the sharp clarity of a mirror. The yellow cupboards she had overpainted with leaves and grasses, the blue ceramic mugs from Portugal, the chrome taps, oranges in a green wooden bowl. She nodded, wanting him to continue.

'She said she was going to get married to someone in California, the guy that wrote the song for her. Jerry something, she said, he played with a group out there. She was excited about it, she talked a lot. She said she was interested in my charity, in Pakistan, that she'd been to India years ago, after she left school, and had been sickened by the poverty, and was happy to give money if it would make better lives for the people who lived there.'

'Yes,' Flora said faintly. Until now, she had completely forgotten Georgie's six-month trip to India. It seemed extraordinary that the gears of her memory should have been shifted by this killer. 'We know you were in the house, but the question is whether you killed her while you were there.'

'I didn't. She gave me a cheque – we prefer people to sign a three-year covenant but because she was going to the States to live, she said that would be too complicated to set up. And then the little . . . the little . . . little g-g-girl—' Blackett was stammering suddenly. The skin round his eyes grew pink, his eyes reddened as though he were about to weep.

'Not Matty.' Flora put both her hands flat on the edge of the table and half rose. The ghosts of his victims seemed to hover behind his head. Was that why Matty had been so disturbed? Was she trying to come to terms with memories of this man killing her mother? 'Please don't tell me that—'

'M-M-Matty,' Blackett said.

'*No!*' Flora said, loudly. 'You have no right.'

At the edge of the room, the officer put his paper down on the floor beside his chair and stood up. 'All right over there, Don?' he asked.

'F-f-fine,' Blackett said.

'Mrs Treffyn?'

Flora made a great effort. 'Yes, thank you.' The officer sat down again.

Blackett took several deep breaths. 'She couldn't sleep. She came wandering into the room, wanted to know what I was doing there.'

It was another picture Flora could clearly envisage. She couldn't look at him.

'You probably find that a repellent idea,' he said. 'The

innocent child and the multiple murderer.' His chin quivered with the effort he was making not to stammer.

'I do, since you mention it.'

'I only told you to show how impossible it would be for me to have killed your sister. After talking to her? After sitting next to the . . . to . . . to M-Matilda? She was so happy, your sister, so full of her plans to live in America.'

'She had a child and no husband. Isn't that the kind of woman you killed?' Flora was not worried by her brutality. This man had veered too sharply away from the accepted social norms to be concerned by conversational discourtesies.

'From time to time.' His mouth twitched slightly, as though he recognised that while there was nothing entertaining about the situation in which they found themselves, none the less he was amused. 'If I'd killed every woman I came across in a similar situation, there'd have been a sharp fall in single parent families, believe me.' He registered Flora's frozen expression and all trace of humour vanished. He held up one hand, the palm facing her as though he were taking an oath. 'Mrs Treffyn, you have to accept that I'm telling the truth. I did not murder Georgina Flynn.'

'And I say again: why should I believe you?'

'Because I've admitted the other murders. Because I've admitted being in the house on the day – so I discovered later – that she was murdered. What possible reason could I have for refusing to admit that I killed her too? What have I got to gain by lying about it?'

'I don't know.' He sounded so convincing. She had come here today for Georgie's sake, simply to prove to herself that Georgie's death had been avenged and the right man was behind bars. Now uncertainty confused her.

'Nothing. The answer is that I gain nothing. But if I could persuade you to accept what I say, then a terrible injustice to the memory of your sister could be put right. Because – don't you see? – if it wasn't me, then it has to be someone else. And whoever it was is out there right now, ready to kill again.'

'The police think you're lying.'

'That's what they're paid to do. And I can understand that.' He shook his head. 'When I first joined the charity, I would never in a million years have expected to find myself on the opposite side of the fence from the police. I've always believed in the concept of guardians of the law. The thin blue line. All that sort of thing. And on the whole, through this whole business, they've been pretty fair, given the way . . . the way things are. But you can see it's not in their interest to resurrect the Georgie Flynn case, even if it stays on the files. They've got other things to get on with, now that I've been put away. Why should they bother when they think they've got the right man? Except that they haven't.' He banged the side of his hand softly on the table for emphasis. 'I beg you to believe me, Mrs Treffyn. I did not kill your sister.'

'So who did? If I accept what you say, can you tell me who did? Who else but you, or someone like you, would want to kill her?'

'Someone like me,' he said softly. 'You think I'm a rarity, but believe me, there are plenty out there who have the same terrors, the same instincts, as I did – and still do. They're just better able to control them than I was, that's the only difference between me and all the hollow men out there walking the streets.'

Flora could see why Beth Harding had been so convinced that Blackett was innocent of Georgie's death. She herself was being drawn into the fly-trap of his persuasiveness. There seemed to be almost no malevolence in the man, merely a huge and wearying sadness. 'In the letter you wrote me, you spoke of growing up in a house where the light of love never shined,' she said, her voice low.

'Yes.' He looked agitated, as though even this far away, the traumas of childhood still haunted him. 'You can't begin to imagine—' The unfinished sentence fell softly into the room like the drifting petals of a flower. Behind him clouds scudded across a blue sky, bringing a reminder that spring was on its way. She could hear men's voices, a distant clang, a car engine revving outside the windows. 'I can,' she said. 'I truly can.'

He shook his head.

'Really. I mean it.' What could it matter whether he accepted the truth of what she said or not? 'My mother hated me.'

'Everybody thinks that when they're an adolescent. In my case, it was true.'

'And in mine.' Yet saying it, she wondered just how correct the statement was.

His smile was quizzical, disbelieving. 'You can't possibly have experienced the things I had to endure.'

'Endure,' Flora said. 'That's exactly what I did. I endured, because I knew that eventually, one day, I'd be free of her.'

'And are you?'

'I—' She broke off. Perhaps she never would be. Perhaps it was something she must learn to absorb, let it simply become part of her, rather than regarding it as an incubus which she constantly sought to cast off. 'One of these—' Flora stood up. So did Blackett.

'Don't leave it too late to do something about it.' He leaned towards her, putting both hands on the table between them, fingers splayed flat, thumbs over the edge. He lowered his voice. 'By the way, the coppers never got on to it,' he said, with a sideways glance at the prison officer. 'But there was someone else in the house that night.'

'What?'

'Someone else,' he repeated.

'Who? How do you know?'

'I don't know who it was, because I didn't see them. But after the . . . the little girl . . . little girl came in and had a bit of a cuddle with her . . . her . . . your sister—' His throat jerked, as though the words were bones lodged in his gullet.

Why did he find it so difficult to speak of Matty? Or was it young things themselves which disturbed him? He'd claimed to kill in order to spare other children what he'd endured himself as a child. 'After that, what?'

'She . . . um . . . Your sister took her to the door and gave her this kind of pat on the bottom and bent down, put her face right close and said something in her ear.'

'Said what?'

'Something about going upstairs to play with—' He shrugged. 'I didn't hear who with. Could have been one of her toys. Like, 'Go and play with Teddy.' Something like that. A name. She was laughing, you know, the way you do when you're saying something silly. A couple of times I thought I'd heard footsteps up there, someone walking about. And water running, as if they were having a bath or a shower.'

'How very convenient for you.' But it was true. In the cottage, footsteps in the bedrooms, however soft, were perfectly audible downstairs. As was the sound of water draining away from the bathroom.

'You don't have to believe me about that,' said Blackett impatiently. 'What about the other? Do you believe me or not?'

'I'll have to think about it.'

But in fact, he had convinced her. In spite of the terrible crimes he had committed, he had not killed Georgie. The more she reviewed the conversation with him, the more convinced she was of that fact though it was only a gut feeling, based on nothing tangible. She could not have produced any evidence, nor offered the kind of proof which would have satisfied the police. What astonished her as she drove home through the slate-grey afternoon was the fact that, despite the crimes Blackett had committed, she couldn't hate him. He was still a human being, a man who could laugh or cry, who ate and thought, made jokes, reacted to things as she herself did. In her mind, she had expected to find him separated from the rest of humanity. But he was just a man, as Bob Martyn had said months ago. Just an ordinary man.

She could see no reason why he should insist on his innocence except because it was true. Perhaps it was gullible of her to be swayed by detail, but the way he had described Georgie making coffee for him in the kitchen while they talked about Billie Holliday had only served to reinforce what he said. How could he have produced a knife and stabbed Georgie to death after that? The two images were impossible to reconcile.

Which left her with a dilemma. If she believed his innocence, she had to believe in someone's else guilt. But how was she to persuade the police of this, based only on the word of a murderer? Bob Martyn was not going to agree to reopen the investigation into Georgie's murder unless she could come up with new evidence that supported Blackett's innocence. Or someone else's guilt. But she had absolutely no idea how she was going to find that, nor even how to start looking. As for the suggestion that someone else was in the house, she was inclined to dismiss that as attention-seeking. If there really had been someone there that night, why had he waited until she was about to end the interview before mentioning it? Why hadn't he told the police? Or had he done so, but they hadn't bothered to follow it up?

The first thing, obviously, was to consider who else might have wanted Georgie dead, and why. And having once decided on that, to establish whether they had the means to do it. But even if she could produce an alternative theory, she did not have the competence, let alone the resources, to reinforce it. Nor did she know anyone who had. If she said anything to Oliver or Angus, they would simply laugh or, worse, be concerned, make it obvious that they considered her misguided or crazy. Yet the authenticity of Blackett's claim seemed to increase with every mile she put between her and the prison. And with it, the strength of his declaration that a man who was a murderer still roamed free. With Oliver still away, who could she talk to about it? Who might help her?

Back home, she went into the room at the back of the house which she used as her studio and looked at the angels on the walls. She was gathering new ones for a third book, painting them as they came into her head, knowing that once she had enough, her storyline would follow. There was one she had no recollection of drawing, an angle with a patchwork robe and stormy hair. It was then she remembered Beth Harding.

'It makes no difference to what Don's done,' Beth said. 'I'm fully aware of that. But I'm so very glad that you believe him.'

'Believing him means that we've got quite a problem on our hands. If it wasn't Blackett—'

'—Who was it?'

'Precisely.'

The two women were sitting in a stuffy little room at the top of the building which housed the headquarters of the charity for which Beth and Blackett had worked. It looked out over narrow back gardens separated from each other by sodden wooden fencing. Wet trees shuddered in the spasms of wind which gusted between the houses, reminding Flora that though spring might be coming, it was nonetheless still winter. Beth had responded with energy to Flora's phone call, and the two women had arranged to meet in London the following day. Flora had arrived in the morning and the two of them had walked round and round Hyde Park while Beth's questions drew out details of her sister and her family. Now, as the afternoon faded, they each sat with a paper cup of coffee in front of them, and tried to work out where they should go from here.

'I don't know enough about you or your sister, obviously,' Beth said. 'I can't offer any theories as to who could possibly have wished her dead. But perhaps if you just talked about her to me, you might come up with a suspect yourself.'

'But people *don't*,' Flora said helplessly. 'Commit murder, I mean.' She remembered Blackett's phrase about the hollow people out on the streets with murder in their hearts. 'There are times when we've all thought we could kill someone – I've done it myself – but that doesn't mean you go out and actually do it.'

'Except that in this case someone did.'

'Yes.'

'What about her fiancé?' probed Beth. 'Jerry.'

'Jerry Long. He was the first person I thought of, though God knows he couldn't be less like a murderer—'

'Any more than Don is.'

'But what possible reason could he have?'

'Didn't you say that he and your sister split up once before because he felt he wasn't ready to settle down with her? Maybe he still wasn't.'

'He wouldn't have had to *kill* her.' The idea was so bizarre that Flora actually found herself laughing.

'Or perhaps the responsibility of taking on another man's child started to weigh on him.'

'But in that case he'd just break it off. He wouldn't come over to England and murder her'

'He might have felt that he couldn't let her down a second time.'

'So rather than see her hurt, he takes a plane from California and stabs her to death? Oh, come on.' Flora was surrpised that she could discuss her sister's death with such objectivity. Over the past few days, it had changed from a personal trauma to a problem which had to be solved. There was no room for emotion.

'Put him down on your list. Maybe he'd taken out insurance on her. Or she on him. There could be all sorts of things we don't know about him. Maybe he'd met another woman, and Georgie was refusing to let him go.'

'Look, I know this man.'

'How well?'

'I've spent time with him. He's just not like that. Besides, Georgie was going to marry him.'

'She wouldn't be the first woman to have fallen for a bad apple. He's a musician, isn't he?'

'That doesn't make him more capable of murder than the rest of us.'

'No, but it does make him capable of putting on a performance.' Beth's wild hair glittered in the light of the desk lamp behind her chair. 'Now, who else might have wanted to kill her. What about someone in the band?'

'A quarrel, you mean? One of them hating her enough to kill her?'

'Why not?'

'Firstly, because none of them seem in the least homicidal. And secondly, if one of them hated her that much, she was leaving in a couple of weeks, anyway, and they'd be rid of her.'

'Revenge,' said Beth.

'What?'

'Suppose it wasn't enough for her to get away with whatever it was that had made them hate her. Suppose she'd damaged someone – not necessarily deliberately – and that person wanted her dead.'

'I don't know what you—'

'Suppose, for instance, she'd been having an affair with one of them, during this last tour of theirs, for instance. It might have affected a relationship back here in England, and the wife or girlfriend was determined to punish her for it.'

'It's possible – just. I suppose that might explain why there was no—' Flora broke off, embarrassed, unwilling to mention to Blackett's champion the sexual activity which Martyn had mentioned in the other cases.

'Put down the names of the people in the band,' Beth said.

Unwillingly, Flora did so. It seemed bizarre to be suspecting Georgie's friends of murder, but she could see that Beth's approach was necessary. If she was right, and Georgie had been having an affair with Frankie or Dave or one of the others, it would obviously provide a motive and a suspect. 'She met up again with Jerry Long on this last trip,' she said. 'It doesn't seem very likely that she'd have been playing around with one of the Ragbags as well.'

'It could have been a long-term thing. Or one of those on-again, off-again affairs. Write down the names of the wives and girlfriends, too. You never know. Maybe one of the guys is the father of your little niece: if you're insanely jealous and you find that your partner's had a child by another woman, that could be reason enough to kill someone. Now, what about your parents?'

'My *parents*? What possible—'

'Because by marrying Jerry, she would be taking their grandchild away. From what you've told me, they must have been aware that *you* didn't want to have children. Perhaps they saw Matilda as their only chance, and now she was going to be snatched away from them.'

'My parents—' Flora rolled her eyes. 'I haven't spoken to my mother since my sister's funeral. I don't even know where she is. Nobody does. As for my father: I hadn't seen him for over thirty years until he suddenly turned up on my doorstep a month ago.'

'Is that suspicious or what?'

'There *is* something odd about him,' conceded Flora. 'He claims to have been keeping an eye on my sister and me for years.' She hadn't believed it when he told her and, repeating it for Beth, believed it even less now.

'Put him on the list,' commanded Beth. 'And your mother as well.'

'This is ridiculous.'

'It's a starting point.' Beth picked up her cup. 'This coffee's absolutely vile, isn't it? Now, who else?'

'I don't know.'

'This Angus man: what about him? You said he used to know her. Or your former husband. Orlando—'

'Oliver. Why him?'

'He might have been in love with her and didn't want her to be happy with another man.'

Flora laughed to hide the sudden fear this possibility raised. 'That's a bit unlikely. He was living with another woman at the time. And Georgie didn't even like him very much. She thought he was far too dominating and selfish.'

'Is he?'

'A bit, I suppose. But not the way Georgie suggested he was. She thought he kept me under his thumb, didn't allow me to grow, but that wasn't true. Or at least, only as far as I was willing to go along with it. Which I was.'

'I see. I think. Now, what about that man you've mentioned several times? This birdwatching person. Gregor.'

'How on earth does he come into it? What motive could he possibly have for killing my sister?'

'It's a bit far-fetched, I agree, but for the moment, everybody who knew Georgie is a suspect.'

'He didn't know her. He only knew me.' Flora remembered with sudden vividness how Gregor had come down the wooden steps of the station footbridge, how she had told him that her sister would be alone in the house. There couldn't have been any connection between Georgie and Gregor, none at all.

'There *is* someone else,' she said. 'Someone was writing to Georgie in the months before she died.' She explained about the anonymous letters Georgie had been sent which she had handed over to the police. 'Not that they'd be much help in finding him if we got them back. He didn't put his address on them. From something Georgie said, I think he was from up north, but that's about the only thing we know about him. The police didn't look into him, obviously, because they thought Blackett was the man, but if he wasn't—'

'He has to be a suspect.' Beth pulled Flora's notebook across the table and looked down at the names written down. 'There's certainly enough to be going on with.'

'How exactly *do* we go on?' Flora enquired. 'We can't just walk up and ask them if they murdered Georgie.'

'We can start by finding out where they were on the night in question.' Beth reached across and touched Flora's hand. 'Don't worry. They've probably all got perfectly good alibis and we can eliminate them from our enquiries. Then we extend our investigation further. But it's always a good idea to start with people your sister knew. As I'm sure you're aware, ninety-eight percent of all murders are committed between people who know each other. And as you know, whoever it was that killed her, she did let the person in, that night. There was no forced entry.'

'How do you know so much about all this stuff?'

Beth laughed. Stretching her arms in front of her, she laced her fingers together. The lamp on the bookcase behind her showed up gold highlights in her hair. 'I don't really. But there's not much night-life in Pakistan, so when we go back after being on leave, we tend to take suitcases full of second-hand paperbacks with us. Mostly crime fiction.'

'Let me get this absolutely right,' Flora said. 'We're going to approach my mother and my father, my former husband and some of my closest friends, and ask them where they were when my sister was killed, on the offchance that one of them was responsible?'

'It shouldn't be too difficult. And when they've told us, we can discreetly check it out. Once we've proved to our satisfaction that it was none of them, we start the second line of enquiry, which will be much more difficult.' Beth's vivid gaze rested on Flora's face. 'You *are* convinced, aren't you, that it wasn't Don?'

'Not entirely. But enough to see that it's worth making an effort to see who else might have done it if not him. It certainly won't hurt to check elsewhere, though I'm not thrilled about this list. I mean, I'm not that fond of my mother, but I find it difficult to go along with the idea that she could be a murderer.'

'We don't really believe she is, do we?' said Beth quietly. 'And if, for instance, we discover that she was on stage somewhere that night, it would mean she couldn't have done it and we can strike her off the list.'

'She could have hired someone to do it for her, of course,' Flora said, twisting her mouth at such a ridiculous notion. 'You read about that sort of thing in the paper.'

'We can fall back on that. Meanwhile, we've got to question these people so we can eliminate them.'

'How are we going to do that? I can't imagine casually asking. If one of them is guilty, he – or she – would know immediately that something was up. They might take steps to cover their tracks and then we'd never be able to pin anything on them.'

'It's a bit tricky, I know. But if you remember, I originally suggested a private detective. It probably wouldn't take a professional very long to at least check alibis.'

'Jane Glass,' Flora said suddenly.

'Who's she?'

'She's a reporter I met.' Quickly Flora explained the circumstances. 'If she'd be willing to help us, she'd have exactly the right cover. She could say she was writing a feature on the case – or even a book. She could easily ask them. You know: something along the lines of everybody remembering where they were when Kennedy was murdered and I've no doubt you'll always remember where you were the night that your . . . your daughter or your friend or your colleague was killed. And then, when they've told her, we can check up on it.'

'And if there's any discrepancy, we could look into it further.' Beth grinned. 'That's a great idea!'

'But won't the police already have checked out alibis for Georgie's friends?'

'Did they ask you for names?'

'Yes.'

'They probably checked them out in a cursory way. Don't forget that they thought it was—' Beth pressed her lips together for a moment, '—it was Don who killed her, so they probably weren't as thorough as they might have been.'

'I'll give this Jane Glass a ring – I've got her card in my wallet.'

Jane Glass's appearance had deteriorated considerably in the three or four months since her last meeting with Flora. She had lost weight, and her hair seemed very much in need of a wash. There were stains on the black trousers she wore, and a button missing from her coat. She had agreed to come to the charity headquarters and now sat opposite them both, a sad figure.

'It's a very good idea' she said. Some animation had come into her face as Flora and Beth outlined their proposals. 'I've been thinking of writing something about my sister's death, and about the other women who were terrorised by the guy who killed her. Fiction, a crime novel, that sort of thing. Doing this: it would be like research. And it would give me something to . . . It would be therapeutic.'

'And as a reporter, presumably you're good at questioning people,' Beth said.

'Yes – and at sussing them out.' A tic jumped in Jane's eyelid. 'I mean, if any of them starts acting shifty, I'll be able to tell. I've interviewed a number of politicians in my time and you can't get much shiftier than them, believe me. Bloody eels, the lot of them.'

Flora had a number of reservations about joining forces with a woman who sometimes seemed perilously close to mental breakdown. But there was no doubting the professionalism with which Jane approached the matter of interviewing the people on the list that Beth and she had drawn up. In addition, she recognised that the two women were going to need help, and that she was someone who could provide it.

'Obviously we'll pay for your time,' Flora said.

'Absolutely,' agreed Beth. 'My charity's set aside some money to covcr costs.'

'Keep it for the people who need it most,' said Flora. 'There's money in my bank account at the moment, and my sister left me some, too. Obviously, most of it is for Matty, but there's still some to spare.'

'I'll do it for nothing,' said Jane. When she smiled, she looked like a different creature. 'But I wouldn't mind being paid my expenses. I won't overcharge you, and I'll produce an invoice so you can see what I've done. It might only be a few hours' work. I'm going to need names and addresses and any background information you can give me on any of these people. And when do you want me to report back to you?'

'Telephone me when you've got something,' Flora said. 'We'll set up another meeting then.'

That evening, she listened to a concert on the radio while she ate supper. Some Bach, some Handel. And then an aria from

Julius Caesar, sung by Grigori Angelos, the man who would be singing on the Russian opera tour next year. Angelos was the Greek word for messenger: as the magnificent, androgynous voice soared, she wondered what message it had for those who heard it. That thought led on to Oliver. She missed him and wished he would come home. It was time to start a new life. To begin again.

Jane Glass's defeated air had vanished, replaced by a crisp efficiency. Even her appearance had changed: she had cut her hair, and was wearing a confident suit of red wool, with a silk blouse underneath. She sat across the table from Flora and Beth, as though she were about to address a meeting. In front of her was a clipboard with a number of sheets of typescript attached.

'As you can imagine, there was a bit of an attitude problem at first. It wasn't easy to get these people to talk to me,' she began. 'When I told them I wanted to write a book about the Cotswold Murders, they seemed to think I was some kind of ghoul, out to make money from someone else's tragedy.' With one hand she fiddled with the buttons on her blouse. 'In the end, I decided to approach it from a different angle. I told them about my own circumstances, about my sister's death. They were much more cooperative after that.'

'The freemasonary of the bereaved,' said Beth.

'Could be.'

'So. Did you discover anything useful?' asked Flora.

'Not a lot. But definitely something. Though you may not like it, Flora.'

Flora took a breath. What skeleton was about to pop out from which cupboard? She wondered how her life had become so complicated. Let me go back to where I was, she thought. To my limited but contented life on my own, before Georgie got pregnant and everything changed.

'I haven't been able to contact everyone yet,' Jane was saying. 'Neither of your parents, Flora, for a start. You gave me your dad's address, but he was never home. And I called your mother's agent, but he said he hadn't been able to get hold of her for ages, which was irritating because two or three good parts had come up.'

'How long is "ages"?'

'He thought a year or so. At least nine months. I even rang your former mother-in-law, like you said, and she told me the same thing. Nobody's heard anything of Jessica Glanville since she dropped out of *Hedda Gabler* when your sister was killed, apart from a tour in Scotland a year ago.'

'That's a bit odd, isn't it?' said Beth. 'An actress not keeping in touch with her agent?'

Flora frowned. 'I don't know enough about my mother to know if it's odd or not.' But Beth was right. She should have wondered long before this why Jessica hadn't tried to visit Matty. Especially when she had disappeared so completely that even Marguerite Treffyn, for all her computer wizardry, couldn't track her down. Flora had learned this only last week, in the course of a conversation when Marguerite had telephoned to ask how Matty was. She had gone on to ask whether Flora had made up her differences with her mother and if so, could she provide an address where Jessica could be got hold of?

'I believe she's moved,' Flora had told her.

'Any idea where to?'

'No. But my father—'

'You're in touch with Rupert?'

'Yes.'

'After all this time? Oh, my dear, that's marvellous. I'm so pleased.'

'Me, too,' said Flora, though she was not entirely sure what her reaction to her new-found father was.

'I'd love to hear all about it, Flora. But at the moment, I have an article to write and I really would like to check a few facts with your mother.'

'I can't help you, I'm sorry.'

'I tried her agent but he said she hadn't been in touch for ages. He said he had money waiting to be paid, but didn't know where she was. Flora—'

'Yes?'

'How long is it since you last saw Jessica? Or heard of her?'

'Nine months or more,' Flora had said, after some thought. She was instantly ashamed, remembering that she had promised herself she would keep in touch with her mother, would share Matty with her.

Now, she stared at the two younger women. How could so much time have elapsed? Where had her mother gone? If she wasn't acting, what was she living on? Even if she had no desire to see her elder daughter, why had she made no attempt to visit Matty? Was it because the child was now living with someone Jessica knew to be antagonistic to her? Straightening her shoulders as though preparing for battle, Flora said firmly: 'She can't really have disappeared.'

'Your father did,' said Jane. There was no need for her to add that she thought the Flynns were a decidedly strange family; it was obvious from her voice.

'He went to the States, and then worked in Europe. It's not quite the same thing.'

'Perhaps that's what your mother's done too.'

'Why should she?'

'Why shouldn't she?' Beth put in. 'You often hear of English people – writers, pop groups, actors and so on – who are huge hits in other countries whereas we've hardly heard of them here.'

'Maybe. But surely she would have contacted me.' But even as she spoke the words, Flora knew it was not true. The relationship between mother and daughter was such that Jessica would have felt no obligation to tell Flora of her movements. Nor did Flora believe that Jessica would have gone to work abroad, when there seemed to be plenty of opportunities for her here. Her uneasiness grew. Oliver had pointed out that just as she had lost a sister, so Jessica had lost a daughter. Georgie's death must be as devastating and traumatic for her as it was for Flora. What might such a trauma have caused her mother to do? How could she have let so long go by without trying again to contact her? Suicide: the word crossed her mind like an ugly shadow. But she'd have heard, someone would have told her, it would have been in the papers. Before she allowed herself to sink into a trough of guilt, reason asserted itself. There was nothing to stop Jessica contacting Flora, if she wished. Therefore, she presumably did not want to do so. And God knew how many times, Flora thought, she herself had tried to get in touch with her.

She remembered the last conversation she had had with Jessica, almost a year ago. As always, her mother's voice had been remote. 'I thought I should congratulate you on your literary success,' she said. There had been no greeting, no preliminaries of the How-are-you-I'm-just-fine-and-you? kind.

'Thank you.'

'I hadn't realised how talented you were. I know you went to art college but I never saw any of your work.'

'No.' Because at that time, Flora never came home, except occasionally to visit Georgie if she knew that Jessica was elsewhere.

'How is my granddaughter?' Jessica had continued.

'Very well.'

'I'd have thought she would have been traumatised, to say the least.'

She is, desperately, Flora should have said. But Jessica's voice was so cool, so aloof, that the words withered. Why couldn't she have been given a warm, loving mother, instead of this icy creature on the other end of the phone? 'She seems all right. Nightmares now and then.'

'You suffered from nightmares when you were that age,' said Jessica.

'Perhaps it's part of childhood. Oliver's been wonderful with—'

'Who?'

'Oliver.' When there was no response, Flora added: 'My former husband.'

'I know who you mean,' Jessica said. 'In what way is Oliver being wonderful?'

'Mainly by being around a lot. I'm sure it helps to have a father figure.'

'That would rather depend on the father figure, wouldn't it?' Jessica's voice held the sarcastic note which Flora had so hated as a child. Now, as then, it made her belligerent.

'What's that supposed to mean?' she demanded.

'Nothing at all.'

'Look, I know Georgie despised Oliver, and she obviously must have said something negative about him to you—'

'I'm perfectly capable of forming my own opinions.'

'—But I love him, and he's a marvellous father to Matty and I'm probably going to end up married to him again.' She said it defiantly, though until then she had not made a decision one way or another.

'Good for you,' her mother said, and her air of indifference brought back to Flora all the turmoil of being Jessica's unloved daugher.

'Oh, mother.' It was pointless quarrelling. It was pointless hoping for something other. 'I wish you liked me.' And gently she had laid down the phone.

Almost a year ago, Flora thought worriedly. That's such a long time. Where is she?

Jane had continued her briefing. 'I went through Georgie's address book and the names in the diary you gave me, Flora. There wasn't much there, actually. I visited the ones who weren't too far from London and telephoned the others. On the night Georgie died, most of them seem to have been watching television with their other halves. I know they could have been lying, but in my judgement, they weren't. There are still three people I haven't been able to get in touch with yet, but I'll keep trying.' She flipped over a sheet of typewritten paper and put her finger at the top of the next sheet. 'Any questions so far?'

Yes, Flora wanted to say. What are you doing? This is my life you're dissecting as though it were a body on a mortuary slab. My life and Georgie's. Stop. Leave it. Instead, she shook her head. 'Go on.'

'If you think about it,' said Jane, 'the person who killed your sister is probably not someone from the address book.'

'Why not?'

'It's more likely to be someone she's had dealings with in the recent past. Most of the people in her address book had been in there for a while.'

'How do you know?'

'Because the writing's different. The entries in her diary are from this year, and the writing's much looser and more relaxed than in the address book. I don't know a lot about it, but I did once research an article on handwriting experts for one of the colour supplements, and I learned that your writing gets more assured, more flowing, as you get older.' She smoothed the pages in front of her. 'Because of that, we can assume that if it was someone in the address book who wanted to kill her, they could have done so ages ago.'

'That makes sense,' Beth said.

'Maybe,' said Flora. 'What about if she'd had a recent quarrel with an old friend, rather than a new one?'

'That's a possibility, but for the moment, I need to make some preliminary eliminations.' Jane pursed her mouth, as though she disliked having her reasoning questioned.

'All right,' Flora said. 'Go on.'

Jane gave a managing director's cough. 'After the address book, I moved on to the guys in Georgie's band. The Ragbags. All but one of them knew exactly where they'd been the night your sister died. Frankie was at home minding the children while his wife was out with her bowling group. Dave and some mates were watching a football match in his local pub. Two of the others – Bill and Gus – went to France together: Gus's sister works in Calais, and they wanted to get the duty-free. The only one who seemed a bit dodgy was Paul Hapgood.'

'Who's he?' said Flora.

'The one with the shaved head and the earrings.'

'That's Spick.' It came as something of a surprise to learn that he had a real name.

'Is it? I dunno. He answered to the name of Paul in a perfectly civilised manner. He said he *thought* he was at the cinema that night, that he'd gone to see *Clueless*. Then, when I pushed him, he said he was *definitely* there. He went on his own, he said, but if you want my opinion, he wasn't there at all.' Jane glanced in turn at the other two. 'He was being evasive. I could tell. Wouldn't meet my eyes, stumbled a bit. I'm sure he's seen the movie, but I'd be prepared to bet that it wasn't that night. He was definitely worried by my question. So much so that I started to wonder what exactly he *was* doing that night.'

'I just can't believe he could have had anything to do with it. He comes down here quite a lot to visit Matty and me – he always seems so gentle,' Flora said.

'From the way he reacted when I mentioned your sister, I think the two of them were almost certainly an item at some point,' said Jane. 'Did she ever say anything about him to you?'

'Never.' But even as she spoke, Flora began speculating. It was perfectly possible that Georgie had been having an affair with Spick. There was no reason why she shouldn't: both of them were free and, working together over the years, they'd obviously spent a lot of time together. He was younger than she was, but that wouldn't have mattered.

'There were photographs of her all over the place when I got to his flat,' Jane continued. 'Taped up on the wall, or framed. Some of her alone, but a lot of the two of them together. And though the other guys were obviously very upset by what had happened to Georgie, this Paul bloke was distraught. I mean, he was really out of it. He even started to cry at one point.'

'In that case, why would he have wanted to kill her? What would his motive be?'

'Suppose they're in love, having an affair, whatever, like Jane says,' said Beth. Flora found her eagerness almost ghoulish: again she repressed the urge to tell them to stop, to leave the matter where it now lay.

'Go on,' said Jane, magisterially.

'Then, on this last tour in the States, Georgie meets up again with her old flame, Jerry Long, and throws Spick over, announces she's getting married, and thanks a lot but no thanks. He's hurt, humiliated, angry. He knows she going to be staying with you in the Cotswolds, and there's this very handy local murderer around. Then he finds out that she's going to be alone one evening, so he comes down, she lets him in, not suspecting anything, and—'

'He lives in a basement flat in Muswell Hill, on his own,' Jane said. 'He could easily have driven down and back: he's got a motorbike, and I know he's also got a car, a Peugeot 205, because I asked him. And when he got back, at that time of night in London – it needn't have been very late – who's going to notice a car parking outside, or car doors slamming?' She tugged gently at the middle button on her blouse, which was loose.

'Didn't you say your sister's never admitted who the father of the little girl is?' said Beth. 'Maybe it's him. Spick.'

It was certainly possible, given the late nights the two of them must have shared, the high after playing to an audience, and afterwards the booze and smokes. Flora remembered Georgie saying that she'd been taken by surprise. If Spick was Matty's father – or suspected that he might be – it would certainly explain his visits, his particular tenderness with the little girl. She'd never noticed any likeness between the two of them, but then she hadn't been looking. She asked: 'Even if he was Matty's father, why should he want to kill Georgie?'

'Perhaps he wasn't too keen on the idea of another man bringing up his child,' Jane said. 'He wanted Matty here, where he could see more of her.'

'That's a bit far-fetched,' said Flora, sounding more certain than she felt. 'As if anyone in his right mind would commit murder for such a reason—'

'Maybe he's *not* in his right mind,' suggested Jane.

'Or maybe he adores the little girl so much he just couldn't stand the idea of not having her close by.'

'If he adores her, the last thing he's going to do is deprive her of her mother.'

'Not necessarily.'

'That's utterly ridiculous.'

'No, it's not.'

'Who else did you see?' Beth asked hastily, before Jane and Flora could square up to each other.

Jane clucked her tongue against her teeth to indicate exasperation before turning the pages on her clipboard with unnecessary vigour. 'I spoke on the phone to Jerry Long, out in California. He told me exactly where he was that night, even gave me a couple of names I could call who'd confirm it. Which I did. In fact I only rang one of them: the manager of the club in San Francisco where his group was playing that night. It seemed about as conclusive proof as one could need that the guy was there, and therefore couldn't have secretly hopped on a plane to England to dispose of his fiancée.'

'What about the band's wives and girlfriends?'

'I checked them all. One was there with her husband when I spoke to him. That was Frankie's wife.'

'You said she was out bowling the night my sister was killed.'

'I verified that, too.' Jane grinned. 'I'd make an ace detective! She was gone three hours, and there was a entire team of women to confirm she was with them the whole time. And incidentally, that also left Frankie in the clear: he couldn't have left his kids on their own all that time, even if he'd had time to drive down to your house, do the deed and get back before his wife came home.'

'Particularly if you remember that Don was there in your house, Flora, between seven-thirty and nine,' Beth pointed out.

Flora nodded silently. She was being taken over by these two strangers. She felt like a leaf blowing in the wind; any minute she would pull clear of the branch to which she clung and be wafted away into nowhere. A vision of the beach at Gran's house came to her: the brittle air, the shining beach, the low whistle of wind through the sea thistles. If only she could go back, relive her life, change things.

'Dave's then girlfriend – they split up two weeks ago, so it was nothing to do with Georgie – was at her mum's the night Georgie was killed. I confirmed that, too—'

'You've really been thorough,' Beth said admiringly.

Jane pulled at the loose button of her blouse. 'The other two in the band are gay, according to Frankie, so even if they hadn't been in France, not only would they not have been interested in Flora's sister in the first place, but they didn't have girlfriends who might have been jealous enough to kill her. Which leaves us with Mr Paul Hapgood. Spick. He didn't have a girlfriend then, he said. And doesn't now. Which is kind of strange if you think about it: a youngish hetero guy like that, nice-looking in spite of the haircut, unattached, in the kind of profession where girls throw themselves at you. He's got lovely eyes: I almost fancied him myself. Plus there was his shifty behaviour.'

'So he definitely has to go down on our shortlist,' said Beth.

'I think so, don't you, Flora?'

'What about the other people you spoke to?' Flora said, avoiding the question.

Jane glanced down at her clipboard. 'I called on Philip Chapman and his partner.'

'Dodie,' Flora said.

'Right. They were in London at a dinner party that night. He admitted, when the partner – Dodie – went out to get coffee, that he'd had a fling with Georgie, years ago, but it hadn't lasted for very long. He asked me not to mention it in front of her. I asked if he'd seen Georgie after shacking up with, um, Dodie, and he went all red and embarrassed. A bit of a Jack the lad, I thought.'

'He is, yes,' Flora said.

'Well, that particular night, he wasn't on the prowl, being otherwise engaged. Then . . . I spoke to Angus Macfarlane.' Jane stared significantly at Flora.

'And what did you discover?' Flora said. Her heart began

to pound and sweat prickled in her armpits. What now? What was Jane going to say?

'Not only did Mr Macfarlane not have an alibi, but he was extremely hostile and irritable when I asked him where he was that night. I got some very clear vibes: wherever he was, he didn't want to talk about it.'

'So what?' Flora said defensively, as though she herself were being accused of something. 'Why should he?'

'He *claimed* he couldn't remember where he was that night, but if he's as close to you as you told us, he must do.'

'Why should he?'

'When he first heard the news about your sister, he'd have thought back, wondered what he was doing while poor Georgie was being killed. He *must* have. It's human nature. On top of that, I also picked up on the fact that he'd once known Georgie pretty well.'

'There's no crime in that,' said Flora. 'They were both involved with bands, even if Angus's is only amateur.' Had Angus continued to see Georgie after he'd come on to her, Flora? She remembered the first time she'd gone out with him, how he'd said that Georgie was tall and beautiful, impossible to miss, whereas she . . . Anyway, he told me himself.' Flora tried not to show the hurt which had started up inside her.

'Would you put him on the shortlist?' asked Beth.

'I think we have to.' Jane looked down at her lists. 'Moving on, there's this Gregor person you mentioned, but since you don't seem to have a phone number or address for him, not even—' Jane examined her notes again, '—a surname, I obviously couldn't get in touch with him.'

'I don't know his surname or where he lives, though I might be able to find a post office box number,' Flora said. That was if Gregor was still advertising in the birdwatching magazines. They always seemed to meet by chance. Next time, she would have to make sure she got his phone number. 'Besides, as I said before, as far as I'm aware, he never met my sister and had absolutely no connection with her whatsoever.'

Beth became brisk. 'So, of the first wave of suspects, the

people Flora knows who knew Georgie, we've got the three from the address book that you haven't yet contacted, we've got Flora's parents, we've got Paul Hapgood and we've got Angus Macfarlane.'

'Right.'

Flora resented the way the two of them were playing detectives with her life even though she knew that they had no choice. Once they'd accepted Don Blackett's innocence in the matter of Georgie's death, how else were they to find other suspects, in the first instance, except by looking closely at friends and relatives?

'Next we have to investigate the people Georgie knew but I didn't,' she said. 'I can't really be much help there; my sister and I led very different lives.'

'I thought of that already,' Jane said. 'I took my tape recorder along and asked all the people I spoke to who else she might have known, or had any kind of dealings with. Also asked which of them, if any, she might have got up the nose of. In other words, who might have wanted to kill her from sheer rage or even hatred. I got another list of names and got in touch with the people on it. Nearly all of them have been eliminated, because they were somewhere else at the time.'

Flora could not rid herself of Jane's description of Angus being hostile and defensive. And without an alibi. There was absolutely no reason why he should have had one, she told herself, nor why, whether he had or not, he should talk to some complete stranger who showed up without warning. For years, almost as long as she'd known him, she had taken for granted Angus's fondness – perhaps even his love – for her. It had glowed somewhere in the background of their relationship, warming her when she was her lowest ebb, something she could always rely on for comfort. She thought of him at Christmas, on New Year's Eve, the way his eyes had rested on her, the expression on his face. Perhaps he had grown tired of waiting. Perhaps he'd been with another woman the night Georgie died and didn't want her to know, in case she was hurt. What form had his hostility to Jane taken, anyway?

Maybe she was exaggerating. Maybe he'd simply been a bit brusque. Flora had seen him that way once or twice, when business was going badly or some commission he'd hoped for fell through.

'Much as I don't like the idea, it does seem as if one of the Ragbags is our best bet,' she said, shaking herself loose of such thoughts.

'I agree,' said Jane. 'Especially since it had happened so soon after they got back from the States. Maybe one of them was narked about losing their singer, just when the *"Falling Angel"* cassette was doing so well.'

'Was it?' said Flora.

'Didn't you know?' Jane raised her eyebrows. 'It got into the top twenty while they were in the States. Perhaps they were pissed off that she was running out on them, just when they were beginning to hit the big time.'

'I imagine things get pretty tense when you're on a tour like that,' Beth was saying. 'Bound to, when you're together, day in, day out, for three months on end. Perhaps Georgie had clashed with one of the guys in the band. A personality problem. I know what it can get like when we're doing our tour of duty in Pakistan, and we at least have time to get away from each other, which the band – the Ragbags – wouldn't have had.'

Selfish, self-obsessed, that's me, Flora was thinking. Too preoccupied with the success of the angel book to bother about Georgie's achievements, too concerned with my own problems and grievances to give a thought to anyone else. What kind of a sister had she been to Georgie? There was only one answer to that: a lousy one. 'Did any of them mention anything like that?' she said, her voice unsteady.

'No,' said Jane, 'But I didn't specifically ask them.'

'Wht about the anonymous letter writer I told you about?'

'Frankie said your sister was getting pretty stressed out towards the end of the tour. By then, the letters were arriving nearly every day. Sometimes they'd even be waiting for her when the band showed up for the next gig, either in their motel or at the venue where they were playing.'

'Did he say what they were about? The ones I found in my sister's flat were fairly standard, according to the police.' Flora tried to remember what the five letters had said. Georgie herself had described them as insinuating that she and the writer of the letters had a relationship, were lovers. 'Not particularly menacing.'

'According to Frankie, they were getting increasingly raunchy and threatening. So much so that in the end, he'd told their road manager to pick them up before Georgie could.'

'What kind of threatening?' Beth asked.

'Calling her a slag, saying she was his and if she thought she could go off with someone else, she was mistaken, he'd see to it that she didn't. He said if he couldn't have her, nobody could, all the things these nutters usually write. In the two or three weeks before they came home, he'd moved on to stuff like, even if you try to come back to me now, it's too late, you've ruined what we had, I wouldn't have you back, you must be punished for what you've done to me, that sort of macho crap. Or so Frankie said.'

'From what Frankie's saying, it's sound as though this guy was getting more and more obsessed. How would you ever track someone like that down?' asked Flora.

'If Frankie came with us, backed us up,' said Beth, 'wouldn't we have enough reason to convince the police that Don's not the one who did it? Or at least get them to look into it some more?'

'But how do we find out who he was? The letters in her flat didn't have any address on them, and the signature was illegible.'

'I've got a theory about it,' Jane said. She looked across at the other two and straightened her papers. 'It was his odd behaviour which got me wondering in the first place, and the more I thought about it, the better it fitted.'

'What did?' demanded Beth. 'Who're you talking about?'

'Spick. Paul Hapgood. Look at it logically. How could an anonymous nutcase have known what the band's itinerary was? I mean, he could have done, but only with a lot of difficulty. Whereas Spick knew exactly where they'd be next, *and* what motel they'd be staying at, so he could send the letters in advance. On top of that, if they were having an affair, him and Georgie, like Beth suggested, naturally he's going to be pretty hacked off when she and Jerry Long decide to get married. And there's the question of Matty. I nicked one of the photos of him and Georgie together, when he wasn't looking.' Jane lifted the papers on her board and pulled out a snapshot which had been tucked beneath them. 'What do you think, Flora? You're the only one who could say whether there's any likeness between him and the little girl.'

Flora looked down at Georgie's face. Her hair was flipped over to one side of her head and tied with a chiffon rag. She nestled against Spick, who stood with his arm round her shoulder, gazing proudly at the camera. Both of them were laughing. Behind them were the vague shapes of other people, tables with glasses on them, the glint of something which caught the light from the camera's flash. Did she recognise any similarity to Matty? 'I can't say,' she said, handing back the photograph. 'His eyes are a different colour, and his face is screwed up with laughter, so it's impossible to tell.' Seeing his face, however, brought him into sharper focus in her mind. Certainly, when he held Matty on his knee, they had seemed amazingly close: it was something she'd noticed several times. But a physical resemblance? She tried to remember. 'No,' she repeated. 'I can't say.'

'If it was him who murdered Georgie,' said Beth, 'maybe someone saw his car in the neighbourhood. Now we know what he drives, it might be easier to pin it down.'

'Couldn't we ask the police?' Flora asked.

'We could,' Jane said. 'Whether they'd tell us is another matter. My family had a hard enough time getting all the facts about my own sister's murder.'

'I could ask Bob Martyn. He worked on the murders for years.'

'I can almost guarantee you'll get nowhere,' said Beth. 'I

tried, believe me. So did the director of my charity, Peter Sharman. We went to see the officers who'd been in charge of the case but they couldn't have cared less. They listened very politely. Wrote down what we said. But basically they didn't want to know, even when we pointed out that Don hadn't been charged with your sister's murder. They just kept on saying they weren't looking for anyone else in connection with the case.'

Jane cleared her throat. 'There are two other people I haven't mentioned.'

'Who're they?'

'Oliver Treffyn. And—' Jane hesitated. 'Flora herself.'

'What?'

'*Me*?'

'It seems to me that the motives for both of you might be the same as for Spick.'

'Nonsense. Rubbish.' Heart pounding, Flora pushed back her chair. 'If I had anything to do with it, why would I have contacted either of you?' She glared at them both. 'And if either of you think I could possibly be involved in the murder of my own sister, then you shouldn't be here talking to me.'

'Calm down,' Beth said. 'Nobody's accusing you of—'

'There's nothing I can say to convince you, but – and however much I loved Matty, I could not possibly—' Flora's throat was dry with the intensity of her emotion. 'I was in my hotel that night.'

'What about Oliver?'

'Everything that goes for me goes for him too.'

'How can you be sure?'

'Because I know him. As well as I know myself.' She thought about how much she had learned about her own psyche in the past couple of years. 'Better, in fact.'

'Well, since he's away, there's not much we can do about him. But when he comes back, I'll certainly talk to him.'

'He's not a violent man. Nobody in the world would be less likely to do Georgie any harm. And depriving a child of her mother is the worst thing anyone could do: Oliver *adores* Matty, he'd never do the slightest thing to hurt her.'

'Fine.' Jane lifted both hands in the air. 'I believe you.'

As she wrote out a cheque for Jane, and thanked her for the hard work already done, kissed Beth goodbye, Flora could hardly restrain her impatience to be getting away from London. Her car was waiting for her at the station and she pulled away, soothed by the familiar smell of the upholstery, the firmness of the steering wheel in her hands. Driving down the High Street, she went past the red-brick house where Angus had his office. On a whim, she pulled into the small hard-topped parking space behind it. She had plenty of time: Matty wouldn't need picking up until teatime.

This was the very first time she had initiated a meeting between the two of them. She had always waited for him to suggest a time and a place, or to drop in to her house. He must think she didn't really care about him; she knew that if she'd lost his friendship, it was her own fault. She went in through the wide carved front door and asked the receptionist where he was.

'Down the passage, third on the right,' the girl called after her. 'But he's on—'

Flora was already knocking on the door of Angus's office. His voice told her to come in. He was standing by the window, talking on the phone. When he saw her, he said quietly into the receiver: 'I'll call you back later.'

'Was that another woman?' Flora said, trying to make it sound like a joke. Seeing his familiar face, the way it crinkled when he smiled, she was suddenly awkward. Why was she interrupting a man during his working hours, a man she'd kept at arm's length for years on end, a man, moreover, whom she had cheerfully ignored when Oliver was around? Was it because she couldn't bear to believe Jane Glass's insinuations that Angus might be the person behind Georgie's death?

'As a matter of fact, yes, it was.' Angus said. He crossed the room with brisk steps and kissed her cheek.

'Do you love her?' The words were out before Flora could stop herself.

'Yes, I do. Very much indeed.'

'Oh.' Flora bit her lip. 'I see.'

Angus held her by the arms. 'This is unlike you, Flo, bursting into my office, asking personal questions.'

'It is, yes, I know.' Flora looked round. 'Have you got five minutes?'

'I've got as long as you want. Tea?'

'Yes, that would be nice, thank you.' She sat down on a black leather upright chair and leaned her arm along the black ash surface of his desk, wishing she had not surrendered to impulse. She thought of the few times they had slept together, how good it had been, how desirable he always made her feel, whereas with Oliver, lovemaking was more a matter of two people sating their appetites with each other. 'Do you have other women, Angus?'

'Oh dear. What's this all about?'

'Do you sleep with other women than me?'

'What do you think, Flora?'

She sighed, dropping her tense shoulders. 'That you do.'

'And?'

'And why shouldn't you? You're handsome, virile, lovable.'

'Quite right.'

'Naturally you have other women. Were you with one the night Georgie was killed?'

'Flora, I have absolutely no intention of answering such a loaded question.'

'But you're so—' She broke off.

'So what?'

So dear to me, so precious . . . It had seemed important to tell him so, yet, now that she was here, she could not do so. Especially when Oliver would be back from Moscow next week. She looked down at the polished grain of the wood, frowned, bit her lip. She had been too precipitate, too eager.

'Flora, my love. What is it?'

'I don't know. I just felt I had to . . . see you, I suppose. Reassure myself.'

'Of what?'

'About you.'

He seemed astonished. 'What's that mean?'

'Oh—' She couldn't say that she'd wanted to see for herself whether he looked like a murderer. '—' Just that you were here.'

'I'll always be here, Flora.'

She couldn't meet his eyes. 'I've no right. Especially if you're in love with somebody else.'

'Am I?'

'Aren't you?'

'Aren't *you*?' He laughed again. Took her hands in his. 'Last time I had a conversation like this, I was seventeen years old and had just been stood up by the school vamp. Melanie Hastings. I remember her well. God, how miserable she made me.'

The door of the office opened as the receptionist came in with a tray. Someone in another office was listening to the radio. As the girl poured tea for them both, the sound of someone singing a Handel aria came drifting towards them. The voice which filled the air seemed neither male nor female; all three of them listened in silence for a moment, the receptionist with the teapot suspended in midair, Angus with his head on one side, Flora remembering innocence, remembering those shiny, polished days by the sea and Gran, singing.

Then Angus said: 'Where's that music coming from, Terry?'

'I don't know, Mr Macfarlane. There's no one in the offices at the moment: they're not back from lunch yet.'

Angus stood. 'Stay here, Flora, I'll just go and check that nobody's got in through a window or something. We're rather vulnerable, stuck here on the High Street.'

'Fine.'

He was away long enough for Flora to pull herself together. When he came back he picked up the cup of tea which had been poured for him. 'Strange,' he said, leaning against the desk, close to her. 'There was nobody about, no open windows, I couldn't even hear that music outside this room. Must be a trick of the acoustics: we get some odd ones from time to time, with all the brick buildings and side passages and so on.'

'I imagine you do.' Flora was embarrassed by her presence in his office and felt a need to explain it. 'Um . . . I came by because I was passing and wondered if you'd like to come for supper on Sunday evening.'

'That would be great.' Angus's eyes were warm. 'I'll bring some wine.'

But as he escorted her to the front door, she could see that he didn't believe she had dropped in just to issue her invitation. Did he suspect her hidden motive?

That evening, she played the tape of *'Falling Angel'*. The range and depth of Georgie's voice astonished her; once again she realised how much she could have shared if she had been more open to other people. In imagination, she saw herself as a small, crunched-up creature, half-hedgehog, half-armadillo, closed, prickled, armour-plated against the hurts the world could dish out. Why hadn't she realised how good her sister was? Georgie had been singing professionally since she was eighteen and yet Flora had only once attended one of her gigs, and that was years ago. She wondered if there were any videos available and telephoned Frankie, in London to ask.

'As a matter of fact, we've got two or three different ones,' he said.

'I'd love to see them.'

'I'll send copies down. Don't know why I didn't think of it before. It'd be something for Matty to have, too.'

'That's exactly why I called.' Flora paused. In the background, she could hear the sound of a television and beyond it, someone inexpertly drawing sound from a trombone. 'Is that Robbie?'

'It's enough to turn you vegetarian, isn't it?' Frankie said. 'Dunno why he wanted to start with it in the first place. Still, he's good on the guitar, I'll give him that. I've got hopes of the boy.'

'Listen, Frankie.' Flora had not intended to ask this when she lifted the receiver; now she wondered if subconsciously that was why she had done so in the first place. 'I wanted to ask you something else.'

'Yeh?'

'About Georgie and . . . um . . . Spick.'

'What about them?'

'Were they—' Having an affair sounded so 1930s, so uncool, but to this relative stranger, she couldn't bring herself to use a more direct terminology. '—bonking each other?'

There was a pause in which the would-be trombonist lurched unsteadily up the scale. 'Yeh,' Frankie said, after a silence. 'I think there was something going on there for a while. Yeh.'

'Was it a serious sort of something?' Frankie took so long to answer that she added: 'For either of them? Or perhaps for both?'

'OK. I'll tell you. I never thought it was that serious for her. But for Spick, right? It was pretty seriously serious, if you know what I mean. He's younger than her. I don't think he'd been in love before.'

'So he *was* in love with her? It wasn't just a fling?'

'Definitely not. The thing is, Georgie wasn't cheap. She didn't sleep around. But . . . I guess you heard about the Jerry Long bit?'

'She wanted to marry him, a while back, and he broke it off?'

'Something like that, yeh. That really broke Georgie up. After that, there was a while in there when she didn't seem to care much about what she did, who she went with. Young Paul stepped in. Started to look out for her, take care of her, cheer her up: I guess that's what she needed. After a while, it led on to . . . something more.'

'How long did the something more last?'

'Maybe a couple of years? Had its ups and downs.'

'Was it still going on when she bumped into Jerry again?'

'Only sort of. They were definitely on the outs when she and Jerry . . . Man! That was like two heat-seeking missiles coming into contact. I mean I'm talking major combustion here. Powee!'

'How did Paul take it?'

'She tried to be nice, did Georgie. She was like that. But there wasn't much she could do. We all knew Jerry'd always been the one, and now it'd all come right, we were glad for them both. But Spick, yeh, well, he was kinda knocked off his perch.'

Enough to murder her? Flora wanted to ask. 'Is there any possibility that Paul is Matty's father?'

There was another pause in which the background trombone hesitantly climbed towards a top note. Then Frankie said quietly: 'What's going on, Flora? I already had some snippy journalist on my doorstep, asking questions about where I was when Georgie got killed. If she hadn't've finally got round to admitting that she'd come from you, I'd have slammed the door on her.'

'It's just that . . . there's some doubt about whether the man they put away for it really did kill Georgie. The police don't believe him when he says he didn't do it, but I do.'

'So you're looking for someone else to take the can for it and Spick just happens to fit the frame, is that it?'

'Of course not. I'm exploring possibilities, that's all. You can see why I'd want to find out as much as I can about it: if Don Blackett didn't do it, someone else did, and I want to know who before he kills someone else.'

'Why'd you pick on young Paul?'

'I *didn't* pick on him, Frankie. But when that journalist – Jane – asked him where he was the night Georgie was killed, he gave her an alibi which she didn't believe, and behaved shiftily enough for us to start to wonder about him. And once we'd started, it was logical to ask *why* it might have been him. Until then, it never occurred to me for a moment that he might have been Georgie's lover. But you can see that it fits. If he couldn't forgive her for dumping him, and especially if he was Matty's father – well, you can see how our thinking went.'

'Oh Jesus,' Frankie said quietly.

'What is it?'

'If it *was* him . . . He's been acting really strange since it happened. We've all gone along with it, thought it was his way of coping with losing her, not just once, either, but twice.'

'Poor Spick.'

'But if by any insane chance it *was* him . . . It hadn't crossed my mind, but now you mention it . . . I'll have to go away and think about it. Maybe have a word with Dave.'

'Before you go, there's another thing I'd like to ask.'

'What's that?'

'Those anonymous letters Georgie kept getting. Is it possible that Spick wrote them?'

'Fuckin' A—' Again Frankie fell silent. In the pause, his breathing sounded harshly down the line. 'I don't want to know about this, I really don't.'

'But is it possible?'

'Yeah. It's possible. Since you've brought it up, I gotta say it's more than possible.'

He swallowed audibly, then said: 'Listen. I'll have to give this one a bit of time, I really will.'

'I'm not accusing him of anything, Frankie. Just asking.'

'I'll get back to you, girl.' He put down the telephone.

For a moment Flora stood there without moving. Obviously she'd hit a nerve with Frankie: perhaps he himself had wondered about Spick. He fitted in so many ways, particularly if he proved to be Matty's father. In the sitting room, she could hear her sister's voice: *Falling, falling angel, through the lonely dark* . . . and behind it the back-up, sax and acoustic guitars, trombone and percussion. Once she would have heard music, sound, nothing more than that. Now behind the melody were names, personalities: Frankie and Dave, Bill and Gus. And Spick.

Despite his brutal appearance, he seemed an unlikely murderer: she tried to picture him with a knife, stabbing at the body of the woman he loved, turned into a killer by anger, grief, despair. If Spick was the one who had killed her, there was a still a long way to go. Proof had to be sought, searches made. Because he looked so frightening, so exactly the sort of man you would cross the street to avoid, would that have made it worse for Georgie? Or would she have seen his clear eyes, as she died, and a mouth she had once kissed, rather than the tattoos and the shaven head?

Standing in the darkened hallway . . . *you have my heart*, Georgie sang, fading out on a minor key, a blues note of despair, *you'll always have my heart* . . . Flora wished she could take a step backwards in time, to when she still believed in Don Blackett's guilt. It would be so much easier than believing in Spick's.

She'd come upstairs to draw the curtains. Despite the fact that winter should be over, the weather had taken a freezing turn. She remembered the first days in the other cottage, and how cold it had been, despite the heat of the Aga. The mark on the ceiling came back to her and the sense that when it looked like an angel, the day ahead would be a good one. Perhaps it was the mark which had subconsciously urged her into producing the first of her angels, the one in the DMs and the denims.

Her bedroom was brilliant with light from the plump March moon and she walked over to the windows without bothering to switch on the lamps. As she looked down at the garden, where hoarfrost glittered in the cold shine, a rabbit suddenly dashed across the lawn. About to tug at the curtains, she saw something else move at the edge of the grass. A fox? A badger? Despite the clarity of the moonlight, it was hard to be certain of detail. She stepped back against the curtains and stared harder.

Her heart began to jump. Perhaps it wasn't an animal at all. Was that a face she could see staring up at the window like a pale reflection of the moon? Was someone was out there, standing in close to the apple tree? It was impossible to decide whether it was simply the black shadow of the tree trunk which lay across the frosty lawn, or something more.

Her mind began to assess, to remember. Ages ago, someone had suggested that all along *she* was the intended target of the man who had murdered Georgie. She'd forgotten this in the aftermath of Blackett's arrest and conviction. But what if they were right? If someone was out there in the chilly garden, could it be the murderer, come back to finish his bungled job?

Scarcely breathing, she tried to focus her attention on the tree. Far away, behind the low hills, the horizon was edged with a pumpkin-coloured layer of lights from the nearest town. An owl hooted; a mouse squeaked. Otherwise, the silence outside was absolute. There was no movement, nothing.

She stayed watching for ten or fifteen minutes, until her eyes burned and her heartbeat gradually slowed to normal, but there was nothing further to suggest that she was being spied on. In the end, deciding that she must have been mistaken, she pulled the curtains across the window before going downstairs again to check that the doors and windows were locked, before checking on Matty and then getting into bed.

But she found it difficult to sleep. Too many thoughts whirled about in her head. It was bad enough to feel that the house might no longer be the safe refuge she had thought it. There was also the question of Jessica's continuing absence, which was beginning to assume a sinister twist. And the problem posed by Spick's possible involvement in Georgie's death, although Flora found it difficult to envisage him as a murderer. Even the prospect of Oliver's return now seemed somehow daunting, although she had been looking forward to it for days.

Shifting her pillows around to get comfortable, she reflected that getting through childhood had been hard enough, that by now she ought to have achieved some kind of peace. Instead she felt increasingly beleaguered. Sleep falling about her at last, she wondered if there was anywhere now where she could find the peace she sought.

Wide seas, wide skies, the sound of the sea advancing up the shingle. There is a place for her. A haven. Curved beaks, red legs brilliant against the mud flats. The ever-shifting dunes, the whisper of sand as it trickles down between the tough sea plants, folds over on itself, falls, infinitesimally moving. The beat of many wings. And always the unending suck and roar of the sea.

Yes. There is a place.

Around five o'clock, she got up and made a thermos of tea and some sandwiches. When she opened the back door, the chill air stung like fire, bringing tears to her eyes and cutting short the breath in her throat. If there had been anybody outside last night – and with the new day beginning, she knew she must have imagined it – they would have gone hours ago, if only to escape from the cold.

She started up the car and went back into the house to gather together clothes and toys before scooping Matty up in a duvet and carrying her, still sleeping, down to the by-now warm car. Reaching for her seat belt, buckling it round her, she thought: We'll be safe now, though she could not have said from what. She felt a sense of freedom as she wound down the window and put her head out before making the sharp turn into the road. There was not much room for reversing and more than once she had almost hit the gate posts. Having manoeuvred the car into position and changed gear, she was about to roll up the window when she heard a voice softly calling her name.

'Flora.'

Oh God! The unexpected sound paralysed her. Incapacitated by terror, she could neither think nor act. Horror poured along her veins, flowed towards her heart, set it wildly pumping. Her hands did not feel the wheel beneath her fingers, her feet would not function on the pedals. Breathing through her mouth, like a trapped creature, she heard it again. 'Flora.'

Who was it? Although she twisted in her seat, whoever had said her name was beyond her line of vision. She heard it clearly, however, a sad, elongated cry, a ribbon laid across the winter morning darkness: 'Flora.'

Someone *was* out there. Calling her. Hunting her. The

shock of that thought brought back the warm blood and set her body moving again. Sobbing with fright, she slammed her foot down on the accelerator, gunned the motor, skidded across the gravel towards the gate. She felt the left hand post graze the side of the car as she hammered out into the road and tore away from the house. Only the fact that there was a child in the back of the car prevented her from breaking into hysterical screams.

What made it worse was that she almost recognised the voice. Or at least, knew she had heard it before. Whose was it? Angus's? Rupert's? Spick's? None of those. She could not even have said whether it was a man's voice or a woman's. She raced along the winding country road, swinging round the corners, scraping against the hawthorn hedges, once almost swerving into the ditch at the side. It wasn't until she had reached the main Oxford road that she slowed down. Despite the early hour, there was already plenty of traffic about and the fact that she was no longer isolated enabled her to calm down and think rationally.

Had she really heard a voice? Had she mistaken the cry of a hunting owl or the despairing shriek of its prey for the sound of her name? The further she drove from the house, the more she was able to convince herself that she was suffering from an overheated brain. Yet the half-recognised voice remained with her long after she had turned north and then east again, and was finally heading through the flat, unpeopled areas beyond Halesworth and Harleston towards the sea.

Wind and weather had peeled off the paint and left dribbles of rust running down from the roof. One of the storm shutters on the upper windows had come loose and was hanging forlornly sideways. The house looked dowdy and despairing. Pulling up alongside the wooden fence which separated the garden from the unmade-up road which ran parallel to the beach, Flora turned off the engine. The wind rushing off the sea buffeted the car, rocking it from side to side. When she got out, it whipped savagely round her head, deafening, painful, the force of it drowning out every other sound except the rattle of the loose shutter. Even the seabirds were inaudible, though she could see them wheeling and curving above her, almost invisible against the gull-coloured sky. How long was it since she was last here? She couldn't remember. She and Georgie had come once, to check on the place, make sure the shutters were tight and the roof still sound. It was the summer before she died. Matty had been left with Frankie's obliging sister Denise. They'd brought food with them, and drink, and sleeping bags. The house had been damp and salt-smelling; a spoon left out on the counter was green with corrosion and soft to the touch; there were silvery snail-trails on the porch and sand seeping through the back door. They had flung open all the doors and windows before going out to collect driftwood, stacks of it, for there had been late spring storms that year. They had piled some in the main room, ready to light later on, the rest they had stowed under the verandah. It was not yet June but the sun had been brilliant that day, the sea almost mediterraneanly green; the breeze which had ruffled their hair as they walked barefoot along the edge of the water was midsummer-warm.

'We'll come again soon,' they had promised each other, as they packed up to go home, 'very soon,' but they never had and now Georgie was dead and would never come back again. Flora tried not to think of her. She should have returned before now to this place so crammed with memories. With happiness.

Since Matty was still asleep on the back seat, Flora went up the warped wooden steps of the porch and put her key into the lock. The door was stiff, swollen by rain and the spray constantly blown in from the sea, but she finally managed to force it open. Stepping into the cold gloom, she reached for the light switch, knowing the electricity was connected because she had gone on paying the bills even though it made little sense to do so. The house smelled musty, even faintly disgusting, as though a bird had been trapped in the chimney and died there.

At first, everything looked exactly as it had when she and Georgie left it before locking up behind them. Then she saw that it was not.

The pile of driftwood by the blackened hearth was much smaller. They had stowed all the cushions of the wickerwork suite in plastic bags, yet two of them had been taken out and set on one of the armchairs. Gingerly she touched them: they were greasy with salt-damp. Straightening, she saw a teacup and saucer on the floor beside the chair, the dregs long since dried to a brown stain. Neither she nor Georgie had left it there, of that she was convinced. They had discussed the possibility of renting the house to summer visitors and, because of that, had been meticulous in checking that it was immaculate before they left.

Someone had been here.

Yet there was no sign of a break-in. Frowning, Flora walked into the little kitchen. The fridge was disconnected, just as they had left it, the door propped open with a rolling pin. The stiff crust of a dishcloth lay twisted in the sink, together with a piece of soap so dried out that it looked like a sliver of bone. Sticky grey spider webs clogged the corners of the window, dead flies lay face up on the windowsill. The mat which covered the trap down into the vegetable cellar was dusty, as were the counters. There was no sign of intrusion in here. Yet someone had definitely lit a fire; someone had fished out cushions and left a teacup almost hidden under the chair. Which meant that the kettle must have been used, that supplies had been brought. She opened one of the cupboards and saw a sprinkle of tea-leaves, a few grains of sugar.

Curious now, she went round the house, examining the windows and doors, front and back. Nothing had been broken or forced. Upstairs, the mattresses were still rolled to the foot of the beds and wrapped in polythene, together with the pillows and blankets. However, because she was looking for signs, she found one or two more indications that the house had been used. There was a black hair lying on the dressing-table in the room which had been Gran's. A faint smear of pinkish toothpaste was visible round the plughole of the bathroom basin. And hanging on the back of the bedroom door, where it might easily have been overlooked, was a red woollen scarf. Man's or woman's? Flora sniffed at it but the faint scent could have been aftershave or perfume: it was impossible to tell. Added to the diminished pile of driftwood, the cushions in the armchair and the cup and saucer, it was fairly conclusive proof that an intruder had been in the house.

A chill settled at the base of Flora's spine. She was the only person who would have been in a position to realise that the cushions should have been in the garbage sacks, that the teacup was not left there by her or Georgie. Anyone trying to hide signs of occupancy would have taken a look round and thought the living room looked as deserted and unused as it had been when they arrived. Anyone, that is, who had not actually been the one to take out the cushions or build the fire. That same person might have stood at the threshold of the bedroom with the door pushed back against the wall, or gone into the room to make sure that the old-fashioned wardrobe was empty, and missed the scarf hanging on the curved brass hooks at the back of the door.

She returned to the front door and looked again round the living room, glad to have open space at her back and the prospect of quick escape. Behind her the wind roared, whistling between the bars of the verandah, knocking at the tumbledown struts of the fence, catching at the wooden overhang below the roof. Between the noisy gusts, she could hear breakers crashing onto the beach and the solitary boom of a foghorn. She examined the room again, searching for any clue as to who could have been here, who could have entered the house without forcing their way in. It had to be someone with a key.

She had one, Georgie had had one. Though the house had been left to the two sisters, Jessica probably had one. And almost certainly the family solicitor. No one else. She knew that she had not lent hers to anyone, but Georgie might have.

To some of her musician friends, to one of her lovers. Perhaps – and as soon as she thought of it, Flora realised that could be the answer – she'd come up here by herself, or with Matty, or with someone else, one weekend, seeing no need to tell Flora because she never went there.

Of course, that must be what had happened. The relief Flora felt at solving the problem was disproportionate.

'It's a bit cold,' Matty said.

'It is, rather. Do you want to go indoors?'

'Yes, please.' Matty was tired, having spent the morning running along the beach, racing the waves, throwing stones into the sea.

'And I think it's going to rain.'

'So do I.' Matty looked at the sky and held out a hand to test for drops, looking so solemn that Flora began to laugh, knowing she must have picked up the gesture from Angus. 'It's very nice out here, ack'shully,' Matty continued, anxious that Flora shouldn't think she wasn't enjoying herself, 'but not very warm.'

'Absolutely right.'

Hand in hand, the two of them walked back up to the dunes, pushing through the purple sea holly and the rattling marram grass. 'What we'll do is have a cuppa and a picnic lunch, and then go home,' said Flora. 'Would you like that?'

'Yes.'

'We could even light a fire. There's plenty of wood.'

'Yes, please.'

'We used to come here in the holidays, your mother and I.'

'When you were little like me?'

'Yes.'

Matty thought about that.

'We could come lots in the summer,' Flora said. 'It's our house, you know. It used to be your mother's and mine, and now it's yours and mine.'

'Is it Angus's too?'

'Not really, unless we share it with him.'

'Is it Spick's?'

Flora tried not to react, but her hand tightened on Matty's. 'No,' she said carefully. 'Why do you ask?'

Instead of answering, Matty asked another question. 'Is Spick part of our family?'

Steady, Flora told herself. She could not decide what answer Matty hoped for. 'Sort of,' she said tentatively.

'Is Oliver?'

'Oliver is, yes, definitely.'

'Why is he?'

'Because . . . he and I were married.'

'But you don't live together all the time like married peoples.'

Again, Flora was at a loss. How to explain to a four-and-a-half-year-old about divorce and love and mutual need? 'Not at the moment.' She waited a beat. 'Would you like it if we did?'

'No.' Matty shook her head.

'Why not?'

'Because it's nice when it's just you and me.'

'What about Spick? Would you like him to live with us all the time?'

Matty considered. 'Would he be my father then?'

'Would you like it if he was?'

'No. I don't like fathers.'

'Why not?'

'Because they interfere. And they're men. Bad men.'

'Not all of them, sweetheart.'

'Some.'

'How do you feel about Angus?'

Matty considered this. 'I wouldn't mind Angus some of the time.'

'But not Oliver or Spick?'

'Not for a father. I *hate* fathers.'

'What about the Man in the Moon?' Flora asked, wondering where this fierce dislike had sprung from. Had Matty somehow picked up on Georgie's contempt for Rupert Flynn?

'That's silly,' Matty said severely. 'He hasn't got any childrens.'

As they clambered over the tilt of the dune and crossed the sandy path to the gate of the house, someone called to them. 'I say! Ahoy there!' A man was approaching them, waving a walking stick as he came.

Matty clutched at Flora's legs, half hiding herself behind them. 'No,' she said, very definitely. 'No.'

'It's all right,' said Flora, wincing at the potential terrors which beset the little girl each time she was faced with the unexpected.

'I say!' The man was heavily wrapped in sweaters, waxed jacket and yellow corduroys tucked into wellingtons. 'So sorry to shout at you like that.' He lifted a tweed pork pie hat briefly from his head and replaced it, before smiling down at Matty. 'Hope I didn't frighten you, my dear.'

'What can I do for you?' Flora said.

'The name's Wetherall,' the man said. 'Guy Wetherall. I just wondered how Mrs Flynn got on.'

'What?' Flora didn't understand what he meant.

'Mrs Flynn. The actress. Comes here from time to time.' He gestured at Gran's house.

'What about her?' Her mother came here? It was the first Flora had known of it.

'She seemed a little distressed when she was here last. I felt bad about leaving her on her own, to be honest. Saw you going in and thought you might know how she was. Friend of yours, is she?'

Flora couldn't help smiling. In his delicate, middle-class way, Guy Wetherall was establishing her right to be in the house. At the same time, he was offering her information more valuable than he could have known. 'You could call her that,' she said, and thought how very far from the truth it was. 'How long ago was this?'

He pursed his mouth. 'Ooh, nine, ten months ago. Perhaps a bit longer.'

Last summer, then. It seemed odd that Jessica should have

used the house without reference to Flora, but she probably knew that it was left unused all year round. Since Jessica didn't drive, she wondered how she could have got out here. Were there buses? Had she hired a cab? Had a friend brought her? 'How long was shc here, do you know?'

'Came for a week, she said. Wanted a bit of piece and quiet. I gathered she'd just finished acting in a play of some kind, touring the north, I believe she said, and wanted a break, so naturally I didn't wish to disturb her. I've seen her here before, of course.'

'Have you?' How often had Jessica come? Was this where she was when Flora was trying to get in touch with her?

'Her house, is it?' asked Wetherall.

'No, actually, it's mine.'

'It's ours,' Matty said, deciding that Wetherall meant no harm, despite the brandished stick. 'It's Flora's and mine.'

'Sorry, yes,' said Flora. 'I should introduce us. This is Miss Matilda Flynn, and I'm Flora Treffyn.'

'How do you do, ladies.' Wetherall tipped his hat. 'Flynn, did you say?' He raised interrogative eyebrows.

'Mrs Flynn is Matilda's grandmother.'

'Ah. Well, the reason I asked about the good lady is that she didn't look too good at all, last time we met. And I wasn't awfully impressed with the chap she went off with. Rude sort of fellow, I thought, wouldn't even say good evening, and shoved Mrs Flynn about in a pretty damned offhand manner. None of my business, of *course*, free agent and all that sort of thing, but you can't help wondering, as I say.'

He gazed expectantly at Flora, obviously hoping that she would enlighten him further.

'What chap was this?' Flora said. 'I'll be honest with you, Mr Wetherall. My mother has been keeping a pretty low profile for the past year or two and nobody, including her agent, has known where to find her.'

'*My* mother's dead,' Matty said.

Wetherall's mouth dropped open. He looked at Flora for confirmation of this and when she nodded, said: 'That's a damned shame. Isn't right, if you ask me. Little girls ought to have a mother. Need one, really.'

'I've *got* a mother,' Matty said, trying to make him understand. 'I've got Flora.'

'You're a lucky young woman, my dear. Well, I'd better be on my way.' Wetherall lifted his hat yet again and made as if to walk on, but Flora stopped him. 'This . . . *chap*.'

'Youngish,' Wetherall said. He whistled suddenly, and two golden retrievers bounded from the dunes onto the road along which he had come, stared at him, barked once each and disappeared again. 'Though it was hard to be sure. I didn't get too good a look at him, frankly. It was latish, dark, all I had was a torch because there's no lighting on this road, but I did get the impression that all was not quite as well as it ought to have been with Mrs Flynn. To be honest, I'd have said she was definitely the worse for wear. Drink taken.' He glanced down at Matty and made lifting motions with one arm. 'But even so, there was no call to shove her about the way he was doing. And I didn't care for his manners.'

'I wonder who it could have been.' Perhaps Jessica had a younger lover, a toy boy. It was possible, though Jessica was not someone Flora associated with strong sex urges. *Cold fish, ice maiden*: the long-ago barbs seemed suddenly no more than that. Simply barbs, something said for momentary effect, rather than as an in-depth character analysis. 'Was he staying here with her?'

'I don't think so. I mean, I walk the girls – the dogs – twice a day past the house and I'd have noticed a car. Used to see Mrs Flynn walking along the beach sometimes, but she was always on her own.' Wetherall cleared his throat and kicked at a stone with his rubber boot. 'Feel a bit of a cad, actually.'

'Why?'

'Letting her go off like that. Thing is, I shone my torch around for a minute, just to check, you realise, and she looked as if she'd been in an accident of some kind. Face all swollen, one eye badly bruised, split lip. If he'd been halfway civil, I'd have offered to help or something, but you know how it is, you don't like to interfere.'

'The English disease.'

'I'm afraid it is. I wondered afterwards, after he'd driven her off, if he could have beaten her up. Felt pretty bad about it. But perhaps she'd fallen down. Like I said, she smelled as though she'd—' With a nod at Matty's bent head, he again mimed lifting a glass to his mouth.

'Well, thank you, Mr Wetherall. I am most grateful. I just wish I knew who she was with and where they were going. Or where she is now, for that matter.'

'Nine months ago,' he said, more positively. 'She hasn't been here since then. I'd have noticed. I kind of keep an eye out, now, you see. Wanted to know how she was.'

'Quite.'

When they set off again for home, the moon was already full at the edge of the sky. Matty was soon asleep, which left Flora time to think. If Jessica had visited the house, it explained the cup on the floor, the driftwood used. But why should she have gone leaving the cushions unwrapped? Either she had intended to return, or whoever had driven her away had not realised that they should have been put back in the bags when he checked the house before leaving. The more Flora thought about it, the less she liked it. Jessica with her face battered? Jessica drunk? Her mother rarely drank alcohol, maintaining that as an actor she couldn't afford to let herself go. To be so pissed that she fell over and smashed up her face seemed almost inconceivable.

But if Wetherall was as reliable as he appeared to be, what else was there to believe? That she had taken up with a younger man, a violent woman-beater? That she had come here with him, let him abuse her, gone off with him without protest, even when a friendly neighbour appeared? Again, it was inconceivable. Was it possible that in the dark, Wetherall could have made assumptions which were false? That the man was older than he thought? That shadows in the darkness had made Jessica's look face banged about? That he had been wrong about the rough treatment?

Suppose he was right. Irresistibly, she remembered Rupert

Flynn. Could it have been him, by any chance, who had bundled Jessica into a car? Perhaps the smell of drink had been coming from him, rather than from her. But even if he had, for some reason, arrived at the beach house in the first place, why would Jessica have gone off with him? Why not ask Wetherall for help, if she needed it?

She realised that the notion of a surviving relationship between her two parents was less startling than it ought to have been. She'd always assumed that the lines of communication had been firmly portcullised more than thirty years ago, but perhaps subconsciously she had known they were not. Certainly, her father had spoken of contacting Jessica over Georgie's funeral, as though he knew where she was. But even so, it still didn't explain why Jessica was at the beach house at all, and what Rupert Flynn might have been doing there with her, if it was him. The Wetherall man had last seen her nine months ago, which tallied with what Margeurite had said about a theatrical tour of Scotland.

Where had she been since then?

The question wouldn't go away, could not be dismissed with the glib justification that Jessica could get in touch if she really wanted to.

Suppose she wasn't able to?.

Once allowed into her mind, the thought lodged there. *Suppose she wasn't able to?* Suppose she couldn't get in touch because she was dead? Once again, the idea of her mother's suicide crossed her mind. But how did that fit in with the man who had driven her away from Gran's house? If it was a lover, perhaps she hadn't realised what he was like until it was too late. Perhaps the fact that she had allowed herself to form a relationship with someone like that was the last straw and she had decided to kill herself. The same objections as last time came rushing to deny this theory. Flora would have been informed. Jessica wasn't entirely unknown. Someone would have found her body, someone would have contacted her daughter. Even if they had not, there would have been obituaries, a memorial service. No, Jessica was simply lying low somewhere. And there was nothing Flora could do about that.

Overtaking a lorry, she was half-blinded by the glare of an oncoming car whose driver didn't bother to dim his headlights. Idiot. She shook her head in exasperation. It began to rain, heavy drops which plopped onto the windscreen and rolled sideways, flattened by the slipstream. She switched on the wipers and thought about Spick. Matty's response to him was unfathomable. If she had seen something the night that Georgie died, if she had seen *Spick*, if she had seen him harming her mother, wouldn't she have said so? On the other hand, even if she had witnessed the violence, she had been so little at the time that she might not have comprehended what she was watching. Certainly she had not appeared hostile to Spick. Any more than she did to Oliver. And she loved Oliver. Flora smiled. There was nothing important to be gleaned about Spick from Matty's remarks.

Blackett had said there was someone else in the house the night he was there. Someone upstairs. She could so easily imagine Georgie inviting someone down, saying that Flora would be away overnight, this would be a perfect chance for . . . for what? Could she have offered Spick one last fling, a farewell fuck, so to speak. *For the good times*, as the song said. Surely not, not just before Georgie was preparing to spend the rest of her life with Jerry Long. Georgie had a generous heart, yes, but not that generous. Especially if she knew Spick was the person behind the anonymous letters.

A scenario for murder opened like a puppet show inside Flora's head. Spick invited down while Flora is absent, expecting one last night with Georgie, Georgie deciding she can't go through with it – or perhaps even going through with it, or even astonished that Spick should have thought she had any intention of sleeping with him – Spick hoping he can persuade her not to leave for the US, Georgie laughing at the idea, Spick pulling a knife on her. What more did it need?

Except proof.

22

He took ages to answer the telephone. Only as she was about to break the connection, did he pick up the receiver. 'Rupert Flynn here,' he said in his mellifluous voice.

'Oh, I . . . uh—' Dad? Father? Rupert? Still awkward with him, Flora could not bring herself to call him anything. She had thought once that when she found him, they would slip back into the intimacy she remembered with such longing. Instead, she had found that she was almost more at home with Jessica's spikiness, if only because it was more familiar. 'It's Flora.'

'Flora!' The voice beamed, glowed, bathed her in a warmth she felt sure must be spurious. 'How very nice.'

'How are you?'

'Much better for hearing from you.'

'Good.' Flora tried to psych herself up to come straight out with the question she wanted answered.

He held the pause for a beat of five seconds then said: 'Do you need help?'

'Yes. Maybe. It's Jessica. She's disappeared completely. I wondered if you—'

'I've no idea where she is,' he said. 'As I told you, I've tried to call her many times and now the phone's been disconnected.'

'Her agent hasn't heard from her, either.'

'That *is* serious.' She could tell he was amused. 'I've never heard of an actor who doesn't keep in touch with her agent.'

'I'm worried.' Something about the visit to Norfolk had disturbed her, and it was not just the fact that Jessica had been there with a man who might have been mistreating her. Like a splinter in the flesh, some overlooked detail was nagging at her subconscious, making itself disproportionately felt. There'd been something . . . She'd taken note but not given it the attention it deserved. If she couldn't remember, she would have to go back there.

'I shouldn't be. Jessica's always been – what's the best word? – *removed* from the rest of the world.'

Flora plunged in with her question. 'Since you two split up, have you kept in touch?'

He didn't seem surprised. 'On and off. In a sporadic sort of way. Even though she didn't . . . In spite of the breakdown, there's a great deal between us still. Until recently, that is.'

'How recently?'

'Um.' He thought about it. 'Not all that recently, now you mention it. It must be a year or so since we last spoke.'

'What did she talk about?'

'Georgina's death, mostly.'

'I knew it.' All Flora's worries that her mother might have killed herself in a fit of depression came flooding back.

'She had some idea that the man who was put away for the murder wasn't in fact the one responsible.'

'You're joking.'

'Not in the least.'

'Did she offer any alternative to Don Blackett?'

'Not over the phone. We were going to meet to discuss it and I've vaguely been waiting for her to ring to say where and when.'

'Weren't you worried about the amount of time that's gone by?'

'Not really. Jessica's always been like that. Arranging things according to her own agenda. But you're right.' Now he sounded anxious. 'It was an awfully long time ago.'

Flora changed tack. 'You said there's always been a great deal between you. What of – sex?'

'Oh, yes. Very much so.' His voice assumed a lustre which she found embarrassing.

'Even when Georgie and I were young?'

'Especially then.'

Flora envisaged the two of them in bed somewhere, taking pleasure from each other's bodies, while somewhere, a child wept. An abandoned child. Herself. 'Where? In our house?'

'No. Jessie wouldn't allow that. She came to me. Or we went away somewhere.'

The use of the diminutive infuriated Flora. 'While we went to Gran's?'

'That's right.'

So one childhood mystery at least was explained. As always, she felt impotent against the armour of her parents' apparent indifference to her. 'Why?' she demanded. 'Why was she perfectly happy to fuck you, even though she'd kicked you out? And yet she wouldn't allow us to see you?' And when he didn't answer, she said: 'I have a right. I'm not a child. I have a right to know why the two of you treated us like that.'

'Like what, exactly? As your mother told you, I believe, you weren't hungry, or frightened, or homeless. You were educated, allowed to take up the careers you wanted.'

'That's not enough!' Flora was shouting now. That her mother should have repeated conversations to him, kept him up to date on family quarrels, seemed like a betrayal. 'She beat me, abused me. She—'

'Abused you? If anyone abused you, Flora, it was not your mother.'

'We were deprived of our father. You were too busy shagging your former wife to bother coming to and see us at your own mother's house.'

'Anything else?' Again the calm, infuriating amusement.

'She didn't . . . *love* me.' Even after all these years, the acknowledgement of it was sharp as a knife in her heart. Yet how infantile the complaint was beginning to sound. How immature. She prayed he would not answer as Oliver had once done, that perhaps she was unlovable.

He didn't. He sighed breathily into the phone. 'We'll have to talk about all that. But now now. Not down a phone line.'

'I don't know if I could bear to see you again. Or her,' raged Flora.

'That has to be your choice.' He sighed again. 'I have the very strong impression, my dear, that you've not yet come to terms with the imperfectibility of the human species.'

'What the *hell* is that supposed to mean?'

'So few of us come anywhere near being even halfway adequate, let alone reasonable. Perfection is for the angels, not for men. And if you think about it, not even angels can stand too much perfection, or Lucifer and all his hosts wouldn't have been flung out of heaven for insurrection.'

'What exactly are you trying to say?' she asked with rudely exaggerated patience.

'That you should look at people with a less judgemental eye than you do. Perhaps especially at yourself. Even as a child, you refused to accept anything less than the best.'

She did not have time to digest that. Nor did she want this total failure of a father talking to her as though he had rights over her, or knowledge. 'Have you been to the beach house in Norfolk recently?' she asked coldly.

'Why do you want to know?'

From his tone, she knew he had. 'Have you, or not?'

'I may have been.'

'With Jessica?'

'Possibly.'

'With anyone else?'

'No.'

'Could you give me a straight answer: have you been to the beach house? You and Jessica together?'

'It might well be so.'

'In the past nine or ten months.'

'Um.'

'For God's sake,' she exploded. 'Can't you see that I'm serious?'

He believed her at last. 'All right. Yes, I have often been to my mother's beach house, with Jessica Glanville, my wife. But the last time was longer ago than nine months. It must have been well over a year since we were there.'

'Somebody saw Jessica there, with some man.'

'How do you know?'

'Because I drove up there today. One of the neighbours had seen her being pushed around a bit by the man she was with. I wondered if it could have been you.'

'Pushing women about is not my style.'

'The point is that since then, nobody seems to know what's happened to her. As I said, I'm getting rather concerned about it.'

'Why? I thought you didn't give a damn about her.'

'I don't.' Or I didn't, Flora thought. Yet, as she approached middle age herself – God, she'd be thirty-nine soon and after that would come the watershed of forty – she had begun to see that perhaps she yearned more than she hated, that she needed something from her mother which Jessica was totally unfitted to give and it was that inability which she could not forgive, any more than she could forgive herself for the need. Rupert was right: she was far too quick to blame people for their inadequacies rather than accepting them for what they were. Yearning for something she couldn't have was a waste of time. She knew that. She'd been forced to come to terms with the fact after the divorce from Oliver.

Unease coiled inside her. 'Something's wrong,' she said. 'Did she talk to you about the effect on her of Georgie's murder? How she was coping with it? Because sometimes I've seriously wondered whether she might have wanted to kill herself. And it's so long since anyone heard from her.'

'We've had many rows over the years, gaps when we didn't meet, but there's never been one this long,' Flynn said slowly. 'Something I'm absolutely certain of, however, and that's that she's not the sort to do away with herself. She's much too strong.'

'Oh God.' Flora could feel the tears welling up. Why had she left everything so late? If anything had happened to Jessica . . . 'But with Georgie gone, and only me left, whom she hates, and knowing—'

'Flora!' Flynn's voice was strong.

'What?'

'Your mother does not hate you.'

'She does. And because of that, I've always hated her back, and now Matty's living with me and maybe she felt that she'd never see her again and—'

'She doesn't hate you, Flora. She's a difficult woman, I grant you that. She can be over-severe with other people, just as you can. And like you, she finds it difficult to show love. But then—' she could hear his smile, '—you're the image of her.'

'Me?'

'Yes, you. You must have been told that before.'

'Never. No one's ever suggested that I—'

He rolled over her protestations. 'But she wasn't brought up in a loving home so she's never known how to show love. And she married me, which didn't help. But she's immensely tough. She wouldn't have killed herself.'

There was so much which ought to be put right. Which still could be. So why did she have this desperate sense of time running out. This fear? 'I wish,' Flora said, 'I just wish things had been different.'

'Don't we all,' said Rupert. 'Now look, Flora. Do you want me to come and see you? Be with you until Oliver gets back.'

'It's all right.' She softened her voice. 'And . . . thanks. Dad.' Her voice cracked on the last word.'

Her restless night, the long drive, the stress of Jessica's apparent disappearance, had combined to make her too exhausted to worry about shadows under the apple tree or mysterious voices calling her name. There was a message from Jane Glass, saying she had contacted Flynn, who had been in Manchester the night that Georgie died, that she had also been in touch with two of the three names left from the address book and had eliminated them. She spoke of something which Flora couldn't make out: it sounded like DNA.

She set her alarm and went very early to bed, to be woken around two in the morning by a call from Oliver. 'Darling,' he said, shouting down a line which kept fading in and out. 'I'm sorry to ring so late. You wouldn't believe how difficult it is to get through to England. Is everything all right?'

'Of course,' she lied.

'I've got a flight booked for two days from tomorrow.'

'That's wonderful.'

'Except for the fact that the mere thought of getting on a plane makes me ill. But I can't wait to see you both. How's Matty?'

They chatted for a while. There was no point in worrying him about Jessica. Nor in explaining about her belief in Blackett's innocence of Georgie's murder, nor the involvement of Jane Glass and Beth Harding. There'd be time enough for that when he got back. 'Have you met the singer yet, the one you've been working with, Grigori Angelos?' she said. 'I heard him on the radio not long ago.'

'He's been around but I always seem to arrive just after he's left. Next time I'm here, I might be luckier.'

'Next time?'

'I'll have to come back here in the summer. But it won't be for anything like as long as this stint. We've broken the back of it now. Perhaps you and Matty could come with me – if you think she can handle it.'

'I don't see why not. She's so much more settled than she used to be. I really think she's beginning to come through it.'

'Still having nightmares?'

'They seemed to have stopped.'

'That's the best news possible.'

A foreign voice broke in and began to gabble and she could hear Oliver responding with his inexpert Russian. He said: 'I'll have to go, Flo. The hotel operator's getting bolshie. I'll see you in three days' time.'

'Can't wait.' Flora put the phone down.

The alarm was set for three in the morning. Since she was now awake, she repeated her routine of yesterday morning, and was driving away from the house by two-thirty. The air was still chilly, but not as piercingly cold as the previous morning; above her head, stars shone sharp and bright as needles against the blue-black sky. As she drove towards the main road, she saw a star shoot across the horizon, amid a shower of sparks. Someone had told her once – was it Jessica? – that shooting stars were much more common in wintertime, and she found the memory warming, evidence of a normality which must have existed in her childhood, even if she had forgotten about it until now.

She reached the beach house as dawn was breaking over the sea. A few stars still hung in the pale sky at the edge of the water, and she sat for a moment, searching for the precise word to describe its colour. Less than turquoise, more subtle than aquamarine: she settled for duck-egg blue, and remembered, years ago, her mother in the fishmonger, showing her a duck's egg, saying how beautiful the colour was.

The shingle stretched smoothly away, unbroken. The tide was coming in, had already covered the mud. When she opened the car door, the air was windless and surprisingly warm. She pushed open the gate and walked between the dry bushes of sea lavender which edged the shingle path.

The front door was open.

But she had locked it yesterday. Distinctly she remembered the screech of the warped wood against the frame as she tugged it shut. It could not have blown open. Someone must be in there. But there was no car visible. She looked up and down the path. There was nobody around. Further along towards the town, the houses were unawake, curtains drawn, shutters closed. Even if she screamed, would she be heard?

She stepped back to the gate and out onto the beach path. No car anywhere. If someone was in there, they had walked. Where from? In the distance, where the beach path curved along the shore and turned into the promenade, she could see the beginning of the town, the flintstone building which had once housed the lifeboat, the stucco wall of the cinema turned bingo hall, the time-ball tower. Should she drive back there and wait? Maybe find the police station and get someone to come with her? Wait for Guy Wetherall to show up with his dogs?

In the end, she did none of these things. From the driftwood piled beneath the verandah, she selected a hefty piece of wood which must once have been a piece of planking but had been whittled and smoothed by the sea to a gnarled grey stake. Grasping this, she went slowly up the wooden steps and pushed at the open door. There were no lights on inside, and the living room was dark. She heard something creak. As she felt for the light switch, a voice said: 'Hello, Flora.'

'Oh, Jesus.' Her heart drummed with sudden terror. Round the stick she carried, her fingers felt boneless. 'Who's that?'

She found the switch and pressed it down. Facing the door was her father, sitting on the cane chair. The damp cushions had been piled on the sofa beside him. As she stared at him, he shifted, and the chair creaked again. 'What are you—?' Her lips were so tight with fear that she couldn't complete the sentence. 'What're you—?'

'After we spoke, I was so worried about your mother that I decided to come down and see for myself.' He pushed himself to his feet like an old man, pressing his hands down on the arms of the chair, and levering himself up. He stepped towards her and she retreated to the door. Despite the fresh air from the beach, the nauseating smell seemed stronger today, fouler, and she glanced involuntarily at the fireplace, thinking of chimneysweeps and then, in the swift episodic manner of imagination, of *The Water Babies* which Gran used to read to them, here in this very room, and of the little golden-haired boys forced to climb up the chimney into the sooty darkness.

'Did you find anything?' Over her shoulder was freedom. And this was her father. There was no need to fear him. But she did. Why was he here? After she had spoken to him yesterday, had he hurried down here to check that he'd left no traces behind, no indications of . . . of whatever it was he was trying to hide? Blood from Jessica's bruised face? Whisky bottles with his fingerprints on? Details which could prove that he had been in this abandoned house? She realised that she was already finding him guilty, condemning him, though she was not sure precisely of what.

'There's an empty half-bottle of whisky outside the back door,' Flynn said.

'What does that prove?'

'Jessica doesn't drink whisky.'

'You do.'

'Not that brand. I can't afford it.'

'What brand is it?'

'Johnny Walker Black label.'

A cold hand seemed to grab at Flora's gut and cruelly twist it. 'Lots of people drink that,' she said. Like Angus, for instance.

'Duty-free.'

'That doesn't prove anything.' Not Angus, surely. How could he have anything to do with any of this?

Flynn took another step, and she moved correspondingly backwards. 'I've got Matty outside in the car,' she said, as though that would deter him if he had villainy in mind.

'And there's this.' He extended his hand.

'What is it?'

'Jessica's wedding ring. She's never taken it off. Never. Not to wash her hands or put cream on them. Even when she . . . when things were at their very worst, she always wore it.'

It was true. Flora could see her mother's hands clearly in her mind. A diamond set in white gold, and a flat wedding band to match. As a child, she had not understood what the difference was between silver and white gold until Jessica had explained that white gold didn't tarnish. 'Where did you find it?' The ring seemed tiny, as though made for a child's finger.

'Underneath the cup.' Flynn pointed to the cup and saucer beside his chair. 'She must have put it there as a sign, a warning.' Closing his hand over it, he repeated: 'She never took it off.'

'A warning.' Biting her lip, Flora surveyed the room again. It was lighter now, the sun up over the horizon, the sky blue and cloudless. 'Of what?'

'God knows.' He looked at her with his head on one side. 'Why did you come back?'

'There was something wrong,' she said. 'I can't quite fix what it is.' She took a deep breath, grimaced. 'Shall we go outside? It smells revolting in here.'

'Something in the chimney?'

'That's what I thought, yesterday. It'll have to be cleaned.'

They stood outside on the porch and watched the sea in silence. Then Flora said loudly: 'It can't be.'

'What do you mean?'

She realised what it was that had been bothering her. 'It's not something in the chimney. Jessica lit a fire while she was here. If there was anything stuck up there, it'd have been burned away or else the house would have smelled of smoke.' Her lips trembled. 'That awful stink. I thought it was a dead bird . . . but it's not.'

The blood fell from his face, so that each bristle of his unshaven morning beard was sharply visible. 'Oh my God.'

The thought occurred to them at the same time. 'The root cellar,' gasped Flora.

They hurried back into the house. Kneeling on the worn lino of the kitchen floor, Flora pushed away the dusty rug to uncover the wooden trap. Beneath it was a recess in the floor, the size and depth of a cabin trunk. Or a coffin.

She tugged at the tarnished metal hook and peered into the space revealed. The stale air rushed out, smelling of earth and salt and decayed matter. 'I can't see.'

Flynn reached above his head and pulled the ceiling light in its age-darkened parchment shade back and forth, illuminating the corners of the hole. 'Anything there?'

'No.' Flora sat back on her heels. 'Oh, Lord.' She pushed the hair back from her forehead. 'For a minute there, I really thought—' Reaching up a hand, she let Flynn help her to her feet. As easily as that, she thought. And thought too: My father and I.

He stared at her. 'Then what's making that awful smell?' It was stronger now, a nose-wrinkling stench of something gone bad, of mould and rotten meat. 'Where's it coming from?'

'The space under the roof?'

They went reluctantly up to the first floor and looked up at the square, boarded hole in the ceiling. 'She couldn't be up there,' Flora said. 'How would you get into it? There's no ladder.'

Memories came back. The plumber had been called out one summer: there had been something wrong with the water tank up there, and for nearly two days they had used water saved in the bathtub for tea and teeth-brushing. She could still remember the sticky feel of her skin from swimming, and Gran saying that they might be salty but at least they were clean, and now they knew what cockles felt like when they were pickled in brine. But the plumber had brought his own ladder, and while he climbed up into the roof space, his mate, a spotty boy called Jarvis, had stood at the bottom to make sure that it didn't slip on the bare floorboards.

They went downstairs again. 'We're imagining things.' Flynn opened his palm and looked again at the ring. 'We bought this in Chester,' he said.

Flora looked out at the car. Matty was standing up at the window, a finger in her mouth. She went out and got her. As she walked back to the house with the little girl in her arms, she could see the grey piles of driftwood stashed beneath the porch, far more than anyone could use in a summer, and thought: We should light a fire, and then thought, wretchedly: That's where she is.

It didn't take long to uncover her body. While Flora and Flynn stood on the verandah, nerving themselves to begin pulling the driftwood from beneath the house, Guy Wetherall had appeared with his dogs. After a brief exchange, he had gone back and roused another neighbour. The three men had pulled the driftwood out, masses of it, collected over the years, while Flora took Matty for a walk towards the town, desperate to distract her from what was going on.

Jessica lay on her side, fully clothed, lightly buried in sand. She might never have been discovered if Flora had not come to the house. By the summer, the processes of decay might have been completed and the smell disappeared. Because the driftwood pile would have been used so seldom, she could have stayed hidden for years. How long had it taken the killer to remove the wood, scoop out a hole and place the body in it, cover it and replace the wood? Perhaps an hour, perhaps longer. But there would have been nobody about. The people who lived hereabouts were for the most part elderly, television watchers, going to bed early, and rising late. The chances of them noticing anything were remote. There was no telephone in the house to summon help; if Jessica had screamed for help, they would not have heard her.

Flora was shocked by her father's reaction to the fact of Jessica's death. In a few hours, he had aged ten years. Though he was making a desperate effort to hide his shock and grief from Matty, tears kept welling up in his eyes and spilling down his face. Flora was beyond tears. The discovery of her mother's body was cataclysmic. There could be no rapprochement now, no coming to terms. She had left it too late. She would grow old, she would die, without the unfinished business between herself and Jessica being resolved. There was fault on both sides, she could see that. Perhaps if she had been more forgiving, Jessica less awkward, they could have come together sooner. She remembered Georgie's funeral, her mother's face, the feel of her arms around her. It was the only occasion she could remember being hugged by her mother, but surely memory was wrong, surely there had been other times when? . . . Hadn't there? There must have been . . . *Must* have been.

According to the police pathologist who came out from Norwich, Jessica's neck had been broken. Perhaps with a sudden violent blow to the back of the head, though there was no occipital fracturing, perhaps via strangulation. If the latter, no sign of a ligature was found round the neck.

'Why?' Flynn said, over and over again, in the hours which followed. 'Why?' But Flora could not answer his questions, and besides, there was Matty to protect now, and no time for speculation.

'Come home with us,' she said to him, but he refused, saying that it would not help the child. 'Perhaps later,' he said. 'I should like that . . . somewhere to go—' He bent his head, so forlorn that Flora put her arms around him and held him close, the first time she had ever done so.

Jane Glass telephoned ten minutes after she walked through the door. 'Did you get my message?' she asked.

Message? All that seemed years ago. 'Oh yes. You've tracked everyone down, haven't you?'

'I have now. But the other bit was the important one, about DNA testing.'

Flora felt stupid. 'I thought that's what you said, but—'

'We could test them both, don't you see? Matty and Paul Hapgood. Find out if he really is her father. If so, it would be another piece of evidence against him. Because I've turned up something more. *Clueless* wasn't actually showing at the cinema he said he'd gone to. And also, I drove down to where you used to live and nosed about a bit, not saying anything about you or your sister. Guess what!'

'I can't.' Flora was dog tired, exhausted by her short night and the horror of seeing Jessica's body being loaded onto a stretcher. She'd never realised how small her mother was; in childhood, she had towered like a giantess, full of resentful rage. Jessica had been wearing a cashmere sweater when she died. Although it was stained with body fluids and discoloured by exposure to the sea air, it was still possible to see that it had been pink when the topcoat she was wearing fell away from the corpse. The long overcoat of thick green wool had to a large extent protected her, according to the police pathologist, from predators.

'Someone thinks she may have seen his car that night. Right in the village.'

'How could she possibly know it was his?'

'She doesn't, not for sure. But it was definitely a white

Peugeot. And the girl who thinks she saw it – she works in the general store – remembered a bit of the number plate because she said she rather fancied the bloke driving it. Thought she might have seen him somewhere before. It's only circumstantial, I know, but it's adding up.'

'Jane, it doesn't mean a thing. There're hundreds of white Peugeots on the road. I'm going to need a lot more convincing that the one this girl saw was his. And how on earth do you propose testing his DNA?' Flora wanted to burst out laughing, the idea was so ludicrous. They rolled about in her chest, the mad hyena laughs which, if she let them out, would pour out of her for days and weeks on end. A black court shoe was still in place on Jessica's foot when they finally found her; she'd always had tiny feet and spent a lot of money on her footwear.

'We can sort that out later. But what do you think?'

'You're doing a great job.'

'Thanks.'

'Listen, Jane. There's been a new development.' Wearily, Flora told her about the discovery of Jessica's body and listened detachedly to the young woman's expressions of dismay and commiseration.

'Do you think it's linked in any way with your sister's death?' Jane asked finally.

'It almost has to be, doesn't it?'

'But it's not suicide.'

'The police say not.' The diamond engagement ring which matched the wedding band was still on Jessica's finger when they had zipped her into a black polythene body bag and taken her away.

'Then why did someone want to kill her?'

'That's what I keep asking myself.'

'There's one very obvious reason.'

'What's that?'

'She saw something. That night when your sister was killed. Didn't Don Blackett say there was someone else in the house the night he was there?

'He did.' The clouds which filled Flora's head parted a little. 'Yes, someone was upstairs, he heard them walking about.'

'Suppose it was your mother. Suppose she came downstairs, thinking Georgina was alone in the sitting room, and saw her being murdered by Paul Hapgood.'

'Wouldn't she have tried to stop him?'

'Perhaps it was too late by the time she came down.'

'Why would he wait for two years or so to kill her?'

'Perhaps he didn't know he'd been seen. Perhaps she didn't know who he was so she couldn't identify him.'

'But she only had to tell the police that she'd seen a shaven-headed man with an earring, and they'd have been onto Spick like a shot. At the time, they interviewed everyone in the band, several times.'

'He could have been disguised. Been wearing a balaclava or something. Or maybe she was so terrified that she blocked it, afterwards. People do that, you know, when they've had a dreadful shock. And then later, she got her memory back about the incident, and realised who he was – perhaps your sister had introduced them once when she was having this affair with him – and let him know that he'd been seen, and he decided to get rid of her. Lured her to the house in Norfolk. Or followed her there.'

'It's all much too suppositious,' Flora said. 'So far you've put Spick and my mother and Don Blackett in my cottage all on the same night. It's too much of a coincidence.'

'Maybe. But if we could prove some of it—'

When Flora didn't answer, Jane said: 'I'm sorry, Flora. I know you and your mother didn't get on all that well, but even so, it must have been a horrible shock for you.'

'Must it? I'm not sure about that. I'm afraid I hardly knew her. And now I never shall.'

'It's the same with me and my sister. That's almost the worst thing about her dying like that: there were so many things we never got around to saying.'

* * *

Two days later, Flora drove to Heathrow to pick up Oliver. As she walked through the swishing automatic doors into the arrivals area, she saw Gregor. He was coming towards her, almost as though he expected to see her there, had been waiting for her to come.

'Flora,' he said and, as always, the stress and the pain fell away.

For a moment, she closed her eyes and leaned against his chest. Over the past three days she had not allowed her guard to drop; she knew that for a long time to come, she would have to be tougher than she wanted to be. But for this short moment, she could give way. As they stood there together, the sounds of the concourse gradually faded. She felt as though she had been lifted up and swept away, as though she were floating in space, adrift in the timeless, lightless regions above the earth, freed from all her burdens.

How long they stood like that, she didn't know. But gradually she was aware of sound returning, the shriek of engines through the thick glass, the mechanical voice of the tannoy, someone shouting, the squeak of rubber wheels across the polished floor.

'Your mother. I'm sorry,' he said.

'How did you know?'

'I can read.'

With a sigh she lifted her head. 'I've come to meet someone off the plane from Moscow.'

'Be strong, Flora.'

He'd said that to her before. 'If I can.'

'You can.'

Behind him, on the gantry, lights flickered and rolled. Oliver's flight had landed safely and on time. He would be coming through the barriers soon. The thought of him was comforting; she would no longer have to cope with everything alone.

'I'd better go,' she said.

'Be strong,' he said again. 'And not guilty.'

She thought she saw Oliver appear through the doors from

customs and stepped forward. It wasn't him; when she looked round, Gregor had gone, and though she stared about her, she could not see him anywhere.

Damn: she'd meant to get his telephone number the next time she saw him, and once again she'd forgotten. As passengers began to emerge, she wondered what he was doing at the airport. He had seemed to know all about her problems; she felt as though they had talked for a week, as though she had poured out her troubles to him, and had her sorrows soothed, and yet they had not exchanged more than a dozen words. Then Oliver appeared and she dashed forward to greet him, and did not think of Gregor again.

He'd brought painted wooden spoons and icons, he'd brought babushka dolls nesting one inside the other, and hats of grey wolf-fur for him and her and a tiny one for Matty. He'd brought silver cups and ribboned dresses. He'd brought caviar, gloomy-looking pots of little pewtery eggs which tasted wonderful eaten with chopped hardboiled eggs and washed down with vodka. He looked at her across the dinner table and his eyes were warm and loving.

'Will you wear your wolf hat when you go to bed tonight?' he murmured.

'Won't I be too hot?'

'Not if you don't wear anything else.'

She smiled. 'I do like to keep my head warm.'

He poured more vodka, pure as water, into the silver cups and toasted her. 'To us, Flora.'

'To us.'

She told him, the vodka icy in her chest, about Jessica and he reacted as she had known he would. 'Don't feel guilty,' he said, as Gregor had done. His hand was warm over hers.

'I don't.' She could not feel sorrow for her dead mother. But regret islanded her, a continually moving tide which she sensed would never now be still. They could have discovered each other, but they had not. All she could do now was to learn Jessica through other people.

They scarcely slept, devouring each others' bodies as though they had been parted for years rather than weeks. At one point, Oliver, flushed and sweating, said: 'You haven't taken anything, have you, Flora?' and not knowing what he meant, she shook her head from side to side on the pillow and smiled, saying no, there was no need, it was enough to love and to be together.

'We'll have such beautiful children,' he said then, parting her, touching her, sliding his fingers up inside her while she moaned and melted and leaped. 'Beautiful,' she agreed, 'more beautiful than you can imagine,' and in her mind, she saw Jessica and Rupert, passionate in hotels, in rented beds. Why had Jessica sent him away? Why had he gone? It was something she would have to find out. Tomorrow. Or the day after.

Once more death lies beside her, a familiar companion. Bones rattle. Wolves howl at the moon. She weeps, and as each tear falls, it hardens until she is encased in crystal. Mist looms beyond the glassy barricade and behind it, hidden, the moon silvers the opaque air. Out there, stars shoot, angels soar. If she climbs high enough, pushes far enough, she will emerge into the light where white birds sing. 'Be strong,' she tells herself. She knows that she must break through her crystalline barrier, banish the skeletons, reclothe the bones, if she is ever to be free to hear the birdsong and the rushing wings.

23

Two days later, Oliver returned to London; Flora found herself glad to see him go so that she could concentrate on Matty. After a period of tranquillity, the little girl had suddenly regressed: her first nightmare for weeks occurred the day after Oliver got back from Moscow, and she went off to school the next morning looking pale and unhappy. Flora dreaded hearing from Anne Barker that Matty had become a disruptive influence again. She wished she could work out what it was that triggered the disturbed dreams.

She also welcomed some time on her own. This was the first real opportunity she had been allowed in which to assimilate the fact of her mother's death. After the discovery of the body at the beach house, there had been the endless questioning from the police which had become so familiar after Georgie's murder. Answering the same questions over and over again induced a feeling of numbness which pervaded ordinary life until even the most mundane of tasks appeared unreal.

Yet, when Angus rang, she found herself inviting him to come round that evening.

'Are you sure?'

No, she was not at all sure. The image of that empty half-bottle of duty-free whisky still lingered, but she insisted to herself that someone like Angus, someone so kind, so good with Matty, could not possibly be involved. She said: 'Since I had to cancel my last invitation, I owe you supper, anyway.'

'Then I'll be there, bottle in hand.'

'Bottle? Of what?'

'Whatever you like, my love.'

'Johnny Walker?'

There was a pause which she could sense was cold. 'I was thinking of wine,' he said eventually. 'Red, white, rosé: you name it and I'll bring it.'

She was being stupid. 'Red, please.'

'Eightish all right? I've got to visit a site with a client and he can't make it until seven. We'll be at least an hour.'

'You'll miss Matty.'

'Couldn't she stay up, just for once? There's no school tomorrow.'

She smiled at his eagerness. 'We'll see.'

'Flora, I'm so terribly sorry to hear about your mother.'

'Yes.'

'The papers were full of it yesterday. I tried to telephone but I only got the machine.'

'I know. Thank you, anyway.'

She telephoned her father. 'I wondered if you'd like to come and stay,' she said abruptly, not sure she wanted him to even as she issued the invitation.

'That's kind of you, Flora.' His beautiful voice was hoarse.

'I don't think you should be on your own.' She realised that she saw him as a responsibility, which in turn meant that she must, somewhere along the way, have accepted him as her father.

'I'm grateful for your concern.'

'Well? Will you come?'

'I don't think I deserve to, Flora.'

'What do you mean?' When he didn't answer, she said: 'Please come. For my sake.'

'After the funeral, maybe.'

'That might not be for weeks.'

'I'll telephone you then, in the next few days.'

'Don't forget.'

Matty had been asked out to tea by a child in her class and the mother had promised to bring her home afterwards, which gave Flora a chance to get on with some work. She still had a commission to complete, illustrating a children's story which followed the adventures of a family of trolls who had inadvertently become stowaways and found themselves transported from the wilds of northern Scandinavia to the terrors of London. She was also putting the finishing touches to an Angel Alphabet, a project which gave her imagination absolutely free rein and would, the publishers hoped, sell in its tens of thousands on the back of the success of her first two angel books.

It was dark by the time she finally started cleaning her brushes and covering up her work. Although the days were lengthening with the onset of spring, the clocks had not yet gone back which is how she was able to see, through the long window which took up most of one wall, some movement in the semi-darkness under the apple tree. Swift, furtive: it might have been nothing more than wind in the branches or a bird settling for the night. She stopped, tensing, listening, a paint-stained sheet in her hands. The media had not yet discovered her whereabouts, but it was only a matter of time before their representatives came hammering on the door for lubricious detail about Jessica Glanville's murder. Was this some over-intrusive reporter who'd finally tracked her down? Or a journalist looking for authentic detail to tart up his column about the family where death had struck brutally not once but twice?

Quickly she finished and, with the door of the studio shut behind her, walked slowly to the kitchen. As she reached it, there was a tap on the back door. 'Who's there?' she said loudly, and hoped she sounded unafraid.

'It's me.'

'Who?' Was it Angus, come earlier than he said? Cautiously she opened the door and a figure stepped out of the deeper shadows. Light from the kitchen caught the shine of his shaven head.

'Spick!' Her hand covered her mouth, as though to stifle a scream. Jane Glass had warned her and she had refused to accept it. Now she wondered why she had been so dismissive. Had Jane been right all along? What was he doing here? Why hadn't he called out as he came round the side of the house?

She had not heard the crunch of his feet on the gravel: was that because he had crept along the grass verge, or simply because the windows had been shut?

Fear made Flora's knees unsteady. Her best hope lay in behaving as if she believed this to be a normal visit. 'Have you come down to see Matty? I'm afraid she's not here at the moment, she's gone out to tea with a friend but she should be back, goodness it's so much later than I thought and I've got somebody coming—' She rattled on, the frightened blood racing round her body, making her dizzy.

'Didn't come to see her.' Spick pressed so close to the door that she had no choice but to open it wider. He stepped into the kitchen.

Don't show fear. Even though your mouth is dry and your pulse pounding with terror, pretend. 'Didn't you?' Flora almost ran across the big, flagged kitchen in order to put the table between the two of them.

'Came to see you, didn't I?'

'Oh? Why?' *In order to kill me?*

'I came before the other night, but you'd gone to bed. So I went away again.'

Had it been Spick out there, looking up at her bedroom window? The thought was not pleasant.

Putting the kettle on to boil, hands trembling so much that they barely functioned, Flora thought of Angus. He'd be coming at eight, he'd said. By then it might be too late. 'I'm sorry if I sound inhospitable,' she said, brightly – too brightly – knowing she had to get him out of the house, 'but this isn't really a good time. Like I said, I've got people coming.' She opened the cutlery drawer and pulled out a wide-bladed chopping knife which she laid on the counter, then, just in case Spick had noticed, pulled a couple of wooden spoons from the stoneware jar on the dresser and put them alongside it. Not a woman preparing to defend herself, nothing like that, just a housewife about to get supper ready for her guests. She added, unconvincingly: 'Very soon. Any minute now, in fact.'

'It's OK,' he said. 'I'm not planning on staying long.'

Just long enough to commit another murder? Flora set a mug of coffee in front of him and pulled out a chair, hoping he would follow suit. Sitting down, he would be less of a threat. Watching him across the table, she assured herself that she was perfectly safe. Someone would be bringing Matty home very soon. Till then, just get through the next thirty minutes or so.

Act normal.

In these circumstances, what was normal? 'Are you all right?' she said.

The question scarcely needed asking. It was obvious that there was something very wrong with Spick. He looked ill and exhausted. His eyes were blank. A half-healed scratch ran down one cheek, and dried blood was smeared across it, as though he had wiped it with his hand several days ago but not bothered to wash the blood away. Under an open leather jacket he wore a T-shirt; the neck was rimmed with grime and torn above the heart, as though something had been ripped off it. His skull was still largely naked, but as he moved his head about she could see the dark bristles growing back in uneven patches.

'Not really. Feel like death.' Spick ran a hand across his scalp. 'Probably look like it, too.'

Death: she tried to suppress a shiver. Had he chosen the word deliberately? 'You don't look too good, I must say.'

'Thing is, Flora, I've got to talk to you. Got something to tell you.'

'What's that?'

He played nervously with the handle of his mug. His fingers were grubby and nicotined, the nails black with ingrained dirt. She'd read somewhere that one of the first signs of incipient mental breakdown was a neglect of personal hygiene. 'It's about Georgie and me.' A gold ring in one of his earlobes glittered briefly when he turned his head.

'Yes?' she said encouragingly.

'We were . . . I don't know if you knew, but we were . . .

The fact is, I loved her. I really thought we was gonna get married and that. Settle down. Have some more babies. I know I look—' he stroked the top of his head again, '—but in the music game, you gotta have a gimmick, a personality, otherwise you don't stand out, right? Nobody sees you.'

Her eyes strayed to the clock above his head. Another twenty minutes to go before someone would bring Matty home. Fifteen, if she was lucky. 'What are you trying to say?'

'All I wanted was the same things everyone wants: home, kids, enough money to not be worrying about the bills. I thought we was gonna have them. Georgie and me. And then she goes and tells me she's marrying Jerry Long. Just like that. I was gutted, I can tell you.'

'I can imagine.'

'I didn't know nothing about it till she told me. Didn't have a bloody clue.' From the pocket of his jacket, Spick produced a wooden object which Flora did not at first recognise until he pulled out a folded blade and ran the flat side of it between his thumb and first finger. A knife. Christ. How was she going to get out of this? She began to sweat. Was this the weapon which had killed Georgie? If so, had he come here to use it on her? But why would he do that? She'd done him no harm.

Unless he was mad.

Before she could think of anything to say, he added: 'She didn't have no right.'

'It was her right to choose who she was going to spend the rest of her life with, wasn't it?' Flora said gently.

'I know that,' he said, his voice suddenly tight with anger. 'I'm not bloody stupid.' His face had begun to jump about, a nerve twitching here, a pulse beating there, muscle pulling at flesh so that it almost seemed at though some small animal was trapped beneath the skin. She wondered if he was high on something.

'I know you're not,' she said quickly.

'After that bastard threw her over for Lianne, I knew what she was going through. Where was bloody Jerry Long when she was spewing out her guts in cheesy hotel rooms, and throwing all the stuff she could get her hands on down her throat, trying to find the quickest route to hell? Christ, it was me who was cleaning her up and sorting her out, not him. It was me who saw to it she got some food down her throat, went to bed, bloody *washed* herself. I got her dressed when she could hardly stand up, I got her standing in front of the mike at the right time. And then she fucking goes back to him without so much as a fucking—'

He was getting increasingly agitated. Reflections danced on the edge of his earring.

Flora didn't want to think of Georgie sunk so low. She interrupted him: 'Who's Lianne?'

'Lianne Walker. She's a singer. Nothing like as good as Georgie was. Bit of a slag, I never knew what Long saw in her. Anyway, he chucks over Georgie and I'm the one who's picking up the pieces. And then he decides perhaps he'll have her back after all, and off she waltzes without so much as a backward look.'

'What did Lianne think about it?' Jerry Long had not struck Flora as a philanderer.

'Not fucking much. She's a tough lady, is Lianne. She didn't give in easy. First of all she trashed his apartment, then she trashed his car. Tried to trash his recording studio, too, but the bodies wouldn't let her in.'

Lianne Walker: a new factor in the equation. Did that make her a possible suspect? Could she have come over from the States and killed Georgie in the hope of getting Jerry Long back? It could be checked, but it sounded unlikely. This was the stuff movies and thrillers were made of, nothing to do with ordinary people living ordinary lives. But then murder itself was out of the ordinary. One part of her brain was recording the information to pass on to Jane Glass and she realised that, disturbed as he obviously was, she still did not want to believe Spick would—

'Fuck her!' Spick shouted suddenly. He jabbed the blade of his knife into the table top. 'And him too!'

His unexpected fury was terrifying. She could smell him

now, the feral scent of a trapped animal, compounded of sweat and anger and desperation. Paralysed, she tried to think what was the best thing to do.

'I hated her!' Spick said, and now he sounded close to tears. 'She destroyed me, do you know that? Fucking destroyed me.'

'I'm sorry.' Although he was obviously beyond soothing words or listening to reason, she reached a hand across the table towards him. He raised his knife and she snatched it back again just before the blade hit the place where it had been, knocking over his mug. Coffee spilled across the table before the mug fell to the floor and skidded in pieces across the tiles.

'Sorry?' he shouted. 'What the hell good is sorry?' He half rose and leaned across the table towards her. His eyes were wide and blank, the pupils so dilated that they looked like a cat's; there was spittle in the corners of his mouth. 'What is the fucking point of saying you're sorry? It's not going to bring her back, is it? It's not going to change anything.'

'*Nothing*'s going to change anything,' Flora said bravely. 'She's gone. She's never coming back to us. It's terrible but there's nothing we can do about it.'

'Yes, there bleeding well is. Somebody's gonna pay.'

'Hasn't Georgie already done that?'

'It's not enough.' Suddenly he was sobbing, harsh dry moans coming from his open mouth. Again she was reminded of an animal. Strings of saliva hung between his tongue and the roof of his mouth. Silver glinted among his teeth. 'It's not enough . . . Not—' he shook his head, light sliding across his scalp, '—nearly enough!' He jabbed the knife into the table again, splintering the wood.

Flora dared not look away from him. Above his head, the clock showed her that it would be at least ten minutes before she could reasonably expect Matty to arrive, and with her, the supportive presence of another adult. 'What more do you want?' she asked.

'I don't *know*.' The naked head moved from side to side. 'But something.'

Flora felt a huge sadness inside her. For his pain now. And for hers to come. The natural reaction would have been to comfort a fellow creature who was in such obvious need but she was too frightened to move closer to him. If only she had believed Jane Glass. By not doing so, she had landed herself in this situation. If killing Georgie had not appeased his anger, would killing Georgie's sister do so? And if not, who was next?

Part of her had melted into a small pool of panic, the rest was planning her own survival. Casual. That was the way to handle it. Be absolutely casual. Keep him talking. Act as though there was nothing wrong.

And perhaps there *was* nothing wrong. She tried to see herself flinging open the front door, screaming for help. Tried to imagine Spick's bewilderment if she accused him of intending to kill her when all he had wanted to do was talk about Georgie. After all, who better to do that with than Georgie's sister? What an idiot she would look if she had misjudged him. But how many women were dead because they had misjudged someone – or had been afraid that they might look like idiots? At what point do you admit that your instincts are right – only when it's too late?

A sudden image of Jessica alone with Spick in the beach house flashed across her mind. Jessica would have presented him with no problem: she was frail and small while he was young and big and brutal. At the thought, anger gave her strength. He would not find it so easy if he turned on her.

'I wish I could help you, Spick,' she said. 'But I can't. Nobody can except yourself.' She got up, leaned against the counter, felt behind her for the knife. If she could only stall him until someone arrived, she would be safe. Once she heard the car pull up outside the front door she could make a dash for it. She tried to remember if the bolts and the chain were in place and decided it didn't matter. However murderous his intentions, Spick was not likely to stab her to death with someone waiting out in the drive.

He stood suddenly, his knife in his hand. Started to walk

round the table towards her. A nerve tremored at the lower edge of his left eye. If the mother bringing Matty back was on time, she had ten minutes to get through, maybe five, before help arrived.

'Spick,' she said rapidly. 'Do help yourself to more coffee. I must just go and—' She didn't specify what she had to do. Still holding the knife she ran out of the kitchen and upstairs to the bathroom, turned the key in the door and leaned against it, panting. The window looked out over the front of the house; if he didn't break the door down first, she could call for help when Matty came home. She put one hand on her chest to still her breathing. What was he doing? Had he guessed why she'd run from the kitchen? She put an ear against the door and as she did so, he knocked. Only the thickness of the door separated them: he could break it down in a matter of seconds, if he wanted to.

She couldn't help it. She screamed.

He said something which she didn't hear because at that moment a car turned in at the gate and crunched to a stop outside the door just below. The security lights on the roof of the house came on.

Thank God. She ran to the window and threw it up. Paused. How was she going to get downstairs? She would have to get past Spick before she could reach the safety of the drive. She was trapped. She peered out. Directly below her were the slanting sides of the porch roof which jutted out at right angles to the house. If she got out onto it, she ought to be able to lower herself to ground level. The mother of Matty's friend had got out of the driver's seat and was coming round the back of the car to let Matty out. Calling, Flora began to ease herself out onto the bathroom windowsill. As she did so, she saw the woman turn and smile as someone came out of the front door. The smile changed to bewilderment as she saw that it was not Flora but a stranger. In the car, Matty began to pound on the window and shout Spick's name, but he stumbled past without noticing her or acknowledging the woman. He looked up at the window. 'She fucking destroyed me,' he shouted, and the break in his voice made her lips tremble. 'But whatever you think, I wouldn't never have harmed her. I *loved* her.'

He disappeared into the darkness. A motorbike briefly revved and, after a few seconds, the raucous sound disappeared in the direction of the main road.

Flora unlocked the bathroom door and went unsteadily downstairs. Adrenalin knocked at the inside of her skull.

'Who was that?' the woman asked. 'Funny-looking man, wasn't he?'

'Yes.' Flora picked Matty up and hugged her.

The woman looked at her watch, clearly anxious to be back for the supper, bath and bed routine of her own children. 'Well—'

'And the thing is, I still don't know,' Flora said. 'Maybe I completely misjudged him.'

'And maybe you didn't.'

'You should have heard his voice. He was so . . . so terribly anguished.' Another victim, Flora thought, even if he had made himself so.

'He's gone now. And I'm here.' Angus refilled their glasses. They had ended up eating scrambled eggs in the kitchen. 'Meanwhile, you can either move in with me, or I'm going to move in with you. Take your choice.'

If she was going to do one or the other, moving in with him seemed much the safest option, but there was Matty to consider. And Oliver. How to explain about Oliver? 'You're so kind to me,' Flora said, stalling.

'Nonsense, woman. I love you. As you must be aware.'

'What about that woman you were talking to on the phone when I came to your office?'

'Woman?'

'You said you loved her.'

'I do. That was my eldest daughter.'

'Oh.' Flora felt foolish. She glanced at his glass. 'No Johnny Walker today?'

He stared at her. 'What's this about whisky?' he said coldly. 'That's the second time you've mentioned it today. Are you implying that I drink too much?'

'No.'

'Or that I'm too mean to bring my expensive booze over here?'

'Of course not.'

'That's all right, then. Now, at the risk of sounding domineering, I would suggest that I move in with you. For the moment. Mostly because of Matty. It would be less disrupting for her.'

'When were you thinking of?' It seemed difficult to imagine Angus being anything but thoughtful.

'As soon as possible.'

'My father may be coming to stay.'

'If he does, that's all right. I'll move out again.'

'And there's—' At some point, she really would have to explain about Oliver.

'There's what?'

'Nothing.'

'Meanwhile, this may sound like a cliché, but I really do know the acting chief constable – we were in a jazz ensemble at university – and I'm going to give him a ring, tell him everything you've told me. See if I can get him to put somebody on to investigating this chap, check if there're grounds for arresting him, or at least bringing him in for questioning.'

Even though he had terrified her, and still did, part of her still couldn't see Spick as a killer. Or else didn't want to. Yet Flora conceded that what Angus said made sense. 'The problem is, it's all so long ago now. Any traces he might have left in my cottage – fingerprints or whatever – must be long gone.'

'The police will still have anything they found on record. They can compare anything he left here with those. Not that it'll get Skip – Spick, whatever he's called – off the hook: he could have worn gloves that night – if he *is* the guilty party – or wiped the place down, anything. Anyway, we've got to do something. We can't sit around waiting for him to come back again, can we?'

'It doesn't seem a particularly attractive idea, I must admit.'

'Darling,' Angus said. He raised his glass at her. 'To us.'

She lifted hers in response. Smiled. Thought: What about Oliver?

He rang the next morning. 'How's things?' he said.

'Just fine.' She felt guilty. And sleazy. Yesterday morning, she had made love with Oliver; last night, another man had been in her bed. Though Angus had not touched her, beyond a quick hug, she wished he had. If he had made the smallest overture, she would have responded with enthusiasm, but he had simply kissed her, murmured something she hadn't caught, turned over and slept, leaving her wakeful and disappointed.

'Oh darling, how can they be?' Oliver asked, concerned. 'With your mother and everything.'

'You're right. Since you ask, things are terrible.'

'In any particular way, or just the general awfulness of the past couple of years?'

'Matty's in a bad way again, just when I thought she was getting over it. And on top of that—' She took a deep breath, reluctant even now. 'I think I know who killed Georgie. And why.'

He was silent for so long that she said: 'Are you still there?'

'Slightly confused, but still here.'

'Why confused?'

'I thought the police already had someone for killing Georgie. Don Blackett.'

'He says he didn't do it. And I believe him.'

'Have you told the police?'

'I told them I don't think Blackett did it. But I haven't said anything about this other chap. Not yet. I still need a bit more hard evidence.'

'Who is it, Flora? And why are you so sure it's him?'

Flora explained at some length, marshalling the facts,

getting things straight in her own mind. The more she talked the clearer the case against Spick seemed to be.

'He didn't look like a murderer to me,' Oliver said, when she'd finished.

'I know. But if you'd seen him in my kitchen, you'd have seen that he's definitely unbalanced.'

'How are you going to get more evidence on him?'

'Now we've got something to work on, we'll investigate him more thoroughly.'

'Just like that.'

'Yes.'

'Who's we?'

Flora told him about Beth Harding and Jane Glass. She'd forgotten that he'd been away in Moscow when the three of them had decided to probe further into Georgie's murder.

When she'd finished, he said: 'Sounds as though you've been busy. Look, can I come down tomorrow lunchtime? Things are starting to hot up, work-wise, and I don't know when I'll next have the opportunity.'

'Fine.'

'You don't sound very enthusiastic.'

'Of course I am, Oliver.'

But when she had replaced the receiver, she realised that she was not. Too much had happened too fast. She needed time to regroup. There was too much going on: Jessica's death. Rupert. Spick and his knife. Angus's insistence on moving in. She'd have to come up with some convincing explanation for why he shouldn't come home – how cosy that sounded – tomorrow. How devious she was. How fundamentally deceitful. And with the thought came the sound of her mother's voice: . . . *what a disruptive little liar you've always been.* With shame she remembered episodes from childhood. The time she had hidden her mother's car keys knowing she had to pick someone up from the airport, and sworn that she had no idea where they were. The time she had not passed on an important message from her mother's agent and later, when found out, insisted that it was not her who had answered the phone.

The day when she . . . But what was the point in going over it all again? Her mother had been right. Her perceptions of herself had fundamentally altered. She was not who she had believed herself to be. She wanted to discover who in fact she was. When Oliver was around, he demanded more of her than she sometimes felt she had energy to supply.

Her attention. Her love.

Her self.

She must tell him. It couldn't wait any longer. She had lied for years. Lying sleepless, she saw how much it had held her back. She had been unable to come to any rapprochement with her mother; she did not want that to happen with Oliver. If they were to start again, then it must not be on the basis of a lie. And if it didn't work, then at least she would know that she had done the right thing.

Matty screamed.

Flora was out of bed before the terrified sound had died away. The house was cold; the polished pine floor felt icy under her bare feet as she ran towards the child's bedroom. There was another scream, and then a confusion of frightened babbling. 'No! No! Stop!'

She had heard it so often in the past months, as she scooped the struggling little body into her arms, whispered soothing words, wished with all the strength she had that she could take Matty's pain and terror onto herself, and give the child peace.

'It's all right,' she said. 'I'm here. You're safe.' In the dim glow of Matty's nightlight, she could see her rigid face, eyes fixed on nothing, lips pulled back across her teeth as she shrieked again.

'Oh Matty.' Holding the trembling body, Flora closed her eyes, wracked with impotence. She repeated the soothing formula: 'I'm here, you're safe, it's all right,' but it was not all right and might never be.

'Mummy,' sobbed Matty. 'Mummymummymummymum-mymummy—'

Flora rocked and soothed. *Mummy* . . . This was the first

time she had mentioned her mother within the context of her nightmares. The word was something of a breakthrough in unlocking the fears which lurked in Matty's mind. She had never been able to articulate the substance of her nightmares so it had been impossible to decide whether they were simply a subconscious acknowledgement of loss or whether they were based on something far more specific. The question which always haunted Flora was whether Matty had witnessed her mother's murder; if Blackett was telling the truth, she had been wakeful that night and might have come down a second time. But however gently she had probed in the past, Matty had always pressed her lips together and shaken her head, refusing to say any more.

'Mummeeee—'

'I'm here,' Flora murmured, not sure whether the little girl referred to Georgie or to herself. 'I'm here.'

'Why is he hurting her?' Matty said, out of sleep. Her whole body shook. 'Why? Why is he?'

'I don't know, love, but it's all right, you're all right, you're safe, it's all right,' Flora repeated, over and over again, hoping that if it was said often enough Matty might eventually believe it. As she whispered comfort, her mind hooked onto Matty's words. She must have seen something. She *must* have.

'Why is he hurting her?' Matty said again. She was feverishly hot, her face damp with sweat. She began to struggle again. 'I don't like blood. It hurts. It's horrid. It makes people cry.' She stiffened in Flora's arm, rigid as wood. 'No!' she screamed. 'Stop it!'

Oh, God: had Matty heard her mother scream? Watched in horror as she was hacked to pieces? Blackett had said that someone was upstairs during his visit. Was that someone the murderer? Had he come down after Blackett had left?

If so, who could it be? As the little girl thrashed and sobbed in her arms, caught in her unspeakable nightmares, Flora recalled Blackett saying that Georgie had told Mattie to go upstairs. *Go upstairs and play with . . . I didn't hear who with.*

Could have been one of her toys. Like, 'Go and play with Teddy.' Something like that. Someone's name.

Flora tried to think of names which sounded like Teddy. Eddy? Freddy? Georgie had whispered it: suppose Blackett had misheard and she had been saying 'Daddy'? Or: 'your daddy.' *Go and play with your daddy* . . . If so, why had she told Matty but no one else, and why had Matty not said? She had been barely two years old at the time: *if* that was what Georgie had said, perhaps the child hadn't heard, or had not understood. Or had Georgie just said it to frighten Blackett, persuade him that there was another man in the house?

It couldn't be that. She'd already told him that she was going to the States to get married. And in any case, Flora was working on the assumption that he was telling the truth when he denied killing Georgie.

Was it possible that Georgie's murderer had been Matty's father? If so, why? What reason did he have to kill her? Was it because, as Jane Glass had suggested, he didn't want the child – *his* child – taken away? In that case, the evidence pointed even more strongly towards Spick. She shivered at the thought that she had been alone in the house with him; she thought of his grubby fingers caressing the knife blade.

But if Spick was the father, why didn't he come out and say so?

Rocking the screaming child back and forth in her arms, the answer seemed self-evident. Because the police would have looked at him much more searchingly if they'd known. He would have become an obvious suspect.

Where and why did Jessica come into it? Recalling the last conversation she had had with her mother, she was overcome with regret for all that could have been but was not.

'Stop! Please stop!' Matty said. She buried her head against Flora, burrowing into her breasts. 'Make him stop, Mummy,' she begged.

'Make who stop, Matty?'

'Him. The man.' The voice drifted into a wail and Matty rubbed her eyes, and began to cry, sobbing against Flora's chest. 'I don't like fathers,' she said, in a chill little voice, as she had said on the Norfolk beach only a few days ago.

'Are you talking about Spick?' Flora asked. If the child could admit it, it would not only provide proof for the police but it might help to cauterise the wound.

Matty jerked as though electrocuted. She screamed again. After that, she didn't speak, but gradually reduced to a tearstained shivering bundle. Flora took her down to the kitchen and made cocoa for them both. They sat together on the sofa, wrapped in a blanket, and eventually Matty fell asleep again, but Flora sat on, full of dread.

Why had Spick killed Jessica? What was her part in all this? What possible reason could he have had to murder Georgie's mother? Perhaps Jessica was the person upstairs and Spick had arrived after Don Blackett had left. Perhaps Jessica had come downstairs and seen him – but if she had, she would have told the police. Even if he'd used his motorbike instead of his car, and been dressed in leathers, she would at least have said something to them. She would have tried to protect her daughter – she would probably have been wounded, if not killed herself.

So the person upstairs during Blackett's visit *wasn't* Jessica. In that case, who had murdered her? It couldn't have been a random killing, the result of a bungled robbery. The beach house was empty most of the year; why wait until it was occupied to break in? Besides, there was nothing at the beach house to steal and it was too much of a coincidence that two women from the same family should be murdered within two years of each other without there being a connection.

But though she stayed awake till dawn, she could not think of one.

The telephone woke her, urgent and undismissable. Groaning, she got out of bed. Matty had been awake most of the night, but had insisted on going to school that morning. Flora, less resilient, had fallen into a heavy sleep as soon as she returned from dropping her off. Flora had been reluctant to do so: the little girl had brown smudges of sleeplessness under her dark eyes and there was a frenetic intensity about her which Flora sensed was masking a much deeper trouble.

'Yes?' she said, yawning.

'It's Jane Glass here.' Jane sounded both excited and apprehensive. 'Something awful's happened.'

'What?' Dully, trying to clear her head, Flora wondered what else *could* happen.

'It's Paul Hapgood.'

'Who? Oh, Spick.'

'After you phoned and told me about him coming at you with a knife—'

'I didn't exactly say that.'

'As good as. Anyway, I went round to see him this morning, and found the place swarming with policemen. That tape they use, the black and yellow stuff, over the entrance down to his flat, flashing blue lights, a crowd gathered.'

'Why?'

'Turns out he killed himself last night.'

'Oh no.'

'Hanged himself.' Listen as she might, Flora could hear in Jane's voice no note of regret for a life so sadly taken. Had her personal experience of violent death somehow repressed any compassion for others in the same situation?

'That's *terrible*,' she said, appalled at the surge of relief which filled her, wondering why this death seemed almost worse than the others. 'He was so young.'

'And almost certainly a murderer.'

'You still don't know that.'

'I'm pretty sure. Which makes it difficult to feel too sad about him.'

'Did he leave a note to say why?'

'Nothing specific, from what I could gather. I hung about for a while and got talking to one of the SOCOs and he told me they'd found a writing pad full of rambling stuff about your sister and how meaningless life was without her.'

'No confession that he killed her?'

'If there was one, they weren't telling me about it. According to my bloke, the police think he was probably on a downer after getting high on something, and he just did it on impulse.'

Flora pictured Spick at the kitchen table, the gold hoop in his ear and the light glancing off the dome of his head. 'He had such gentle eyes,' she said. She wanted to put her head back on her pillow and howl.

'So did Hitler,' Jane said briskly.

'Where does that leave us?' she said. 'We still haven't established beyond any doubt that he murdered my sister.'

'No. But the police are going to be investigating his suicide and the reasons for it. If we tell them all the stuff we found out, they can probably come up with the necessary proof. Don't forget, they weren't looking at him as a possible murderer before. They thought it was Blackett.'

'Yes.' Somehow, Flora didn't feel comforted. If a man's death diminishes me, she thought, how much more so does a man's suicide? Yet what alternative did Spick have? If he'd killed Georgie, he would either have to live for the rest of his life with not only the deed hanging over him but also the possibility that the police would eventually find him. Or else he would have to confess, and spend most of the rest of his life in prison? Suicide might have come to seem the better option.

If he had not, what pressures could have driven him to such an irreversible action?

She went back to bed, trying not to think of him but none the less haunted by images of Spick turning slowly in his basement flat, tongue protruding, eyes bulging, lips tinged with blue. She had no wish to envisage such details, would not have said she knew anything about the effects of hanging, but reflected that contemporary life involves such a pitiless and constant bombardment of visual information that little needs to be left to the imagination. She thought, pensively: we know far more than previous generations about everything, and because of that, we probably feel less.

Oliver was in energetic mode when he arrived. He strode into the house, hugged Flora vigorously, pulled a bottle of champagne from the pocket of his loosely belted overcoat and poured them a glass each. 'Oh, Flora, my darling,' he said. 'It's good to be back with you.'

She gazed up at him. 'You're looking so well,' she said.

'I *am* well.' His eyes were very bright. 'I'm feeling terrifically optimistic at the moment.'

'About anything in particular?'

'Oh, this and that. Problems solved, obstacles overcome, that sort of thing. Sometimes, I feel as if I'm swimming in stormy waters, way out of my depth, with bits of wreckage all around me, and other times, as though I'd reached the crest of a wave. One of those big Atlantic rollers – do you remember, when we were in North Carolina? I can see it rolling, and me on top of it, riding the great curve of water for miles and miles and it's the most exhilarating thing in the world.' He laughed hugely, flinging out his arms, slopping wine onto the carpet. 'Of course, it never lasts. The wave breaks onto shore and leaves me lying in a wet heap, but while it lasts, it's wonderful.'

'If I didn't know you better, I'd say you were drunk.'

'Drunk? Moi?'

'Or that you've been indulging in illegal substances.'

'Me, a user? No way.' He laughed again, placed a hand on

his heart and shook his head. 'Never. Not that I haven't been tempted, from time to time. You've no idea how easy it is to find the stuff if you're looking for it. You should have talked to Georgie about it.'

'I didn't talk to her much about anything.'

'Don't blame yourself, sweetheart. You had things to work through, and it was horribly unfortunate that she died before you'd completed the programme.' He put down his glass and came over to her. 'I brought you a present, by the way.'

'Oliver, how nice.'

'It's a book.' He handed her a package and hovered as she looked at the midnight blue wrapping paper sprinkled with silver stars. 'Aren't you going to open it?'

'Of course I am.' Carefully she undid the ribbon and pulled off the paper. It was a book about angels, a kind of dictionary. 'Oh, Oliver. This is lovely.'

'Since you're obviously set fair to making your first million with these angels of yours, I thought you'd better have a source book.'

She could never say that part of her pleasure in the gift was the fact that he took her work seriously at last. 'Sweetheart: I'll so much enjoy browsing through this.' She put it down and gave him a hug. 'Thank you.'

'Hey,' he said softly. 'Did I say that you look beautiful today?'

'You mean I don't always?'

'You know you do. But especially so right now. Your face is so . . . It has a kind of glow.'

Flora took his hand. 'Perhaps you ought to check if it's just my face which glows.'

'Now you mention it, I'd say it was a matter of urgency.'

Before he came into her bed she heard him in the bathroom, opening the doors of the cabinet, and the old pine cupboard where she kept fresh towels and toiletries. When he came back to the bedroom in his dressing-gown, she said: 'Got a headache?'

'No.'

'You were looking for something.'

He dropped the dressing-gown on the carpet and pulled back the covers. 'Just checking.'

'Checking what?'

'That you aren't on the pill. Or using something else.'

She drew away from him, feeling slightly sick. This was it. After all these years. The moment she had dreaded. The opportunity had crept up on her before she had properly prepared herself, but she knew she had to seize it now. 'I never have,' she said levelly.

'What?'

'I've never used any form of contraception.'

'You must have done. All the years we were married, all the times we've fucked, and you never got pregnant.'

'I did.'

'You always said it was because of your mother and you didn't—What did you say?'

'I did get pregnant. Three times, actually.'

'What happened?'

'I got rid of it. Them.'

She watched apprehensively as he closed his eyes. Dropped his shoulders. Breathed in through his nose. She could almost see the progress of the anger building up inside him, slow burning at firs, then catching, igniting, bursting into flame. But he had a right to be angry. 'Are you telling me,' he said through his teeth, 'that you got rid of my children?'

'*Our* children.'

He moaned. 'I can't believe this. Why? All this time and you've never told me. Why, Flora?' Although he was holding himself tightly in check, his jaw trembled.

'It was ages ago. And it's all too painful for me to talk about.'

'Painful for *you*? What about *me*? Don't you think *I* had a right to know about *my* child?'

She didn't correct him again. 'The first time was about a year after we were married. Do you remember?'

'Of course I bloody remember,' he shouted. 'We were just about to go to Sydney for a year.'

'And I found I was pregnant. And I had an abortion.'

'For fuck's sake *why*?'

'Because I thought it was the wrong time. A baby at that point was going to jeopardise everything. Your career. You even said something once: *I hope you don't get pregnant just yet*, you said. *It'd really bugger things up*. Remember that?'

He sat down heavily on the edge of the bed and she felt it quiver with the intensity of his fury. 'So it's my fault, is it?'

'I didn't say that. But I thought it was the best thing. You didn't really want to start a family until we came back and settled in London, years later. And by then, it was all too late.'

'What do you mean?'

'Because the third time—' she swallowed apprehensively, 'the third time, something went wrong. I got an infection. And when it cleared up, I found I couldn't have any more.'

'Oh Jesus, Flora. Why didn't you tell me?'

'I was afraid you'd leave me.'

He hit her. His fist smashed against her mouth, knocking her back against the pillows. In the split second before the blood began pouring down her face, she felt only surprise. Oliver didn't do things like this. Oliver wasn't a violent man, never had been. Once he'd thrown a vase across the room, and on a couple of occasions he'd hammered his fists against the wall in frustration at some stupidity of his director or scenery builders, but nothing more than that.

She looked down at her naked breasts and the blood dripping onto them from her upper lip, then reached for the box of tissues beside the bed and tried to mop it up. He stood up and reached for his clothes. Half-dressed, he clenched his fists and held them tightly against his cheeks as though he feared his face might otherwise fly apart. 'I simply cannot believe you did this to me,' he said.

'And to myself.' How could she begin to express the pain she'd felt, lying there, legs apart, knowing that they were tearing a child out of her? Not the physical agony, she didn't mean that, but the emotional one. Three times. She'd gone through it three times, each time alone.

'You bitch. You goddamned utter *bitch*,' Oliver raged. '*Why*?'

'I just told you why.' She was frightened. More so, she realised than when Spick had come. Oliver's anger was far more threatening than Spick's knife had been.

'All those lies you told me, about being afraid you'd be like your mother. Those damned fucking lies.'

'I'm so—'

'I can't believe it, I just can't believe it. Do you know, once we'd decided to start a family—'

'You,' she managed to say through the pain of her swollen lip.

'What?'

'Once *you'd* decided.'

'Every single time I fucked you I thought: this time, maybe this time we'll start a baby. Before I went to Moscow, I watched you all day and you didn't take a pill, I swear it. I couldn't understand why you never got pregant. I even rang our GP once, made some excuse to see if you'd had a coil inserted, but you hadn't. I figured you'd hidden the pills so I wouldn't find them and stop you from taking them. I used to look everywhere for them, watch you when we went to bed, but I never saw you at it.'

'I couldn't tell you,' she said sadly. 'I wanted you and you wanted children which I couldn't give you.'

She hoped he would hit her again. She deserved it. She'd lied and cheated and deceived, in order to preserve her marriage, and in the end it was for nothing because they'd split up anyway. She'd known how much he wanted children and she'd been too cowardly to tell him the truth in case he walked out on her and she'd lost him anyway, the marriage had been destroyed. It would have been more honest to tell him, but would it have been any better? She'd wanted to spare him the misery of knowing that they could never have children of their own, because she'd already known that he wouldn't adopt. So now, although she cringed in imagination away from the pain of it, she wanted him to beat her, she needed to expiate the wrong she'd done him. She began to sob.

He looked down at her, his mouth curled with contempt, his eyes cold. 'Stay there,' he said. She heard him down in the kitchen, turning on taps, opening a cupboard, and then he was back with a bowl of warm water, milky with disinfectant. He sat beside her on the bed and wiped her face clean of blood, and then her body.

'Every time we made love,' he said, 'I used to wonder what it would be like to see my own child drinking at your breast. It used to turn me on, thinking about it. Thinking about you and our children. It was always part of why I fucked you. Always.'

'I'm so desperately sorry, Oliver,' she wept. 'I know I should have told you.' Especially since, even though she'd kept the secret all these years, in the end, it hadn't made the slightest difference. Their marriage had foundered despite all her lies. 'I just couldn't bear to hurt you. Disappoint you.' She felt as if her heart was breaking all over again. 'Can you understand that?'

He put the bowl down on the small round table beside her bed. Above the medical smell of disinfectant, she became aware of another odour. The scent of violence; the smell of hatred. Her lungs seemed to contract so that in order to draw enough air into her lungs she had to breathe twice as fast as usual. She was suddenly frightened. Looking into his dark eyes, she knew he did not understand and that he would never forgive her.

With a sudden vicious movement, he jerked the covers off the bed so that she was exposed naked to his gaze. Uselessly, she tried to cover herself with her hands, but he yanked at her arm so that she could not.

'I loved you, Flora,' he said. The quiet voice was more chilling than shouting could ever have been. 'I loved your body. More than you could possibly imagine. You were so soft and so pliable. I thought I could mould you. I thought you'd make a wonderful mother to my children. All these years I've continued to hope – and now I discover that you deliberately killed my future.'

She wanted to shout that it was his fault, but there was no point. It was because of him that she'd done it. He had said so often in those early years that a baby now would be a catastrophe, it would ruin his career, that they must wait until they had money and a home and were settled, and she'd taken it for a message, for an indication, maybe even for an order, and because she was used to obedience, she'd gone out and found someone who would remove the child from her womb and hated the doing of it, and him for making her, until the love came back each time, slower the third time than the first, because she'd wanted those babies then just as much as he wanted them later, and she'd always known they'd have managed, they'd have got by, even if Oliver did depend on her to help him with his work. She'd even asked him once what he'd say if she got pregnant and he'd groaned and run his hands through his hair the way he did and grinned at her and said; 'Disaster, darling, pure disaster,' so the next day she had done it, found an abortion clinic, had her baby removed. That was the second time. And after the third, she'd been really ill – they were in Stockholm by then – and he'd stood at her bedside, so loving and so worried, and she knew how much he needed her to be strong and she'd gone on to the pill when she was finally better so that it wouldn't have to happen again, and it wasn't until they were back in London and she stopped taking it that she realised she couldn't get pregnant, that she was never going to have any more babies.

'They haunted me,' she said. 'I used to dream about them.'

He leaned over her and drove his fist into her stomach. 'What?'

Those three children, she wanted to say, would have said if the pain of the blow hadn't doubled her up so that she had to curl into a ball in order to bear it. I see them in my dreams, the two boys and a girl I killed, for your sake, Oliver, not for mine. She clasped her hands across her stomach until he pulled them savagely away.

'Why are you bothering to protect yourself?' he demanded. His face was blotched with red along the cheekbones and there were white patches on either side of his nose. 'I loved your body, worshipped it. Did you know that? I thought it would carry my children and now I discover that there was nothing in there but emptiness. Barrenness.' He punched her again, hard, the blow landing on her breast, above her heart, turning her stomach to fire with the pain of it.

'Don't,' she gasped, not sure if the word had emerged or had clogged somewhere in her throat. At the same time, she accepted that she deserved this, just as she had deserved the punishment her mother had meted out, after she'd discovered what Flora had done. She had a sudden flash of that peaceful summer afternoon and the green discs of the beech leaves exquisite against the sun.

He yanked her up by the hair, pulling it until she thought her scalp would come away in his hand, then cracked her head as hard as he could against the wall behind it. She moaned, thinking of Matty, thinking that if Oliver killed her, Matty would lose out a second time. Another thought flickered in her fear-soaked brain and was gone again before she could seize it. At least the child wasn't here now, to see this. To hear it. Because she was screaming now, tugging at her own hair, terrified at the strength in his fists. Had it been like this when Georgie was killed? What had Matty seen, coming backwards down the stairs with her little nightdress rucked up over her backside? *Whom* had she seen?

Oliver threw her across the bed. He was panting. 'If Georgie was still alive, I'd kill you, you fucking cow,' he said. He'd never spoken to her like that before, not even during the height of their rows in the unsteady days before she'd left and moved into the cottage.

'Georgie?' How did Georgie come into it?

'Yes. Your sister.'

'What about her?'

He grabbed her hair again and pulled her head back so that

she was looking into his face. He stared coldly down at her. 'She's the mother of my child.'

'What?' She tried to move her head but he held it immovable, his fingers tight on her scalp. He leaned closer to her and she could smell something on his breath, sweetish, faintly rancid. 'Which child?'

'Matty, of course.'

'Matty is yours?'

'I didn't meant to let you know. If she'd bloody stayed in England, none of this would ever have happened.'

'It was you?' She was truly astonished. '*You're* Matty's—'

'Father? Yes. I'm surprised you haven't guessed by now. She looks just like me.'

'You made love with my own sister?'

'Why not? You'd left me, darling Annabel had just calmly informed me, in her own inimitable way, that she couldn't have children, I headed blindly to the nearest place I knew for some sort of reassurance. Which happened to be my former sister-in-law.' He laughed harshly. 'I'll say this: neither of us meant it to happen. She didn't like me, I always knew that. Thought I was bad for her big sister, thought I repressed you. But one thing started leading to another, the way it always does, and I thought, what the hell.'

He let her go again, and she fell backwards on to the bed. Behind her eyes a series of scenes began to roll, a long Atlantic roller of belated comprehension crashing onto the shore of her mind, the way the green waves used to roll in at Norfolk. She recalled how she had fought to save Matty from the same fate as her own three unborn babies, and realised at last why Georgie had been so uneasy, wanting the child but not wanting it to be Oliver's.

'When did she tell you about Matty?'

'She didn't. I asked her when I finally cottoned on to the fact that Matty could be mine.'

'How long ago was that?'

'Just before she—'

'She *what*?'

'Went back to the States.'

'You saw her?'

'Yes.'

'Where?'

He clenched his jaw together. 'Does it fucking matter? It was one of the days she came up to London – if you remember she had a lot of business to attend to. I . . . I asked her about Matty then, not really expecting her to say yes.'

Knowing him so well, Flora could tell he was lying. 'I see.'

She tried to scramble away from him but he came round the bed and took hold of her, squeezing his fingers together painfully in the soft flesh of her bare arm. 'It would've been all right,' he said softly. 'We'd have made a go of it, I'm sure. We could have got married and brought Matty up together.'

Who was he talking about, Flora or Georgie? Did he know himself?

He said: 'But she had to go and fall in love, didn't she?'

Oh, Jesus. Breathing through her mouth, to ease the pain, Flora wondered why she hadn't seen any of this coming, hadn't guessed. *Be strong*, Gregor always said. *You are strong*. She sat up. 'Let me get dressed, and we'll talk this over,' she said.

Oliver seemed to be reassured by her reasonable tone. He let go of her arm. 'Yes. Why not.'

'Maybe we can still work something out,' she said, though she felt nothing but a gut-wrenching disgust at the possibility.

You are strong. It was true. Only someone strong could so calmly go down to the kitchen, pull out the bowl of salad from the fridge, turn up the gas under the soup she'd made last night, behave as though they were an ordinary couple on an ordinary day. She'd had a friend whose husband used to beat her up; she clearly remembered the woman sobbing as she described it, telling her how unreal it was to be bloodied and bruised and yet, each time, to find herself continuing to carry out the every-day functions of a wife as though nothing untoward had happened.

She ladled the angry red borscht into a bowl and added a swirl of sour cream. Set it in front of him, a brilliant, wine-coloured red, glimmering against the white porcelain. It reminded her of the first time she had opened her paint-box and heard the litany of colours it contained, had envisaged that crimson lake, its translucent scarlet waters lapping against encarmined reeds, blood-red swans smoothing their feathers, spreading their ruby wings.

'Flora—'

The dazzling birds faded, the rosy lake receded. 'What?'

'I'm sorry, Flora,' Oliver said. 'I shouldn't have hit you.'

'I'll get over it.' She even managed to look him in the eye and smile.

'Till death do us part,' he said.

'Talking of death, I had some rather horrible news this morning.' She sat down opposite him, passed butter, the salad bowl, salt. *Be ordinary. Be strong*. Told him about Spick, the bare details, that he had hanged himself, that he was dead.

He clicked his tongue in pity. 'That's sad. He was – what? – twenty-eight? Still young. And a damned fine musician.'

'Did you know him?'

'I've met him a couple of times. After you moved down here, I used to go to some of the group's gigs. What where they called? The Ragbags?' He screwed his face up, trying to remember, then said: 'But if you're right about what you said the other day, and he did kill Georgie, perhaps this is the best way out for him.'

'Maybe.'

He shook his head. 'Dreadful to think of him hanging there all night, waiting to be found.'

'Yes.'

'I often wonder if suicides regret it when it's too late. You know: wish they hadn't jumped off the bridge or taken all those pills, hadn't kicked the chair away.'

'It's too awful to think about.' Yet Flora had done so, often. In the high and windy places, who hadn't wondered about casting themselves off? And then contemplated the horror or realising too late that this was not what you wanted after all?

The two of them sat silently, absorbed by unpleasant thoughts. Then Oliver shook himself, like a dog emerging from a river. 'Let's talk about something else. I can't bear to imagine poor Spick swinging on that bit of nylon rope.'

When he left, he looked down at her face. 'We'll make it come right,' he said.

She forced herself to meet his gaze, even reached up and brushed her lips against his cheek. 'Yes, I really think we will.'

Once he'd gone, she started to work out how.

Dense with lack of sleep, she made herself a cup of tea and sat in the kitchen, mindlessly staring into the mud-brown liquid. Curiously, she was able to consider the matter of Oliver and Georgie philosophically, with acceptance rather than with the pain she had expected. Gran's voice echoed in her mind. 'These things happen . . . What can't be cured . . . It's an ill wind—' And there was Matty. That had to be good.

When the doorbell rang, she scarcely had the energy to get up and answer it. Dragging herself down the hall, she shot the bolts and blinked at the blazing light outside. Gregor was on the step.

'May I come in?' he asked.

Once again, Flora's depression and anxiety dropped away from her. She hadn't realised how beautiful an afternoon it was, buds beginning to form on bare branches, a brilliantly blue sky, birdsong. She led the way to the kitchen.

'Things will get better,' Gregor said. He touched her thickened lip with his finger.

'I hope so.' She smiled wearily. 'I don't know how much more of this I can take.'

'It's nearly over.'

'I wish I could be sure of that.'

'Trust me, Flora.'

'I do,' she said. 'I don't know why, but I do. I scarcely know you, and yet it's as though you've been around all my life. You're always there when I need you.'

'That's what I'm here for.'

'I don't even have to explain my troubles: you just instinctively seem to know what they are.'

He smiled and moved across to look out of the window at the garden.

'You told me once that you weren't married,' she said.

'*The sons of God saw the daughters of men that they were fair and they took them wives of all which they chose.*'

'You're quoting from the Bible.'

'Yes.'

'What kind of an answer to my question is that?'

'Some questions will never be answered.'

She laughed. Once, his enigmatic seesaw mode of speech had irritated her. Now, more accepting, she saw it was simply his way, as it was hers to fume and fuss. 'My sister once told me I was born angry,' she said.

'Angry people are often strong people.'

'I don't know how strong I am.'

'Strong enough.'

'Will you be running your birdwatching course this year?'

'That depends on the need.'

'Do you mean take-up?'

'Need.'

She wasn't going to argue with him. He turned to look out of the window again, staring up at the sky as though he longed to take wing and soar into that unseasonable blue. Watching him, she decided that he was not handsome in any conventional sense, but his face possessed an amazing beauty, as though it had been carved from something golden, like amber, or alabaster. She wanted to preserve it for herself after he was gone. Before she could pull back from the impulse, she said: 'Could I draw you?'

'It won't do any good.'

'That's not why I want to do it.'

He shrugged. 'You can try, if you wish.'

'Come into my studio.' She walked down the passage in front of him, aware that her earlier lethargy had been replaced with a fizzing vitality. 'It won't take long.'

'Won't it?'

'I only want your head.'

'That's not a lot to ask.'

She paused, looked at him over her shoulder, teasing him. 'Is that a joke, Gregor? Goodness, what's happened to you?'

Drawing him wasn't easy. Each time she looked up from her drawing block, his face seemed the same, and yet entirely different, as though behind the glowing skin there lived a hundred, a thousand, a host of other Gregors. He'd said to her once: *We are many*. She hadn't really understood him then, thinking he spoke of humanity at large. Now she could see that he had intended to point out that there are many personae inside each one of us. Which, of course, was why she couldn't get his face down on paper. She tried three separate times but finally put down her charcoal stick, defeated. 'I don't know what it is,' she said. 'I'm not getting it right. Perhaps I'm just too exhausted. It's not that you keep moving, just that no single expression seems to capture you properly.'

'Capture,' he repeated. 'Nobody can capture someone else.'

'That never stops us trying. But I really meant that I can't pin you down.' As she said this, she realised that it was, of course, his essential quality. However long she knew him, he would forever remain elusive. She understood, too, that if she needed him, he would be there, but that she could never call him to her side. She smiled at him. 'I'll just have to remember you in my mind.'

'In that case, I shall go.' He stood up and moved towards the door. 'Remember, Flora. It will get better.'

Shyly, she said: 'Everything always gets better when I see you.'

'Then I'm doing things right.'

As he walked away from her, down the drive and out into the road beyond, she said: 'Gregor.'

'Yes.'

'I am in need.'

'I'll be there,' he said.

* * *

'What on earth have you done to your lip?' Katie Vernon was nervous. She sat on the edge of an armchair in Flora's sitting room, her back held rigid, the way they'd been taught at school. 'You look as if you've been in a fight.'

'I banged into a door.' Flora looked at her father sitting opposite, knowing he would appreciate the self-mockery which loaded the remark, even if Katie didn't.

What was this all about? Katie had arrived at the house ten minutes ago, with Rupert in tow, and since then had behaved as though this was simply a routine visit. 'You'll be wondering what we're doing here, I expect.'

'Yes.' Flora had far more important things to think about than social niceties.

'What happened was, I was standing in the queue behind Mr Fl – behind your father – in the dry cleaner's, you see.'

'Yes?' Flora tried to look encouraging.

'Well, he'd lost his ticket, so he had to give his details, and as soon as I heard his name, Rupert Flynn—' she looked over at him, '—I thought: can it possibly be Flora and Georgie's father, so I asked him, and it was. So then he asked if I'd bring him over to see you and since I was driving in this direction anyway, I was delighted to do so.'

'I see,' said Flora, who saw nothing.

'And I've been meaning to pop over and see you for ages,' rattled Katie. 'So it seemed a good opportunity.'

Except that she could scarcely sit still, much less think of anything to say, her gaze constantly tangling itself with Flynn's expression and then sliding off again, only to return once more. Rupert himself had said nothing, sitting hunched and grey-faced in the corner of the sofa, staring down at his hands.

Katie drained her coffee cup and stood up. 'Look, I've still got some shopping to do and I noticed a supermarket on the way here. Why don't I leave the two of you together, and I'll come back later, Mr Flynn, drive you back?'

He roused himself. 'That would be most kind of you. I'm exceedingly grateful to you.'

'It's just lovely to see you again.' As Flora escorted her to the front door, she whispered: 'I don't think he's at all well, Flora.'

'Really?'

'Your mother's death has obviously upset him terribly, even though they'd been apart for so long. Like I said, I just meant to say hello, when I heard his name, and before I quite knew it, we were driving over here. I don't think he really has the faintest idea who I am, though I explained I'd known you when we were children.'

'Strange.'

'I know. Look, I'm so sad about all the dreadful things which have happened to you, Flora. I think about you such a lot.'

'You're kind, Katie.'

Katie fiddled with her string driving gloves. 'How long do you think you'll need together to sort out whatever's bothering him?'

'I've absolutely no idea. I can't think why he asked you to bring him. He's got his own car.'

'An hour? Or shall I ring first?'

'Yes, ring when you're ready, and by then I'll have more idea what this is all about. If necessary, I'll drive him home myself.'

Katie leaned towards her and kissed her cheek then stepped back and smiled. 'You know, I hope you won't mind me saying this, but there's a whole world out here, Flora, if you'd just allow yourself to join it.'

'She's a good woman,' Rupert said, when she went back into the sitting room. He hadn't moved from his corner, and spoke with his eyes fixed on his lap.

'What's this all about?'

'I'm not really sure, except I've felt for some time, especially since your mother's death, that there are things which ought to be explained. And then your friend spoke to me in Cheltenham—'

'What were you doing there?'

'I don't really know.'

'Where's your car?'

'I'm afraid I don't know that either, Flora.'

'For heaven's sake,' she said impatiently, then more gently: 'Dad. What's the matter?' What, she wondered, had Katie meant about joining the world, and why had she said it?

'It's time I talked to you. I should have done it after your sister died, but I was too cowardly, too afraid of what you'd think.'

Flora hated to see him looking so defeated. 'I think we've all travelled too far,' she said, 'to worry about what we might feel about each other. You're right when you say I haven't learned to accept that things – people – aren't always perfect, don't even come near it. But I'm trying. Starting with myself.'

'You weren't treated well,' he said.

'I've always thought that. Now I wonder if I was wrong. I've been realising recently just how much Jessica did for us, not just materially but in other ways.'

'She certainly tried. She could have gone right to the top of the acting profession but she decided to give up her career for you two. Perhaps it wasn't the right decision, but Jessica was always a very . . . dominant woman. A controller. Not that that would have mattered if she'd ever learned to express affection.'

'Why hadn't she?'

'I told you she had a harsh upbringing.'

'You implied it, but you didn't actually tell me anything.'

Words suddenly began to gush from him. 'Her father was a Baptist minister, from a little village near Aberdeen. The coldest, grimmest man you could ever hope to see – or hope not to see. I only met him a few times, but being in his company was like walking into a deep freeze. I've never met anyone so joyless. And so determined to stay that way. You'd think a man whose life was dedicated to preaching the word of God would have a bit more humanity about him.' A little colour had come into his face as he spoke. He reached for his coffee and drank it. 'When I said you weren't treated well, I didn't just mean by your mother, but by both of us. I went along with her because I loved her, even though I knew that what she was doing was wrong. I should have argued more, I can see that now. I shouldn't have left you.'

'Why did you?'

He glanced to the side, avoiding her, lacing his fingers together round his cup. 'This is so difficult,' he murmured.

'Tell me.'

Visibly he braced himself. 'The fact is that your mother thought I had—'

'Had what?'

He forced the words out. '—Abused you.'

For a moment what he said didn't make any sense. 'Abused me? In what way?' Then she realised. A deep blush overtook her. 'Sexually, do you mean?'

He nodded. 'That's what she thought.'

'And had you?'

He started to shake his head, then stopped. 'No.'

'Then why did she think you had?'

'I hadn't, not in any true sense of the word. But—'

'But what?'

'Jessica adored you, Flora. We both did. But particularly your mother. You were the little girl she'd always wanted, someone she could love and be loved by in the way she never had been by her parents. And because she loved you, she was always on the lookout for harm coming to you.'

'And she saw harm in you?'

'The potential for harm.'

'I'm sorry. I'm not following this.'

He grimaced. 'I'm not being clear. The thing is, Flora, I never abused you. Never treated you in any way that I could be in the least ashamed of. We had this ritual, your mother and I. A drink together before dinner, playing with you. Then I'd take you upstairs and give you your bath while she got things ready, then we'd read to you, and put you down and have supper.'

'And?'

'It's difficult to say this. But – I suppose a lot of fathers have this problem. An adored female object, clean and powdered and utterly cute, sitting on their knee, cuddling up, kissing them. And, I have to say, arousing them.'

'What?'

'Yes.' For the first time, he looked at her squarely. 'I was aroused by you. I'm not going to pretend I didn't get an erection sometimes. Fathers do. Ninety-nine percent of them do nothing about it, wouldn't dream of doing so, would rather die than do so.'

'So what happened? Why did she kick you out?' Flora asked harshly. From the dim regions of her mind where forgotten experience lurked, she had an image of his hands. His beautiful hands on her body, his cheek against her, a voice whispering to her. The sense of being loved. 'It can't have been just on a whim.' She wondered whether Angus had felt the same about his daughters as Rupert had, and if so, what he had felt at discovering his own betraying flesh.

'She came in, once, when I was drying you after your bath. She . . . saw the state I was in and was afraid that maybe, one day, I might – I w-would—' Rupert's mouth quivered and he put down the cup he'd been holding. 'And God help me, Flora, I couldn't say she might not be right.'

'That's the most ridiculous reason for breaking up a marriage that I ever heard.'

'It is. Looking back, I can see that. At the time, I went along with it because, frankly, I was appalled at the knowledge of my own potential guilt. We were young: such things were unmentionable. There wasn't anybody I could talk to. Now, of course, I realise that it was a perfectly natural reaction, and one shared by millions of men. Nothing to be ashamed of. But Jessica was a fierce woman and she told me I must go.' He smiled wryly. 'It was like the expulsion from the Garden of Eden. Never darken my doors again sort of thing. The Baptist father had got to her, however much she was determined not to be the kind of unloving parent he was.'

'Which is just what she became.'

'Ironic, isn't it?' His expression was tentative. 'You don't seem shocked or surprised by what I've told you.'

'I think my capacity for being shocked has disappeared over the past year or so,' said Flora.

He hadn't abused her, he said, and she believed him. She certainly had no memory of him doing so, though she could still remember the doctor who had come one day and reached under the bedclothes to touch her while her mother was fetching something, the father who had brought her home from dancing class and dropped his daughter off before doing incomprehensibly odd things to her which she had never thought to mention to her mother. But in that case, where had those childhood nightmares come from, those sudden terrors?

The prettiest little girl in the world, he used to say, and his hands, those beautiful hands had caressed her, those fine eyes had looked into hers and asked for things she knew even then she should not give him. No, he hadn't abused her, but he might well have done. One day the hands would have probed further, the arousal would have been irresistible, the urge ungainsayablc.

Jessica had seen the potential too. Jessica the controller, the manager, so certain she knew how things would be. That was why she'd sent him away. Given him up. Sacrificed both herself and Flora. Although she had loved him, she'd loved her elder daughter more. The acknowledgement was almost too painful for Flora to bear.

She started weeping. Now that she'd allowed herself to, she could recall other instances of Jessica's love. A prickly adult herself, she could see how prickly her mother had been, with the added difficulty of undemonstrative parents to handicap her in the showing of affection. Georgie had seen the loving mother underneath; Flora had not.

'She told me to stay away from you until you were grown up,' Rupert said. 'I don't know why she said I was dead.'

'She didn't tell us that until Gran died.'

'Perhaps she was afraid that with Gran gone, you might start looking for me.'

'Why didn't Gran say anything?'

'Because I asked her not to. In those days, I went along with what Jessica wanted. I know now what a mistake that was.'

'She wouldn't let us go to Gran's funeral.'

'We talked about that. She was afraid that if you saw me there you'd try and move in with me.'

'Couldn't she have told me some of . . . of what you've just said?'

'If she'd done that, first of all you probably wouldn't have believed her. And secondly, she didn't want to make negative remarks about me. She knew how you worshipped me. And she also knew by then that she'd somehow failed with you.' He shooked his head. 'You never knew how much she longed for you to love her.'

Under her sweater, the long scar on Flora's arm throbbed, as though reminding her of something. She pulled up her sleeve, feeling rather than seeing the long line of ridged flesh which ran down from her shoulder. 'It was an accident,' she whispered. 'I knew it was. But I pretended to myself that she'd done it on purpose. That's what I told Georgie, too.'

'Freudian, wasn't it?' Rupert leaned across the space between them and ran his finger the full length of the scar, before she pulled away from it. 'You slashed her arm, and then she slashed yours.'

'Yes.' She could feel her memory, like an under-used muscle, sluggishly coming into play. How could she have forgotten? Or had she deliberately suppressed the truth, preferring to hate her awkward mother rather than herself?

'It cost a fortune,' Rupert said reminiscently, 'to have it repaired.'

'I can imagine.'

'Do you even remember why you did it?'

'Not really. Something to do with her refusing to let me do something with Katie and her family.'

Katie had come round and asked if she wanted to go camping with her family. A week in Cornwall. It'd be terrific fun, Katie had said, and Flora had never been camping.

Besides, Katie had two older brothers. Waiting for her mother to finish a telephone conversation in the drawing room, Flora and Katie had rehearsed all the arguments in favour of the arrangement, though they decided not to emphasise the brothers. Educational, Flora would say. The two of them could get on with their holiday reading together, and the French essay they were supposed to write. And healthy. Being out in the open air was so good for you, too, and there'd be sea bathing instead of the horrid municipal swimming pool crowded with strangers who had all sorts of germs.

And Jessica had said no. Flora had asked why, and been rude in front of Katie, and said she wished she lived with her father, *he'd* have let her go, and Jessica had refused to give any reason after that. Katie had gone home, and Jessica, not looking at Flora, had said she was going shopping, and when she'd gone, Flora had taken a knife from the kitchen and gone in and slashed the portrait of her mother which hung above the fireplace.

'It was by John Russell,' said her father. 'He was a famous portrait painter of the time.'

'Jessica Glanville as Rosalind in *As You Like It*,' said Flora. It had been written in black letters on a small gold plaque set into the lower frame. 'By John Russell, RA.'

She could still remember how the canvas had parted under the blade, and the chips of pigment had flaked off as she ran it down the length of her mother's painted arm. As soon as she'd done it, she'd known it was unforgivable. An action which went far beyond the bounds of ordinary mother-daughter dispute. The two edges had curled slightly inward and she'd realised that there was nothing she could do about it, no way of making good the damage, though her panicking brain thought of glue and sticky tape, and even a needle and thread. Nothing would help: she'd just have to wait until Jessica noticed and then take her punishment.

'My poor faltering wife,' Rupert said, and he too looked close to tears. 'And my poor daughter.'

'And,' Flora said, 'poor you. What a lot you missed out on.'

'We all missed out on.'

Before she could explore it too much, she said awkwardly: 'Why don't you take Matty out sometime? She'd love to have a grandfather.'

'Do you trust me?' Rupert said, staring into her eyes, and she knew that deep down, he recognised his own reality. We all pretend we are different from ourselves, she thought. What saves us, is acknowledging the truth.

'I have to,' she said.

Final Curtain

26

It was earlier in the year than on her last visit, and consequently colder. The wind rushing down from the hills had frost on its breath and there was an amber ring of ice around the moon. As the train dragged away from her into the darkness, the peace of the place fell upon her again with the soft strength of feathers. She could smell the sea.

He was there to greet her. 'It's been a long journey,' he said, and she knew he did not mean the train ride. How far back did the trek begin: with Georgie's pregnancy, with Rupert Flynn's departure from the family, with Jessica's stern parents and their inability to love?

'I'm nearly where I want to be.'

'Good.'

He had arrived at the cottage a few days ago, out of the blue, as always, and sat neutrally across from her while she dreamed up this plan, put the various parts of it together. Now, as the Range Rover pulled away from the little station, she touched his arm. 'Thanks to you, Gregor.'

'It's what I'm here for.'

As before, they arrived to find a fire burning in the hearth and wine open on the table in front of it. Flora filled two glasses and they looked into the fire, watching the flames hiss and the driftwood logs crumble. They didn't talk. After they had eaten, they sat again by the fire and the flames cast flickering shadows on the the staircase, making the balustraded angels appear ready to fly away.

Pictures passed through her head: Oliver on Primrose Hill in the snow, Angus, the earring glinting in Spick's ear,

Jessica's awkward gaze, so like her own. Matty in her too-big velvet hat.

He would come tomorrow. If not tomorrow, then definitely the day after. She was sure of that. She'd prepared the ground too carefully. When he came, she would be ready.

'When you aren't here, what do you do?' she asked.

'Does it matter?'

'What do you do?'

'Many things.'

'But what do you *do*? What fires you, what enthuses you?'

'Like your sister. I sing. We all do.'

'All?' Was this another of his enigmatic utterances? Did he mean that inside all of us there was a place of singing? 'Will you sing for me?' She sensed his reluctance. 'Please?'

He got up and went over to the harpsichord under the open stairs. 'I made this.' He stroked the painted ribbons and the fat cherubs.

'I know. I thought at first you were a carpenter.'

'That's not me.'

He sat down and opened the lid. Ran his fingers over the keys, and played a couple of chords. Lifted his head so that he was staring up at the ceiling rather than at the instrument. *Falling angel, dropping past a star*, he sang. *Do you know, do you care, how lonely you are*?

His voice was beautiful, both familiar and, at the same time, like nothing Flora had ever heard before. She remembered the unearthly voice heard in Angus's office and felt a shiver of almost-comprehension. Why had he chosen that song? Had he known Georgie?

Falling angel, drifting past the sun. You will always be my shining one, sang Gregor, and on some of the words it seemed as though a multiplicity of others, a vast choir, were harmonising with and around his voice. . . . *Sad angel, lost angel come back to me*.

He sounded as though his heart was breaking. Flora remembered the first time she had come here and the sense she had had then of irretrievable loss, of someone who had been offered a glimpse of paradise and then been turned away before he could step in through the gates. Back then, her own paradise had been lost; now she felt she might be about to regain it. If she could be strong. Perhaps he too would be allowed back, perhaps he had completed his task. The sound of his voice moved her. She suspected that he found as much solace in singing as she did in her angels. Whatever angels were. Heavenly messengers, epiphanic moments made solid: it was enough that they existed.

Remember, angel, you have my heart. Yes, you'll always have my heart. Gregor stopped singing and sat at the keys with his head bowed.

Flora could not bear to see his unhappiness. She went over and stood behind him, taking his head between her hands and holding it against her breast. 'Is there anything I can do to help you?'

'You have already.'

'Anything.' But she knew there was not. Like her, whatever it was, he had to deal with it alone. She touched his closed eyes and felt the blueness beneath the fragile golden skin which covered them. There were tears on his cheeks. Sadness leaked from him; his hair was like sorrowful silk under her fingers.

He said: 'Oh, God,' the words sounding as though they had been torn from him, and his hands reached up to cover hers.

'What is it you want, Gregor?' she whispered.

'Something I had once and lost.'

'Can you get it back?'

'I don't know. I can only go on hoping.'

He came late the following afternoon. Night was starting to drop onto the surface of the sea and the wheeling birds had already begun to settle when he drove up. She was alone in the big room when he came in through the door. His face took in the fire and the wine, the glasses on the table in front of the hearth. He sniffed appreciatively at the woodsmoke and the scent of timber which came from the wooden walls.

'This is nice,' he said. He rubbed his hands together and

walked briskly towards the fire. 'I hope you don't mind me coming after you, Flora,' he said. 'But it seems to me there are some things we have to sort out.'

'I agree.'

'When Eithne rang, all excited about the prospect of you getting married again, to someone else . . . Well, I thought we should talk.'

'Yes.'

He shook his head. 'Married again: I can't let you do that. Surely I mean something to you.' He moved towards her. 'We mean something to each other.' He stopped short as Gregor came silently down the stairs.

He frowned. 'Should I know you?'

'Yes,' Gregor said.

'But I don't.'

'No.'

'Are you the one Flora wants to marry?'

Gregor shook his head, looking amused.

'Who are you?'

'It doesn't matter.'

He raised his eyebrows at this. 'We've got to talk, Flora.' He glanced at the window and then back at Gregor. 'We could go for a walk.'

'All right.' Flora got her coat while he stood impatiently at the door with his hands in the pockets of his waxed jacket.

Now that the moment had come, she was perfectly calm. She had baited the trap and, as she had known he would, he had sprung it. Eithne had needed little persuasion to play her part. 'Sure, and I'll be glad to help,' she said. 'Just be giving me my instructions and I'll do the rest.'

'He needs to be told that I've decided, for Matty's sake, to get married again, but not to him.'

'Will he believe it?'

'He won't be able to accept it,' Flora had said. 'So believing won't come into it.'

'And he'll be able to reach you in this godforsaken place you're off to?'

'If he wants to enough.'

'And you're betting that he will do.'

'Yes. He'll be confident he can change my mind.'

And here he was. All she had to do now was put an end to it. She stepped outside into the cold wind and he followed. 'Strange sort of chap, isn't he?' he said, nodding back at the building.

'Not as other men,' she said. 'That's true.'

'Couldn't he see I wanted to talk to you alone?'

'It's his place, not ours.'

'Right.'

They walked together along the path to the cliff. There was a band of brilliant white sky lying between the edge of the sea and the dark line of night cloud. A single star gleamed above the water.

'Where should we start?' he asked.

'What about with Jessica's death?'

He stopped. Shivered a little as the wind roared round his ears. 'I didn't think you knew about her.'

'I put it together.'

'I didn't mean to kill her,' he said. 'Really I didn't. But she telephoned me, she asked me to come and visit her in that godforsaken beach house. So I went. And when I got there – it's a hellish drive – she was as nice as pie. I'd brought some whisky—'

'Black Label.'

'How did you – anyway, we talked about this and that, and then went out in the car and got fish and chips. Ate them in one of the shelters along the front, shared a joke or two. When we got back, we had a cuppa and then she suddenly told me that if I didn't stay away from you, she'd go to the police.'

'Did she know you'd killed Georgie?'

'She said Georgie had told her who Matty's father was. She said she thought I'd killed her. She said I was to leave you and Georgie alone.'

Poor Jessica, so blind to the fact that well-intentioned actions could have entirely unexpected results. 'She has a history of trying to protect her daughters from unsuitable men,' Flora said.

He pulled the ends of his scarf tighter round his neck and shivered. 'It's bloody cold up here, isn't it?'

'It is.'

'The point was, she kept on and on saying I wasn't ever to talk to you again, that she wasn't going to have you hurt in any way. Said enough harm had already been done. She wouldn't listen to a word I said. And I got so irritated that at some point I pushed her, and she kind of staggered and fell sideways and caught the back of her head on the edge of the mantelpiece. Before I quite knew what had happened, she was dead. It was a complete accident, I swear it.'

'So you carried her outside and put her under the house.' She knew he was lying. Even if he'd had no intention of murdering Jessica when he went to Norfolk, he'd ended by using violence, if Guy Wetherall's account was to be trusted. Why hadn't she asked him for help? Had she been so sure that she could handle it, so sure she could still remain in control?

'It seemed the best thing. I wiped everything round, washed up our glasses and my cup and saucer so nobody'd know I'd been there.' But not noticed Jessica's, down by the side of the chair. And Jessica, brave Jessica, had managed to leave a clue to indicate that all was not what it seemed. She must have realised by then that she wouldn't be able to get away from him.

She nodded.

'It was an accident, Flo. I didn't mean to leave her under the porch, but I couldn't get back for a bit and when nobody came after me, or even seemed aware that she'd gone missing, I thought I might as well leave her there while I thought about what to do.'

How could he speak so calmly of the terrible things he'd done? He was, she realised, so self-obsessed that it had become a madness in him. Nothing could be allowed to stand in the way of what he wanted.

They'd come to the edge of the cliff. The sea churned on the pebbles below, but darkness was welling up from the beach and they couldn't see anything clearly. Out towards the horizon, a lightship flashed, and she could make out the lamps of fishing boats between them and the far edge of the black water.

'What about my sister?'

He bent and plucked a piece of grass out of the ground. 'Yes. Well. It's not something I'm proud of.'

'Proud?' She almost laughed. '*Proud*?'

'You know what I mean,' he said uneasily.

I could do it now, she thought. But there was more she needed to know. 'Those letters she was getting.'

Nothing to do with me. She often got them when she was touring. And the ones in the States: Spick told me he wrote them.

'Ah yes. Tell me about Spick.'

'You know about that, do you?'

'I worked it out.'

'It seemed like the perfect solution. There was all this agitation about the other chap – Don Blackett – being innocent, which meant everything was going to be raked over again. It seemed to me that since Spick – stupid name, isn't it? – was in such a state anyway, and you and your friends thought he'd murdered Georgie, I might as well kill two birds with one stone.' He considered his words and added: 'So to speak.'

'I can't believe what a monster you really are,' she said softly.

'You know that's not true,' he said. 'You know why I did it. For Matty.'

'You did it for yourself.' Why hadn't she realised long ago how their entire lives had been built around his whims and desires? She realised that although she had always wished that Marguerite and Theo were her parents, they had, with their love and indulgence, created something dangerously, fatally, flawed. Whereas Jessica, for all her own imperfections, had not. For a moment, she was overwhelmed by feelings of loss and grief for the mother she had never tried to come to terms with.

'Spick.' The wind was so strong that the ground under their feet seemed to shake with each gust. Her lips were salty with blown spray. 'I know you killed him.'

'How can you—'

'Because you said something about him hanging all night, and mentioned a piece of rope. It hadn't even got into the papers by then.'

'It was a mistake. I wondered if you'd notice.'

She closed her eyes for a moment, defeated by his disregard for any intelligence but his own.

'I went round there – I don't really know why I'm telling you all this – and said I wanted to talk about Georgie. There were all these diaries and exercise books sitting round, and I sneaked a look while he was out of the room. They were full of stuff about her: fantasies and so on. That's what gave me the idea. And there were photos of her everywhere. It was like a shrine, almost. I hadn't decided to do anything, but it suddenly came to me what a perfect answer to everything it would be if he killed himself. So I knocked him out and . . . Jesus, Flora, I only did it for us – anyway, I saw this nylon rope in one corner, climbing rope, so I tied it round his neck and slung it over a pipe in the basement passage.'

'Why didn't you make him write a confession?'

'Silly, really. But by the time I'd thought of it, it was too late. He was already dead. Besides, I figured there was enough in the diaries for the police to assume he must have hanged himself for love of her.'

Flora felt sick. How could he be so unemotional about such inhuman actions? Not boastful or repentant, just matter-of-fact. And to think that she had seriously contemplated moving herself and Matty in with him, the three of them setting up as a family. 'And it was you who murdered my sister.'

'Look, you're making me out to sound like some kind of serial killer or something. Like that Blackett fellow. I didn't plan to do any of this, you know. It just happened.'

'Blackett probably feels the same.'

'Flora, we do still love each other, don't we? I mean, we can put all this behind us, can't we? Start again? Us two, and Matty?'

'Of course we can.'

'The thing is, if Georgie hadn't said she was going to take Matty to the States, none of this would have happened.'

'So it's all her fault, is it?'

'Yes,' he said defiantly. 'It is.'

'So how exactly did she make you murder her?'

'Don't be like that, Flora. You sound so bitter.'

'I am bitter.'

'What happened was that I knew you were staying in London overnight, because of your working breakfast the next day.' He looked pained. 'If you'd agreed to stay with me that night, it wouldn't have happened.'

'Not your fault, then?'

'Absolutely not. Anyway, I went down to the cottage. I wanted to ask Georgie straight out if I was right in thinking Matty was my child. And if she yes, have another go at persuading her not to take Matty away. And we'd started talking when there was a ring at the door, and Matty started whingeing, so I offered to take her upstairs and read her a story while Georgie dealt with whoever was at the door. For some reason she invited him in, so I got Matty ready for bed, and sent her downstairs to say goodnight. Hoping to give the fellow a nudge, you see. Make him go. He hung about for ages, something to do with a charity, you see, and a convenant. And it wasn't until he'd finally gone that I had a chance to ask Georgie about Matty, and she said I was right, so I told her not to go to the States.'

'And when she wouldn't agree, you killed her.'

'Something like that.'

'Using a knife.'

'I had this idea that the police would just think it was another of Blackett's victims.' He gave a small laugh. 'When I discovered later that it was actually him who'd come to the door, I simply couldn't believe my luck. But then I've been lucky all my life.'

'Or made your own luck,' Flora said. 'Did Matty see you . . . see you murdering her mother?'

He stared. 'What? Of course she didn't.'

'She must have done. It's the only explanation. She came downstairs, maybe she heard the two of you talking. Maybe she heard Georgie admitting you were the father, and picked up the bad vibes between the two of you so she didn't dare come into the room and then . . . then watched as you, as you—'

'No,' he said, appalled. 'Please. Not that.'

'Hadn't it occurred to you before?'

'Never. Not once. I checked on her before I left the house and she was fast asleep. I figured she'd be safe enough, you'd be home early in the morning.'

'You left her alone in the house with the body of her mother.'

'What else could I do?'

Now.

She pushed him.

He wasn't expecting danger. Caught off-balance, he took two or three involuntary steps towards the edge of the cliff and stood there, teetering, black against the dark sky, his arms flailing for a second or two. Then he dropped out of her sight. She stepped cautiously forward and looked over and down. He lay on the air as though it were a bed, falling away from her, further and further towards the waiting beach.

Imagine, she thought, being flung out into space, an angel banished, disgraced. Imagine the dark air rushing past you. Imagine the terror and the knowledge of the huge void below, the inevitability of it, the loneliness.

She'd called him monstrous, but he was no monster, just a man, an ordinary man with an ordinary dream that was never going to come true. As he fell, he stared up at her, his eyes dark in his white face, arms and legs held out from his body, curiously still. He made no sound. Could he see her watching him? she wondered. What was he thinking?

As his body hit the rocks below, she thought she might have heard his back breaking. After that, there was only the sound of the sea and the shriek of the wind and the scream of a bird.

Falling, falling angel, she thought, staring down at the white smudge which was all she could see of him. You have my heart.

You'll always have my heart.

Gregor was waiting when she got back. 'The train goes early in the morning.'

'I know.'

'And somebody's meeting you at the other end?'

'Yes.'

'Will you be happy?' His face shone. Literally. As though it were polished stone under a strong light.

'Contented, perhaps. It may be too late for happiness.' She suspected she might not see him again for years. Or ever. He had done what he was sent to do. 'But I'll see to it that Matty is happy. And there's my father. Something can be rescued from all this.'

'Rescue is often the best we can do.'

On the train, she took from her bag the gift Oliver had brought her, the book about angels. Leafing through it, something caught her eye, a diagram of a familiar pattern. *These are the seals of the seven angels*, she read, *as reproduced in ancient magical works*. One of them corresponded almost exactly to the marks on Gregor's chest. And then she found something which she realised she had instinctively known already. In legendary lore, one entry ran, the *grigori* are the watchers, a superior sort of angel who keeps guard over men.

She smiled at that. A superior sort of angel . . . She hoped that Gregor would get back soon to wherever it was he so desperately wanted to be.

* * *

When she got off the train, he was waiting. Matty held his hand. She had one of Flora's scarves wrapped round her neck and across her coat. She was holding a primrose. 'I found it in the garden,' she said. 'It's for you.'

'Thank you, darling,' Flora said. As she took the flower, she felt fêted. Celebrated. With all the accompanying connotations of birthday candles, presents, of Christmas trees, of fanfares and warmth and laughter.

'The first sign of spring,' Angus said.

She reached across Matty's head and kissed him. 'What now?'

'The rest of our lives, don't you think?'

'I do.'